The
Best of
R. A.
Lafferty

The Best of

R. A. Lafferty

Edited by Jonathan Strahan

TOR ▰ ESSENTIALS

A TOM DOHERTY ASSOCIATES BOOK
NEW YORK

THE BEST OF R. A. LAFFERTY

Copyright © 2019 by The Locus Science Fiction Foundation

All introductions and afterwords are copyright © 2018 by their respective authors and are used with permission.

A Tor Essentials Book
Published by Tom Doherty Associates
120 Broadway
New York, NY 10271

www.tor-forge.com

Tor® is a registered trademark of Macmillan Publishing Group, LLC.

Library of Congress Cataloging-in-Publication Data

Lafferty, R. A., author.
   The best of R. A. Lafferty / edited by Jonathan Strahan.—First edition.
     p. cm.
   "A Tom Doherty Associates book."
   ISBN 978-1-250-79481-9 (hardcover)
   ISBN 978-1-250-77853-6 (trade paperback)
   ISBN 978-1-250-77868-0 (ebook)
1. Science fiction, American—Fiction. I. Title.
   PS3562.A28
   813'.54—dc23

                                        2020044266

ISBN 978-1-250-77853-6 (trade paperback)
ISBN 978-1-250-79481-9 (paper over board)
ISBN 978-1-250-77868-0 (ebook)

Our books may be purchased in bulk for promotional, educational, or business use. Please contact your local bookseller or the Macmillan Corporate and Premium Sales Department at 1-800-221-7945, extension 5442, or by email at MacmillanSpecialMarkets@macmillan.com.

First published in Great Britain in 2019 by Gollancz, an imprint of the Orion Publishing Group Ltd

First U.S. Edition: February 2021

Printed in the United States of America

D   10   9   8   7   6   5   4   3

Copyright Acknowledgments

"Seven-Day Terror" by R. A. Lafferty © The Locus Science Fiction Foundation. First published in *If*, March 1962.

"Slow Tuesday Night" by R. A. Lafferty © The Locus Science Fiction Foundation. First published in *Galaxy Magazine*, April 1965.

"In Our Block" by R. A. Lafferty © The Locus Science Fiction Foundation. First published in *If*, July 1965.

"Nine Hundred Grandmothers" by R. A. Lafferty © The Locus Science Fiction Foundation. First published in *If*, February 1966.

"Narrow Valley" by R. A. Lafferty © The Locus Science Fiction Foundation. First published in *The Magazine of Fantasy and Science Fiction*, September 1966.

"The Primary Education of the Camiroi" by R. A. Lafferty © The Locus Science Fiction Foundation. First published in *Galaxy Magazine*, December 1966.

"Thus We Frustrate Charlemagne" by R. A. Lafferty © The Locus Science Fiction Foundation. First published in *Galaxy Magazine*, February 1967.

"Land of the Great Horses" by R. A. Lafferty © The Locus Science Fiction Foundation. First published in *Dangerous Visions*, Harlan Ellison ed.

"Cliffs That Laughed" by R. A. Lafferty © The Locus Science Fiction Foundation. First published in *The Magazine of Horror*, March 1969.

"Ride a Tin Can" by R. A. Lafferty © The Locus Science Fiction Foundation. First published in *If*, April 1970.

"Continued on Next Rock" by R. A. Lafferty © The Locus Science Fiction Foundation. First published in *Orbit 7*, Damon Knight ed.

"Old Foot Forgot" by R. A. Lafferty © The Locus Science Fiction Foundation. First published in *Orbit 7*, Damon Knight ed.

"Interurban Queen" by R. A. Lafferty © The Locus Science Fiction Foundation. First published in *Orbit 8*, Damon Knight ed.

"Nor Limestone Islands" by R. A. Lafferty © The Locus Science Fiction Foundation. First published in *Universe 1*, Terry Carr ed.

"Sky" by R. A. Lafferty © The Locus Science Fiction Foundation. First published in *New Dimensions I*, Robert Silverberg ed.

"Boomer Flats" by R. A. Lafferty © The Locus Science Fiction Foundation. First published in *If*, July-August 1971.

"Eurema's Dam" by R. A. Lafferty © The Locus Science Fiction Foundation. First published in *New Dimensions II*, Robert Silverberg ed.

"The World as Will and Wallpaper" by R. A. Lafferty © The Locus Science Fiction Foundation. First published in *Future City*, Roger Elwood ed.

"Days of Grass, Days of Straw" by R. A. Lafferty © The Locus Science Fiction Foundation. First published in *New Dimensions 3*, Robert Silverberg ed.

"Funnyfingers" by R. A. Lafferty © The Locus Science Fiction Foundation. First published in *Funnyfingers & Cabrito*.

"Selenium Ghosts of the Eighteen Seventies" by R. A. Lafferty © The Locus Science Fiction Foundation. First published in *Universe 8*, Terry Carr ed.

"Thieving Bear Planet" by R. A. Lafferty © The Locus Science Fiction Foundation. First published in *Universe 12*, Terry Carr ed.

Contents

Not to Mention R. A. Lafferty: A Personal Introduction

Neil Gaiman

Objectivity is a good thing. We rely on our commentators, our observers, our critics to be objective. It's what makes a critic a good critic and a reviewer a good reviewer. We trust them to tell us about books and films, music and authors.

You cannot trust me to tell you anything about R. A. Lafferty. It would be like asking a string tuned to G to give its opinion on the strings of a lower octave. When it hears another G, it's going to thrum in joyous recognition. That's the way of it. It's just how it is.

I was about nine years old, and somebody had left a copy of Judith Merril's *SF-12* in our house. I don't know who. It might conceivably have been my father's. Whoever owned it, I appropriated it, and proceeded to have my mind turned inside out. William Burroughs and Samuel R. Delany, Carol Emshwiller and Kit Reed, Brian Aldiss and Harvey Jacobs and John Updike and Tuli Kupferberg, J. G. Ballard and Hilary Bailey, Sonya Dorman and Tommaso Landolfi, none of them authors one would automatically recommend to nine-year-olds. I didn't care. I read the stories and took what I could from them. I had a bunch of new favorite authors. I had new rules about what fiction could be. The Brian Aldiss short story, "Confluence," was a dictionary. And one of the two stories by R. A. Lafferty was a school curriculum.

It was called "The Primary Education of the Camiroi," and it was the curriculum for the schools of an alien race, who would need to learn how to create life and run planets as part of their schooling. It was really funny. It also struck several nerves with me. I was certain that they should be teaching us that sort of thing in school anyway.

The second story, "Narrow Valley," was one of the best things in the book, and one of my favorite short stories to this day. It's a tall tale, about a beautiful valley that's, well, narrow. It told me things about America and Native Americans, about scientists, about ways of viewing the world, even things about magic, that spoke to me and made me happy.

When I was ten my father brought me copies of three of the Carr-Wollheim *World's Best Science Fiction* collections, all the way from America. I read "Nine Hundred Grandmothers," and "In Our Block." I read "Thus We Frustrate Charlemagne." I was in love.

I was also lucky. Why the library in the little Sussex town I lived in had, on their shelves, all the R. A. Lafferty books published in the UK in hardback by

Dennis Dobson & Co is still a mystery to me. Someone who ordered books had good taste, I suppose. But they had them. I read, and loved, *Fourth Mansions* (a story about secret societies and animals and men with hairy ears) and *The Reefs of Earth* (about a family of alien children who are stranded on Earth) and *Space Chantey* (which is the Odyssey set in space). (All of these descriptions are at best incomplete and at worst wildly misleading.) I remember the world-shaking moment when I realized that the contents page of *The Reefs of Earth*, the chapter titles, actually rhymed and made a poem. I remember the joy I took in this.

I bought my own copy of the paperback of *Nine Hundred Grandmothers*, the first Lafferty short story collection, from Dark They Were And Golden Eyed, in Berwick Street. I made all my friends read it. As far as I was concerned, Lafferty was the most interesting author out there: I loved what he did with words. I loved the tune of the sentences, the way they sang and jigged and the sheer delight the author took in words.

For Christmas in 1978 my parents gave me a copy of *The Encyclopedia of Science Fiction*, edited by Peter Nicholls and John Clute. I did not know at the time that Peter and John would, each in their own way, become close and valued friends. I did not know that I would one day, write with John Clute the entry on Lafferty for the second edition of *The Encyclopedia of Science Fiction*. All I knew was there were lots and lots of Lafferty books listed that I had not read and did not know existed. I spent years happily hunting for them, not knowing that most of them were, at the time of writing, actually unpublished, something that would drive Clute and Nicholls to distraction.

I was twenty-one, and I did not know what I wanted to do or to be, but I suspected that I wanted to be a writer. The only story I had completed by then was an R. A. Lafferty pastiche. In the back room of the same library in which I had found the Lafferty books was an *Author's Who's Who*. I looked up Lafferty in it, knowing that he would not be in there. There was an address listed, in Tulsa, Oklahoma. I would never have dared to write to an agent or a publisher, but this looked like a home address.

I wrote him a letter, and with it, I sent the story.

The address was out of date, but the letter was eventually forwarded and it reached him, and to my genuine astonishment, he wrote back, thanking me for the "pretty good sketch or pastiche or something, not a short story, however, although the title page says that it is. It might be saleable, depending on the quirks of the market when you send it out. A good piece wakens a spark of recognition in every breast, so somebody once said. This, of course, wakens a special spark of recognition." And he added, "Why don't you write another piece or two? Things are fun to write and there doesn't have to be any other reason."

My favorite writer told me I should write some more, so I did.

I wanted to write an article about him, but nobody wanted to publish it, back then. Still we wrote back and forth, and I asked impertinent questions about writing and his work, and he answered them as best he could.

There are few enough authors who simply make me happy. There are authors who make me think, or who trouble me in good ways, or make me worry for their characters. Lafferty did those things, and did them so very well. But he does more than that. I start to smile with pleasure when I start reading a Lafferty story. It's the way the tale is told, the voice of the teller, that brings me so much joy.

There isn't anyone out there with whom it's easy to compare Lafferty: Avram Davidson wrote unclassifiable and brilliant stories, and knew more of the world, but his stories did not feel like tall tales, nor were they such great lies told with so straight a face. The Irish novelist Flann O'Brien (aka Myles na Gopaleen, real name Brian O'Nolan) did the tall tales and the straight-faced lies, but he didn't take us so far out of this world. Gene Wolfe is as deep, but seldom as funny.

I read all the Lafferty I could. I followed him as the work got darker, then more personal. I followed him from the big publishers to the small presses and the pamphlets. I read the work that I understood and the work that I didn't (I suspected it was being written for an audience of only himself, but even then, I took joy in the sentences and the world). I have seen Lafferty's office door, on display in a museum in Tulsa, Oklahoma.

What else do you need to know? And as I write that, it occurs to me that I've missed out all the biographical stuff, the important information I am sure you actually need in an introduction like this.

Raphael Aloysius Lafferty, Ray to his friends, was from Tulsa, Oklahoma. He trained as an electrical engineer and worked for an electrical supply company until he retired, aged forty-five. He was a professional writer from then until he retired again. He was Catholic ("Catholicism plays a big part in my life. Without it I would be in the gutter entirely. With it, I have only one foot in the gutter.") and an alcoholic ("Drinking has influenced my writing all in the wrong direction. I am an alcoholic and shouldn't drink at all. But once or twice a year I forget this and the results are usually sad. More of my writing has been ruined by my drinking than improved by it. Yet there's always a goose there, it's part of the 'to seek and not to find' motif. Somewhere, somewhere there must be this mind-expanding elixir! Such delusions are part of life. When I was younger I got a lot of pleasure and companionship out of drinking, but probably no creative impetus.")

He was in the army in WWII, and was sent to the South Pacific, but maintained that, at twenty-eight, he was ten years too old when this happened to properly enjoy or appreciate it.

He published his first science fiction story, "Day of the Glacier," in *Original Science Fiction Stories* in 1960 when he was forty-six. "I was moderately successful," he said of his writing. "It didn't put me on easy street, but it put me on easy alley."

He won the Hugo Award in 1973 for "Eurema's Dam," which was a good story, but he lost awards with much better stories, and some of his finest stories were never noticed by the people who nominate you for awards. He retired from writing in 1984, having published over two hundred short stories and over twenty novels.

He had a stroke in 1994, and Alzheimer's in his final years. He died in 2002, in a nursing home in Broken Arrow, Oklahoma, twenty minutes from Tulsa.

In a brief piece he wrote to accompany a photo of himself in Patti Perret's 1985 book *The Faces of Science Fiction*, he said, "When I was forty-five years old, I tried to be a writer. I became the best short story writer in the world. I've been telling people that for twenty years, but some of them don't believe me."

I believed.

It is not impossible that, once you also have read this book, you may become a believer as well.

Slow Tuesday Night

Introduction by Michael Dirda

While loosely categorized as a science fiction writer, R. A. Lafferty was—to use the old phrase—*sui generis*. His stories, with their surrealist plots and breathless pace, revel in excess, parenthetical asides, and gonzo bizarreness of every sort. Lafferty fans seldom have any clear idea where his absurdist tall tales are going, but who cares? We're here for the ride.

Think back to the first time you read a "Lafferty." It might have been "Land of the Great Horses," which explains the origin of the gypsies and was included in Harlan Ellison's groundbreaking *Dangerous Visions*. Perhaps you happened upon "Eurema's Dam" in an anthology of Nebula Award winners. Or just maybe you unearthed an old issue of *If* in a run-down charity shop and discovered "Boomer Flats," in which a trio of eminent scientists travel to a Texas backwater in search of the missing link and there encounter hairy giants, a gorgeous woman named Crayola Catfish, a race of near immortals, and a space traveler known as the Comet.

My own introduction to Lafferty came through Gene Wolfe, back in the early 1980s. I was interviewing Wolfe about the just completed *Book of the New Sun* and asked him what contemporary writers he admired. He immediately answered, "R. A. Lafferty," so I sensibly went out and bought a copy of the Ace Science Fiction Special, *Nine Hundred Grandmothers*. For some reason—perhaps the title attracted me—the first story I turned to was "Slow Tuesday Night." That was enough. I read it with the same delight I had experienced when, as a teenager, I opened Lord Dunsany's *Jorkens Remembers Africa* or *The Most of S. J. Perelman*. You know that feeling: you just want to hug yourself with pleasure, while sometimes laughing quietly or murmuring, "This is soooo good."

No précis can convey the sheer exuberance of "Slow Tuesday Night." Lafferty mixes courtly diction and comic-strip names, sets up expectations and immediately undercuts them, and gradually reveals a world that now seems all too familiar. In 1965, when "Slow Tuesday Night" first appeared in *Galaxy*, Lafferty was obviously using the American obsession with speed to critique our idolization of wealth, status, and celebrity. Read today, the story uncannily foretells the viral culture of the internet.

In its opening scene a panhandler accosts a strolling couple: "'Preserve us this night,' he said as he touched his hat to them, 'and could you good people advance me a thousand dollars to be about the recouping of my fortunes?'"

The diction here recalls the arch formality of W. C. Fields or Popeye's scrounging friend J. Wellington Wimpy ("I'll gladly pay you Tuesday for a hamburger today"). Neither the panhandler nor the couple seem to think it unusual for a beggar to ask for a thousand dollars. We soon learn why: after removing the "Abebaios block" from our brains, people found that "things that had once taken months and years now took only minutes and hours. A person could have one or several pretty intricate careers within an eight-hour period."

Soon everything—absolutely everything—goes much, much faster, which also means that nothing lasts for very long. That panhandler—his name is Basil Bagelbaker—"would be the richest man in the world within an hour and a half. He would make and lose four fortunes within eight hours; and these not the little fortunes that ordinary men acquire, but titanic things."

In the course of a single evening, Ildefonsa Impala, the most beautiful woman in the city, marries again and again. Her honeymoon with newly rich inventor Freddy Fixico is utterly kitsch—"the reticulated water of the famous falls was tinted gold; the immediate rocks had been done by Rambles; and the hills had been contoured by Spall." After a luxurious hour, Ildefonsa consults "a trend indicator" and realizes that Freddy's invention would soon be outmoded and his wealth gone, so she immediately divorces him. "Whom shall I marry next?" Ildefonsa asks herself on this slow Tuesday night.

Meanwhile, Basil has been wheeling and dealing in the Money Market. "He caused to collapse certain industrial empires that had grown up within the last two hours, and made a good thing of recombining their wreckage." Naturally enough, his wife, Judy, is chosen "one of the ten best-dressed women during the frou-frou fashion period about two o'clock." In such a mayfly world, plays and films run no longer than six minutes and Stanley Skuldugger can be voted "the top Actor-Imago of the middle hours of the night." Having decided to produce a philosophical masterpiece, Maxwell Mouser is willing to devote an entire seven minutes to the task. He turns to "the ideas index," sets the "activator" for the amount of wordage needed, and, for that extra bit of sparkle, switches on a "striking analogy blender" calibrated to his particular "personality-signature." The resulting monograph quickly goes viral—"This was truly one of the greatest works of philosophy to appear during the early and medium hours of the night"—but by dawn it will already be dismissed and forgotten.

In "Slow Tuesday Night" Lafferty—politically conservative and devoutly Catholic—depicts a society of meaningless flux and impermanence, where there is "no abiding city" nor any sense of the spiritual. People surrender to the passing moment, nothing seems to matter very much, no hearts are permanently broken. Yet all this meretricious shallowness is conveyed through a simple yet brilliant conceit: if you speed up the world enough, everything starts to resemble the frenetic climax of a Keystone Kops farce.

In "Seven-Day Terror" Lafferty mentions "an untidy suite that looked as though it belonged to a drunken sultan." That's a wonderful simile, but also a fair description of his own gorgeous, shambolic abundance. What we love about Lafferty's stories is the joyfulness of their telling, the playful diction, the topsy-turvy plot surprises, the knowing winks. To expect from them any logic but that of Wonderland is to miss the party. After all, as the Rabelaisian hero of "One at a Time" says, if you insist on realism and perfect sense, "you put unnatural conditions on a tale." I'm pretty sure his creator would agree.

Slow Tuesday Night

A panhandler intercepted the young couple as they strolled down the night street.

"Preserve us this night," he said as he touched his hat to them, "and could you good people advance me a thousand dollars to be about the recouping of my fortunes?"

"I gave you a thousand last Friday," said the young man.

"Indeed you did," the panhandler replied, "and I paid you back tenfold by messenger before midnight."

"That's right, George, he did," said the young woman. "Give it to him, dear. I believe he's a good sort."

So the young man gave the panhandler a thousand dollars, and the panhandler touched his hat to them in thanks and went on to the recouping of his fortunes.

As he went into Money Market, the panhandler passed Ildefonsa Impala, the most beautiful woman in the city.

"Will you marry me this night, Ildy?" he asked cheerfully.

"Oh, I don't believe so, Basil," she said. "I marry you pretty often, but tonight I don't seem to have any plans at all. You may make me a gift on your first or second, however. I always like that."

But when they had parted she asked herself: "But whom will I marry tonight?"

The panhandler was Basil Bagelbaker, who would be the richest man in the world within an hour and a half. He would make and lose four fortunes within eight hours; and these not the little fortunes that ordinary men acquire, but titanic things.

When the Abebaios block had been removed from human minds, people began to make decisions faster, and often better. It had been the mental stutter. When it was understood what it was, and that it had no useful function, it was removed by simple childhood metasurgery.

Transportation and manufacturing had then become practically instantaneous. Things that had once taken months and years now took only minutes and hours. A person could have one or several pretty intricate careers within an eight-hour period.

Freddy Fixico had just invented a manus module. Freddy was a Nyctalops, and the modules were characteristic of these people. The people had then divided themselves—according to their natures and inclinations—into the Auroreans, the Hemerobians, and the Nyctalops—or the Dawners, who had their most active hours from four A.M. till noon; the Day-Flies, who obtained from noon to eight P.M.; and the Night-Seers, whose civilization thrived from eight P.M. to four A.M. The cultures, inventions, markets, and activities of these three folk were a little different. As a Nyctalops, Freddy had just begun his working day at eight P.M. on a slow Tuesday night.

Freddy rented an office and had it furnished. This took one minute, negotiation, selection, and installation being almost instantaneous. Then he invented the manus module; that took another minute. He then had it manufactured and marketed; in three minutes it was in the hands of key buyers.

It caught on. It was an attractive module. The flow of orders began within thirty seconds. By ten minutes after eight every important person had one of the new manus modules, and the trend had been set. The module began to sell in the millions. It was one of the most interesting fads of the night, or at least the early part of the night.

Manus modules had no practical function, no more than had Sameki verses. They were attractive, of a psychologically satisfying size and shape, and could be held in the hands, set on a table, or installed in a module niche of any wall.

Naturally, Freddy became very rich. Ildefonsa Impala, the most beautiful woman in the city, was always interested in newly rich men. She came to see Freddy about eight-thirty. People made up their minds fast, and Ildefonsa had hers made up when she came. Freddy made his own up quickly and divorced Judy Fixico in Small Claims Court. Freddy and Ildefonsa went honeymooning to Paraiso Dorado, a resort.

It was wonderful. All of Ildy's marriages were. There was the wonderful floodlighted scenery. The recirculated water of the famous falls was tinted gold; the immediate rocks had been done by Rambles; and the hills had been contoured by Spall. The beach was a perfect copy of that at Merevale, and the popular drink that first part of the night was blue absinthe.

But scenery—whether seen for the first time or revisited after an interval—is stirring for the sudden intense view of it. It is not meant to be lingered over. Food, selected and prepared instantly, is eaten with swift enjoyment; and blue absinthe lasts no longer than its own novelty. Loving, for Ildefonsa and her paramours, was quick and consuming; and repetition would have been pointless to her. Besides, Ildefonsa and Freddy had taken only the one-hour luxury honeymoon.

Freddy wished to continue the relationship, but Ildefonsa glanced at a trend indicator. The manus module would hold its popularity for only the first third of the night. Already it had been discarded by people who mattered. And Freddy Fixico was not one of the regular successes. He enjoyed a full career only about one night a week.

They were back in the city and divorced in Small Claims Court by nine thirty-five. The stock of manus modules was remaindered, and the last of it would be disposed to bargain hunters among the Dawners, who will buy anything.

"Whom shall I marry next?" Ildefonsa asked herself. "It looks like a slow night."

"Bagelbaker is buying," ran the word through Money Market, but Bagelbaker was selling again before the word had made its rounds. Basil Bagelbaker enjoyed making money, and it was a pleasure to watch him work as he dominated the floor of the Market and assembled runners and a competent staff out of the corner of his mouth. Helpers stripped the panhandler rags off him and wrapped him in a tycoon toga. He sent one runner to pay back twentyfold the young couple who had advanced him a thousand dollars. He sent another with a more substantial gift to Ildefonsa Impala, for Basil cherished their relationship. Basil acquired title to the Trend Indication Complex and had certain falsifications set into it. He caused to collapse certain industrial empires that had grown up within the last two hours, and made a good thing of recombining their wreckage. He had been the richest man in the world for some minutes now. He became so money heavy that he could not maneuver with the agility he had shown an hour before. He became a great fat buck, and the pack of expert wolves circled him to bring him down.

Very soon he would lose that first fortune of the evening. The secret of Basil Bagelbaker is that he enjoyed losing money spectacularly after he was full of it to the bursting point.

A thoughtful man named Maxwell Mouser had just produced a work of actinic philosophy. It took him seven minutes to write it. To write works of philosophy one used the flexible outlines and the idea indexes; one set the activator for such a wordage in each subsection; an adept would use the paradox feed-in, and the striking-analogy blender; one calibrated the particular-slant and the personality-signature. It had to come out a good work, for excellence had become the automatic minimum for such productions.

"I will scatter a few nuts on the frosting," said Maxwell, and he pushed the lever for that. This sifted handfuls of words like chthonic and heuristic and prozymeides through the thing so that nobody could doubt it was a work of philosophy.

Maxwell Mouser sent the work out to publishers, and received it back each time in about three minutes. An analysis of it and reason for rejection was always given—mostly that the thing had been done before and better. Maxwell received it back ten times in thirty minutes, and was discouraged. Then there was a break.

Ladion's work had become a hit within the last ten minutes, and it was now recognized that Mouser's monograph was both an answer and a supplement to it. It was accepted and published in less than a minute after this break. The reviews of the first five minutes were cautious ones; then real enthusiasm was shown. This was truly one of the greatest works of philosophy to appear during the early and medium hours of the night. There were those who said it might be one of the enduring works and even have a holdover appeal to the Dawners the next morning.

Naturally, Maxwell became very rich, and naturally Ildefonsa came to see him about midnight. Being a revolutionary philosopher, Maxwell thought that he might make some free arrangement, but Ildefonsa insisted it must be marriage. So Maxwell divorced Judy Mouser in Small Claims Court and went off with Ildefonsa.

This Judy herself, though not so beautiful as Ildefonsa, was the fastest taker in the city. She only wanted the men of the moment for a moment, and she was always there before even Ildefonsa. Ildefonsa believed that she took the men away from Judy; Judy said that Ildy had her leavings and nothing else.

"I had him first," Judy would always mock as she raced through Small Claims Court.

"Oh that damned urchin!" Ildefonsa would moan. "She wears my very hair before I do."

Maxwell Mouser and Ildefonsa Impala went honeymooning to Musicbox Mountain, a resort. It was wonderful. The peaks were done with green snow by Dunbar and Fittle. (Back at Money Market Basil Bagelbaker was putting together his third and greatest fortune of the night, which might surpass in magnitude even his fourth fortune of the Thursday before.) The chalets were Switzier than the real Swiss and had live goats in every room. (And Stanley Skuldugger was emerging as the top Actor-Imago of the middle hours of the night.) The popular drink for that middle part of the night was Glotzenglubber, Eve Cheese, and Rhine wine over pink ice. (And back in the city the leading Nyctalops were taking their midnight break at the Toppers' Club.)

Of course it was wonderful, as were all of Ildefonsa's—but she had never been really up on philosophy so she had scheduled only the special thirty-five-minute honeymoon. She looked at the trend indicator to be sure. She found that her current husband had been obsoleted, and his opus was now referred to sneeringly as Mouser's Mouse. They went back to the city and were divorced in Small Claims Court.

The membership of the Toppers' Club varied. Success was the requisite of membership. Basil Bagelbaker might be accepted as a member, elevated to the presidency, and expelled from it as a dirty pauper from three to six times a night. But only important persons could belong to it, or those enjoying brief moments of importance.

"I believe I will sleep during the Dawner period in the morning," Overcall said. "I may go up to this new place, Koimopolis, for an hour of it. They're said to be good. Where will you sleep, Basil?"

"Flop house."

"I believe I will sleep an hour by the Midian Method," said Burnbanner. "They have a fine new clinic. And perhaps I'll sleep an hour by the Prasenka Process, and an hour by the Dormidio."

"Crackle has been sleeping an hour every period by the natural method," said Overcall.

"I did that for half an hour not long since," said Burnbanner. "I believe an hour is too long to give it. Have you tried the natural method, Basil?"

"Always. Natural method and a bottle of red-eye."

Stanley Skuldugger had become the most meteoric Actor-Imago for a week. Naturally he became very rich, and Ildefonsa Impala went to see him about three A.M.

"I had him first!" rang the mocking voice of Judy Skuldugger as she skipped through her divorce in Small Claims Court. And Ildefonsa and Stanley-boy went off honeymooning. It is always fun to finish up a period with an Actor-Imago who is the hottest property in the business. There is something so adolescent and boorish about them.

Besides, there was the publicity, and Ildefonsa liked that. The rumor-mills ground. Would it last ten minutes? Thirty? An hour? Would it be one of those rare Nyctalops marriages that lasted through the rest of the night and into the daylight off-hours? Would it even last into the next night as some had been known to do?

Actually it lasted nearly forty minutes, which was almost to the end of the period.

It had been a slow Tuesday night. A few hundred new products had run their course on the market. There had been a score of dramatic hits, three-minute and five-minute capsule dramas, and several of the six-minute long-play affairs. *Night Street Nine*—a solidly sordid offering—seemed to be in as the drama of the night unless there should be a late hit.

Hundred-storied buildings had been erected, occupied, obsoleted, and demolished again to make room for more contemporary structures. Only the mediocre would use a building that had been left over from the Day Fliers or the Dawners, or even the Nyctalops of the night before. The city was rebuilt pretty completely at least three times during an eight-hour period.

The period drew near its end. Basil Bagelbaker, the richest man in the world, the reigning president of the Toppers' Club, was enjoying himself with his cronies. His fourth fortune of the night was a paper pyramid that had risen to incredible heights; but Basil laughed to himself as he savored the manipulation it was founded on.

Three ushers of the Toppers' Club came in with firm step.

"Get out of here, you dirty bum," they told Basil savagely. They tore the tycoon's toga off him and then tossed him his seedy panhandler's rags with a three-man sneer.

"All gone?" Basil asked. "I gave it another five minutes."

"All gone," said a messenger from Money Market. "Nine billion gone in five minutes, and it really pulled some others down with it."

"Pitch the busted bum out!" howled Overcall and Burnbanner and the other cronies.

"Wait, Basil," said Overcall. "Turn in the President's Crosier before we kick you downstairs. After all, you'll have it several times again tomorrow night."

The period was over. The Nyctalops drifted off to sleep clinics or leisure-hour hide-outs to pass their ebb time. The Auroreans, the Dawners, took over the vital stuff.

Now you would see some action! Those Dawners really made fast decisions. You wouldn't catch them wasting a full minute setting up a business.

A sleepy panhandler met Ildefonsa Impala on the way.

"Preserve us this morning, Ildy," he said, "and will you marry in the coming night?"

"Likely I will, Basil," she told him. "Did you marry Judy during the night past?"

"I'm not sure. Could you let me have two dollars, Ildy?"

"Out of the question. I believe a Judy Bagelbaker was named one of the ten best-dressed women during the froufrou fashion period about two o'clock. Why do you need two dollars?"

"A dollar for a bed and a dollar for red-eye. After all, I sent you two million out of my second."

"I keep my two sorts of accounts separate. Here's a dollar, Basil. Now be off! I can't be seen talking to a dirty panhandler."

"Thank you, Ildy. I'll get the red-eye and sleep in an alley. Preserve us this morning."

Bagelbaker shuffled off whistling "Slow Tuesday Night."

And already the Dawners had set Wednesday morning to jumping.

Narrow Valley

Introduction by Michael Swanwick

"Narrow Valley" is possibly Ray Lafferty's single most approachable and humane tale. It fairly bulges with people you'd like to have for neighbors: Clarence Little-Saddle and his father, Clarence Big-Saddle, of course, but also the beefy man with the land office in his desk, the farmer Tom Dublin who enjoys firing his rifle at friends for a joke, the inexplicably ubiquitous Willy McGilly, and not one but two smart-mouthed little girls. (Their brothers are OK, too, but Lafferty had a particular gift for precocious little girls.) Admittedly, Robert Rampart *père* is a blowhard, but one out of a family of seven isn't bad. I've lost track of how many people I've converted to Lafferty fans by thrusting forward a copy of *Nine Hundred Grandmothers*, with a thumb bookmarking "Narrow Valley," and saying, "Here—read this!" It's easy to like.

This is one of the stories responsible for the notion that Lafferty was principally influenced by American tall tales. It's true that he accomplished a great deal of his effects using deadpan narration of wondrous events. Also that he pretty much ignored the internal psychology of his characters. Henry James he wasn't. If a man's possessions were taken away from him, Lafferty had him throw back his head and lament this fact in words. If a woman lost interest in an enterprise, he indicated it by having her say exactly that. So, yes, the assertion is, in part, valid.

But a lot of people have written modern-day tall tales and not one of them has come close to writing like the Bard of Tulsa. Consider such digressions as Clarence Little-Saddle's riff on the significance of the war bonnet and the lecture on how much larger the moon appears at the horizon than overhead. Consider his beautiful use of dialect. Consider his lovely comic asides and delightful parodies of scientific argot. Tall tales are nothing if not straightforward. "Narrow Valley" is anything but. This is a sophisticated work, written by a sophisticated man.

You can tell a lot about a writer by what he chooses to celebrate. There is a grim backstory underlying this tale and Lafferty, who knew Oklahoma history inside and out, was well aware of it. In the early seventeenth century, there were sixty thousand Pawnee in possession of a great deal of land and by 1875 . . . well, you can read that for yourself in the opening sentence. But "Narrow Valley" is, almost paradoxically, one of Lafferty's sunniest works, a comedy, and a paean to resilience and human decency.

It's also, as I said, easy to like. You'll see.

Narrow Valley

I n the year 1893, land allotments in severalty were made to the remaining eight hundred and twenty-one Pawnee Indians. Each would receive one hundred and sixty acres of land and no more, and thereafter the Pawnees would be expected to pay taxes on their land, the same as the White-Eyes did.

"Kitkehahke!" Clarence Big-Saddle cussed. "You can't kick a dog around proper on a hundred and sixty acres. And I sure am not hear before about this pay taxes on land."

Clarence Big-Saddle selected a nice green valley for his allotment. It was one of the half dozen plots he had always regarded as his own. He sodded around the summer lodge that he had there and made it an all-season home. But he sure didn't intend to pay taxes on it.

So he burned leaves and bark and made a speech:

"That my valley be always wide and flourish and green and such stuff as that!" he orated in Pawnee chant style. "But that it be narrow if an intruder come."

He didn't have any balsam bark to burn. He threw on a little cedar bark instead. He didn't have any elder leaves. He used a handful of jack-oak leaves. And he forgot the word. How you going to work it if you forget the word?

"Petahauerat!" he howled out with the confidence he hoped would fool the fates.

"That's the same long of a word," he said in a low aside to himself. But he was doubtful. "What am I, a White Man, a burr-tailed jack, a new kind of nut to think it will work?" he asked. "I have to laugh at me. Oh well, we see."

He threw the rest of the bark and the leaves on the fire, and he hollered the wrong word out again.

And he was answered by a dazzling sheet of summer lightning.

"Skidi!" Clarence Big-Saddle swore. "It worked. I didn't think it would."

Clarence Big-Saddle lived on his land for many years, and he paid no taxes. Intruders were unable to come down to his place. The land was sold for taxes three times, but nobody ever came down to claim it. Finally, it was carried as open land on the books. Homesteaders filed on it several times, but none of them fulfilled the qualification of living on the land.

Half a century went by. Clarence Big-Saddle called his son.

"I've had it, boy," he said. "I think I'll just go in the house and die."

"OK, Dad," the son Clarence Little-Saddle said. "I'm going in to town to shoot a few games of pool with the boys. I'll bury you when I get back this evening."

So the son Clarence Little-Saddle inherited. He also lived on the land for many years without paying taxes. There was a disturbance in the courthouse one day. The place seemed to be invaded in force, but actually there were but one man, one woman, and five children. "I'm Robert Rampart," said the man, "and we want the Land Office."

"I'm Robert Rampart Junior," said a nine-year-old gangler, "and we want it pretty blamed quick."

"I don't think we have anything like that," the girl at the desk said. "Isn't that something they had a long time ago?"

"Ignorance is no excuse for inefficiency, my dear," said Mary Mabel Rampart, an eight-year-old who could easily pass for eight and a half. "After I make my report, I wonder who will be sitting at your desk tomorrow."

"You people are either in the wrong state or the wrong century," the girl said.

"The Homestead Act still obtains," Robert Rampart insisted. "There is one tract of land carried as open in this county. I want to file on it."

Cecilia Rampart answered the knowing wink of a beefy man at the distant desk. "Hi," she breathed as she slinked over. "I'm Cecilia Rampart, but my stage name is Cecilia San Juan. Do you think that seven is too young to play ingénue roles?"

"Not for you," the man said. "Tell your folks to come over here."

"Do you know where the Land Office is?" Cecilia asked.

"Sure. It's the fourth left-hand drawer of my desk. The smallest office we got in the whole courthouse. We don't use it much any more."

The Ramparts gathered around. The beefy man started to make out the papers.

"This is the land description," Robert Rampart began. "Why, you've got it down already. How did you know?"

"I've been around here a long time," the man answered.

They did the paperwork, and Robert Rampart filed on the land.

"You won't be able to come onto the land itself though," the man said.

"Why won't I?" Rampart demanded. "Isn't the description accurate?"

"Oh, I suppose so. But nobody's ever been able get to the land. It's become a sort of joke."

"Well, I intend to get to the bottom of that joke," Rampart insisted. "I will occupy the land, or I will find out why not."

"I'm not sure about that," the beefy man said. "The last man to file on the land, about a dozen years ago, wasn't able to occupy the land. And he wasn't able to say why he couldn't. It's kind of interesting, the look on their faces after they try it for a day or two, and then give it up."

The Ramparts left the courthouse, loaded into their camper, and drove out to find their land. They stopped it at the house of a cattle and wheat farmer named Charley Dublin. Dublin met them with a grin which indicated he had been tipped off.

"Come along if you want to, folks," Dublin said. "The easiest way is on foot across my short pasture here. Your land's directly west of mine."

They walked the short distance to the border.

"My name is Tom Rampart, Mr. Dublin." Six-year-old Tom made conversation as they walked. "But my name is really Ramires, and not Tom. I am the issue of an indiscretion of my mother in Mexico several years ago."

"The boy is a kidder, Mr. Dublin," said the mother Nina Rampart, defending herself. "I have never been in Mexico, but sometimes I have the urge to disappear there forever."

"Ah yes, Mrs. Rampart. And what is the name of the youngest boy here?" Charley Dublin asked.

"Fatty," said Fatty Rampart.

"But surely that is not your given name?"

"Audifax," said five-year-old Fatty.

"Ah well, Audifax, Fatty, are you a kidder too?"

"He's getting better at it, Mr. Dublin," Mary Mabel said. "He was a twin till last week. His twin was named Skinny. Mama left Skinny unguarded while she was out tippling, and there were wild dogs in the neighborhood. When Mama got back, do you know what was left of Skinny? Two neck bones and an ankle bone. That was all."

"Poor Skinny," Dublin said. "Well, Rampart, this is the fence and the end of my land. Yours is just beyond."

"Is that ditch on my land?" Rampart asked.

"That ditch *is* your land."

"I'll have it filled in. It's a dangerous deep cut even if it is narrow. And the other fence looks like a good one, and I sure have a pretty plot of land beyond it."

"No, Rampart, the land beyond the second fence belongs to Holister Hyde," Charley Dublin said. "That second fence is the *end* of your land."

"Now, just wait a minute, Dublin! There's something wrong here. My land is one hundred and sixty acres, which would be a half mile on a side. Where's my half-mile width?"

"Between the two fences."

"That's not eight feet."

"Doesn't look like it, does it, Rampart? Tell you what—there's plenty of throwing-sized rocks around. Try to throw one across it."

"I'm not interested in any such boys' games," Rampart exploded. "I want my land."

But the Rampart children *were* interested in such games. They got with it with those throwing rocks. They winged them out over the little gully. The stones acted funny. They hung in the air, as it were, and diminished in size. And they were small as pebbles when they dropped down, down into the gully. None of them could throw a stone across that ditch, and they were throwing kids.

"You and your neighbor have conspired to fence open land for your own use," Rampart charged.

"No such thing, Rampart," Dublin said cheerfully. "My land checks perfectly. So does Hyde's. So does yours, if we knew how to check it. It's like one of those trick topological drawings. It really is half a mile from here to there, but the eye gets lost somewhere. It's your land. Crawl through the fence and figure it out."

Rampart crawled through the fence, and drew himself up to jump the gully. Then he hesitated. He got a glimpse of just how deep that gully was. Still, it wasn't five feet across.

There was a heavy fence post on the ground, designed for use as a corner post. Rampart up-ended it with some effort. Then he shoved it to fall and bridge the gully. But it fell short, and it shouldn't have. An eight-foot post should bridge a five-foot gully.

The post fell into the gully, and rolled and rolled and rolled. It spun as though it were rolling outward, but it made no progress except vertically. The post came to rest on a ledge of the gully, so close that Rampart could almost reach out and touch it, but it now appeared no bigger than a match stick.

"There is something wrong with that fence post, or with the world, or with my eyes," Robert Rampart said. "I wish I felt dizzy so I could blame it on that."

"There's a little game that I sometimes play with my neighbor Hyde when we're both out," Dublin said. "I've a heavy rifle and I train it on the middle of his forehead as he stands on the other side of the ditch apparently eight feet away. I fire it off then (I'm a good shot) and I hear it whine across. It'd kill him dead if things were as they seem. But Hyde's in no danger. The shot always bangs into that little scuff of rocks and boulders about thirty feet below him. I can see it kick up the rock dust there, and the sound of it rattling into those little boulders comes back to me in about two and a half seconds."

A bull-bat (poor people call it the night-hawk) raveled around in the air and zoomed out over the narrow ditch, but it did not reach the other side. The bird dropped below ground level and could be seen against the background of the other side of the ditch. It grew smaller and hazier as though at a distance of three or four hundred yards. The white bars on its wings could no longer be discerned; then the bird itself could hardly be discerned; but it was far short of the other side of the five-foot ditch.

A man identified by Charley Dublin as the neighbor Hollister Hyde had appeared on the other side of the little ditch. Hyde grinned and waved. He shouted something, but could not be heard.

"Hyde and I both read mouths," Dublin said, "so we can talk across the ditch easy enough. Which kid wants to play chicken? Hyde will barrel a good-sized rock right at your head, and if you duck or flinch you're chicken."

"Me! Me!" Audifax Rampart challenged. And Hyde, a big man with big hands, did barrel a fearsome jagged rock right at the head of the boy. It would have killed him if things had been as they appeared. But the rock diminished to nothing and disappeared into the ditch. Here was a phenomenon: things seemed real-sized on either side of the ditch, but they diminished coming out over the ditch either way.

"Everybody game for it?" Robert Rampart Junior asked.

"We won't get down there by standing here," Mary Mabel said.

"Nothing wenchered, nothing gained," said Cecilia. "I got that from an ad for a sex comedy."

Then the five Rampart kids ran down into the gully. Ran *down* is right. It was almost as if they ran down the vertical face of a cliff. They couldn't do that. The gully was no wider than the stride of the biggest kids. But the gully diminished those children, it ate them alive. They were doll-sized. They were acorn-sized. They were running for minute after minute across a ditch that was only five feet across. They were going, deeper in it, and getting smaller. Robert Rampart was roaring his alarm, and his wife, Nina, was screaming. Then she stopped. "What am I carrying on so loud about?" she asked herself. "It looks like fun. I'll do it too."

She plunged into the gully, diminished in size as the children had done, and ran at a pace to carry her a hundred yards away across a gully only five feet wide.

That Robert Rampart stirred things up for a while then. He got the sheriff there, and the highway patrolmen. A ditch had stolen his wife and five children, he said, and maybe had killed them. And if anybody laughs, there may be another killing. He got the colonel of the State National Guard there, and a command post set up. He got a couple of airplane pilots. Robert Rampart had one quality: when he hollered, people came.

He got the newsmen out from T-Town, and the eminent scientists, Dr. Velikof Vonk, Arpad Arkabaranan, and Willy McGilly. That bunch turns up every time you get on a good one. They just happen to be in that part of the country where something interesting is going on.

They attacked the thing from all four sides and the top, and by inner and outer theory. If a thing measures half a mile on each side, and the sides are straight, there just has to be something in the middle of it. They took pictures from the air, and they turned out perfect. They proved that Robert Rampart had the prettiest hundred and sixty acres in the country, the larger part of it being a lush green valley, and all of it being half a mile on a side, and situated just where it should be. They took ground-level photos then, and it showed a beautiful half-mile stretch of land between the boundaries of Charley Dublin and Hollister Hyde. But a man isn't a camera. None of them could see that beautiful spread with the eyes in their heads. Where was it?

Down in the valley itself everything was normal. It really was half a mile wide and no more than eighty feet deep with a very gentle slope. It was warm and sweet, and beautiful with grass and grain.

Nina and the kids loved it, and they rushed to see what squatter had built that little house on their land. A house, or a shack. It had never known paint, but paint would have spoiled it. It was built of split timbers dressed near smooth with axe and draw knife, chinked with white clay, and sodded up to about half its height. And there was an interloper standing by the little lodge.

"Here, here what are you doing on our land?" Robert Rampart Junior demanded of the man. "Now you just shamble off again wherever you came from. I'll bet you're a thief too, and those cattle are stolen."

"Only the black-and-white calf," Clarence Little-Saddle said. "I couldn't resist him, but the rest are mine. I guess I'll just stay around and see that you folks get settled all right."

"Is there any wild Indians around here?" Fatty Rampart asked.

"No, not really. I go on a bender about every three months and get a little bit wild, and there's a couple Osage boys from Gray Horse that get noisy sometimes, but that's about all," Clarence Little-Saddle said.

"You certainly don't intend to palm yourself off on us as an Indian," Mary Mabel challenged. "You'll find us a little too knowledgeable for that."

"Little girl, you might as well tell this cow there's no room for her to be a cow since you're so knowledgeable. She thinks she's a short-horn cow named Sweet Virginia; I think I'm a Pawnee Indian named Clarence. Break it to us real gentle if we're not."

"If you're an Indian where's your war bonnet? There's not a feather on you anywhere."

"How you be sure? There's a story that we got feathers instead of hair on—aw, I can't tell a joke like that to a little girl! How come you're not wearing the Iron Crown of Lombardy if you're a white girl? How you expect me to believe you're a little white girl and your folks came from Europe a couple hundred years ago if you don't wear it? There are six hundred tribes, and only one of them, the Oglala Sioux, had the war bonnet, and only the big leaders, never more than two or three of them alive at one time, wore it."

"Your analogy is a little strained," Mary Mabel said. "Those Indians we saw in Florida and the ones at Atlantic City had war bonnets, and they couldn't very well have been the kind of Sioux you said. And just last night on the TV in the motel, those Massachusetts Indians put a war bonnet on the President and called him the Great White Father. You mean to tell me that they were all phonies? Hey, who's laughing at who here?"

"If you're an Indian where's your bow and arrow?" Tom Rampart interrupted. "I bet you can't even shoot one."

"You're sure right there," Clarence admitted. "I never shot one of those things but once in my life. They used to have an archery range in Boulder Park over in T-Town, and you could rent the things and shoot at targets tied to hay bales. Hey, I barked my whole forearm and nearly broke my thumb when the bow-string thwacked home. I couldn't shoot that thing at all. I don't see how anybody ever could shoot one of them."

"OK, kids," Nina Rampart called to her brood. "Let's start pitching this junk out of the shack so we can move in. Is there any way we can drive our camper down here, Clarence?"

"Sure, there's a pretty good dirt road, and it's a lot wider than it looks from the top. I got a bunch of green bills in an old night charley in the shack. Let me get them, and then I'll clear out for a while. The shack hasn't been cleaned out for seven years, since the last time this happened. I'll show you the road to the top, and you can bring your car down it."

"Hey, you old Indian, you lied!" Cecilia Rampart shrilled from the doorway of the shack. "You *do* have a war bonnet. Can I have it?"

"I didn't mean to lie, I forgot about that thing," Clarence Little-Saddle said. "My son Clarence Bare-Back sent that to me from Japan for a joke a long time ago. Sure, you can have it."

All the children were assigned tasks carrying the junk out of the shack and setting fire to it. Nina Rampart and Clarence Little-Saddle ambled up to the rim of the valley by the vehicle road that was wider than it looked from the top.

"Nina, you're back! I thought you were gone forever," Robert Rampart jittered at seeing her again. "What—where are the children?"

"Why, I left them down in the valley, Robert. That is, ah, down in that little ditch right there. Now you've got me worried again. I'm going to drive the camper down there and unload it. You'd better go on down and lend a hand too, Robert, and quit talking to all these funny-looking men here."

And Nina went back to Dublin's place for the camper.

"It would be easier for a camel to go through the eye of a needle than for that intrepid woman to drive a car down into that narrow ditch," the eminent scientist Dr. Velikof Vonk said.

"You know how that camel does it?" Clarence Little-Saddle offered, appearing of a sudden from nowhere. "He just closes one of his own eyes and flops back his ears and plunges right through. A camel is mighty narrow when he closes one eye and flops back his ears. Besides, they use a big-eyed needle in the act."

"Where'd this crazy man come from?" Robert Rampart demanded, jumping three feet in the air. "Things are coming out of the ground now. I want my land! I want my children! I want my wife! Whoops, here she comes driving it. Nina, you can't drive a loaded camper into a little ditch like that! You'll be killed or collapsed!"

Nina Rampart drove the loaded camper into the little ditch at a pretty good rate of speed. The best of belief is that she just closed one eye and plunged right through. The car diminished and dropped, and it was smaller than a toy car. But it raised a pretty good cloud of dust as it bumped for several hundred yards across a ditch that was only five feet wide.

"Rampart, it's akin to the phenomenon known as looming, only in reverse," the eminent scientist Arpad Arkabaranan explained as he attempted to throw a rock across the narrow ditch. The rock rose very high in the air, seemed to hang at its apex while it diminished to the size of a grain of sand, and then fell into the ditch not six inches of the way across. There isn't anybody going to throw across a half-mile valley even if it looks five feet. "Look at a rising moon sometimes, Rampart. It appears very large, as though covering a great sector of the horizon, but it only covers one-half of a degree. It is hard to believe that you could set seven hundred and twenty of such large moons side by side around the horizon, or that it would take one hundred and eighty of the big things to reach from the horizon to a point overhead. It is also hard to believe that your valley is twelve hundred times as wide as it appears, but it has been surveyed, and it is."

"I want my land. I want my children. I want my wife," Robert chanted dully. "Damn, I let her get away again."

"I tell you, Rampy," Clarence Little-Saddle squared on him, "a man that lets his wife get away twice doesn't deserve to keep her. I give you till nightfall; then you forfeit. I've taken a liking to the brood. One of us is going to be down there tonight."

After a while a bunch of them were off in that little tavern on the road between Cleveland and Osage. It was only half a mile away. If the valley had run in the other direction, it would have been only six feet away.

"It is a psychic nexus in the form of an elongated dome," said the eminent scientist Dr. Velikof Vonk. "It is maintained subconsciously by the concatenation of at least two minds, the stronger of them belonging to a man dead for many years. It has apparently existed for a little less than a hundred years, and in another hundred years it will be considerably weakened. We know from our checking out folk tales of Europe as well as Cambodia that these ensorcelled areas seldom survive for more than two hundred and fifty years. The person who first set such a thing in being will usually lose interest in it, and in all worldly things, within a hundred years of his own death. This is a simple thanatopsychic limitation. As a short-term device, the thing has been used several times as a military tactic.

"This psychic nexus, as long as it maintains itself, causes group illusion, but it is really a simple thing. It doesn't fool birds or rabbits or cattle, or cameras, only humans. There is nothing meteorological about it. It is strictly psychological. I'm glad I was able to give a scientific explanation to it or it would have worried me."

"It is continental fault coinciding with a noospheric fault," said the eminent scientist Arpad Arkabaranan. "The valley really is half a mile wide, and at the same time it really is only five feet wide. If we measured correctly, we would get these dual measurements. Of course it is meteorological! Everything including dreams is meteorological. It is the animals and cameras which are fooled, as lacking a true dimension; it is only humans who see the true duality. The phenomenon should be common along the whole continental fault where the earth gains or loses half a mile that has to go somewhere. Likely it extends through the whole sweep of the Cross Timbers. Many of those trees appear twice, and many do not appear at all. A man in the proper state of mind could farm that land or raise cattle on it, but it doesn't really exist. There is a clear parallel in the Luftspiegelungthal sector in the Black Forest of Germany which exists, or does not exist, according to the circumstances and to the attitude of the beholder. Then we have the case of Mad Mountain in Morgan County, Tennessee, which isn't there all the time; and also the Little Lobo Mirage south of Presidio, Texas, from which twenty thousand barrels of water were pumped in one two-and-a-half-year period before the mirage reverted to mirage status. I'm glad I was able to give a scientific explanation to this or it would have worried me."

"I just don't understand how he worked it," said the eminent scientist Willy McGilly. "Cedar bark, jack-oak leaves, and the world 'Petahauerat.' The thing's impossible! When I was a boy and we wanted to make a hide-out, we used bark from the skunk-spruce tree, the leaves of a box-elder, and the word was 'Boadicea.' All three elements are wrong here. I cannot find a scientific explanation for it, and it does worry me."

They went back to Narrow Valley. Robert Rampart was still chanting dully: "I want my land. I want my children. I want my wife."

Nina Rampart came chugging up out of the narrow ditch in the camper and emerged through that little gate a few yards down the fence row.

"Supper's ready and we're tired of waiting for you, Robert," she said. "A fine homesteader you are! Afraid to come onto your own land! Come along now; I'm tired of waiting for you."

"I want my land! I want my children! I want my wife!" Robert Rampart still chanted. "Oh, there you are, Nina. You stay here this time. I want my land! I want my children! I want an answer to this terrible thing."

"It is time we decided who wears the pants in this family," Nina said stoutly. She picked up her husband, slung him over her shoulder, carried him to the camper and dumped him in, slammed (as it seemed) a dozen doors at once, and drove furiously down into the Narrow Valley, which already seemed wider.

Why, that place was getting normaler and normaler by the minute! Pretty soon it looked almost as wide as it was supposed to be. The psychic nexus in the form of an elongated dome had collapsed. The continental fault that coincided with the noospheric fault had faced facts and decided to conform. The Ramparts were in effective possession of their homestead, and Narrow Valley was as normal as any place anywhere.

"I have lost my land," Clarence Little-Saddle moaned. "It was the land of my father, Clarence Big-Saddle, and I meant it to be the land of my son, Clarence Bare-Back. It looked so narrow that people did not notice how wide it was, and people did not try to enter it. Now I have lost it."

Clarence Little-Saddle and the eminent scientist Willy McGilly were standing on the edge of Narrow Valley, which now appeared its true half-mile extent.

The moon was just rising, so big that it filled a third of the sky. Who would have imagined that it would take a hundred and eighty of such monstrous things to reach from the horizon to a point overhead, and yet you could sight it with sighters and figure it so.

"I had a little bear-cat by the tail and I let go," Clarence groaned. "I had a fine valley for free, and I have lost it. I am like that hard-luck guy in the funny-paper or Job in the Bible. Destitution is my lot."

Willy McGilly looked around furtively. They were alone on the edge of the half-mile-wide valley.

"Let's give it a booster shot," Willy McGilly said.

Hey, those two got with it! They started a snapping fire and began to throw the stuff onto it. Bark from the dog-elm tree—how do you know it won't work?

It *was* working! Already the other side of the valley seemed a hundred yards closer, and there were alarmed noises coming up from the people in the valley.

Leaves from a black locust tree—and the valley narrowed still more! There was, moreover, terrified screaming of both children and big people from the depths of Narrow Valley, and the happy voice of Mary Mabel Rampart chanting, "Earthquake! Earthquake!"

"That my valley be always wide and flourish and such stuff, and green with money and grass!" Clarence Little-Saddle orated in Pawnee chant style, "but that it be narrow if intruders come, smash them like bugs!"

People, that valley wasn't over a hundred feet wide now, and the screaming of the people in the bottom of the valley had been joined by the hysterical coughing of the camper car starting up.

Willy and Clarence threw everything that was left on the fire. But the word? The word? Who remembers the word?

"Corsicanatexas!" Clarence Little-Saddle howled out with confidence he hoped would fool the fates.

He was answered not only by a dazzling sheet of summer lightning, but also by thunder and raindrops.

"Chahiksi!" Clarence Little-Saddle swore. "It worked. I didn't think it would. It will be all right now. I can use the rain."

The valley was again a ditch only five feet wide.

The camper car struggled out of Narrow Valley through the little gate. It was smashed flat as a sheet of paper, and the screaming kids and people in it had only one dimension.

"It's closing in! It's closing in!" Robert Rampart roared, and he was no thicker than if he had been made out of cardboard.

"We're smashed like bugs," the Rampart boys intoned. "We're thin like paper."

"*Mort, ruine, ecrasement!*" spoke-acted Cecilia Rampart like the great tragedienne she was.

"Help! Help!" Nina Rampart croaked, but she winked at Willy and Clarence as they rolled by. "This homesteading jag always did leave me a little flat."

"Don't throw those paper dolls away. They might be the Ramparts," Mary Mabel called.

The camper car coughed again and bumped along on level ground. This couldn't last forever. The car was widening out as it bumped along.

"Did we overdo it, Clarence?" Willy McGilly asked. "What did one flat-lander say to the other?"

"Dimension of us never got around," Clarence said. "No, I don't think we overdid it, Willy. That car must be eighteen inches wide already, and they all ought to be normal by the time they reach the main road. The next time I do it, I think I'll throw wood-grain plastic on the fire to see who's kidding who."

Nor Limestone Islands

Introduction by Michael Bishop

Lafferty strikes the reader as *sui generis,* a literary creator like no other. But he also comes across as *uniquely himself,* a writer so potently fizzy and tipsy-making that one could say his prose Laffervesces.

See the first paragraph of "Nor Limestone Islands," a tale arising from Lafferty's interest in geology, mineralogy, rockhounding, story-mining and architectural and literary lapidaries. (Disarmingly, he had the ability to appear to be an expert in every -ology imaginable.)

That paragraph reads: "*A lapidary is one who cuts, polishes, engraves, and sets small stones. He is also a scrivener who sets in little stones or pieces here and there and attempts to make a mosaic out of them.*"

With that dubious hook, our Oklahoman leprechaun not only defines a term that may not feel wholly familiar, but also compares the intricately fitted jigsaw-puzzle of an architectural mosaic to the mix-and-match literary method by which he has structured "Nor Limestone Islands."

Listen to this tale's limestone salesman make a pitch to a roomful of city officials: "*We . . . want everybody to come and visit us, but hardly anybody wants to. Right now, my country [Sky-High Stutzamutza]* is **about three miles from here**" [my emphasis].

This spiel evokes part three, "A Voyage to Laputa," of my most admired book in the world, *Gulliver's Travels*. Laputa's lodestone-directed flying islands first boggled my starving preteen mind in Tulsa, Oklahoma, *circa* 1958.

Thus, in 1984, I chose "Nor Limestone Islands" to represent R. A. Lafferty in an anthology titled *Light Years and Dark: Science Fiction and Fantasy Of and For Our Time*. And here is how I introduced it:

"How does a 105-pound girl assemble a thirty-million-ton Pink Pagoda in six hours? R. A. Lafferty will tell you in this charming 'article' about floating limestone islands and the intrepid Miss Phosphor McCabe, whose breathtaking photographs of Sky-High Stutzamutza (see plates I to XXII) are unfortunately not included in the text.

"Lafferty, you see, is famous—perhaps *notorious* is the better word—for the inveterate unorthodoxy of his story concepts and narrative strategies. His work is immediately recognizable as his in a way that the work of other writers is not always identifiable as theirs and nobody else's.

"This distinctiveness would seem to leave Lafferty wide open to parody, but he writes with such droll originality that any attempt to burlesque him turns instead into a pale pastiche of his methods and hence into a kind of homage.

"New Wave? Old Wave? Who cares? Lafferty is surfing the crest of a comber whose quirky break only *he* knows how to ride."

That remains pretty much the case today. Indeed, those who manage to create better than passable parodies-cum-*hommages* to Lafferty (like Neil Gaiman) usually come away from the experience understanding both how hard such stories are to write and why no one else tries to build a career emulating our *sui generis* Raphael Aloysius Lafferty.

Nor Limestone Islands

A lapidary is one who cuts, polishes, engraves, and sets small stones. He is also a scrivener with a choppy style who sets in little stones or pieces here and there and attempts to make a mosaic out of them.

But what do you call one who cuts and sets very large stones?

Take a small *lapillus* or stone for instance:

> The origin of painting as an art in Greece is connected with definite historical personages; but that of sculpture is lost in the mists of legend. Its authentic history does not begin until about the year 600 B.C. It was regarded as an art imparted to men by the gods; for such is the thought expressed in the assertion that the earliest statues fell from heaven.
>
> "Statuaria Ars; Sculpture," *Harper's Dictionary*
> *of Classical Literature and Antiquities.*

We set that little stone in one corner, even though it contains a misunderstanding of what fell from heaven: it wasn't finished statues.

Then we set another small stone:

(We haven't the exact citation of this. It's from Charles Fort or from one of his imitators.) It's of a scientist who refused to believe that several pieces of limestone had fallen from the sky, even though two farmers had seen them fall. They could not have fallen from the sky, the scientist said, because there is no limestone in the sky. (What would that scientist have done if he had been confronted with the question of Whales in the Sky?)

We set that little stone of wisdom into one corner. And we look around for other stones to set.

The limestone salesman was making his pitch to the city commissioners. He had been making a poor pitch and he was a poor salesman. All he had was price (much less than one tenth that of the other bidders) and superior quality. But the limestone salesman did not make a good appearance. He was bare-chested (and colossally deep-chested). He had only a little shoulder jacket above, and a folded drape below. On his feet he had the *crepida* or Hermes-sandals, made of buckskin apparently: a silly affectation. He was darkly burned in skin and hair, but the roots of his hair and of his skin indicated that he was blond in both. He was golden-bearded, but the beard (and in fact the whole man) was covered with chalk-dust or rock-dust. The man was sweaty, and he smelled. His was a composite smell of limestone and edged bronze and goats and clover and honey and ozone and lentils and sour milk and dung and strong cheese.

"No, I don't believe that we want to deal with you at all," the mayor of the city was saying. "The other firms are all reputable and long established."

"Our firm is long established," the limestone salesman said. "It has been doing business from the same—ah—cart for nine thousand years."

"Balderdash," the streets and sewers commissioner swore. "You won't even give us the address of your firm, and you haven't put in a formal bid."

"The address is Stutzamutza," the limestone salesman said. "That's all the address I can give you. There isn't any other address. And I will put in a formal bid if you will show me how to do it. I offer you three hundred tons of the finest marble-limestone, cut exactly to specification, and set in place, guaranteed to take care of your project, guaranteed to be without flaw, in either pure white or variegated; I offer this delivered and set within one hour, all for the price of three hundred dollars or three hundred bushels of cracked corn."

"Oh take it, take it!" a Miss Phosphor McCabe cried out. "We elect you gentlemen to do our business for us at bargain prices. Do not pass up this fine bargain, I beg you." Phosphor McCabe was a lady photographer who had nine fingers in every pie.

"You be quiet, young lady, or we will have you put out of the hearing room," said the parks and playgrounds commissioner. "You will wait your turn, and you will not interfere in other cases. I shudder to think what your own petition will be today. Was ever a group so put upon by cranks as ourselves?"

"You have a very bad reputation, man," the finance commissioner said to the limestone salesman, "insofar as anyone has heard of you before. There is some mumble that your limestone or marble is not substantial, that it will melt away like hailstones. There is even a rumor that you had something to do with the terrible hailstorm of the night before last."

"Ah, we just had a little party at our place that night," the limestone salesman said. "We had a few dozen bottles of Tontitown wine from some stone that we set over in Arkansas, and we drank it up. We didn't hurt anybody or anything with those hailstones. Hey, some of them were as big as basketballs, weren't they! But we were careful where we let them fall. How often do you see a hailstorm as wild as that that doesn't do any damage at all to anything?"

"We can't afford to look silly," the schools and activities commissioner said. "We have been made to look silly in quite a few cases lately, not all of them our own fault. We can't afford to buy limestone for a project like this from someone like you."

"I wonder if you could get me about a hundred and twenty tons of good quality pink granite?" asked a smiling pinkish man in the hearing room.

"No, that's another island entirely," the limestone salesman said. "I'll tell them if I see them."

"Mr. Chalupa, I don't know what your business is here today," the mayor said severely to the smiling pinkish man, "but you will wait your turn, and you will not mix into this case. Lately it seems that our open hearings are just one nut after another."

"How can you lose?" the limestone salesman asked the commissioners. "I will supply and cut and set the stones. If you are not satisfied, I will leave the stones at no cost, or I will remove them again. And not until you are completely satisfied do you pay me the three hundred dollars or the three hundred bushels of cracked corn."

"I want to go to your country with you," Miss Phosphor McCabe burst out. "I am fascinated by what I have heard of it. I want to do a photographic article about it for the *Heritage Geographical Magazine*. How far away is your country now?"

"All right," the limestone salesman said. "I'll wait for you. We'll go just as soon as I have transacted my business and you have transacted yours. We like everybody and we want everybody to come and visit us, but hardly anybody wants to. Right now, my country is about three miles from here. Last chance, gentlemen: I offer you the best bargain in quality marble-limestone that you'll ever find if you live two hundred years. And I hope you do all live to be two hundred. We like everybody and we'd like to see everybody live two hundred years at least."

"Absolutely not," said the mayor of the city. "We'd be the laughing-stock of the whole state if we did business with someone like you. What kind of a country of yours are you talking about that's only three miles from here? Absolutely not. You are wasting your time and ours, man."

"No, no, it just couldn't be," said the streets and sewers commissioner. "What would the papers print if they heard that we had bought limestone from somebody nearly as disreputable as a saucerian?"

"Rejected, rejected," said the parks and playgrounds commissioner. "We were elected to transact the city's business with economy *and dignity*."

"Ah well, all right," the limestone salesman said. "You can't sell a stylobate every time you try. Good day, commissioners. No hurry, lady. I'll wait for you." And the limestone salesman went out, leaving, as it seemed, a cloud of rock-dust in his wake.

"What a day!" the schools and activities commissioner moaned. "What a procession of jokers we have had! Anyhow, that one can't be topped."

"I'm not so sure," the mayor grumbled. "Miss Phosphor McCabe is next."

"Oh, I'll be brief," Phosphor said brightly. "All I want is a permit to build a pagoda on that thirty-acre hill that my grandfather left me. It won't interfere with anything. There won't be any utilities to run to it. And it will be pretty."

"Ah, why do you want to build a pagoda?" the streets and sewers commissioner asked.

"So I can take pictures of it. And just because I want to build a pagoda."

"What kind of a pagoda will it be?" the parks and playgrounds commissioner asked.

"A pink pagoda."

"How big will it be?" the schools and activities commissioner asked.

"Thirty acres big. And four hundred feet high. It will be big and it won't bother anything."

"Why do you want it so big?" the mayor asked.

"So it will be ten times as big as the Black Pagoda in India. It'll be real pretty and an attraction to the area."

"Do you have the money to build this with?" the streets and sewers commissioner asked.

"No, I don't have hardly any money. If I sell my photographic article 'With Camera and Canoe on Sky-High Stutzamutza' to the *Heritage Geographical Magazine* I will get some money for it. And I have been snapping unrehearsed camera portraits of all you gentlemen for the last few minutes, and I may be able to sell them to *Comic Weekly* if I can think of cute headings for them. As to the money to build the Pink Pagoda, oh, I'll think of something."

"Miss McCabe, your request is remanded or remaindered or whatever, which is the same thing as being tabled," the mayor said.

"What does that mean?"

"I'm not sure. The legal commissioner is absent today, but he always says something like that when we want to pass the buck for a little while."

"It means come back in one week, Miss McCabe," the streets and sewers commissioner said.

"All right," Miss Phosphor McCabe agreed. "I couldn't possibly start on the Pink Pagoda before a week anyhow."

And now we set this odd-shaped stone over in the other corner:

The seventeenth century discovery of the Polynesian Islands by common seamen was one of the ancient paradise promises fulfilled. The green islands, the blue sea, the golden beaches and the golden sunlight, the dusky girls! Fruit incomparable, fish incomparable, roast pig and baked bird beyond believing, breadfruit and volcano, absolute and continuing perfection of weather, brown-skin paradise maidens such as are promised in alcoran, song and string-music and surf-music! This was the Promised Paradise of the Islands, and it came true.

But even this was a weak thing beside the less known, the earlier and continuing discovery of the Floating Islands (or the Travertine Islands) by more intrepid farers. The girls of the Floating Islands are lighter (except for the cool blacks on the Greenstone Dolomites) than the Polynesian maidens; they are more intelligent and much more full of fun; are more handsome and fuller bodied; are of an artier and more vital culture. They are livelier. Oh how they are livelier! And the regions themselves defy description. For color and zest, there is nothing in Polynesia or Aegea or Antilla to compare at all. And all the Travertine people are so friendly! Perhaps it is well that they are little known and little visited. We may be too weak for their experience.

—*Facts of the Paradise Legend* by Harold Bluewater

Look closely at that little stone ere we leave it. Are you sure that you have correctly noted the shape of it?

Then a still smaller stone to be set in, here where there seems too empty a little gap. It's a mere quotation:

"In Lapidary Inscription a Man is not upon Oath."

—Doctor Johnson

Miss Phosphor McCabe did visit the limestone salesman's country, and she did do the photographic article "With Camera and Canoe in Sky-High Stutzamutza." The stunning, eye-blowing, heart-swelling, joy-filled color photography cannot be given here, but these are a few extracts from the sustaining text:

"Stutzamutza is a limestone land of such unbelievable whiteness as to make the eyes ache with delight. It is this super-whiteness as a basis that makes all the other colors stand out with such clarity. There cannot be anywhere a bluer sky than, for most of the hours and days, surrounds Stutzamutza (see plates I and II). There cannot be greener fields, where there are fields, nor more silvery water (plates IV and V). The waterfalls are absolute rainbows, especially Final Falls, when it flows clear off the high land (plate VI). There cannot be more variegated cliffs, blue, black, pink, ochre, red, green, but always with that more-white-than-white basic (plate VII). There cannot be such a sun anywhere else. It shines here as it shines nowhere on the world.

"Due to the high average elevation of Stutzamutza (there will be some boggled eyes when I reveal just what I do mean by the *average* elevation of this place), the people are all wonderfully deep-chested or deep-breasted. They are like something out of fable. The few visitors who come here from lower, from more mundane elevations, are uniform in their disbelief. 'Oh, oh,' they will say. 'There can't be girls like that.' There are, however (see plate VIII). 'How long has this been going on?' these occasional visitors ask. It has been going on for the nine thousand years of recorded Stutzamutza history; and, beyond that, it has been going on as long as the world has been going on.

"Perhaps due to their deep-breastedness the Stutzamutza people are superb in their singing. They are lusty, they are loud, they are beautiful and enchanting in this. Their instruments, besides the conventional flutes and bagpipes (with their great lung-power, these people do wonderful things with the bagpipes) and lyric harps and tabors, are the thunder-drum (plate IX) and the thirteen-foot-long trumpets (plates X and XI). It is doubted whether any other people any-where would be able to blow these roaring trumpets.

"Perhaps it is due also to their deep-breastedness that the Stutzamutza people are all so lustily affectionate. There is something both breath-taking and breath-giving in their Olympian carnality. They have a robustness and glory in their man and woman interfluents that leave this underdeveloped little girl more than amazed (plates X to XIX). Moreover, these people are witty and wise, and always pleasant.

"It is said that originally there was not any soil at all on Stutzamutza. The people would trade finest quality limestone, marble, and dolomite for equal amounts of soil, be it the poorest clay or sand. They filled certain crevices with this soil and got vegetation to begin. And, in a few thousand years, they built countless verdant terraces, knolls, and valleys. Grapes, olives, and clover are now grown in profusion. Wine and oil and honey gladden the deep hearts of the people. The wonderful blue-green clover (see plate XX) is grazed by the bees and the goats. There are two separate species of goat: the meadow and pasture goat kept for its milk and cheese and mohair, and the larger and wilder mountain goat hunted on the white crags and eaten for its flavorsome, randy meat. Woven mohair and dressed buckskin are used for the Stutzamutza clothing. The people are not voluminously clothed, in spite of the fact that it becomes quite chilly on the days when the elevation suddenly increases.

"There is very little grain grown on Stutzamutza. Mostly, quarried stones are bartered for grain. Quarrying stone is the main industry, it is really the only one on Stutzamutza. The great quarries in their cutaways sometimes reveal amazing fossil deposits. There is a complete fossilized body of a whale (it is an extinct Zeuglodon or Eocene Whale) (see plate XXI).

'If this is whale indeed, then this all must have been under ocean once,' I said to one of my deep-chested friends. 'Oh certainly,' he said, 'nowhere else is limestone formed than in ocean.' 'Then how has it risen so far above it?' I asked. 'That is something for the Geologists and the Hyphologists to figure out,' my friend said.

"The fascinating aspect of the water on Stutzamutza is its changeableness. A lake is sometimes formed in a single day, and it may be emptied out in one day again by mere tipping. The rain is prodigious sometimes, when it is decided to come into that aspect. To shoot the rapids on the sudden swollen rivers is a de-light. Sometimes ice will form all over Stutzamutza in a very few minutes. The people delight in this sudden ice, all except the little under-equipped guest. The beauty of it is stupendous; so is its cold. They shear the ice off in great sheets and masses and blocks, and let it fall for fun.

"But all lesser views are forgotten when one sees the waterfalls tumbling in the sunlight. And the most wonderful of all of them is Final Falls. Oh to watch it fall clear off Stutzamutza (see plate XXII), to see it fall into practically endless space, thirty thousand feet, sixty thousand feet, turning into mist, into sleet or snow or rain or hail depending on the sort of day it is, to see the miles-long rainbow of it extending to the vanishing point so far below your feet!

"There is a particularly striking pink marble cliff toward the north end of the land (the *temporary* north end of the land). 'You like it? You can have it,' my friends say. That is what I had been fishing for them to say."

Yes, Miss Phosphor McCabe did the really stunning photographic article for *Heritage Geographical Magazine*. *Heritage Geographical* did not accept it, however. Miss Phosphor McCabe had arrived at some unacceptable conclusions, the editor said.

"What really happened is that I arrived at an unacceptable place," Miss Phosphor said. "I remained there for six days. I photographed it and I narrated it."

"Ah, we'd never get by with that," the editor said. Part of the trouble was Miss Phosphor McCabe's explanations of just what she did mean by the average elevation of Stutzamutza (it was quite high), and by "days of increasing elevation."

Now here is another stone of silly shape. At first glimpse, it will not seem possible to fit it into the intended gap. But the eye is deceived: this shape will fit into the gap nicely. It is a recollection in age of a thing observed during a long lifetime by a fine weather eye.

Already as a small boy I was interested in clouds. I believed that certain clouds preserve their identities and appear again and again; and that some clouds are more solid than others.

Later, when I took meteorology and weather courses at the university, I had a classmate who held a series of seemingly insane beliefs. At the heart of these was the theory that certain apparent clouds are not vapor masses at all but are floating stone islands in the sky. He believed that there were some thirty of these islands, most of them composed of limestone, but some of them of basalt or sandstone, even of shale. He said that one, at least, of them was composed of pot-stone or soap-stone.

This classmate said that these floating islands were sometimes large, one of them being at least five miles long: that they were intelligently navigated to follow the best camouflage, the limestone islands usually traveling with masses of white fleecy clouds, the basalt islands traveling with dark thunderheads, and so on. He believed that these islands sometimes came to rest on earth, that each of them had its own several nests in unfrequented regions. And he believed that the floating islands were peopled.

We had considerable fun with Mad Anthony Tummley, our eccentric classmate. His ideas, we told each other, were quite insane. And, indeed, Anthony himself was finally institutionalized. It was a sad case, but one that could hardly be discussed without laughter.

But later, after more than fifty years in the weather profession, I have come to the conclusion that Anthony Tummley was right in every respect. Several of us veteran weathermen share this knowledge now, but we have developed a sort of code for the thing, not daring to admit it openly, even to ourselves. "Whales in the Sky" is the code-name for this study, and we pretend to keep it on a humorous basis.

Some thirty of these floating stone islands are continuously over our own country (there may be more than a hundred of them in the world). They are tracked on radar; they are sighted again and again in their slightly changed forms (some of them, now and then, seem to slough off small masses of stone and deposit it somehow on earth); they are known, they are named.

They are even visited by some persons of odd character: always a peculiar combination of simplicity, acceptance, intelligence, and strange rapport. There are persons and families in rural situations who employ these peopled islands to carry messages and goods for them. In rural and swampland Louisiana, there was once some wonder that the people did not more avail themselves of the Intercoastal Canal barges to carry their supplies, and their products to market. "How are the barges better than the stone islands that we have always used?" these people ask. "They aren't on a much more regular schedule, they aren't much faster, and they won't give you anything like the same amount of service in exchange for a hundredweight of rice. Besides that, the stone-island people are our friends, and some of them have intermarried with us Cajuns." There are other regions where the same easy cooperation obtains.

Many of the stone-island people are well known along certain almost regular routes. These people are all of a powerful and rather coarse beauty. They are good-natured and hearty. They actually traffic in stone, trading amazing tonnages of top grade building stone for grain and other simple provisions.

There is no scientific explanation at all of how these things can be, how the stone islands are able to float in the sky. But that they do so is the open secret of perhaps a million persons.

Really, I am now too wealthy to be put in a madhouse (though I made my money in a rather mad traffic which would not be generally believed). I am too old to be laughed at openly: I will merely be smiled at as an eccentric. I have now retired from that weather profession which served me as a front for many years (which profession, however, I loved and still love).

I know what I know. There are more things in the zone fifteen miles above the earth than are dreamed of in your philosophy, Horatio.

—*Memories of 52 Years as a Weather Observer*
by Hank Fairday (Privately printed, 1970)

Miss Phosphor McCabe did another really stunning photographic article for the *Heritage Geographical Magazine.* It had a catchy title: "All Right, Then You Tell *Me* How I Did It, or The Building of the Pink Pagoda."

"The Pink Pagoda is complete, except for such additions as I shall have made whenever the notion strikes me, and whenever my high-flying friends are in the neighborhood. It is by far the largest structure in the world and also, in my opinion, the most beautiful. But it is not massive in appearance: it is light and airy. Come see it in the stone, all of you! Come see it in the color photography (plates I to CXXIX) if you are not able to come yourself. This wonderful structure gives the answers to hundreds of questions, if you will just open your eyes and your ears.

"Of ancient megalithic structures it has sometimes been asked how a hundred or more of one-hundred ton blocks of stone could have been piled up, and fitted so carefully that even a knife-blade could not be inserted between the blocks. It's easy. You usually don't set a hundred one-hundred ton blocks, unless for a certain ornamentation. You set one ten-thousand ton block, and the joinings are merely simulated. In the Pink Pagoda I have had set blocks as heavy as three hundred thousand tons of pink limestone (see plate XXI).

"They bring the whole island down in place. They split off what block is wanted at that location (and, believe me, they are some splitters); then they withdraw the island a little bit and leave the block in place.

"Well, how else was it done? How did I get the one-hundred-and-fifty-thousand ton main capstone in place four-hundred-and-fifty-feet in the air? With ramps? Oh stop it, you'll scare the cuckoos. The stone pillars and turrets all around and below it are like three-dimensional lace-work, and that main capstone had to go on last. It wasn't done by rocking it up on ramps, even if there had been a place for the ramps. It was all done on one Saturday afternoon, and here are the sequence pictures showing just how it was done. It was done by using a floating island, and by detaching pieces of that island as it was floated into place. I tell you that there is no other way that a one-hundred-and-five pound girl can assemble a thirty-million ton Pink Pagoda in six hours. She has got to have a floating island, with a north cliff of pink limestone, and she has got to be very good friends with the people on that island.

"Please come and see my Pink Pagoda. All the people and all the officials avert their eyes from it. They say that it is impossible that such a thing could be there, and therefore it cannot be there. But it is there. See it yourself (or see plates IV, IX, XXXIII, LXX especially). And it is pretty (see plates XIX, XXIV, V, LIV). But best, come see it as it really is."

Miss Phosphor McCabe did that rather astonishing photographic article for the *Heritage Geographical Magazine. Heritage Geographical* refused to publish it, though, stating that such things were impossible. And they refused to come and see the Pink Pagoda itself, which is a pity, since it is the largest and most beautiful structure on earth.

It stands there yet, on that thirty-acre hill right on the north edge of town. And you have not heard the last stone of it yet. The latest, a bad-natured little addition, will not be the last: Miss Phosphor swears that it will not be.

There was a flimsy-winged enemy flew down, shortly after the first completion of the pagoda, and set the latest very small stone (it is called the egg-of-doubt stone) on top of the main capstone. 'Twas a crabbed written little stone, and it read:

> "I will not trow two-headed calves,"
> Say never-seens, and also haves.
>
> "I'll not believe a hollow earth,"
> Say skepticals of doubtful birth.
>
> "I'll not concede Atlantis you,
> "Nor yet Lemuria or Mu,
>
> "Nor woodsmen in northwestern lands,
> "Nor bandy-legg'd saucerians,
>
> "Nor ancient technologic myth,
> "Nor charm of timeless megalith.
>
> "I will not credit Whales that fly,
> "Nor Limestone Islands in the Sky."
>
> —Unfolk Ballad

That crabby little ballad-stone on the top almost spoils the Pink Pagoda for me. But it will be removed, Miss Phosphor McCabe says, just as soon as her traveling friends are back in this neighborhood and she can get up there.

That is all that we have to say on the subject of stone setting.

Does anyone else have something further to add?

Interurban Queen

Introduction by Terry Bisson

Although his *Okla Hannali* will surely someday take its proper place alongside *Huckleberry Finn* and *Moby-Dick* as one of the Great American Novels, Raphael Aloysius Lafferty is more known for his short stories than his novels. And not all that widely known.

For Lafferty is that most tender, wretched, and essential of creatures, the writers' writer: celebrated by, beloved of, but mostly visible only (check the intros) to his own proud, primitive tribe.

And even in the cult we call SF, Lafferty is an outlier, a dark star, a visitor from the Oort Cloud of literature. Our poet. Not Romantic (how much more pallid, Bradbury!) but rather Elizabethan in the exuberant precision of his words; metaphysical in the playful contrariness of his ideas. Difficult but fun.

No, not the most Important Writer of SF's post-Golden Age. How could such an original prevail? But how not persist! Once discovered, he is never let go. He is with us forever. His is a slant spell but once you fall under it you remain enchanted.

So here is "Interurban Queen." Not his greatest story: it's a middling Lafferty which places it in the top rank of short fiction worldwide. It's an Alternate History, a form Lafferty (a conservative Midwestern engineer) often used as a lever to upend his familiar Oklahoma quotidian. It's a Utopian Tale (another field in which Lafferty liked to romp) with a solid business engine and a sunny, murderous heart.

Come along.

You are on an outing with your great-granddaughter through the green and pleasant landscape of your dreams.

Rifles are handed out.

Interurban Queen

"I t was the year 1907 when I attained my majority and came into a considerable inheritance," the old man said. "I was a very keen young man, keen enough to know that I didn't know everything. I went to knowledgeable men and asked their advice as to how I might invest this inheritance.

"I talked with bankers and cattlemen and the new oilmen. These were not stodgy men. They had an edge on the future, and they were excited and exciting about the way that money might be made to grow. It was the year of statehood and there was an air of prosperity over the new state. I wished to integrate my patrimony into that new prosperity.

"Finally I narrowed my choice to two investments which then seemed about of equal prospect, though you will now smile to hear them equated. One of them was the stock-selling company of a certain Harvey Goodrich, a rubber company, and with the new automobile coming into wider use, it seemed that rubber might be a thing of the future. The other was a stock-selling transportation company that proposed to run an interurban railway between the small towns of Kiefer and Mounds. It also proposed (at a future time) to run branches to Glenpool, to Bixby, to Kellyville, to Slick, to Bristow, to Beggs, even to Okmulgee and Sapulpa. At that time it also seemed that these little interurban railways might be things of the future. An interurban already ran between Tulsa and Sand Springs, and one was building between Tulsa and Sapulpa. There were more than one thousand of these small trolley railroads operating in the nation, and thoughtful men believed that they would come to form a complete national network, might become the main system of transportation."

But now the old man Charles Archer was still a young man. He was listening to Joe Elias, a banker in a small but growing town.

"It is a riddle you pose me, young man, and you set me thinking," Elias said. "We have dabbled in both, thinking to have an egg under every hen. I begin to believe that we were wrong to do so. These two prospects are types of two futures, and only one of them will obtain. In this state with its new oil discoveries, it might seem that we should be partial to rubber which has a tie-in with the automobile which has a tie-in with petroleum fuel. This need not be. I believe that the main use of oil will be in powering the new factories, and I believe that rubber is already oversold as to industrial application. And yet there *will be* a new transportation. Between the horse and the main-line railways there is a great

gap. I firmly believe that the horse will be eliminated as a main form of transportation. We are making no more loans to buggy or buckboard manufacturers
nor to harness makers. I have no faith in the automobile. It destroys something
in me. It is the interurbans that will go into the smallest localities, and will so
cut into the main-line railroads as to leave no more than a half dozen of the
long-distance major lines in America. Young man, I would invest in the interurban with complete confidence."

Charles Archer was listening to Carl Bigheart, a cattleman.
    "I ask you, boy, how many head of cattle can you put into an automobile? Or
even into what they call a lorry or trook? Then I ask you how many you can put
into an honest cattle car which can be coupled onto any interurban on a country run? The interurban will be the salvation of us cattlemen. With the fencing
regulations we cannot drive cattle even twenty miles to a railroad; but the little
interurbans will go into the deep country, running along every second or third
section line.
    "And I will tell you another thing, boy: There is no future for the automobile.
We cannot let there be! Consider the man on horseback, and I have been a man
on horseback for most of my life. Well, mostly he is a good man, but there is a
change in him as soon as he mounts. Every man on horseback is an arrogant
man, however gentle he may be on foot. I know this in myself and in others.
He was necessary in his own time, and I believe that time is ending. There was
always extreme danger from the man on horseback.
    "Believe me, young man, the man in the automobile is one thousand times
as dangerous. The kindest man in the world assumes an incredible arrogance
when he drives an automobile, and this arrogance will increase still further if
the machine is allowed to develop greater power and sophistication. I tell you, it
will engender absolute selfishness in mankind if the driving of automobiles becomes common. It will breed violence on a scale never seen before. It will mark
the end of the family as we know it, the three or four generations living happily
in one home. It will destroy the sense of neighborhood and the true sense of
nation. It will create giantized cankers of cities, false opulence of suburbs, ruin-
ized countryside, and unhealthy conglomeration of specialized farming and
manufacturing. It will breed rootlessness and immorality. It will make every
man a tyrant. I believe the private automobile will be suppressed. *It will have to
be!* This is a moral problem, and we are a moral nation and world; we will take
moral action against it. And without the automobile, rubber has no real future.
Opt for the interurban stock, young man."

Young Charles Archer was listening to Nolan Cushman, an oilman.
    "I will not lie to you, young fellow, I love the automobile, the motorcar. I
have three, custom-built. I am an emperor when I drive. Hell, I'm an emperor
anyhow! I bought a castle last summer that had housed emperors. I'm having it

transported, stone by stone, to my place in the Osage. Now, as to the motorcar, I can see how it should develop. It should develop with the roads, they becoming leveled and metaled or concreted, and the cars lower and lower and faster and faster. We would develop them so, if we were some species other than human. It is the logical development, but I hope it will not come, and it will not. That would be to make it common, and the commonality of men cannot be trusted with this power. Besides, I love a high car, and I do not want there to be very many of them. They should only be allowed to men of extreme wealth and flair. How would it be if the workingmen were ever permitted them? It would be murderous if they should come into the hands of ordinary men. How hellish a world would it be if all men should become as arrogant as myself! No, the automobile will never be anything but a rich man's pride, the rubber will never be anything but a limited adjunct to that special thing. Invest in your interurban. It is the thing of the future, or else I dread that future."

Young Charles Archer knew that this was a crossroads of the world. Whichever turning was taken, it would predicate a certain sort of nation and world and humanity. He thought about it deeply. Then he decided. He went out and invested his entire inheritance in his choice.

"I considered the two investments and I made my choice," said Charles Archer, the old man now in the now present. "I put all I had into it, thirty-five thousand dollars, a considerable sum in those days. You know the results."

"I am one of the results, Great-grandfather," said Angela Archer. "If you had invested differently you would have come to different fortune, you would have married differently, and I would be different or not at all. I like me here and now. I like everything as it is."

Three of them were out riding early one Saturday morning, the old man Charles Archer, his great-granddaughter Angela, and her fiancé Peter Brady. They were riding through the quasiurbia, the rich countryside. It was not a main road, and yet it had a beauty (partly natural and partly contrived) that was as exciting as it was satisfying.

Water always beside the roadway, that was the secret! There were the carp ponds one after another. There were the hatcheries. There were the dancing rocky streams that in a less enlightened age might have been mere gutter runs or roadway runs. There were the small and rapid trout streams, and boys were catching big trout from them.

There were the deep bush-trees there, sumac, witch hazel, sassafras—incense trees they might almost have been. There were the great trees themselves, pecan and hickory and black walnut, standing like high backdrops; and between were the lesser trees, willow, cottonwood, sycamore. Catheads and sedge grass and reeds stood in the water itself, and tall Sudan grass and bluestem on the shores. And always the clovers there, and the smell of wet sweet clover.

"I chose the wrong one," said old Charles Archer as they rode along through the textured country. "One can now see how grotesque was my choice, but I was young. In two years, the stock-selling company in which I had invested was out of business and my loss was total. So early and easy riches were denied me, but I developed an ironic hobby: keeping track of the stock of the enterprise in which I did *not* invest. The stock I could have bought for thirty-five thousand dollars would now make me worth nine million dollars."

"Ugh, don't talk of such a thing on such a beautiful day," Angela objected.

"They heard another of them last night," Peter Brady commented. "They've been hearing this one, off and on, for a week now, and haven't caught him yet."

"I always wish they wouldn't kill them when they catch them," Angela bemoaned. "It doesn't seem quite right to kill them."

A goose-girl was herding her white honking charges as they gobbled weeds out of fields of morning onions. Flowering kale was shining green-purple, and okra plants were standing. Jersey cows grazed along the roadway, and the patterned plastic (almost as patterned as the grasses) filled the roadway itself.

There were clouds like yellow dust in the air. Bees! Stingless bees they were. But dust itself was not. That there never be dust again!

"They will have to find out and kill the sly klunker makers," said old man Charles Archer. "Stop the poison at its source."

"There's too many of them, and too much money in it," said Peter Brady. "Yes, we kill them. One of them was found and killed Thursday, and three nearly finished klunkers were destroyed. But we can't kill them all. They seem to come out of the ground like snakes."

"I wish we didn't have to kill them," Angela said.

There were brightly colored firkins of milk standing on loading stoas, for this was a milk shed. There were chickens squawking in nine-story-high coops as they waited the pickups, but they never had to wait long. Here were a thousand dozen eggs on a refrigeration porch; there a clutch of piglings, or of red steers.

Tomato plants were staked two meters high. Sweetcorn stood, not yet come to tassel. They passed cucumber vines and cantaloupe vines, and the potato hills rising up blue-green. Ah, there were grapevines in their tight acres, deep alfalfa meadows, living fences of Osage orange and white-thorn. Carrot tops zephyred like green lace. Cattle were grazing fields of red clover and of peanuts—that most magic of all clovers. Men mowed hay.

"I hear him now!" Peter Brady said suddenly.

"You couldn't. Not in the daytime. Don't even think of such a thing," Angela protested.

Farm ducks were grazing with their heads under water in the roadway ponds and farm ponds. Bower oaks grew high in the roadway parks. Sheep fed in hay grazer that was higher than their heads; they were small white islands in it. There was local wine and choc beer and cider for sale at small booths, along with limestone sculpture and painted fruitwood carvings. Kids danced on loading stoas to little post-mounted music canisters, and goats licked slate outcroppings in search of some new mineral.

The Saturday riders passed a roadway restaurant with its tables out under the leaves and under a little rock overhang. A one-meter-high waterfall gushed through the middle of the establishment, and a two-meter-long bridge of set shale stone led to the kitchen. Then they broke onto view after never-tiring view of the rich and varied quasiurbia. The roadway farms, the fringe farms, the berry patches! In their seasons: Juneberries, huckleberries, blueberries, dewberries, elderberries, highbush cranberries, red raspberries, boysenberries, loganberries, nine kinds of blackberries, strawberries, greenberries.

Orchards! Can there ever be enough orchards? Plum, peach, sand plum and chokecherry, black cherry, apple and crab apple, pear, blue-fruited pawpaw, persimmon, crooked quince. Melon patches, congregations of beehives, pickle patches, cheese farms, flax farms, close clustered towns (twenty houses in each, twenty persons in a house, twenty of the little settlements along every mile of roadway), country honky-tonks, as well as high-dog clubs already open and hopping with action in the early morning; roadway chapels with local statuary and with their rich-box-poor-boxes (one dropped money in the top if one had it and the spirit to give it, one tripped it out the bottom if one needed it), and the little refrigeration niches with bread, cheese, beef rolls, and always the broached cask of country wine: that there be no more hunger on the roadways forever!

"I hear it too!" old Charles Archer cried out suddenly. "High-pitched and off to the left. And there's the smell of monoxide and—gah—rubber. Conductor, conductor!"

The conductor heard it, as did others in the car. The conductor stopped the cars to listen. Then he phoned the report and gave the location as well as he might, consulting with the passengers. There was rough country over to the left, rocks and hills, and someone was driving there in broad daylight.

The conductor broke out rifles from the locker, passing them out to Peter Brady and two other young men in the car, and to three men in each of the other two cars. A competent-seeming man took over the communication, talking to men on a line further to the left, beyond the mad driver, and they had him boxed into a box no more than half a mile square.

"You stay, Angela, and you stay, Grandfather Archer," Peter Brady said. "Here is a little thirty carbine. Use it if he comes in range at all. We hunt him down now." Then Peter Brady followed the conductor and the rifle-bearing men, ten men on a death hunt. And there were now four other groups out on the hunt, converging on their whining, coughing target.

"Why do they have to kill them, Great-grandfather? Why not turn them over to the courts?"

"The courts are too lenient. All they give them is life in prison."

"But surely that should be enough. It will keep them from driving the things, and some of the unfortunate men might even be rehabilitated."

"Angela, they are the greatest prison breakers ever. Only ten days ago, Mad Man Gudge killed three guards, went over the wall at State Prison, evaded all pursuit, robbed the cheesemakers' cooperative of fifteen thousand dollars, got to a sly klunker maker, and was driving one of the things in a wild area within thirty hours of his breakout. It was four days before they found him and killed him. They are insane, Angela, and the mental hospitals are already full of them. Not one of them has ever been rehabilitated."

"Why is it so bad that they should drive? They usually drive only in the very wild places, and for a few hours in the middle of the night."

"Their madness is infectious, Angela. Their arrogance would leave no room for anything else in the world. Our country is now in balance, our communication and travel is minute and near perfect, thanks to the wonderful trolleys and the people of the trolleys. We are all one neighborhood, we are all one family! We live in love and compassion, with few rich and few poor, and arrogance and hatred have all gone out from us. We are the people with roots, and with trolleys. We are one with our earth."

"Would it hurt that the drivers should have their own limited place to do what they wanted, if they did not bother sane people?"

"Would it hurt if disease and madness and evil were given their own limited place? But they will not stay in their place, Angela. There is the diabolical arrogance in them, the rampant individualism, the hatred of order. There can be nothing more dangerous to society than the man in the automobile. Were they allowed to thrive, there would be poverty and want again, Angela, and wealth and accumulation. And cities."

"But cities are the most wonderful things of all! I love to go to them."

"I do not mean the wonderful Excursion Cities, Angela. There would be cities of another and blacker sort. They were almost upon us once when a limitation was set on them. Uniqueness is lost in them; there would be mere accumulation of rootless people, of arrogant people, of duplicated people, of people who have lost their humanity. Let them never rob us of our involuted countryside, or our quasiurbia. We are not perfect; but what we have, we will not give away for the sake of wild men."

"The smell! I cannot stand it!"

"Monoxide. How would you like to be born in the smell of it, to live every moment of your life in the smell of it, to die in the smell of it?"

"No, no, not that."

The rifleshots were scattered but serious. The howling and coughing of the illicit klunker automobile were nearer. Then it was in sight, bouncing and bounding weirdly out of the rough rock area and into the tomato patches straight toward the trolley interurban.

The klunker automobile was on fire, giving off the ghastly stench of burning leather and rubber and noxious monoxide and seared human flesh. The man, standing up at the broken wheel, was a madman, howling, out of his head. He was a young man, but sunken-eyed and unshaven, bloodied on the left side of his head and the left side of his breast, foaming with hatred and arrogance.

"Kill me! Kill me!" he croaked like clattering broken thunder. "There will be others! We will not leave off driving so long as there is one desolate place left, so long as there is one sly klunker maker left!"

He went rigid. He quivered. He was shot again. But he would die howling.

"Damn you all to trolley haven! A man in an automobile is worth a thousand men on foot! He is worth a million men in a trolley car! You never felt your black heart rise up in you when you took control of one of the monsters! You never felt the lively hate choke you off in rapture as you sneered down the whole world from your bouncing center of the universe! Damn all decent folks! I'd rather go to hell in an automobile than to heaven in a trolley car!"

A spoked wheel broke, sounding like one of the muted volleys of rifle fire coming from behind him. The klunker automobile pitched onto its nose, up-ended, turned over, and exploded in blasting flames. And still in the middle of the fire could be seen the two hypnotic eyes with their darker flame, could be heard the demented voice:

"The crankshaft will still be good, the differential will still be good, a sly klunker maker can use part of it, part of it will drive again—*ahhhiiii.*"

Some of them sang as they rode away from the site in the trolley cars, and some of them were silent and thoughtful. It had been an unnerving thing.

"It curdles me to remember that I once put my entire fortune into that future," Great-grandfather Charles Archer moaned. "Well, that is better than to have lived in such a future."

A young couple had happily loaded all their belongings onto a baggage trolley and were moving from one of the Excursion Cities to live with kindred in quasiurbia. The population of that Excursion City (with its wonderful theaters and music halls and distinguished restaurants and literary coffeehouses and alcoholic oases and amusement centers) had now reached seven thousand persons, the legal limit for any city: oh, there were a thousand Excursion Cities and all of them delightful! But a limit must be kept on size. A limit must be kept on everything.

It was a wonderful Saturday afternoon. Fowlers caught birds with collapsible kite-cornered nets. Kids rode free out to the diamonds to play Trolley League ball. Old gaffers rode out with pigeons in pigeon boxes, to turn them loose and watch them race home. Shore netters took shrimp from the semi-saline Little Shrimp Lake. Banjo players serenaded their girls in grassy lanes.

The world was one single bronze gong song with the melodious clang of trolley cars threading the country on their green-iron rails, with the sparky fire following them overhead and their copper gleaming in the sun. By law there must be a trolley line every mile, but they were oftener. By law no one trolley line might run for more than twenty-five miles. This was to give a sense of locality. But transfers between the lines were worked out perfectly. If one wished to cross the nation, one rode on some one hundred and twenty different lines. There were no more long-distance railroads. They also had had their arrogance, and they also had had to go.

Carp in the ponds, pigs in the clover, a unique barn factory in every hamlet and every hamlet unique, bees in the air, pepper plants in the lanes, and the whole land as sparky as trolley fire and right as rails.

Thus We Frustrate Charlemagne

Introduction by Jack Dann

Rump of Skunk and Madness, or
How to Read R. A. Lafferty

Yes, it looks perfectly simple on the surface . . . Lafferty's prose is short on adjectives and long on what would seem to be the voice of the American tall tale. His characters are ciphers, seemingly one-dimensional caricatures; and the tall voice is innocently jocular as it seems to invent its own convoluted syntax, explains historical incidents at length, punctuates events with impossibly over-the-top details, and tramples through philosophical swamplands like Paul Bunyan in a hurry to get to the end of the story.

We can't help but notice that there is more going on than we can see; and although there are bits and pieces we don't understand—words we don't know, incidents and outré theories that may or may not be historically correct, ostensibly irrelevant sidebars—we can't get off the runaway train until it . . . stops. As is widely acknowledged, Lafferty is a one-off. He can't be imitated. He's been compared to Gene Wolfe because of the influence and presence of Christianity in his work; and he's been compared to Mark Twain, probably for the yarnish nature of his prose. But comparisons don't really work with Lafferty. After all the comparisons are made, we are still left wondering what the hell just happened after we read a Lafferty story. And why do these stories stick in our minds like childhood memory, like fairy tales that scared the bejesus out of us . . . ?

Perhaps it's because they are just that: philosophical fairy tales for adults.

And so to "Thus We Frustrate Charlemagne," which for my money is one of his best short stories; it is quintessential Lafferty, and it works on all the levels, sure to leave you scratching your head as the parable(?) inserts itself firmly into your memory. The story is classic counterfactual fiction: it is an illustration of what happens when you change history to create alternate history; and it comes into being through the writer's choice of a divergence point, which creates a new branch that confounds history as we (think we) know it. Lafferty will leave you to tangle with the possible consequences of the battle of Roncesvalles and William of Occam's concept of terminalism. And if you're as obsessive as I am, you'll probably find yourself looking up some terms.

All that aside, consider as you read whether this is a science fiction story at all . . . or whether it might just be an anti–science fiction story.[1] The author playfully uses the tropes of science fiction, of alternate history; but the science is pretty much just another version of magic, a trope in itself. And the history . . . we believe it because Lafferty sprinkles in such learned esoterica that it somehow *feels* right. And some of it is!

Suffice it to say the story you're about to read is simple and confusing and makes absolute sense! Welcome to the antinomical Lafferty. Welcome to his happily constructed dystopia. As the critic and scholar Don Webb said, "Lafferty's fiction creates the Unknown rather than the Known."

Enjoy the peep show.

---

1. I recommend Paul Kincaid's excellent article in *Through the Dark Labyrinth*, https://www .google.com.au/amp/s/ttdlabyrinth.wordpress.com/2014/08/01/reprint-thus-we-frustrate -charlemagne/amp/

Thus We Frustrate Charlemagne

W e've been on some tall ones," said Gregory Smirnov of the Institute, "but we've never stood on the edge of a bigger one than this, nor viewed one with shakier expectations. Still, if the calculations of Epiktistes are correct, this will work."

"People, it will work," Epikt said.

This was Epiktistes the Ktistec machine? Who'd have believed it? The main bulk of Epikt was five floors below them, but he had run an extension of himself up to this little penthouse lounge. All it took was a cable, no more than a yard in diameter, and a functional head set on the end of it.

And what a head he chose! It was a sea-serpent head, a dragon head, five feet long and copied from an old carnival float. Epikt had also given himself human speech of a sort, a blend of Irish and Jewish and Dutch comedian patter from ancient vaudeville. Epikt was a comic to his last para-DNA relay when he rested his huge, boggle-eyed, crested head on the table there and smoked the biggest stogies ever born.

But he was serious about this project.

"We have perfect test conditions," the machine Epikt said as though calling them to order. "We set out basic texts, and we take careful note of the world as it is. If the world changes, then the texts should change here before our eyes. For our test pilot, we have taken that portion of our own middle-sized city that can be viewed from this fine vantage point. If the world in its past-present continuity is changed by our meddling, then the face of our city will also change instantly as we watch it.

"We have assembled here the finest minds and judgments in the world: eight humans and one Ktistec machine, myself. Remember that there are nine of us. It might be important."

The nine finest minds were: Epiktistes, the transcendent machine who put the "K" in Ktistec; Gregory Smirnov, the large-souled director of the Institute; Valery Mok, an incandescent lady scientist; her over-shadowed and over-intelligent husband, Charles Cogsworth; the humorless and inerrant Glasser; Aloysius Shiplap, the seminal genius; Willy McGilly, a man of unusual parts (the seeing third finger on his left hand he had picked up on one of the planets of Kapteyn's Star) and no false modesty; Audifax O'Hanlon; and Diogenes Pontifex. The latter two

men were not members of the Institute (on account of the Minimal Decency
Rule), but when the finest minds in the world are assembled, these two cannot
very well be left out.

"We are going to tamper with one small detail in past history and note its
effect," Gregory said. "This has never been done before openly. We go back
to an era that has been called 'A patch of light in the vast gloom,' the time of
Charlemagne. We consider why that light went out and did not kindle others.
The world lost four hundred years by that flame expiring when the tinder was
apparently ready for it. We go back to that false dawn of Europe and consider
where it failed. The year was 778, and the region was Spain. Charlemagne
had entered alliance with Marsilies, the Arab king of Saragossa, against the
Caliph Abd ar-Rahmen of Córdova. Charlemagne took such towns as Pamplona, Huesca, and Gerona and cleared the way to Marsilies in Saragossa.
The Caliph accepted the situation. Saragossa should be independent, a city
open to both Moslems and Christians. The northern marches to the border of
France should be permitted their Christianity, and there would be peace for
everybody.

"This Marsilies had long treated Christians as equals in Saragossa, and now
there would be an open road from Islam into the Frankish Empire. Marsilies
gave Charlemagne thirty-three scholars (Moslem, Jewish, and Christian) and
some Spanish mules to seal the bargain. And there could have been a cross-
fertilization of cultures.

"But the road was closed at Roncesvalles where the rearguard of Charlemagne
was ambushed and destroyed on its way back to France. The ambushers were
more Basque than Moslems, but Charlemagne locked the door at the Pyrenees
and swore that he would not let even a bird fly over that border thereafter. He
kept the road closed, as did his son and his grandsons. But when he sealed off
the Moslem world, he also sealed off his own culture.

"In his latter years he tried a revival of civilization with a ragtag of Irish half-
scholars, Greek vagabonds, and Roman copyists who almost remembered an
older Rome. These weren't enough to revive civilization, and yet Charlemagne
came close with them. Had the Islam door remained open, a real revival of
learning might have taken place then rather than four hundred years later. We
are going to arrange that the ambush at Roncesvalles did not happen and that
the door between the two civilizations was not closed. Then we will see what
happens to us."

"'Intrusion like a burglar bent,'" said Epikt.

"Who's a burglar?" Glasser demanded.

"I am," Epikt said. "We all are. It's from an old verse. I forget the author; I
have it filed in my main mind downstairs if you're interested."

"We set out a basic text of Hilarius," Gregory continued. "We note it carefully,
and we must remember it the way it is. Very soon, that may be the way it *was*.

I believe that the words will change on the very page of this book as we watch them. Just as soon as we have done what we intend to do."

The basic text marked in the open book read:

The traitor Gano, playing a multiplex game, with money from the Córdova Caliph hired Basque Christians (dressed as Saragossan Mozarabs) to ambush the rear-guard of the Frankish force. To do this it was necessary that Gano keep in contact with the Basques and at the same time delay the rearguard of the Franks. Gano, however, served both as guide and scout for the Franks. The ambush was effected. Charlemagne lost his Spanish mules. And he locked the door against the Moslem world.

That was the text by Hilarius.

"When we, as it were, push the button (give the nod to Epiktistes), this will be changed," Gregory said. "Epikt, by a complex of devices which he has assembled, will send an Avatar (partly of mechanical and partly of ghostly construction), and something will have happened to the traitor Gano along about sundown one night on the road to Roncesvalles."

"I hope the Avatar isn't expensive," Willy McGilly said. "When I was a boy we got by with a dart whittled out of slippery elm wood."

"This is no place for humor," Glasser protested. "Who did you, as a boy, ever kill in time, Willy?"

"Lots of them. King Wu of the Manchu, Pope Adrian VII, President Hardy of our own country, King Marcel of Auvergne, the philosopher Gabriel Toeplitz. It's a good thing we got them. They were a bad lot."

"But I never heard of any of them, Willy," Glasser insisted.

"Of course not. We killed them when they were kids."

"Enough of your fooling, Willy," Gregory cut it off.

"Willy's not fooling," the machine Epikt said. "Where do you think I got the idea?"

"Regard the world," Aloysius said softly. "We see our own middle-sized town with half a dozen towers of pastel-colored brick. We will watch it as it grows or shrinks. It will change if the world changes."

"There's two shows in town I haven't seen," Valery said. "Don't let them take them away! After all, there are only three shows *in* town."

"We regard the Beautiful Arts as set out in the reviews here which we have also taken as basic texts," Audifax O'Hanlon said. "You can say what you want to, but the arts have never been in meaner shape. Painting is of three schools only, all of them bad. Sculpture is the heaps-of-rusted-metal school and the obscene tinker-toy effects. The only popular art, graffiti on mingitorio walls, has become unimaginative, stylized, and ugly.

"The only thinkers to be thought of are the dead Teilhard de Chardin and the stillborn Sartre, Zielinski, Aichinger. Oh well, if you're going to laugh there's no use going on."

"All of us here are experts on something," Cogsworth said. "Most of us are experts on everything. We know the world *as* it is. Let us do what we are going to do and then look at the world."

"Push the button, Epikt!" Gregory Smirnov ordered.

From his depths, Epiktistes the Ktistec machine sent out an Avatar, partly of mechanical and partly of ghostly construction. Along about sundown on the road from Pamplona to Roncesvalles, on August 14th of the year 778, the traitor Gano was taken up from the road and hanged on a carob tree, the only one in those groves of oak and beech. And all things thereafter were changed.

"Did it work, Epikt? Is it done?" Louis Lobachevski demanded. "I can't see a change in anything."

"The Avatar is back and reports his mission accomplished," Epikt stated. "I can't see any change in anything either."

"Let's look at the evidence," Gregory said. The thirteen of them, the ten humans and the Ktistec, Chresmoeidec, and Proaisthematic machines, turned to the evidence and with mounting disappointment.

"There is not one word changed in the Hilarius text," Gregory grumbled, and indeed the basic text still read:

The king Marsilies of Saragossa, playing a multiplex game, took money from the Caliph of Córdova for persuading Charlemagne to abandon the conquest of Spain (which Charlemagne had never considered and couldn't have effected); took money from Charlemagne in recompense for the cities of the Northern marches being returned to Christian rule (though Marsilies himself had never ruled them); and took money from everyone as toll on the new trade passing through his city. Marsilies gave up nothing but thirty-three scholars, the same number of mules, and a few wagonloads of book-manuscripts from the old Hellenistic librar-ies. But a road over the mountains was opened between the two worlds; and also a sector of the Mediterranean coast became open to both. A limited opening was made between the two worlds, and a limited reanimation of civilization was effected in each.

"No, there is not one word of the text changed," Gregory grumbled. "History followed its same course. How did our experiment fail? We tried, by a device that seems a little cloudy now, to shorten the gestation period for the new birth. It would not be shortened."

"The town is in no way changed," said Aloysius Shiplap. "It is still a fine large town with two dozen imposing towers of varicolored limestone and midland marble. It is a vital metropolis, and we all love it, but it is now as it was before."

"There are still two dozen good shows in town that I haven't seen," Valery said happily as she examined the billings. "I was afraid that something might have happened to them."

"There is no change at all in the Beautiful Arts as reflected in the reviews here that we have taken as basic texts," said Audifax O'Hanlon. "You can say what you want to, but the arts have never been in finer shape."

"It's a link of sausage," said the machine Chresmoeidy.

"'Nor know the road who never ran it thrice,'" said the machine Proaisth. "That's from an old verse; I forget the author; I have it filed in my main mind in England if you're interested."

"Oh yes, it's the three-cornered tale that ends where it begins," said the machine Epiktistes. "But it is good sausage, and we should enjoy it; many ages have not even this much."

"What are you fellows babbling about?" Audifax asked without really wanting to know. "The art of painting is still almost incandescent in its bloom. The schools are like clustered galaxies, and half the people are doing some of this work for pleasure. Scandinavian and Maori sculpture are hard put to maintain their dominance in the field where almost everything is extraordinary. The impassioned-comic has released music from most of its bonds. Since speculative mathematics and psychology have joined the popular performing arts, there is considerably more sheer fun in life.

"There's a piece here on Pete Teilhard putting him into context as a talented science fiction writer with a talent for outré burlesque. The Brainworld Motif was overworked when he tackled it, but what a shaggy comic extravaganza he did make of it! And there's Muldoom, Zielinski, Popper, Gander, Aichinger, Whitecrow, Hornwhanger—we owe so much to the juice of the cultists! In the main line there are whole congeries and continents of great novels and novelists.

"An ever popular art, graffiti on mingitorio walls, maintains its excellence. Travel Unlimited offers a ninety-nine-day art tour of the world keyed to the viewing of the exquisite and hilarious miniatures on the walls of its own restrooms. Ah, what a copious world we live in!"

"It's more grass than we can graze," said Willy McGilly. "The very bulk of achievement is stupefying. Ah, I wonder if there is subtle revenge in my choice of words. The experiment, of course, was a failure, and I'm glad. I like a full world."

"We will not call the experiment a failure since we have covered only a third of it," said Gregory. "Tomorrow we will make our second attempt on the past. And, if there is a present left to us after that, we will make a third attempt the following day."

"Shove it, good people, shove it," the machine Epiktistes said. "We will meet here again tomorrow. Now you to your pleasures, and we to ours."

The people talked that evening away from the machines where they could make foolish conjectures without being laughed at.

"Let's pull a random card out of the pack and go with it," said Louis Lobachevski. "Let's take a purely intellectual crux of a little later date and see if the changing of it will change the world."

"I suggest Ockham," said Johnny Konduly.

"Why?" Valery demanded. "He was the last and least of the medieval schoolmen. How could anything he did or did not do affect anything?"

"Oh no, he held the razor to the jugular," Gregory said. "He'd have severed the vein if the razor hadn't been snatched from his hand. There is something amiss here, though. It is as though I remembered when things were not so stark with Ockham, as though, in some variant, Ockham's Terminalism did not mean what we know that it did mean."

"Sure, let's cut the jugular," said Willy. "Let's find out the logical termination of Terminalism and see just how deep Ockham's razor can cut."

"We'll do it," said Gregory. "Our world has become something of a fat slob; it cloys; it has bothered me all evening. We will find whether purely intellectual attitudes are of actual effect. We'll leave the details to Epikt, but I believe the turning point was in the year 1323 when John Lutterell came from Oxford to Avignon where the Holy See was then situated. He brought with him fifty-six propositions taken from Ockham's Commentary on the Sentences, and he proposed their condemnation. They were not condemned outright, but Ockham was whipped soundly in that first assault, and he never recovered. Lutterell proved that Ockham's nihilism was a bunch of nothing. And the Ockham thing did die away, echoing dimly through the little German courts where Ockham traveled peddling his wares, but he no longer peddled them in the main markets. Yet his viewpoint could have sunk the world if, indeed, intellectual attitudes are of actual effect."

"We wouldn't have liked Lutterell," said Aloysius. "He was humorless and he had no fire in him, and he was always right. And we would have liked Ockham. He was charming, and he was wrong, and perhaps we will destroy the world yet. There's a chance that we will get our reaction if we allow Ockham free hand. China was frozen for thousands of years by an intellectual attitude, one not nearly so unsettling as Ockham's. India is hypnotized into a queer stasis which calls itself revolutionary and which does not move— hypnotized by an intellectual attitude. But there was never such an attitude as Ockham's."

So they decided that the former chancellor of Oxford, John Lutterell, who was always a sick man, should suffer one more sickness on the road to Avignon in France, and that he should not arrive there to lance the Ockham thing before it infected the world.

"Let's get on with it, good people," Epikt rumbled the next day. "Me, I'm to stop a man getting from Oxford to Avignon in the year 1323. Well, come, come, take your places, and let's get the thing started." And Epiktistes's great sea-serpent head glowed every color as he puffed on a seven-branched pooka-dooka and filled the room with wonderful smoke.

"Everybody ready to have his throat cut?" Gregory asked cheerfully.

"Cut them," said Diogenes Pontifex, "but I haven't much hope for it. If our yesterday's essay had no effect, I cannot see how one English schoolman chasing another to challenge him in an Italian court in France, in bad Latin, nearly seven hundred years ago, on fifty-six points of unscientific abstract reasoning, can have effect."

"We have perfect test conditions here," said the machine Epikt. "We set out a basic text from Cobblestone's *History of Philosophy*. If our test is effective, then the text will change before our eyes. So will every other text, and the world."

"We have assembled here the finest minds and judgments in the world," the machine Epiktistes said, "ten humans and three machines. Remember that there are thirteen of us. It might be important."

"Regard the world," said Aloysius Shiplap. "I said that yesterday, but it is required that I say it again. We have the world in our eyes and in our memories. If it changes in any way, we will know it."

"Push the button, Epikt," said Gregory Smirnov.

From his depths, Epiktistes the Ktistec machine sent out an Avatar, partly of mechanical and partly of ghostly construction. And along about sundown on the road from Mende to Avignon in the old Languedoc district of France, in the year 1323, John Lutterell was stricken with one more sickness. He was taken to a little inn in the mountain country, and perhaps he died there. He did not, at any rate, arrive at Avignon.

"Did it work, Epikt? Is it done?" Aloysius asked.

"Let's look at the evidence," said Gregory.

The four of them, the three humans and the ghost Epikt who was a kachenko mask with a speaking tube, turned to the evidence with mounting disappointment.

"There is still the stick and the five notches in it," said Gregory. "It was our test stick. Nothing in the world is changed."

"The arts remain as they were," said Aloysius. "Our picture here on the stone on which we have worked for so many seasons is the same as it was. We have painted the bears black, the buffalos red, and the people blue. When we find a way to make another color, we can represent birds also. I had hoped that our experiment might give us that other color. I had even dreamed that birds might appear in the picture on the rock before our very eyes."

"There's still rump of skunk to eat and nothing else," said Valery. "I had hoped that our experiment would have changed it to haunch of deer."

"All is not lost," said Aloysius. "We still have the hickory nuts. That was my last prayer before we began our experiment. 'Don't let them take the hickory nuts away,' I prayed."

They sat around the conference table that was a large flat natural rock, and cracked hickory nuts with stone fisthammers. They were nude in the crude, and the world was as it had always been. They had hoped by magic to change it.

"Epikt has failed us," said Gregory. "We made his frame out of the best sticks, and we plaited his face out of the finest weeds and grasses. We chanted him full of magic and placed all our special treasures in his cheek pouches. So, what can the magic mask do for us now?"

"Ask it, ask it," said Valery. They were the four finest minds in the world—the three humans, Gregory, Aloysius, and Valery (the *only* humans in the world unless you count those in the other valleys), and the ghost Epikt, a kachenko mask with a speaking tube.

"What do we do now, Epikt?" Gregory asked. Then he went around behind Epikt to the speaking tube.

"I remember a woman with a sausage stuck to her nose," said Epikt in the voice of Gregory. "Is that any help?"

"It may be some help," Gregory said after he had once more taken his place at the flat-rock conference table. "It is from an old (What's old about it? I made it up myself this morning) folk tale about the three wishes."

"Let Epikt tell it," said Valery. "He does it so much better than you do." Valery went behind Epikt to the speaking tube and blew smoke through it from the huge loose black-leaf uncured stogie that she was smoking.

"The wife wastes one wish for a sausage," said Epikt in the voice of Valery. "A sausage is a piece of deer-meat tied in a piece of a deer's stomach. The husband is angry that the wife has wasted a wish, since she could have wished for a whole deer and had many sausages. He gets so angry that he wishes the sausage might stick to her nose forever. It does, and the woman wails, and the man realized that he had used up the second wish. I forget the rest."

"You can't forget it, Epikt!" Aloysius cried in alarm. "The future of the world may depend on your remembering. Here, let me reason with that damned magic mask!" And Aloysius went behind Epikt to the speaking tube.

"Oh yes, now I remember," Epikt said in the voice of Aloysius. "The man used the third wish to get the sausage off his wife's nose. So things were the way they had been before."

"But we don't want it the way it was before!" Valery howled. "That's the way it is now, rump of skunk to eat, and me with nothing to wear but my ape cape. We want it better. We want deer skins and antelope skins."

"Take me as a mystic or don't take me at all," Epikt signed off.

"Even though the world has always been so, yet we have intimations of other things," Gregory said. "What folk hero was it who made the dart? And of what did he make it?"

"Willy McGilly was the folk hero," said Epikt in the voice of Valery, who had barely got to the speaking tube in time, "and he made it out of slippery elm wood."

"Could we make a dart like the folk hero Willy made?" Aloysius asked.

"We gotta," said Epikt.

"Could we make a slinger and whip it out of our own context and into—"

"Could we kill an Avatar with it before he killed somebody else?" Gregory asked excitedly.

"We sure will try," said the ghost Epikt who was nothing but a kachenko mask with a speaking tube. "I never did like those Avatars."

You *think* Epikt was nothing but a kachenko mask with a speaking tube! There was a lot more to him than that. He had red garnet rocks inside him and real sea salt. He had powder made from beaver eyes. He had rattlesnake rattles and armadillo shields. He was the first Ktistec machine.

"Give me the word, Epikt," Aloysius cried a few moments later as he fitted the dart to the slinger.

"Fling it! Get that Avatar fink!" Epikt howled.

Along about sundown in an unnumbered year, on the Road from Nowhere to Eom, an Avatar fell dead with a slippery elm dart in his heart.

"Did it work, Epikt? Is it done?" Charles Cogsworth asked in excitement. "It must have. I'm here. I wasn't in the last one."

"Let's look at the evidence," Gregory suggested calmly.

"Damn the evidence!" Willy McGilly cussed. "Remember where you heard it first."

"Is it started yet?" Glasser asked.

"Is it finished?" Audifax O'Hanlon questioned.

"Push the button, Epikt!" Diogenes barked. "I think I missed part of it. Let's try it again."

"Oh, no, no!" Valery forbade. "Not again. That way is rump of skunk and madness."

In Our Block

Introduction by Neil Gaiman

This was not the first short story of Lafferty's I read, nor even the first I fell in love with.

It was, however, the first story I ever took apart, as best I could, to try and work out how he did it.

I would have been about eleven. I didn't know what an American city block actually was—it was an indeterminate word that meant simply a region, as far as I was concerned. I came from towns and cities with winding, random streets. But I loved the story. It was a shaggy dog story without a punch line, a tall tale without apparent conflict in which all that happened was that two friends walked around a block, and talked to people they found. A letter was dictated. It was about new people coming in, about immigrants, about people working hard and moving on. It was about taking the extraordinary for granted. And I loved the way the words worked.

So I read it, and I reread it, and I read it aloud, and I tried to understand it. I would never know what a Dort Glide was (nor, I suspected, did Lafferty), but I felt that, if I could understand how this short story was built and constructed, I would understand how to write.

I loved the way the people in the shanties spoke. I wanted to speak like the typist, or her sister in the bar. I hoped one day to be able to say, "See how foxy I turn all your questions," but I never had an opportunity to. I only had one tongue, so to reply, "With my other tongue" was also right out.

Coming back to it as an adult, and I have read it every year or so, I find that I love it as much as I ever did. It's cockeyed and joyful, but it's also a glorious, blue-collar, low-rent story about a block in Oklahoma where the people arriving just want to fit in. It's about immigration, and about what people bring to the places they visit. It's about revealing secrets.

And it's a writer's story, too, about the places that ideas come from. I imagine Ray Lafferty walking past a tin shack he had not noticed before, on his way to a local bar, and having a story in his head by the time that he returned home that night.

In Our Block

There were a lot of funny people in that block.

"You ever walk down that street?" Art Slick asked Jim Boomer, who had just come onto him there.

"Not since I was a boy. After the overall factory burned down, there was a faith healer had his tent pitched there one summer. The street's just one block long and it dead-ends on the railroad embankment. Nothing but a bunch of shanties and weed-filled lots. The shanties looked different today, though, and there seem to be more of them. I thought they pulled them all down a few months ago."

"Jim, I've been watching that first little building for two hours. There was a tractor-truck there this morning with a forty-foot trailer, and it loaded out of that little shanty. Cartons about eight inches by eight inches by three feet came down that chute. They weighed about thirty-five pounds each from the way the men handled them. Jim, they filled that trailer up with them, and then pulled it off."

"What's wrong with that, Art?"

"Jim, I said they filled that trailer up. From the drag on it it had about a sixty-thousand-pound load when it pulled out. They loaded a carton every three and a half seconds for two hours; that's two thousand cartons."

"Sure, lots of trailers run over the load limit nowadays; they don't enforce it very well."

"Jim, that shack's no more than a cracker box seven feet on a side. Half of it is taken up by a door, and inside a man in a chair behind a small table. You couldn't get anything else in that half. The other half is taken up by whatever that chute comes out of. You could pack six of those little shacks on that trailer."

"Let's measure it," Jim Boomer said. "Maybe it's bigger than it looks." The shack had a sign on it: *Make Sell Ship Anything Cut Price*. Jim Boomer measured the building with an old steel tape. The shack was a seven-foot cube, and there were no hidden places. It was set up on a few piers of broken bricks, and you could see under it.

"Sell you a new fifty-foot steel tape for a dollar," said the man in the chair in the little shack. "Throw that old one away." The man pulled a steel tape out of a drawer of his table-desk, though Art Slick was sure it had been a plain flat-top table with no place for a drawer.

"Fully retractable, rhodium-plated, Dort glide, Ramsey swivel, and it forms its own carrying case. One dollar," the man said.

Jim Boomer paid him a dollar for it. "How many of them you got?"

"I can have a hundred thousand ready to load out in ten minutes," the man said. "Eighty-eight cents each in hundred thousand lots."

"Was that a trailer-load of steel tapes you shipped out this morning?" Art asked the man.

"No, that must have been something else. This is the first steel tape I ever made. Just got the idea when I saw you measuring my shack with that old beat-up one."

Art Slick and Jim Boomer went to the run-down building next door. It was smaller, about a six-foot cube, and the sign said *Public Stenographer*. The clatter of a typewriter was coming from it, but the noise stopped when they opened the door.

A dark pretty girl was sitting in a chair before a small table. There was nothing else in the room, and no typewriter.

"I thought I heard a typewriter in here," Art said.

"Oh, that is me." The girl smiled. "Sometimes I amuse myself make typewriter noises like a public stenographer is supposed to."

"What would you do if someone came in to have some typing done?"

"What are you think? I do it of course."

"Could you type a letter for me?"

"Sure is can, man friend, two bits a page, good work, carbon copy, envelope and stamp."

"Ah, let's see how you do it. I will dictate to you while you type."

"You dictate first. Then I write. No sense mix up two things at one time."

Art dictated a long and involved letter that he had been meaning to write for several days. He felt like a fool droning it to the girl as she filed her nails. "Why is public stenographer always sit filing her nails?" she asked as Art droned. "But I try to do it right, file them down, grow them out again, then file them down some more. Been doing it all morning. It seems silly."

"Ah—that is all," Art said when he had finished dictating.

"Not P.S. Love and Kisses?" the girl asked.

"Hardly. It's a business letter to a person I barely know."

"I always say P.S. Love and Kisses to persons I barely know," the girl said. "Your letter will make three pages, six bits. Please you both step outside about ten seconds and I write it. Can't do it when you watch." She pushed them out and closed the door.

Then there was silence.

"What are you doing in there, girl?" Art called.

"Want I sell you a memory course too? You forget already? I type a letter," the girl called.

"But I don't hear a typewriter going."

"What is? You want verisimilitude too? I should charge extra." There was a giggle, and then the sound of very rapid typing for about five seconds.

The girl opened the door and handed Art the three-page letter. It was typed perfectly, of course.

"There is something a little odd about this," Art said.

"Oh? The ungrammar of the letter is your own, sir. Should I have correct?"

"No. It is something else. Tell me the truth, girl: how does the man next door ship out trailer-loads of material from a building ten times too small to hold the stuff?"

"He cuts prices."

"Well, what are you people? The man next door resembles you."

"My brother-uncle. We tell everybody we are Innominee Indians."

"There is no such tribe," Jim Boomer said flatly.

"Is there not? Then we will have to tell people we are something else. You got to admit it sounds like Indian. What's the best Indian to be?"

"Shawnee," said Jim Boomer.

"OK then we be Shawnee Indians. See how easy it is."

"We're already taken," Boomer said. "I'm a Shawnee and I know every Shawnee in town."

"Hi cousin!" the girl cried, and winked. "That's from a joke I learn, only the begin was different. See how foxy I turn all your questions."

"I have two-bits coming out of my dollar," Art said.

"I know," the girl said. "I forgot for a minute what design is on the back of the two-bitser piece, so I stall while I remember it. Yes, the funny bird standing on the bundle of firewood. One moment till I finish it. Here." She handed the quarter to Art Slick. "And you tell everybody there's a smoothie public stenographer here who types letters good."

"Without a typewriter," said Art Slick. "Let's go, Jim."

"P.S. Love and Kisses," the girl called after them.

The Cool Man Club was next door, a small and shabby beer bar. The bar girl could have been a sister of the public stenographer.

"We'd like a couple of Buds, but you don't seem to have a stock of anything," Art said.

"Who needs stock?" the girl asked. "Here is beers." Art would have believed that she brought them out of her sleeves, but she had no sleeves. The beers were cold and good.

"Girl, do you know how the fellow on the corner can ship a whole trailer-load of material out of a space that wouldn't hold a tenth of it?" Art asked the girl.

"Sure. He makes it and loads it out at the same time. That way it doesn't take up space, like if he made it before time."

"But he has to make it out of something," Jim Boomer cut in.

"No, no," the girl said. "I study your language. I know words. Out of something is to assemble, not to make. He makes."

"This is funny." Slick gaped. "Budweiser is misspelled on this bottle, the *i* before the *e*."

"Oh, I goof," the bar girl said. "I couldn't remember which way it goes so I make it one way on one bottle and the other way on the other. Yesterday a man ordered a bottle of Progress beer, and I spelled it Progers on the bottle. Sometimes I get things wrong. Here, I fix yours."

She ran her hand over the label, and then it was spelled correctly.

"But that thing is engraved and then reproduced," Slick protested.

"Oh, sure, all fancy stuff like that," the girl said. "I got to be more careful. One time I forget and make Jax-taste beer in a Schlitz bottle and the man didn't like it. I had to swish swish change the taste while I pretended to give him a different bottle. One time I forgot and produced a green-bottle beer in a brown bottle, 'It is the light in here, it just makes it look brown,' I told the man. Hell, we don't even have a light in here. I go swish fast and make the bottle green. It's hard to keep from making mistake when you're stupid."

"No, you don't have a light or a window in here, and it's light," Slick said. "You don't have refrigeration. There are no power lines to any of the shanties in this block. How do you keep the beer cold?"

"Yes, is the beer not nice and cold? Notice how tricky I evade your question. Will you good men have two more beers?"

"Yes, we will. And I'm interested in seeing where you get them," Slick said.

"Oh look, is snakes behind you!" the girl cried. "Oh how you startle and jump!" she laughed. "It's all joke. Do you think I will have snakes in my nice bar?"

But she had produced two more beers, and the place was as bare as before.

"How long have you tumble-bugs been in this block?" Boomer asked.

"Who keep track?" the girl said. "People come and go."

"You're not from around here," Slick said. "You're not from anywhere I know. Where do you come from? Jupiter?"

"Who wants Jupiter?" the girl seemed indignant. "Do business with a bunch of insects there, is all! Freeze your tail too."

"You wouldn't be a kidder, would you, girl?" Slick asked.

"I sure do try hard. I learn a lot of jokes but I tell them all wrong yet. I get better, though. I try to be the witty bar girl so people will come back."

"What's in the shanty next door toward the tracks?"

"My cousin-sister," said the girl. "She set up shop just today. She grow any color hair on bald-headed men. I tell her she's crazy. No business. If they wanted hair they wouldn't be bald-headed in the first place."

"Well, *can* she grow hair on bald-headed men?" Slick asked.

"Oh sure. Can't you?"

There were three or four more shanty shops in the block. It didn't seem that there had been that many when the men went into the Cool Man Club.

"I don't remember seeing this shack a few minutes ago," Boomer said to the man standing in front of the last shanty on the line.

"Oh, I just made it," the man said.

Weathered boards, rusty nails . . . and he had just made it.

"Why didn't you—ah—make a decent building while you were at it?" Slick asked.

"This is more inconspicuous," the man said. "Who notices when an *old* building appears suddenly? We're new here and want to feel our way in before we attract attention. Now I'm trying to figure out what to make. Do you think there is a market for a luxury automobile to sell for a hundred dollars? I suspect I would have to respect the local religious feeling when I make them though."

"What is that?" Slick asked.

"Ancestor worship. The old gas tank and fuel system still carried as vestiges after natural power is available. Oh well, I'll put them in. I'll have one done in about three minutes if you want to wait."

"No. I've already got a car," Slick said. "Let's go, Jim."

That was the last shanty in the block, so they turned back.

"I was just wondering what was down in this block where nobody ever goes," Slick said. "There's a lot of odd corners in our town if you look them out."

"There are some queer guys in the shanties that were here before this bunch," Boomer said. "Some of them used to come up to the Red Rooster to drink. One of them could gobble like a turkey. One of them could roll one eye in one direction and the other eye the other way. They shoveled hulls at the cottonseed oil float before it burned down."

They went by the public stenographer shack again.

"No kidding, honey, how do you type without a typewriter?" Slick asked.

"Typewriter is too slow," the girl said.

"I asked *how,* not *why,*" Slick said.

"I know. Is it not nifty the way I turn away a phrase? I think I will have a big oak tree growing in front of my shop tomorrow for shade. Either of you nice men have an acorn in your pocket?"

"Ah—no. How do you really do the typing, girl?"

"You promise you won't tell anybody."

"I promise."

"I make the marks with my tongue," the girl said.

They started slowly on up the block.

"Hey, how do you make the carbon copies?" Jim Boomer called back.

"With my other tongue," the girl said.

There was another forty-foot trailer loading out of the first shanty in the block. It was bundles of half-inch plumbers pipe coming out of the chute—in twenty-foot lengths. Twenty-foot rigid pipe out of a seven-foot shed.

"I wonder how he can sell trailer-loads of such stuff out of a little shack like that," Slick puzzled, still not satisfied.

"Like the girl says, he cuts prices," Boomer said. "Let's go over to the Red Rooster and see if there's anything going on. There always were a lot of funny people in that block."

Ride a Tin Can

Introduction by Neil Gaiman

When I wrote to R. A. Lafferty as a very young man, I asked him about his favorite of his own short stories. He mentioned three stories that I had read and loved—"Ginny Wrapped in the Sun," "Configuration of the North Shore," and "Continued on Next Rock"—and one that I hadn't. It was called "Ride a Tin Can."

Shortly afterward, I bought a copy of *Strange Doings*, and read "Ride a Tin Can," and was disappointed. It made me sad.

I think I wanted to be uplifted. I wanted the thing that Lafferty did where his apocalypses were joyful things one went into with delight. And here were the Shelni race going into an apocalypse with joyful delight, and I walked away from the story feeling that I might just have read the saddest story in the world. I felt manipulated, because it was an ending that called for tears, told in a way that did not allow for tears. I did not trust tears anyway. "Ride a Tin Can" left me disappointed in Humanity. It was a story I could admire, but I could not love, and which I did not look forward to rereading.

As an older reader, I can love it: I can love it for the shape of the story, the three tiny tales that hover at the end of understanding; I love it for the world-building that is never fully described, for the relationship between the Shelni and the Skokie and the frogs and the trees. I love it for Holly Harkel, a human woman who is goblin enough to talk to goblins under their tree-root home, goblin enough to ride a tin can herself.

It's a story nobody else could have written, pulled off in a way nobody else would have imagined, that describes a genocide that hurts, without a word wasted.

I think, "We are better than this. Surely we must be better than this?" And I think, "How do you write a story like that anyway? Write a story like that, and make it look easy?"

But he does. Somehow he does.

It's OK if you cry.

Ride a Tin Can

These are my notes on the very sticky business. They are not in the form of a protest, which would be useless. Holly is gone, and the Shelni will all be gone in the next day or two, if indeed there are any of them left now. This is for the record only.

Holly Harkel and myself, Vincent Vanhoosier, received funds and permission to record the lore of the Shelni through the intercession of that old correlator John Holmberg. This was unexpected. All lorists have counted John as their worst enemy.

"After all, we have been at great expense to record the minutiae of pig grunts and the sound of earthworms," Holmberg told me, "and we have records of squeakings of hundreds of species of orbital rodents. We have veritable libraries of the song and cackle of all birds and pseudo-ornins. Well, let us add the Shelni to our list. I do not believe that their thumping on tree roots or blowing into jug gourds is music. I do not believe that their singsong is speech any more than the squeaking of doors is speech. We have recorded, by the way, the sound of more than thirty thousand squeaking doors. And we have had worse. Let us have the Shelni, then, if your hearts are set on it. You'll have to hurry. They're about gone.

"And let me say in all compassion that anyone who looks like Miss Holly Harkel deserves her heart's desire. That is no more than simple justice. Besides, the bill will be footed by the Singing Pig Breakfast Food Company. These companies are bitten by the small flea of remorse every now and then and they want to pitch a few coins into some fund for luck. It's never many coins that they want to pitch; the remorse bug that bites them is never a very large one. You may be able to stretch it to cover your project though, Vanhoosier."

So we had our appropriation and our travel, Miss Holly and myself.

Holly Harkel had often been in disrepute for her claims to understand the languages of various creatures. There was special outrage to her claim that she would be able to understand the Shelni. Now that was odd. No disrepute attached to Captain Charbonnett for his claim to understand the planetary simians, and if there was ever a phony claim it was this. No disrepute attached to Meyrowitz for his claim of finding esoteric meanings in the patterns of vole droppings. But there seemed something incredible in the claim of the goblin-faced Holly Harkel that not only would she be able to understand the Shelni instantly and completely but that they were not low scavenger beasts at all, that they were genuine goblin people who played goblin music and sang goblin songs.

Holly Harkel had a heart and soul too big for her dwarfish body, and a brain too big for her curious little head. That, I suppose, is what made her so lumpy everywhere. She was entirely compounded of love and concern and laughter, and much of it bulged out from her narrow form. Her ugliness was one of the unusual things and I believe that she enjoyed giving it to the worlds. She had loved snakes and toads, she had loved monkeys and misbegottens. She had come to look weirdly like them when we studied them. She was a snake when we studied them, she was a toad when they were our subject. She studied every creature from the inside of it. And here there was an uncommon similarity, even for her.

Holly loved the Shelni instantly. She became a Shelni, and she hadn't far to go. She moved and scooted and climbed like a Shelni. She came down trees headfirst like a Shelni or a squirrel. She had always seemed to me to be a little other than human. And now she was avid to record the Shelni things "—before they be gone."

As for the Shelni themselves, some scientists have called them humanoid, and then braced themselves for the blow and howl. If they were humanoid they were certainly the lowest and oddest humanoids ever. But we folklorists knew intuitively what they were. They were goblins pure and simple—I do not use the adjectives here as cliché. The tallest of them were less than three feet tall; the oldest of them were less than seven years old. They were, perhaps, the ugliest creatures in the universe, and yet of a pleasant ugliness. There was no evil in them at all. Scientists who have tested them have insisted that there was no intelligence in them at all. They were friendly and open. Too friendly, too open, as it happened, for they were fascinated by all human things, to their harm. But they were no more human than a fairy or an ogre is human. Less, less, less than a monkey.

"Here is a den of them," Holly divined that first day (it was the day before yesterday). "There will be a whole coven of them down under here and the door is down through the roots of this tree. When I got my doctorate in primitive music I never imagined that I would be visiting Brownies down under tree roots. I should say that I never so much as *hoped* that I would be. There was *so* much that they didn't teach us. There was even one period in my life when I ceased to believe in goblins."

The latter I do not believe.

Suddenly Holly was into a hole in the ground headfirst, like a gopher, like a ground squirrel, like a Shelni. I followed her, letting myself down carefully, and not headfirst. I myself would have to study the Shelni from the outside. I myself would never be able to crawl inside their green goblin skins, never be able to croak or carol with their frog tongues, never feel what made their popeyes pop. I myself would not even have been able to sense out their dens.

And at the bottom of the hole, at the entrance to the den itself, was an encounter which I disbelieved at the time I was seeing and hearing it. There occurred a conversation which I heard with my own ears, they having become transcendent for the moment. It was in the frog-croak Shelni talk between Holly Harkel and the five-year-old Ancient who guarded the coven, and yet it was in a sort of English and I understood it:

"Knockle, knockle." (This from Holly.)

"Crows in cockle." (This from the guard.)

"Wogs and wollie."

"Who you?"

"Holly."

"What's a dinning?"

"Coming inning."

So they let us in. But if you think you can enter a Shelni coven without first riming with the five-year-old Ancient who guards it, then it's plain that you've never been in one of the places. And though the philologists say that the "speech" of the Shelni is meaningless croaking, yet it was never meaningless to Holly, and in flashes it was not meaningless to me. The secret guess of Holly was so.

Holly had insisted that the Shelni spoke English within the limits of their vocal apparatus. And they told her at this very first session that they never had had any language of their own "because no one had ever made one for us"; so they used English as soon as they came to hear it. "We would pay you for the use of it if we had anything to pay you with," they said. It is frog-croak English, but only the pure of ear can understand it.

I started the recorder and Holly started the Shelni. Quite soon she had them playing on those jug-shaped flutes of theirs. Frog music. Ineffably sad *sionnach* skirries. Rook, crow, and daw squabbling melody. They were pleasant, weird little pieces of music that sounded as though they were played underwater. It would be hard to imagine them not played under the ground at least.

The tunes were short just as all tunes of children are short. There was no real orchestration, though that should have been possible with the seven flutes differently jugged and tuned. Yet there was true melody in these: short, complete, closed melody, dwarfed perfection. They were underground fugues full of worms' blood and cool as root cider. They were locust and chaffer and cricket din.

Then Holly got one of the most ancient of the Shelni to tell stories while the jug flutes chortled. Here are the two of them that we recorded that first day. Others who listen to them today say that there is nothing to them but croaking. But I heard them with Holly Harkel, she helped interpret them to me, so I can hear and understand them perfectly in frog-croak English.

Take them, Grisly Posterity! I am not sure that you deserve even this much of the Shelni.

The Shelni Who Lost His Burial Tooth

It is told this way.

There was a Shelni who lost his burial tooth before he died. Every Shelni begins life with six teeth, and he loses one every year. Then, when he is very old and has only one tooth left, he dies. He must give the last tooth to the Skokie burial-person to pay for his burial. But this Shelni had either lost two teeth in one year or else he had lived to too great an age.

He died. And he had no tooth left to pay with.

"I will not bury you if you have no tooth left to pay me with," said the Skokie burial-person. "Should I work for nothing?"

"Then I will bury myself," said the dead Shelni.

"You don't know how," said the Skokie burial-person. "You don't know the places that are left. You will find that all the places are full. I have agreement that everybody should tell everybody that all the places are full, so only the burial-person may bury. That is my job."

Nevertheless, the dead Shelni went to find a place to bury himself. He dug a little hole in the meadow, but wherever he dug he found that it was already full of dead Shelnis or Skokies or Frogs. And they always made him put all the dirt back that he had dug.

He dug holes in the valley and it was the same thing. He dug holes on the hill, and they told him that the hill was full too. So he went away crying for he could find no place to lie down.

He asked the *Eanlaith* whether he could stay in their tree. And they said, no he could not. They would not let any dead folks live in their tree.

He asked the *Eise* if he could stay in their pond. And they said, no he could not. They would not allow any dead folks in their pond.

He asked the *Sionnach* if he could sleep in their den. And they said, no he could not. They liked him when he was alive, but a dead person has hardly any friends at all.

So the poor dead Shelni wanders yet and can find no place to rest his head.

He will wander forever unless he can find another burial tooth to pay with.

They used to tell it so.

One comment on this burial story: the Shelni do have careful burial. But the burial crypts are plainly dug, not by the six-fingered Shelni, but by the seven-clawed Skokie. There must be substance to the Skokie burial-person. Moreover, the Skokie, though higher on the very low scale than the Shelni, do not bury their own. Furthermore, there are no Shelni remains going back more than about thirty equivalent years. There are no random lying or fossil Shelni at all, though such remains are common for every other species here.

The second story (of the first day).

The Shelni Who Turned into a Tree

This is how they tell it.

There was a woman who was neither Shelni nor Skokie nor Frog. She was Sky Woman. One day she came with her child and sat down under the Shelni tree. When she got up to go she left her own child who was asleep and picked up a Shelni child by mistake. Then the Shelni woman came to get her own child and she looked at it. She did not know what was wrong but it was a Sky People child.

"Oh, it has pink skin and flat eyes! How can that be?" the Shelni woman asked. But she took it home with her and it still lives with the Shelni and everyone has forgotten the difference.

Nobody knows what the Sky Woman thought when she got the Shelni child home and looked at it. Nevertheless she kept it, and it grew and was more handsome than any of them.

But when the second year came and the young Shelni was grown, it walked in the woods and said, "I do not feel like a Sky People. But if I am not a Sky People, then what am I? I am not a Duck. I am not a Frog. And if I am a Bird, what kind of Bird am I? There is nothing left. It must be that I am a Tree." There was reason for this. We Shelni do look a little bit like trees and we feel a little bit like trees.

So the Shelni put down roots and grew bark and worked hard at being a tree. He underwent all the hardships that are the life of a tree. He was gnawed by goats and gobniu; he was rough-tongued by cattle and crom; he was infested by slugs and befouled by the nameless animal. Moreover, parts of him were cut away for firewood.

But he kept feeling the jug music creeping up all the way from his undertoes to his hair and he knew that this music was what he had always been looking for. It was the same jug and tine music that you hear even now.

Then a bird told the Shelni that he was not really a tree but that it was too late for him to leave off growing like a tree. He had brothers and sisters and kindred living in the hole down under his roots, the bird said, and they would have no home if he stopped being a tree.

This is the tree that is the roof of our den where we are even now. This tree is our brother who was lost and who forgot that he was a Shelni.

This is the way it has always been told.

On the second day it was remarkable how much Holly had come to look like a Shelni. And she was hardly taller than they were. Ah well, she has come to look like every sort of creature we have ever studied together. Holly insists that the Shelni have intelligence, and I half agree with her. But the paragraph in the basic manual of this world is against us:

—*a tendency to attribute to the Shelni an intelligence which they do not possess, perhaps due to their fancied human resemblance. In maze-running they are definitely inferior to the rodents. In the manipulation of latches and stops they are less adept than the earth raccoons or the asteroid rojon. In tool handling and true mimicry they are far from equal to the simians. In simple foraging and the instinct for survival they are far below the hog or the harzl. In* mneme, *the necessary prelude to intelligence, they are about on par with the turtles. Their "speech" lacks the verisimilitude of the talking birds, and their "music" is below that of the insects. They make poor watchdogs and inadequate scarecrows. It appears that the move to ban shelniphagi, though perhaps sincere, is ill-advised. After all, as an early spaceman put it, "What else are they good for?"*

Well, we have to admit that the Shelni are not as intelligent as rats or hogs or harzls. Yet I, surely due to the influence of Holly, feel a stronger affinity to them than to rats or hogs or coons or crows or whatever. But no creature is so helpless as the Shelni. How do they even get together?

The Shelni have many sorts of songs, but they do not have any romantic songs in our sense. After all, they are small children till they die of old age. Their sexual relationship seems distinguished either by total unawareness or by extreme bashfulness.

"I don't see how they bring it off at all, Vincent," Holly said the second day (which was yesterday). "They are here, so they must have been born. But how do these bashful and scatterbrained three-year-olds ever get together to bring it off? I can't find anything at all in their legends or acting patterns, can you?

"In their legends, all their children are foundlings. They are born or discovered under a blueberry bush (my translation of *spionam*). Or alternately, and in other cycles, they are found under a quicken tree or in a cucumber patch. In common sense we must assume that the Shelni are placental and viviparous. But should we apply common sense to goblin folk?

"They also have a legend that they are fungoid and spring out of the ground at night like mushrooms. And that if a Shelni woman wishes a child, she must buy a fungoid slip from a Skokie and plant it in the ground. Then she will have her child ready the next morning."

But Holly was depressed yesterday morning. She had seen some copy by our sponsor The Singing Pig Breakfast Food Company and it disturbed her:

"Singing Pig! The Children love it! Nourishing Novelty! Nursery Rime Characters in a can for your convenience! Real Meat from Real Goblins! No fat, no bones. If your can has a lucky number tab, you can receive free a facsimile Shelni jug flute. Be the first on your block to serve Singing Pig, the meat from real Goblins. Cornstarch and natural flavor added."

Oh well, it was only an advertisement that they used back on World. We had our recording to do.

"Vincent, I don't know how they got here," Holly said, "but I know they won't be here very long. Hurry, hurry, we have to get it down! I will make them remembered somehow."

Holly got them to play on the tines that second day (which was yesterday). There had been an impediment the day before, she said. The tines may not be played for one until the second day of acquaintance. The Shelni do not have stringed instruments. Their place is taken by the tines, the vibrating, singing forks. They play these many-pronged tuned forks like harps, and in playing them they use the tree roots for sounding boards so that even the leaves in the air above partake a little of the music. The tines, the forks are themselves of wood, of a certain very hard but light wood that is sharp with chert and lime dust. They are wood, I believe, in an early stage of petrifaction. The tine fork music usually follows the jug flute music, and the ballads that are sung to it have a dreamlike sadness of tone that belies the childish simplicity of the texts.

Here are two more of those ballad stories that we recorded on the second day (which was yesterday).

The Skokie Who Lost His Wife

This is the way they tell it.

A Skokie heard a Shelni jug flute jugging one night.

"That is the voice of my wife," the Skokie said. "I'd know it anywhere."

The Skokie came over the moors to find his wife. He went down into the hole in the ground that his wife's voice was coming from. But all he found there was a Shelni playing a jug flute.

"I am looking for my poor lost wife," the Skokie said. "I have heard her voice just now coming out of this hole. Where is she?"

"There is nobody here but myself," the Shelni said. "I am sitting here alone playing my flute to the moons whose light runs down the walls of my hole."

"But I heard her here," said the Skokie, "and I want her back."

"How did she sound?" asked the Shelni. "Like this?" And he jugged some jug music on his flute.

"Yes, that is my wife," said the Skokie. "Where have you hidden her? That is her very voice."

"That is nobody's wife," the Shelni told the Skokie. "That is just a little tune that I made up."

"You play with my wife's voice, so you must have swallowed my wife," the Skokie said. "I will have to take you apart and see."

"If I swallowed anybody's wife I'm sorry," said the Shelni. "Go ahead then."

So the Skokie took the Shelni apart and scattered the pieces all over the hole and some of them on the grass outside. But he could not find any part of his wife.

"I have made a mistake," said the Skokie. "Who would have thought that one who had not swallowed my wife could make her voice on the flute!"

"It is all right," said the Shelni, "so long as you put me together again. I remember part of the way I go. If you remember the rest of the way, then you can put me together again."

But neither of them remembered very well the way the Shelni was before he was taken apart. The Skokie put him together all wrong. There were not enough pieces for some parts and too many for others.

"Let me help," said a Frog who was there. "I remember where some of the parts go. Besides, I believe it was my own wife he swallowed. That was her voice on the flute. It was not a Skokie voice."

The Frog helped, and they all remembered what they could, but it did not work. Parts of the Shelni could not be found again, and some of the parts would not go into him at all. When they had him finished, the Shelni was in great pain and could hardly move, and he didn't look much like a Shelni.

"I've done all I can," the Skokie said. "That's the way you'll have to be. Where is Frog?"

"I'm inside," said Frog.

"That's where you will have to stay," the Skokie said. "I've had enough of both of you. Enough, and these pieces left over. I will just take them with me. Maybe I can make someone else out of them."

That is the way the Shelni still is, put together all wrong. In his wrong form he walks the country by night, being ashamed to go by day. Some folks are startled when they meet him, not knowing this story. He still plays his jug flute with the lost Skokie wife's voice and with Frog's voice. Listen, you can hear it now! The Shelni goes in sorrow and pain because nobody knows how to put him together right.

The Skokie never did find his lost wife.

This is how it is told.

And then there was the second story that we recorded yesterday, the last story, though we did not know it then, that we would record of the Shelni:

The Singing Pigs

This is how they say it.

We have the ancient story of the singing pigs who sing so loud that they fly up into the sky on the tail of their own singing. Now we ourselves, if we can sing loud enough, if we can jug the flutes strong enough, if we can tang the tines deep enough, will get to be the Singing Pigs of our own story. Many already have gone away as Singing Pigs.

There come certain bell men with music carts. They play rangle-dangle Sky music. They come for love of us. And if we can hurry fast enough when they come we can go with them, we can ride a tin can over the sky.

Bong! bong! that is the bell man with the music cart now! All the Shelni hurry! This is the day you may get to go. Come all you Shelni from the valley and the stream and jump on the cart for the free ride. Come all the Shelni from the meadows and the woods. Come up from the tree roots and the holes underground. The Skokie don't get to go, the Frogs don't get to go, only the Shelni get to go.

Cry if the cart is too full and you don't get to go today, but don't cry too long. The bell men say that they will come back tomorrow and every day till there are no Shelni left at all.

"Come all you little Singing-Pig-Shelni," a bell man shouts. "Come get your free rides in the tin cans all the way to Earth! Hey, Ben, what other animal jumps onto the slaughter wagon when you only ring a bell? Come along little Shelni-Pigs, room for ten more on this wagon. That's all, that's all. We'll have lots more wagons going tomorrow. We'll take all of you, all of you! Hey, Ben, did you ever see little pigs cry when there's no more room for them on the slaughter wagon?" These are the high kind words that a bell man speak for love of us.

Not even have to give a burial tooth or other tooth to pay for the ride. Frogs can't go, Skokies can't go, only the Shelni get to go!

Here are the wonderful things! From the wagon, the Shelni get to go to one room where all their bones are taken out. This does never happen to Shelni before. In another room the Shelni are boiled down to only half their size, little as little-boy Shelni. Then they all get to play the game and crawl into the tin cans. And then they get their free ride in the tin cans all the way to Earth. Ride a tin can!

Wipe off your sticky tears you who miss the music cart today. Go to sleep early tonight and rise early tomorrow. Sing your loudest tomorrow so the bell men will know where to come. Jug the flutes very strong tomorrow, tang the tines deep, say *whoop! whoop!* here we are, bell men.

All laugh when they go with the bell men in the music cart. But there is story that someday a Shelni woman will cry instead of laugh when they take her. What can be the matter with this woman that she will cry? She will cry out, "Damn you, it's murder! They're almost people! You can't take them! They're as much people as I am. Double damn you, you can't take *me*! I'm human. I know I look as funny as they do but I'm human. Oh, oh, oh!" This is the funniest thing of the story, the prophecy thing part.

Oh, oh, oh, the woman will say, Oh, oh, oh, the jug flutes will echo it. What will be the matter with the Shelni woman who cries instead of laughs?

This is our last story, wherever it is told. When it is told for the last time, then there will be no more stories here, there will be no more Shelni. Who needs stories and jug flute music who can ride a tin can?

That is how it has been said.

Then we went out (for the last time, as it happened) from the Shelni burrow. And, as always, there was the riming with the five-year-old Ancient who guarded the place:

"What to crowing?"

"Got to going."

"Jinx on Jolly,

"Golly, Holly!"
"Were it other,
"Bug, my brother!"
"Holly crying.
"Sing her flying,
"Jugging, shouting."
"Going outing."

Now this was remarkable. Holly Harkel was crying when we came out of the burrow for the (as it happened) last time. She was crying great goblin tears. I almost expected them to be green.

Today I keep thinking how amazingly the late Holly Harkel had finally come to look like the Shelni. She was a Shelni. "It is all the same with me now," she said this morning. "Would it be love if they should go and I should stay?" It is a sticky business. I tried to complain, but those people were still ringing that bell and chanting, "All you little Pig-Shelni-Singers come jump on the cart. Ride a tin can to Earth! Hey, Ben, look at them jump on the slaughter wagon!"

"It was inexcusable," I said. "Surely you could tell a human from a Shelni."

"Not that one," said a bell ringer. "I tell you they all jumped on the wagon willingly, even the funny-looking one who was crying. Sure, you can have her bones, if you can tell which ones they are."

I have Holly's bones. That is all. There was never a creature like her. And now it is over with.

But it is not over!

Singing Pig Breakfast Food Company, beware! There will be vengeance!

It has been told.

Nine Hundred Grandmothers

Introduction by Patton Oswalt

And the oldest of the oldest grandmothers knows how the universe began. Or does she? And does she—or they—know how to live forever?

This is R. A. Lafferty dangling a simple, delicious carrot in front of his not-simple protagonist, a space plunderer named Ceran Swicegood. Of course, Ceran would like to think of himself as a "special aspects man," a more refined breed than his compatriots who take brutish names like Manbreaker and Barrelhouse. These names, they feel, make it easier for them to pillage. A name like "Ceran Swicegood" is for someone who's searching for more . . . esoteric and rarefied booty.

But it's this rarefied, pretentious (and ultimately greedy) search that destroys poor Ceran quicker than the short-term, cash-money goals of his colleagues. Knowledge is power, but ultimate knowledge juuuuuuust out of reach is soul-poison.

Did I mention this story is also hilarious?

Nine Hundred Grandmothers

Ceran Swicegood was a promising young Special Aspects Man. But, like all Special Aspects, he had one irritating habit. He was forever asking the question: How Did it All Begin?

They all had tough names except Ceran. Manbreaker Crag, Heave Huckle, Blast Berg, George Blood, Move Manion (when Move says "Move," you move), Trouble Trent. They were supposed to be tough, and they had taken tough names at the naming. Only Ceran kept his own—to the disgust of his commander, Manbreaker.

"Nobody can be a hero with a name like Ceran Swicegood!" Manbreaker would thunder. "Why don't you take Storm Shannon? That's good. Or Gutboy Barrelhouse or Slash Slagle or Nevel Knife? You barely glanced at the suggested list."

"I'll keep my own," Ceran always said, and that is where he made his mistake. A new name will sometimes bring out a new personality. It had done so for George Blood. Though the hair on George's chest was a graft job, yet that and his new name had turned him from a boy into a man. Had Ceran assumed the heroic name of Gutboy Barrelhouse he might have been capable of rousing endeavors and man-sized angers rather than his tittering indecisions and flouncy furies.

They were down on the big asteroid Proavitus—a sphere that almost tinkled with the potential profit that might be shaken out of it. And the tough men of the Expedition knew their business. They signed big contracts on the native velvet-like bark scrolls and on their own parallel tapes. They impressed, inveigled, and somewhat cowed the slight people of Proavitus. Here was a solid two-way market, enough to make them slaver. And there was a whole world of oddities that could lend themselves to the luxury trade.

"Everybody's hit it big but you," Manbreaker crackled in kindly thunder to Ceran after three days there. "But even Special Aspects is supposed to pay its way. Our charter compels us to carry one of your sort to give a cultural twist to the thing, but it needn't be restricted to that. What we go out for every time, Ceran, is to cut a big fat hog in the rump—we make no secret of that. But if the hog's tail can be shown to have a cultural twist to it, that will solve a requirement. And if that twist in the tail can turn us a profit, then we become mighty happy about the whole thing. Have you been able to find out anything about the living dolls, for instance? They might have both a cultural aspect and a market value."

"The living dolls seem a part of something much deeper," Ceran said. "There's a whole complex of things to be un-raveled. The key may be the statement of the Proavitoi that they do not die."

"I think they die pretty young, Ceran. All those out and about are young, and those I have met who do not leave their houses are only middling old."

"Then where are their cemeteries?"

"Likely they cremate the old folks when they die."

"Where are the crematories?"

"They might just toss the ashes out or vaporize the entire remains. Probably they have no reverence for ancestors."

"Other evidence shows their entire culture to be based on an exaggerated reverence for ancestors."

"You find out, Ceran. You're Special Aspects Man."

Ceran talked to Nokoma, his Proavitoi counterpart as translator. Both were expert, and they could meet each halfway in talk. Nokoma was likely feminine. There was a certain softness about both the sexes of the Proavitoi, but the men of the Expedition believed that they had them straight now.

"Do you mind if I ask some straight questions?" Ceran greeted her today.

"Sure is not. How else I learn the talk well but by talking?"

"Some of the Proavitoi say that they do not die, Nokoma. Is this true?"

"How is not be true? If they die, they not be here to say they do not die. Oh, I joke, I joke. No, we do not die. It is a foolish alien custom which we see no reason to imitate. On Proavitus, only the low creatures die."

"None of you does?"

"Why, no. Why should one want to be an exception in this?"

"But what do you do when you get very old?"

"We do less and less then. We come to a deficiency of energy. Is it not the same with you?"

"Of course. But where do you go when you become exceedingly old?"

"Nowhere. We stay at home then. Travel is for the young and those of the active years."

"Let's try it from the other end," Ceran said. "Where are your father and mother, Nokoma?"

"Out and about. They aren't really old."

"And your grandfathers and grandmothers?"

"A few of them still get out. The older ones stay home."

"Let's try it this way. How many grandmothers do you have, Nokoma?"

"I think I have nine hundred grandmothers in my house. Oh, I know that isn't many, but we are the young branch of a family. Some of our clan have very great numbers of ancestors in their houses."

"And all these ancestors are alive?"

"What else? Who would keep things not alive? How would such be ancestors?"

Ceran began to hop around in his excitement.

"Could I see them?" he twittered.

"It might not be wise for you to see the older of them," Nokoma cautioned. "It could be an unsettling thing for strangers, and we guard it. A few tens of them you can see, of course."

Then it came to Ceran that he might be onto what he had looked for all his life. He went into a panic of expectation.

"Nokoma, it would be finding the key!" he fluted. "If none of you has ever died, then your entire race would still be alive!"

"Sure. Is like you count fruit. You take none away, you still have them all."

"But if the first of them are still alive, then they might know their origin! They would know how it began! Do they? Do you?"

"Oh, not I. I am too young for the Ritual."

"But who knows? Doesn't someone know?"

"Oh, yes, all the old ones know how it began."

"How old? How many generations back from you till they know?"

"Ten, no more. When I have ten generations of children, then I will also go to the Ritual."

"The Ritual. What is it?"

"Once a year, the old people go to the very old people. They wake them up and ask them how it all began. The very old people tell them the beginning. It is a high time. Oh, how they hottle and laugh! Then the very old people go back to sleep for another year. So it is passed down to the generations. That is the Ritual."

The Proavitoi were not humanoid. Still less were they "monkey-faces," though that name was now set in the explorers' lingo. They were upright and robed, and swathed, and were assumed to be two-legged under their garments. Though, as Manbreaker said, "They might go on wheels, for all we know."

They had remarkable flowing hands that might be called everywhere-digited. They could handle tools, or employ their hands as if they were the most intricate tools.

George Blood was of the opinion that the Proavitoi were always masked, and that the men of the Expedition had never seen their faces. He said that those apparent faces were ritual masks, and that no part of the Proavitoi had ever been seen by the men except for those remarkable hands, which perhaps were their real faces.

The men reacted with cruel hilarity when Ceran tried to explain to them just what a great discovery he was verging on.

"Little Ceran is still on the how-did-it-begin jag," Manbreaker jeered. "Ceran, will you never give off asking which came first, the chicken or the egg?"

"I will have that answer very soon," Ceran sang. "I have the unique opportunity. When I find how the Proavitoi began, I may have the clue to how everything began. All of the Proavitoi are still alive, the very first generation of them."

"It passes belief that you can be so simpleminded," Manbreaker moaned. "They say that one has finally mellowed when he can suffer fools gracefully. By God, I hope I never come to that."

But two days later, it was Manbreaker who sought out Ceran Swicegood on nearly the same subject. Manbreaker had been doing a little thinking and discovering of his own.

"You are Special Aspects Man, Ceran," he said, "and you have been running off after the wrong aspect."

"What is that?"

"It don't make a damn how it began. What is important is that it may not have to end."

"It is the beginning that I intend to discover," said Ceran.

"You fool, can't you understand anything? What do the Proavitoi possess so uniquely that we don't know whether they have it by science or by fool luck?"

"Ah, their chemistry, I suppose."

"Sure. Organic chemistry has come of age here. The Proavitoi have every kind of nexus and inhibitor and stimulant. They can grow and shrink and telescope and prolong what they will. These creatures seem stupid to me; it is as if they had these things by instinct. But they have them, that is what is important. With these things, we can become the patent medicine kings of the universes, for the Proavitoi do not travel or make many outside contacts. These things can do anything or undo anything. I suspect that the Proavitoi can shrink cells, and I suspect that they can do something else."

"No, they couldn't shrink cells. It is you who talk nonsense now, Manbreaker."

"Never mind. Their things already make nonsense of conventional chemistry. With the pharmacopoeia that one could pick up here, a man need never die. That's the stick horse you've been riding, isn't it? But you've been riding it backward with your head to the tail. The Proavitoi say that they never die."

"They seem pretty sure that they don't. If they did, they would be the first to know it, as Nokoma says."

"What? Have these creatures humor?"

"Some."

"But, Ceran, you don't understand how big this is."

"I'm the only one who understands it so far. It means that if the Proavitoi have always been immortal, as they maintain, then the oldest of them are still alive. From them I may be able to learn how their species—and perhaps every species—began."

Manbreaker went into his dying buffalo act then. He tore his hair and nearly pulled out his ears by the roots. He stomped and pawed and went off bull-bellowing: "It don't make a damn how it began, you fool! It might not have to end!" so loud that the hills echoed back:

"It don't make a damn—you fool."

Ceran Swicegood went to the house of Nokoma, but not with her on her invitation. He went without her when he knew that she was away from home. It was a sneaky thing to do, but the men of the Expedition were trained in sneakery.

He would find out better without a mentor about the nine hundred grandmothers, about the rumored living dolls. He would find out what the old people did do if they didn't die, and find if they knew how they were first born. For his intrusion, he counted on the innate politeness of the Proavitoi.

The house of Nokoma, of all the people, was in the cluster on top of the large flat hill, the Acropolis of Proavitus. They were earthen houses, though finely done, and they had the appearance of growing out of and being a part of the hill itself.

Ceran went up the winding, ascending flagstone paths, and entered the house which Nokoma had once pointed out to him. He entered furtively, and encountered one of the nine hundred grandmothers—one with whom nobody need be furtive.

The grandmother was seated and small and smiling at him. They talked without real difficulty, though it was not as easy as with Nokoma, who could meet Ceran halfway in his own language. At her call, there came a grandfather who likewise smiled at Ceran. These two ancients were somewhat smaller than the Proavitoi of active years. They were kind and serene. There was an atmosphere about the scene that barely missed being an odor—not unpleasant, sleepy, reminiscent of something, almost sad.

"Are there those here older than you?" Ceran asked earnestly.

"So many, so many! Who could know how many?" said the grandmother. She called in other grandmothers and grandfathers older and smaller than herself, these no more than half the size of the active Proavitoi—small, sleepy, smiling.

Ceran knew now that the Proavitoi were not masked. The older they were, the more character and interest there was in their faces. It was only of the immature active Proavitoi that there could have been a doubt. No masks could show such calm and smiling old age as this. The queer textured stuff was their real faces.

So old and friendly, so weak and sleepy, there must have been a dozen generations of them there back to the oldest and smallest.

"How old are the oldest?" Ceran asked the first grandmother.

"We say that all are the same age since all are perpetual," the grandmother told him. "It is not true that all are the same age, but it is indelicate to ask how old."

"You do not know what a lobster is," Ceran said to them, trembling, "but it is a creature that will boil happily, if the water on him is heated slowly. He takes no alarm, for he does not know at what point the heat is dangerous. It is that gradual here with me. I slide from one degree to another with you and my credulity is not alarmed. I am in danger of believing anything about you if it comes in small doses, and it will. I believe that you are here and as you are for no other reason than that I see and touch you. Well, I'll be boiled for a lobster, then, before I turn back from it. Are there those here even older than the ones present?"

The first grandmother motioned Ceran to follow her. They went down a ramp through the floor into the older part of the house, which must have been under ground.

Living dolls! They were here in rows on the shelves, and sitting in small chairs in their niches. Doll-sized indeed, and several hundred of them.

Many had wakened at the intrusion. Others came awake when spoken to or touched. They were incredibly ancient, but they were cognizant in their glances and recognition. They smiled and stretched sleepily, not as humans would, but as very old puppies might. Ceran spoke to them, and they understood each other surprisingly.

Lobster, lobster, said Ceran to himself, *the water has passed the danger point! And it hardly feels different. If you believe your senses in this, then you will be boiled alive in your credulity.*

He knew now that the living dolls were real and that they were the living ancestors of the Proavitoi.

Many of the little creatures began to fall asleep again. Their waking moments were short, but their sleeps seemed to be likewise. Several of the living mummies woke a second time while Ceran was still in the room, woke refreshed from very short sleeps and were anxious to talk again.

"You are incredible!" Ceran cried out, and all the small and smaller and still smaller creatures smiled and laughed their assent. Of course they were. All good creatures everywhere are incredible, and were there ever so many assembled in one place? But Ceran was greedy. A roomful of miracles wasn't enough.

"I have to take this back as far as it will go!" he cried avidly. "Where are the even older ones?"

"There are older ones and yet older and again older," said the first grandmother, "and thrice-over older ones, but perhaps it would be wise not to seek to be too wise. You have seen enough. The old people are sleepy. Let us go up again."

Go up again, out of this? Ceran would not. He saw passages and descending ramps, down into the heart of the great hill itself. There were whole worlds of rooms about him and under his feet. Ceran went on and down, and who was to stop him? Not dolls and creatures much smaller than dolls.

Manbreaker had once called himself an old pirate who revelled in the stream of his riches. But Ceran was the Young Alchemist who was about to find the Stone itself.

He walked down the ramps through centuries and millennia. The atmosphere he had noticed on the upper levels was a clear odor now—sleepy, half-remembered, smiling, sad, and quite strong. That is the way Time smells.

"Are there those here even older than you?" Ceran asked a small grandmother whom he held in the palm of his hand.

"So old and so small that I could hold in my hand," said the grandmother in what Ceran knew from Nokoma to be the older uncompounded form of the Proavitus language.

Smaller and older the creatures had been getting as Ceran went through the rooms. He was boiled lobster now for sure. He had to believe it all: he saw and felt it. The wren-sized grandmother talked and laughed and nodded that there were those far older than herself, and in doing so she nodded herself back to sleep. Ceran returned her to her niche in the hive-like wall where there were thousands of others, miniaturized generations.

Of course he was not in the house of Nokoma now. He was in the heart of the hill that underlay all the houses of Proavitus, and these were the ancestors of everybody on the asteroid.

"Are there those here even older than you?" Ceran asked a small grandmother whom he held on the tip of his finger.

"Older and smaller," she said, "but you come near the end."

She was asleep, and he put her back in her place. The older they were, the more they slept.

He was down to solid rock under the roots of the hill. He was into the passages that were cut out of that solid rock, but they could not be many or deep. He had a sudden fear that the creatures would become so small that he could not see them or talk to them, and so he would miss the secret of the beginning.

But had not Nokoma said that all the old people knew the secret? Of course. But he wanted to hear it from the oldest of them. He would have it now, one way or the other.

"Who is the oldest? Is this the end of it? Is this the beginning? Wake up! Wake up!" he called when he was sure he was in the lowest and oldest room.

"Is it Ritual?" asked some who woke up. Smaller than mice they were, no bigger than bees, maybe older than both.

"It is a special Ritual," Ceran told them. "Relate to me how it was in the beginning."

What was that sound—too slight, too scattered to be a noise? It was like a billion microbes laughing. It was the hilarity of little things waking up to a high time.

"Who is the oldest of all?" Ceran demanded, for their laughter bothered him. "Who is the oldest and first?"

"I am the oldest, the ultimate grandmother," one said gaily. "All the others are my children. Are you also of my children?"

"Of course," said Ceran, and the small laughter of unbelief flittered out from the whole multitude of them.

"Then you must be the ultimate child, for you are like no other. If you be, then it is as funny at the end as it was in the beginning."

"How was it in the beginning?" Ceran bleated. "You are the first. Do you know how you came to be?"

"Oh, yes, yes," laughed the ultimate grandmother, and the hilarity of the small things became a real noise now.

"How did it begin?" demanded Ceran, and he was hopping and skipping about in his excitement.

"Oh, it was so funny a joke the way things began that you would not believe it," chittered the grandmother. "A joke, a joke!"

"Tell me the joke, then. If a joke generated your species, then tell me that cosmic joke."

"Tell yourself," tinkled the grandmother. "You are a part of the joke if you are of my children. Oh, it is too funny to believe. How good to wake up and laugh and go to sleep again."

Blazing green frustration! To be so close and to be balked by a giggling bee!

"Don't go to sleep again! Tell me at once how it began!" Ceran shrilled, and he had the ultimate grandmother between thumb and finger.

"This is not Ritual," the grandmother protested. "Ritual is that you guess what it was for three days, and we laugh and say, 'No, no, no, it was something nine times as wild as that. Guess some more.'"

"I will *not* guess for three days! Tell me at once or I will crush you," Ceran threatened in a quivering voice.

"I look at you, you look at me, I wonder if you will do it," the ultimate grandmother said calmly.

Any of the tough men of the Expedition would have done it—would have crushed her, and then another and another and another of the creatures till the secret was told. If Ceran had taken on a tough personality and a tough name he'd have done it. If he'd been Gutboy Barrelhouse he'd have done it without a qualm. But Ceran Swicegood couldn't do it.

"Tell me," he pleaded in agony. "All my life I've tried to find out how it began, how anything began. And you know!"

"We know. Oh, it was so funny how it began. So joke! So fool, so clown, so grotesque thing! Nobody could guess, nobody could believe."

"Tell me! Tell me!" Ceran was ashen and hysterical.

"No, no, you are no child of mine," chortled the ultimate grandmother. "Is too joke a joke to tell a stranger. We could not insult a stranger to tell so funny, so unbelieve. Strangers can die. Shall I have it on conscience that a stranger died laughing?"

"Tell me! Insult me! Let me die laughing!" But Ceran nearly died crying from the frustration that ate him up as a million bee-sized things laughed and hooted and giggled:

"Oh, it was so funny the way it began!"

And they laughed. And laughed. And went on laughing . . . until Ceran Swicegood wept and laughed together, and crept away, and returned to the ship still laughing. On his next voyage he changed his name to Blaze Bolt and ruled for ninety-seven days as king of a sweet sea island in M-81, but that is another and much more unpleasant story.

Afterword by Andy Duncan

I first encountered "Nine Hundred Grandmothers" in *The Norton Book of Science Fiction,* edited by Ursula K. Le Guin and Brian Attebery with Karen Joy Fowler, an anthology that turned out to be important to my fiction-writing career. It was published in fall 1993, during my first year in the graduate creative-writing program at North Carolina State University. I don't think I bought a copy immediately, but in January 1994 I had my first workshop with Nebula Award winner John Kessel, who peered at my manuscript and peered at me and peered at my manuscript again and said, "There's a long, rich history of this sort of thing, and you're part of it whether you know it or not."

From that point Kessel was my sensei, and on his recommendation I snapped up a copy of the *Norton*—a box of marvels that tells a novice SF writer, "You can do anything you want, as long as it's strange." When I flew to the Clarion West Writers Workshop that summer, also on Kessel's recommendation, the *Norton* was one of the two inspirational hardcovers in my luggage. (The other was Faulkner's *Absalom, Absalom!* for which I never will be asked to write an introduction.)

Of all the stories in the *Norton* that spoke directly to me, "Nine Hundred Grandmothers" may have spoken the loudest. In her *Norton* essay, Le Guin discusses science fiction's tendency to literalize metaphors, and Lafferty's story precisely literalizes one of the foundational metaphors of my upbringing in rural South Carolina, where I was taught to venerate a long chain of ancestors growing ever smaller as they receded into the distance. Their secrets were closely guarded, but as I stumbled through the late twentieth century, those generations were often audible in the background, like peepers in the spring; I was pretty sure they were laughing. Moreover, all my important ancestors, the conveyors of culture and especially language, seemed to be women. Lafferty's unforgettable "living dolls" of the planet Proavitus (Latin for "ancestral," I'm told) embody the famous Faulkner line from *Requiem for a Nun*: "The past is never dead. It's not even past."

Rereading Lafferty's story now, I wonder about the fate of the Proavitoi. What happens to them in the space between the story's last two sentences? "With the pharmacopoeia that one could pick up here, a man need never die," says Manbreaker Crag, who envisions his team becoming "the patent medicine kings of the universe." Will these "slight people" survive Manbreaker's unstranding of their organic chemistry? Consider that Lafferty was a lifelong resident of Oklahoma—a state wrested from the natives by any number of

Manbreaker Crags—and many of his writings ponder the exploitation of the indigenous peoples of North America; along with language itself, it is the unavoidable theme of his great novel, *Okla Hannali.*

I believe Lafferty knows exactly what happens to the Proavitoi, but spares us at the end by diverting our attention to "another and much more unpleasant story." As the ultimate grandmother might have said, was too joke a joke to tell a stranger, perhaps; Lafferty could not insult a stranger to tell so funny, so unbelieve.

Land of the Great Horses

Introduction by Harlan Ellison™

Look out your window. What do you see? The gang fight on the corner, with the teenie-boppers using churchkeys on each other's faces; the scissors grinder with his multicolored cart and tinkling bells; a pudgy woman in a print dress too short for her fat legs, hoeing her lawn; a three-alarm fire with children trapped on the fifth story; a mad dog attached to the leg of a peddler of Seventh Day Adventist literature; an impending race riot with a representative of RAM on a sound truck. Any or all? It takes no special powers of observation to catalog the unclassifiable. But now look again. What do you see? What you usually see? An empty street. *Now catalog:*

Curbstones, without which cars would run up onto front lawns. Mailboxes, without which touch with the world would be diminished. Telephone poles and wires, without which communication would screech to a halt. Gutters, sewers, and manholes, without which you would be flooded when it rains. Blacktop, without which the car you own wouldn't last a month on the crushed rock. The breeze, without which, well, a day is diminished. What are these things? They are the obvious. So obvious they become invisible. How many water hydrants and mailboxes did you pass today? None? Hardly. You passed dozens, but you did not see them. They are the incredibly valuable, absolutely necessary, totally ignored staples of a well-run community.

Speculative fiction is a small community. It has its obvious flashy residents. Knight, Sheckley, Sturgeon, Bradbury, Clarke, Vonnegut. We see them and take note of them, and know what they're about. But the community would not run one thousandth as well as it does without the quiet writers, the ones who turn out story after story, not hack work but really excellent stories, time after time. The kind you settle back and think about, after finishing them, saying, "That was a *good* story." And you promptly forget who wrote it. Perhaps later you recall the story. "Oh yeah, remember that one about . . ." and then you wrinkle down and say, "What the hell was the name of the guy who wrote it? He's done a bunch of things, you know, pretty fair writer . . ."

The problem is a matter of cumulativeness. Each story is an excellence, standing alone. But somehow it never makes a totality, an image of a writer, a career in perspective. This is the sad but obvious thing about R. A. Lafferty's place in speculative fiction.

He is a man of substantiality, whose writing is top-flight. Not merely competent fiction, but genuinely exemplary fiction. He has been writing for—how many years? More than six, but less than fifteen? Something like that. Yet he is seldom mentioned when fans gather to discuss The Writers. Even though he has been anthologized many times, been included in Judith Merril's *Year's Best SF* on several occasions, and the Carr-Wollheim *World's Best* anthology twice, and appeared in almost all the science fiction magazines. He is the invisible man. It will be rectified here. Raphael Aloysius Lafferty will emerge, will speak, will declare himself, and then you will read another extra-brilliant story by him. And dammit, this time *remember*!

Lafferty speaking: "I am, not necessarily in this order, fifty-one years old, a bachelor, an electrical engineer, a fat man.

"Born in Iowa, came to Oklahoma when I was four years old, and except for four years in the army have been here all my life. Also, one year on a little civil service job in Washington, D.C. The only college I've ever attended was a couple of years in the University of Tulsa's night school division long ago, mostly math and German. I've spent close to thirty years working for electrical jobbers, mostly as buyer and price-quotation man. During WWII I was stationed in Texas, North Carolina, Florida, California, Australia, New Guinea, Morotai (Dutch East Indies, now Indonesia), and the Philippines. I was a good staff sergeant, and at one time I could talk pretty fair *pasar* Malay and Tagalog (of the Philippines).

"What does a man say about himself? Never the important things. I was a heavy drinker for a few years and gave it up about six years ago. This left a gap: when you give up the company of the more interesting drinkers, you give up something of the colorful and fantastic. So I substituted writing science fiction. Something I read in one of the writers' magazines gave me the silly idea that science fiction would be easy to write. It isn't, for me. I wasn't raised on the stuff like most of the writers in this form seem to have been.

"My hobby is language. Any language. I've got at least a thousand dollars in self-teach grammars and readers and dictionaries and Lingua-phone and Corti-naphone courses. I've picked up a rough reading knowledge of all the languages of the Latin, German, and Slavic families, as well as Irish and Greek; but actually Spanish, French, and German are the only ones I read freely with respectable speed. I'm a Catholic of the out-of-season or conservative variety. As to politics, I am the only member of the American Centrist Party, whose tenets I will one day set out in an ironic-Utopia story. I'm a compulsive walker; turn me loose in a strange town and I'll explore every corner of it on foot inside a week. I don't think of myself as a very interesting fellow."

This is the editor again, for a final comment. Lafferty is about as uninteresting as his stories. Which is to say, not at all. As entered for the prosecution's case against R. A.'s contention that he's a neb, the following story, one of my particular favorites in this book.

Note: The introduction above is reproduced from its original appearance in *Dangerous Visions* and is © 1967 The Kilimanjaro Corporation with the kind permission of the author.

Land of the Great Horses

T *hey came and took our country away from us," the people had always said. But nobody understood them.*

Two Englishmen, Richard Rockwell and Seruno Smith, were rolling in a terrain buggy over the Thar Desert. It was bleak, red country, more rock than sand. It looked as though the top had been stripped off it and the naked underland left uncovered.

They heard thunder and it puzzled them. They looked at each other, the blond Rockwell and the dark Smith. It never thundered in the whole country between New Delhi and Bahawalpur. What would this rainless north India desert have to thunder with?

"Let's ride the ridges here," Rockwell told Smith, and he sent the vehicle into a climb. "It never rains here, but once before I was caught in a draw in a country where it never rained. I nearly drowned."

It thundered again, heavy and rolling, as though to tell them that they were hearing right.

"This draw is named Kuti Tavdavi—Little River," Smith said darkly. "I wonder why."

Then he jerked back as though startled at himself.

"Rockwell, why did I say that? I never saw this draw before. How did a name like that pop into my mind? But it's the low draw that would be a little river if it ever rained in this country. This land can't have significant rain. There's no high place to tip whatever moisture goes over."

"I wonder about that every time I come," said Rockwell, and raised his hand toward the shimmering heights—the Land of the Great Horses, the famous mirage. "If it were really there it would tip the moisture. It would make a lush savanna of all this."

They were mineral explorers doing ground minutiae on promising portions of an aerial survey. The trouble with the Thar was that it had everything—lead, zinc, antimony, copper, tin, bauxite—in barely submarginal amounts. Nowhere would the Thar pay off, but everywhere it would almost pay.

Now it was lightning about the heights of the mirage, and they had never seen that before. It had clouded and lowered. It was thundering in rolling waves, and there was no mirage of sound.

"There is either a very large and very busy bird up there or this is rain," Rockwell said.

And it had begun to rain, softly but steadily. It was pleasant as they chuckered along in the vehicle through the afternoon. Rain in the desert is always like a bonus.

Smith broke into a happy song in one of the northwest India tongues, a tune with a ribald swing to it, though Rockwell didn't understand the words. It was full of double rhymes and vowel-packed words such as a child might make up.

"How the devil do you know the tongues so well?" Rockwell asked. "I find them difficult, and I have a good linguistic background."

"I didn't have to learn them," Smith said, "I just had to remember them. They all cluster around the *boro jib* itself."

"Around the what? How many of the languages do you know?"

"All of them. The Seven Sisters, they're called: Punjabi, Kashmiri, Gujarati, Marathi, Sindhi, Hindi."

"Your Seven Sisters only number six," Rockwell jibed.

"There's a saying that the seventh sister ran off with a horse trader," Smith said. "But that seventh lass is still encountered here and there around the world."

Often they stopped to survey on foot. The very color of the new rivulets was significant to the mineral men, and this was the first time they had ever seen water flow in that country. They continued on fitfully and slowly, and ate up a few muddy miles.

Rockwell gasped once and nearly fell off the vehicle. He had seen a total stranger riding beside him, and it shook him.

Then he saw that it was Smith as he had always been, and he was dumbfounded by the illusion. And, soon, by something else.

"Something is very wrong here," Rockwell said.

"Something is very right here," Smith answered him, and then broke into another song in an Indian tongue.

"We're lost," Rockwell worried out loud. "We can't see any distance for the rain, but there shouldn't be rising ground here. It isn't mapped."

"Of course it is," Smith sang. "It's the Jalo Char."

"The what? Where did you get a name like that? The map's a blank here, and the country should be."

"Then the map is defective. Man, it's the sweetest valley in the world! It will lead us all the way up. How could the map forget it? How could we all forget it for so long?"

"Smith! What's wrong? You're pie-eyed."

"Everything's right, I tell you. I was reborn just a minute ago. It's a coming home."

"Smith! We're riding through green grass!"

"I love it. I could crop it like a horse."

"That cliff, Smith! It shouldn't be that close! It's part of the mir—"

"Why, sir, that is Lolo Trusul."

"But it's not real! It's not on any topography map!"

"Map, sir? I'm a poor *kalo* man who wouldn't know about things like that."

"Smith! You're a qualified cartographer!"

"Does seem that I followed a trade with a name like that. But the cliff is real enough. I climbed it in my boyhood—in my other boyhood. And that yonder, sir, is Drapengoro Rez—the Grassy Mountain. And the high plateau ahead of us which we begin to climb is Diz Boro Grai—the Land of the Great Horses."

Rockwell stopped the terrain buggy and leaped off. Smith followed him in a happy daze.

"Smith, you're wide-eyed crazy!" Rockwell gasped. "And what am I? We're terribly lost somehow. Smith, look at the log chart and the bearings recorder!"

"Log chart, sir? I'm a poor *kalo* man who wouldn't know—"

"Damn you, Smith, you *made* these instruments. If they're correct we're seven hundred feet too high and have been climbing for ten miles into a highland that's supposed to be part of a mirage. These cliffs can't be here. We can't be here. Smith!"

But Seruno Smith had ambled off like a crazy man.

"Smith, where are you trotting off to? Can't you hear me?"

"You call to me, sir?" asked Smith. "And by such a name?"

"Are the two of us as crazy as the country?" Rockwell moaned. "I've worked with you for three years. Isn't your name Smith?"

"Why, yes, sir, I guess it might be englished as Horse-Smith or Black-Smith. But my name is Pettalangro and I'm going home."

And the man who had been Smith started on foot up to the Land of the Great Horses.

"Smith, I'm getting on the buggy and I'm going back," Rockwell shouted. "I'm scared liverless of this country that changes. When a mirage turns solid it's time to quit. Come along now! We'll be back in Bikaner by tomorrow morning. There's a doctor there, and a whiskey bar. We need one of them."

"Thank you, sir, but I must go up to my home," Smith sang out. "It was kind of you to give me a ride along the way."

"I'm leaving you, Smith. One crazy man is better than two."

"*Ashava, Sarishan,*" Smith called a parting.

"Smith, unriddle me one last thing," Rockwell called, trying to find a piece of sanity to hold to. "What is the name of the seventh sister?"

"Deep Romany," Smith sang, and he was gone up into the high plateau that had always been a mirage.

In an upper room on Olive Street in St. Louis, Missouri, a half-and-half couple were talking half-and-half.

"The *rez* has riser'd," the man said. "I can *sung* it like *brishindo*. Let's *jal*."

"All right," the wife said, "if you're *awa*."

"Hell, I bet I can *riker* plenty *bano* on the *beda* we got here. I'll have *kakko* come *kinna* it *aro*."

"With a little *bachi* we can be *jal*'d by *areat*," said the wife.

"*Nashiva*, woman, *nashiva*!"

"All right," the wife said, and she began to pack their suitcases.

In Camargo in the Chihuahua State of Mexico, a shade-tree mechanic sold his business for a hundred pesos and told his wife to pack up—they were leaving.

"To leave now when business is so good?" she asked.

"I only got one car to fix and I can't fix that," the man said.

"But if you keep it long enough, he will pay you to put it together again even if it isn't fixed. That's what he did last time. And you've a horse to shoe."

"I'm afraid of that horse. It has come back, though. Let's go."

"Are you sure we will be able to find it?"

"Of course I'm not sure. We will go in our wagon and our sick horse will pull it."

"Why will we go in the wagon, when we have a car, of sorts?"

"I don't know why. But we will go in the wagon, and we will nail the old giant horseshoe up on the lintel board."

A carny in Nebraska lifted his head and smelled the air.

"It's come back," he said. "I always knew we'd know. Any other Romanies here?"

"I got a little *rart* in me," said one of his fellows. "This *narvelengero dives* is only a two-bit carnival anyhow. We'll tell the boss to shove it up his *chev* and we'll be gone."

In Tulsa, a used-car dealer named Gypsy Red announced the hottest sale on the row:

"Everything for nothing! I'm leaving. Pick up the papers and drive them off. Nine new heaps and thirty good ones. All free."

"You think we're crazy?" the people asked. "There's a catch."

Red put the papers for all the cars on the ground and put a brick on top of them. He got in the worst car on the lot and drove it off forever.

"All free," he sang out as he drove off. "Pick up the papers and drive the cars away."

They're still there. You think people are crazy to fall for something like that that probably has a catch to it?

In Galveston a barmaid named Margaret was asking merchant seamen how best to get passage to Karachi.

"Why Karachi?" one of them asked her.

"I thought it would be the nearest big port," she said. "It's come back, you know."

"I kind of felt this morning it had come back," he said. "I'm a *chal* myself. Sure, we'll find something going that way."

In thousands of places fawney-men and dukkerin-women, kakki-baskros and hegedusies, clowns and commission men, Counts of Condom and Dukes of Little Egypt *parvel'*d in their chips and got ready to roll.

Men and families made sudden decisions in every country. *Athinganoi* gathered in the hills above Salonika in Greece and were joined by brothers from Serbia and Albania and the Rhodope Hills of Bulgaria. *Zingari* of north Italy gathered around Pavia and began to roll toward Genoa to take ship. *Boêmios* of Portugal came down to Porto and Lisbon. *Gitanos* of Andalusia and all southern Spain came to Sanlúcar and Málaga. *Zigeuner* from Thuringia and Hanover thronged to Hamburg to find ocean passage. *Gioboga* and their mixed-blood *Shelta* cousins from every *cnoc* and *coill* of Ireland found boats at Dublin and Limerick and Bantry.

From deeper Europe, *Tsigani* began to travel overland eastward. The people were going from two hundred ports of every continent and over a thousand highroads—many of them long forgotten.

Balauros, Kalo, Manusch, Melelo, Tsigani, Moro, Romani, Flamenco, Sinto, Cicara, the many-named people was traveling in its thousands. The *Romani Rai* was moving.

Two million Gypsies of the world were going home.

At the institute, Gregory Smirnov was talking to his friends and associates.

"You remember the thesis I presented several years ago," he said, "that, a little over a thousand years ago, Outer Visitors came down to Earth and took a sliver of our Earth away with them. All of you found the proposition comical, but I arrived at my conclusion by isostatic and eustatic analysis carried out minutely. There is no doubt that it happened."

"One of our slivers is missing," said Aloysius Shiplap. "You guessed the sliver taken at about ten thousand square miles in area and no more than a mile thick at its greatest. You said you thought they wanted to run this sliver from our Earth through their laboratories as a sample. Do you have something new on our missing sliver?"

"I'm closing the inquiry," Gregory said. "They've brought it back."

It was simple really, *jekvasteskero,* Gypsy-simple. It is the *gadjo,* the non-Gypsies of the world, who give complicated answers to simple things.

"They came and took our country away from us," the Gypsies had always said, and that is what had happened.

The Outer Visitors had run a slip under it, rocked it gently to rid it of nervous fauna, and then taken it away for study. For a marker, they left an immaterial simulacrum of that high country as we ourselves sometimes set name or picture tags to show where an object will be set later. This simulacrum was often seen by humans as a mirage.

The Outer Visitors also set simulacra in the minds of the superior fauna that fled from the moving land. This would be a homing instinct, inhibiting permanent settlement anywhere until the time should come for the resettlement; entwined with this instinct were certain premonitions, fortune-showings, and understandings.

Now the Visitors brought the slice of land back, and its old fauna homed in on it.

"What will the—ah—patronizing smile on my part—Outer Visitors do now, Gregory?" Aloysius Shiplap asked back at the Institute.

"Why, take another sliver of our Earth to study, I suppose, Aloysius," Gregory Smirnov said.

Low-intensity earthquakes rocked the Los Angeles area for three days. The entire area was evacuated of people. Then there was a great whistle blast from the sky as if to say, "All ashore that's going ashore."

Then the surface to some little depth and all its superstructure was taken away. It was gone. And then it was quickly forgotten.

From the *Twenty-second Century Comprehensive Encyclopedia*, Vol. 1, page 389:

ANGELENOS. (See also *Automobile Gypsies* and *Prune Pickers*.) A mixed ethnic group of unknown origin, much given to wandering in automobiles. It is predicted that they will be the last users of this vehicle, and several archaic chrome-burdened models are still produced for their market. These people are not beggars; many of them are of superior intelligence. They often set up in business, usually as real estate dealers, gamblers, confidence men, managers of mail-order diploma mills, and promoters of one sort or other. They seldom remain long in one location.

Their pastimes are curious. They drive for hours and days on old and seldom-used cloverleafs and freeways. It has been said that a majority of the Angelenos are narcotics users, but Harold Freelove (who lived for some months as an Angeleno) has proved this false. What they inhale at their frolics (smog-crocks) is a black smoke of carbon and petroleum waste laced with monoxide. Its purpose is not clear.

The religion of the Angelenos is a mixture of old cults with a very strong eschatological element. The Paradise Motif is represented by reference to a mystic "Sunset Boulevard." The language of the Angelenos is a colorful and racy argot. Their account of their origin is vague:

"They came and took our dizz away from us," they say.

Afterword by Gregory Frost

In 1967 Harlan Ellison's *Dangerous Visions* was first published by Doubleday. I, in high school in Iowa and already devouring the likes of Fredric Brown, Bradbury, Heinlein, Asimov, Zelazny, and Dick, might as well have been the target Harlan put in the crosshairs. In retrospect we peer through many great annual *Best of* anthologies—edited by Gardner Dozois, David Hartwell, Ellen Datlow, Terri Windling, Kelly Link & Gavin Grant, Terry Carr, etc.—and we forget how monumental was Harlan's lashing together of what he termed "Thirty-two Soothsayers." I'm near Philadelphia now, and so I think of Harlan as the Albert Barnes of science fiction. Barnes' collection of impressionists is an extraordinary thing; and to be fair there are a few disappointing works hanging among the Matisses, Van Goghs, Gaunguins, Picassos, and Renoirs—lesser paintings by artists who faded into obscurity, though obviously Barnes thought he saw *something* in them. *Dangerous Visions* really is the Barnes collection of science fiction. A few "what happened to . . ." pieces, but otherwise breathtaking.

Dangerous Visions proved to be my gateway into the worlds of Raphael Aloysius Lafferty through the story Harlan selected, called "Land of the Great Horses." I did not know at the time how extraordinary that would prove to be, just as I didn't know that Lafferty himself was a fellow Iowan (born in the southwestern town of Neola, Iowa—if anyone from Neola is reading this, you need to put up at least a plaque for Heaven's sake!)

As Lafferty stories go, this one is short and seemingly simple, but oh, by the end it has shape-shifted on you more than once. It can be read, in a way, as a companion story to another tale of his called "Narrow Valley," also concerned with unreliable topography.

It is also exemplary of the way Lafferty entered stories sidewise, producing a text that dives straight into a situation already in motion and seems to be about one thing, yet turns out to be about something else. And then when you think you have its measure, the author adds a punch line you never saw coming.

Here, we begin with a sort of dictum: *"They came and took our country away from us," the people had always said. But nobody understood them.*

What country and what people, we must read to discover. We are then introduced to two Englishmen, Richard Rockwell and Seruno Smith, driving across the Thar Desert, which is to say the Great Desert of India. They approach and behold a famous mirage called the Land of the Great Horses, or *Diz Boro Grai*. It's what they've come to see. Things immediately start to go wrong. In this extremely barren desert, they hear the sound of thunder from an approaching storm, and then find their mirage shot with lightning. The improbable climatic event seems to transform Seruno Smith: he suddenly and inexplicably knows the names of places (a draw called *Kuti Tavdavi*, Little River); he bursts into song in tongues he does not speak. When asked how by Rockwell, he explains that he has only to remember these tongues to sing, and that "They all cluster around the *boro jib* itself." Smith seems to be leading this "great life" out of nowhere. He confesses to Rockwell that he speaks all languages in play—the so-called Seven Sisters, but Smith names only six. Rockwell notices and finally requests the name of the missing language: Deep Romany. Rockwell tries to head back, but Smith refuses, and calls him "Sarishan," or "English," as if they are suddenly foreign to each other, and then begins to scale the heights that until moments ago were part of the mirage.

The story shifts then to various small scenes of people speaking various dialects of Romani, Punjabi, Hindi—in each it's clear that someone with Romany blood is feeling the pull of Diz Boro Grai. Some are *Romani Rai,* gypsy gentlemen; some are *dukkerin*-women, that is, fortune-tellers; some perhaps Athinganoi, considered to be the ancestral tribe of the Roma. And so it goes as various people with some percentage of gypsy blood pull up stakes and head "home" because "the *rez* has *riser'*d," and it tugs at them, smells like rain, cannot be ignored. Home is the Land of Great Horses, which became a mirage for thousands of years but now is no longer.

To reveal more would be to spoil the story for the reader. Suffice it to say that once you understand what is going on, Lafferty still has a coda to deliver—one that plays on the "Diz" of "Diz Boro Grai" and "dizz" in a newly coined dialect that refers in all probability to Disneyland.

In "Narrow Valley," where, Michael Swanwick tells me, Lafferty is having his little joke with the Pawnee language, here he effortlessly tosses off terms and phrases in various Romany dialects . . . all of which leads to a final, signature jape that can only exist *because* of his skill with those dialects.

As so often happens in a story by R. A. Lafferty, you are turned and turned and turned again, but always within the framework of the remarkable story itself. As a reader, I'm agog. As a writer, I'm forever asking, "How does he do this?"

Eurema's Dam

Introduction by Robert Silverberg

This is a story about a schlemiel, to use a word probably not too often heard in Raphael Aloysius Lafferty's hometown of Tulsa, Oklahoma. The schlemiel story is a genre I always thought I'd avoid, if I were an editor, for it has seemed to me that stories about schlemiels, losers, twerps, dullards, or schnooks would be of interest only to an audience of schlemiels, losers, twerps, dullards, or schnooks, at best, and no such people would be reading anything I edited. Well, never mind all that. R. A. Lafferty was a cunning and tricky writer and—as can quickly be seen—the schlemiel he created for us here is of an extraordinary sort.

"Eurema's Dam" won a Hugo in 1973 at Toronto. I am not all that awed by stories that win awards, nor all that scornful of those that don't, but Lafferty's feat of winning a Hugo for "Eurema's Dam" deserves some commemoration. Virtually all Hugo-winning stories then were first published in science fiction magazines or in paperback anthologies easily available to a wide segment of the electorate, but my anthology *New Dimensions II* had appeared only in an expensive hardcover edition that had sold perhaps six thousand copies. How, given that handicap, Lafferty's story had ever reached enough people to get the required number of votes, I have no idea. Yet it won, beating out, among other things, a story of mine. I will not pretend that I would not have preferred it the other way around, but I was undilutedly delighted that so fine and special a writer as Lafferty had carried off his first trophy with a story I had published.

Eurema's Dam

He was about the last of them.

What? The last of the great individualists? The last of the true creative geniuses of the century? The last of the sheer precursors?

No. No. He was the last of the dolts.

Kids were being born smarter all the time when he came along, and they would be so forever more. He was about the last dumb kid ever born.

Even his mother had to admit that Albert was a slow child. What else can you call a boy who doesn't begin to talk till he is four years old, who won't learn to handle a spoon till he is six, who can't operate a doorknob till he is eight? What else can you say about one who put his shoes on the wrong feet and walked in pain? And who had to be told to close his mouth after yawning?

Some things would always be beyond him—like whether it was the big hand or the little hand of the clock that told the hours. But this wasn't something serious. He never did care what time it was.

When, about the middle of his ninth year, Albert made a breakthrough at telling his right hand from his left, he did it by the most ridiculous set of mnemonics ever put together. It had to do with the way a dog turns around before lying down, the direction of whirlpools and whirlwinds, the side a cow is milked from and a horse is mounted from, the direction of twist of oak and sycamore leaves, the maze patterns of rock moss and of tree moss, the cleavage of limestone, the direction of a hawk's wheeling, of a shrike's hunting, and of a snake's coiling (remembering that the mountain boomer is an exception, and that it isn't a true snake), the lay of cedar fronds and of balsam fronds, the twist of a hole dug by a skunk and by a badger (remembering pungently that skunks sometimes use old badger holes). Well, Albert finally learned to remember which was right and which was left, but an observant boy would have learned his right hand from his left without all that nonsense.

Albert never learned to write a readable hand. To get by in school he cheated. From a bicycle speedometer, a midget motor, tiny eccentric cams, and batteries stolen from his grandfather's hearing aid, Albert made a machine to write for him. It was small as a doodlebug and fitted onto a pen or pencil so that Albert could conceal it with his fingers. It formed the letters beautifully as Albert had set the cams to follow a copybook model. He triggered the different letters with keys no bigger than whiskers. Sure it was crooked, but what else can you do when you're too dumb to learn how to write passably?

Albert couldn't figure at all. He had to make another machine to figure for him. It was a palm-of-the-hand thing that would add and subtract and multiply and divide. The next year when he was in the ninth grade they gave him algebra, and he had to devise a flipper to go on the end of his gadget to work quadratic and simultaneous equations. If it weren't for such cheating Albert wouldn't have gotten any marks at all in school.

He had another difficulty when he came to his fifteenth year. People, that is an understatement. There should be a stronger word than "difficulty" for it. Albert was afraid of girls.

What to do?

"I will build me a machine that is not afraid of girls," Albert said. He set to work on it. He had it nearly finished when a thought came to him: "But *no* machine is afraid of girls. How will this help me?"

His logic was at fault and analogy broke down. He did what he always did. He cheated.

He took the programming rollers out of an old player piano in the attic, found a gear case that would serve, used magnetized sheets instead of perforated music rolls, fed a copy of Wormwood's *Logic* into the matrix, and he had a logic machine that would answer questions.

"What's the matter with me that I'm afraid of girls?" Albert asked his logic machine.

"Nothing the matter with you," the logic machine told him. "It's logical to be afraid of girls. They seem pretty spooky to me too."

"But what can I do about it?"

"Wait for time and circumstances. They sure are slow. Unless you want to cheat—"

"Yes, yes, what then?"

"Build a machine that looks just like you, Albert, and talks just like you. Only make it smarter than you are, and not bashful. And, ah, Albert, there's a special thing you'd better put into it in case things go wrong. I'll whisper it to you. It's dangerous."

So Albert made Little Danny, a dummy who looked like him and talked like him, only he was smarter and not bashful. He filled Little Danny with quips from *Mad Magazine* and from *Quip*, and then they were set.

Albert and Little Danny went to call on Alice.

"Why, he's wonderful," Alice said. "Why can't you be like that, Albert? Aren't you wonderful, Little Danny. Why do you have to be so stupid, Albert, when Little Danny is so wonderful?"

"I, uh, uh, I don't know," Albert said, "uh, uh, uh."

"He sounds like a fish with the hiccups," Little Danny said.

"You do, Albert, really you do!" Alice screamed. "Why can't you say smart things like Little Danny does, Albert? Why are you so stupid?"

This wasn't working out very well, but Albert kept on with it. He programmed Little Danny to play the ukulele and to sing. He wished that he could program himself to do it. Alice loved everything about Little Danny, but she paid no attention to Albert. And one day Albert had had enough.

"Wha-wha-what do we need with this dummy?" Albert asked. "I just made him to am—to amu—to make you laugh. Let's go off and leave him."

"Go off with you, Albert?" Alice asked. "But you're so stupid. I tell you what. Let's you and me go off and leave Albert, Little Danny. We can have more fun without him."

"Who needs him?" Little Danny asked. "Get lost, Buster."

Albert walked away from them. He was glad that he'd taken his logic machine's advice as to the special thing to be built into Little Danny. Albert walked fifty steps. A hundred. "Far enough," Albert said, and he pushed a button in his pocket.

Nobody but Albert and his logic machine ever did know what that explosion was. Tiny wheels out of Little Danny and small pieces of Alice rained down a little later, but there weren't enough fragments for anyone to identify.

Albert had learned one lesson from his logic machine: never make anything that you can't unmake.

Well, Albert finally grew to be a man, in years at least. He would always have something about him of a very awkward teenager. And yet he fought his own war against those who were teenagers in years, and he defeated them completely. There was enmity between them forever. Albert hadn't been a very well-adjusted adolescent, and he hated the memory of it. And nobody ever mistook him for an adjusted man.

Albert was too awkward to earn a living at an honest trade. He was reduced to peddling his little tricks and contrivances to shysters and promoters. But he did back into a sort of fame, and he did become burdened with wealth.

He was too stupid to handle his own monetary affairs, but he built an actuary machine to do his investing and he became rich by accident. He built the damned thing too good and he regretted it.

Albert became one of that furtive group that has saddled us with all the mean things in our history. There was that Punic who couldn't learn the rich variety of hieroglyphic characters and who devised the crippled short alphabet for wan-wits. There was the nameless Arab who couldn't count beyond ten and who set up the ten-number system for babies and idiots. There was the double-Dutchman with his movable type who drove fine copy out of the world. Albert was of their miserable company.

Albert himself wasn't much good for anything. But he had in himself the low knack for making machines that were good at everything.

His machines did a few things. You remember that anciently there was smog in the cities. Oh, it could be drawn out of the air easily enough. All it took was a tickler. Albert made a tickler machine. He would set it fresh every morning. It would clear the air in a circle three hundred yards around his hovel and gather a little over a ton of residue every twenty-four hours. This residue was rich in large polysyllabic molecules which one of his chemical machines could use.

"Why can't you clear all the air?" the people asked him.

"This is as much of the stuff as Clarence Deoxyribonuclei-conibus needs every day," Albert said. That was the name of this particular chemical machine.

"But we die of the smog," the people said. "Have mercy on us."

"Oh, all right," Albert said. He turned it over to one of his reduplicating machines to make as many copies as were necessary.

You remember that once there was a teenager problem? You remember when those little buggers used to be mean? Albert got enough of them. There was something ungainly about them that reminded him too much of himself. He made a teenager of his own. It was rough. To the others it looked like one of themselves, the ring in the left ear, the dangling side-locks, the brass knucks and the long knife, the guitar pluck to jab in an eye. But it was incomparably rougher than the human teenagers. It terrorized all in the neighborhood and made them behave, and dress like real people. And there was one thing about the teenage machine that Albert made: it was made of such polarized metal and glass that it was invisible except to teenager eyes.

"Why is your neighborhood different?" the people asked Albert. "Why are there such good and polite teenagers in your neighborhood and such mean ones everywhere else? It's as though something had spooked all those right around here."

"Oh, I thought I was the only one who didn't like the regular kind," Albert said.

"Oh, no, no," the people answered him. "If there is anything at all you can do about it—"

So Albert turned his mostly invisible teenager machine over to one of his reduplicating machines to make as many copies as were necessary, and set one up in every neighborhood. From that day till this the teenagers have all been good and polite and a little bit frightened. But there is no evidence of what keeps them that way except an occasional eye dangling from the jab of an invisible guitar pluck.

So the two most pressing problems of the latter part of the twentieth century were solved, but accidentally and to the credit of no one.

As the years went by, Albert felt his inferiority most when in the presence of his own machines, particularly those in the form of men. Albert just hadn't their urbanity or sparkle or wit. He was a clod beside them, and they made him feel it.

Why not? One of Albert's devices sat in the President's Cabinet. One of them was on the High Council of World-Watchers that kept the peace everywhere. One of them presided at Riches Unlimited, that private-public-international instrument that guaranteed reasonable riches to everyone in the world. One of them was the guiding hand in the Health and Longevity Foundation which provided those things to everyone. Why should not such splendid and successful machines look down on their shabby uncle who had made them?

"I'm rich by a curious twist," Albert said to himself one day, "and honored through a mistake in circumstance. But there isn't a man or a machine in the world who is really my friend. A book here tells how to make friends, but I can't do it that way. I'll make one my own way."

So Albert set out to make a friend.

He made Poor Charles, a machine as stupid and awkward and inept as himself. "Now I will have a companion," Albert said, but it didn't work. Add two zeros together and you still have zero. Poor Charles was too much like Albert to be good for anything.

Poor Charles! Unable to think, he made a—(*but wait a moleskin-gloved minute here, Colonel, this isn't going to work at all*)—he made a machi—(*but isn't this the same blamed thing all over again?*)—he made a machine to think for him and to—

Hold it, hold it! That's enough. Poor Charles was the only machine that Albert ever made that was dumb enough to do a thing like that.

Well, whatever it was, the machine that Poor Charles made was in control of the situation and of Poor Charles when Albert came onto them accidentally. The machine's machine, the device that Poor Charles had constructed to think for him, was lecturing Poor Charles in a humiliating way.

"Only the inept and deficient will invent," that damned machine's machine was droning. "The Greeks in their high period did not invent. They used neither adjunct power nor instrumentation. They used, as intelligent men or machines will always use, slaves. They did not descend to gadgets. They, who did the difficult with ease, did not seek the easier way.

"But the incompetent will invent. The insufficient will invent. The depraved will invent. And knaves will invent."

Albert, in a seldom fit of anger, killed them both. But he knew that the machine of his machine had spoken the truth.

Albert was very much cast down. A more intelligent man would have had a hunch as to what was wrong. Albert had only a hunch that he was not very good at hunches and would never be. Seeing no way out, he fabricated a machine and named it Hunchy.

In most ways this was the worst machine he ever made. In building it he tried to express something of his unease for the future. It was an awkward thing in mind and mechanism, a misfit.

Albert's more intelligent machines gathered around and hooted at him while he put it together.

"Boy! Are you lost!" they taunted. "That thing is a primitive! To draw its power from the ambient! We talked you into throwing that away twenty years ago and setting up coded power for all of us."

"Uh—someday there may be social disturbances and all centers of power seized," Albert stammered. "But Hunchy would be able to operate if the whole world were wiped smooth."

"It isn't even tuned to our information matrix," they jibed. "It's worse than Poor Charles. That stupid thing practically starts from scratch."

"Maybe there'll be a new kind of itch for it," said Albert.

"It's not even housebroken!" the urbane machines shouted their indignation. "Look at that! Some sort of primitive lubrication all over the floor."

"Remembering my childhood, I sympathize," Albert said.

"What's it good for?" they demanded.

"Ah—it gets hunches," Albert mumbled.

"Duplication!" they shouted. "That's all you're good for yourself, and not very good at that. We suggest an election to replace you as—pardon our laughter—the head of these enterprises."

"Boss, I've got a hunch how we can block them there," the unfinished Hunchy whispered.

"They're bluffing," Albert whispered back. "My first logic machine taught me never to make anything that I can't unmake. I've got them there and they know it. I wish I could think up things like that myself."

"Maybe there will come an awkward time and I will be good for something," Hunchy said.

Only once, and that rather late in life, did a sort of honesty flare up in Albert. He did one thing (and it was a dismal failure) on his own. That was the night of the year of the double millennium when Albert was presented with the Finnerty-Hochmann Trophy, the highest award that the intellectual world could give. Albert was certainly an odd choice for it, but it had been noticed that almost every basic invention for thirty years could be traced back to him or to the devices with which he had surrounded himself.

You know the trophy. Atop it was Eurema, the synthetic Greek goddess of invention, with arms spread as if she would take flight. Below this was a stylized brain cut away to show the convoluted cortex. And below this was the coat of arms of the Academicians: Ancient Scholar rampant (argent); the Anderson Analyzer sinister (gules); the Mondeman Space-Drive dexter (vair). It was a fine work by Groben, his ninth period.

Albert had a speech composed for him by his speech-writing machine, but for some reason he did not use it. He went on his own, and that was disaster. He got to his feet when he was introduced, and he stuttered and spoke nonsense!

"Ah—only the sick oyster produces nacre," he said, and they all gaped at him. What sort of beginning for a speech was that? "Or do I have the wrong creature?" Albert asked weakly.

"Eurema doesn't look like that!" Albert gawked out and pointed suddenly at the trophy. "No, no, that isn't her at all. Eurema walks backward and is blind. And her mother is a brainless hulk."

Everybody was watching him with pained expression.

"Nothing rises without a leaven," Albert tried to explain, "but the yeast is itself a fungus and a disease. You be regularizers all, splendid and supreme! But you cannot live without the irregulars. You will die, and who will tell you that you are dead? When there are no longer any deprived or insufficient, *who will invent?* What will you do when there are none of us defectives left? Who will leaven your lump then?"

"Are you unwell?" the master of ceremonies asked him quietly. "Should you not make an end to it? People will understand."

"Of course I'm unwell. Always have been," Albert said. "What good would I be otherwise? You set the ideal that all should be healthy and well adjusted. No! No! Were we all well adjusted, we would ossify and die. The world is kept healthy only by some of the unhealthy minds lurking in it. The first implement made by man was not a scraper or Celt or stone knife. It was a crutch, and it wasn't devised by a hale man."

"Perhaps you should rest," a functionary said in a low voice, for this sort of rambling nonsense talk had never been heard at an awards dinner before.

"Know you," said Albert, "that it is not the fine bulls and wonderful cattle who make the new paths. Only a crippled calf makes a new path. In everything that survives there must be an element of the incongruous. Hey, you know the woman who said, 'My husband is incongruous, but I never liked Washington in the summertime.'"

Everybody gazed at him in stupor.

"That's the first joke I ever made," Albert said lamely. "My joke-making machine makes them a lot better than I do." He paused and gaped, and gulped a big breath. "Dolts!" he croaked out fiercely then. "What will you do for dolts when the last of us is gone? How will you survive without us?"

Albert had finished. He gaped and forgot to close his mouth. They led him back to his seat. His publicity machine explained that Albert was tired from overwork, and then that machine passed around copies of the speech that Albert was supposed to have given.

It had been an unfortunate episode. How noisome it is that the innovators are never great men, and that the great men are never good for anything but just being great men.

In that year decree went forth from Caesar that a census of the whole country should be taken. The decree was from Cesare Panebianco, the president of the country. It was the decimal year proper for the census, and there was nothing unusual about the decree. Certain provisions, however, were made for taking a census of the drifters and decrepits who were usually missed, to examine them and to see why they were so. It was in the course of this that Albert was picked up. If any man ever looked like a drifter and decrepit, it was Albert.

Albert was herded in with other derelicts, set down at a table, and asked tortuous questions. As:

"What is your name?"

He almost muffed that one, but he rallied and answered, "Albert."

"What time is it by that clock?"

They had him in his old weak spot. Which hand was which? He gaped and didn't answer.

"Can you read?" they asked him.

"Not without my—" Albert began. "I don't have with me my—No, I can't read very well by myself."

"Try."

They gave him a paper to mark up with true and false questions. Albert marked them all true, believing that he would have half of them right. But they were all false. The regularized people are partial to falsehood. Then they gave him a supply-the-word test on proverbs.

"_ _ _ _ _ _ _ is the best policy" didn't mean a thing to him. He couldn't remember the names of the companies that he had his own policies with.

"A _ _ _ _ _ _ in time saves nine" contained more mathematics than Albert could handle. "There appear to be six unknowns," he told himself, "and only one positive value, nine. The equating verb 'saves' is a vague one. I cannot solve this equation. I am not even sure that it is an equation. If only I had with me my—"

But he hadn't any of his gadgets or machines with him. He was on his own. He left half a dozen other proverb fill-ins blank. Then he saw a chance to recoup. Nobody is so dumb as not to know one answer if enough questions are asked.

"_ _ _ _ _ _ _ _ _ is the mother of invention," it said.

"Stupidity," Albert wrote in his weird ragged hand. Then he sat back in triumph. "I know that Eurema and her mother," he snickered. "Man, how I do know them!"

But they marked him wrong on that one too. He had missed every answer to every test. They began to fix him a ticket to a progressive booby hatch where he might learn to do something with his hands, his head being hopeless.

A couple of Albert's urbane machines came down and got him out of it. They explained that, while he was a drifter and a derelict, yet he was a rich drifter and derelict, and that he was even a man of some note.

"He doesn't look it, but he really is—pardon our laughter—a man of some importance," one of the fine machines explained. "He has to be told to close his mouth after he has yawned, but for all that he is the winner of the Finnerty-Hochmann Trophy. We will be responsible for him."

Albert was miserable as his fine machines took him out, especially when they asked that he walk three or four steps behind them and not seem to be with them. They gave him some pretty rough banter and turned him into a squirming worm of a man. Albert left them and went to a little hide-out he kept.

"I'll blow my crawfishing brains out," he swore. "The humiliation is more than I can bear. Can't do it myself, though. I'll have to have it done."

He set to work building a device in his hide-out.

"What you doing, boss?" Hunchy asked him. "I had a hunch you'd come here and start building something."

"Building a machine to blow my pumpkin-picking brains out," Albert shouted. "I'm too yellow to do it myself."

"Boss, I got a hunch there's something better to do. Let's have some fun."

"Don't believe I know how to," Albert said thoughtfully. "I built a fun machine once to do it for me. He had a real revel till he flew apart, but he never seemed to do anything for me."

"This fun will be for you and me, boss. Consider the world spread out. What is it?"

"It's a world too fine for me to live in any longer," Albert said. "Everything and all the people are perfect, and all alike. They're at the top of the heap. They've won it all and arranged it all neatly. There's no place for a clutter-up like me in the world. So I get out."

"Boss, I've got a hunch that you're seeing it wrong. You've got better eyes than that. Look again, real canny, at it. Now what do you see?"

"Hunchy, Hunchy, is that possible? Is that really what it is? I wonder why I never noticed it before. That's the way of it, though, now that I look closer.

"Six billion patsies waiting to be took! Six billion patsies without a defense of any kind! A couple of guys out for some fun, man, they could mow them down like fields of Albert-Improved Concho Wheat!"

"Boss, I've got a hunch that this is what I was made for. The world sure had been getting stuffy. Let's tie into it and eat off the top layer. Man, we can cut a swath."

"We'll inaugurate a new era!" Albert gloated. "We'll call it the Turning of the Worm. We'll have fun, Hunchy. We'll gobble them up like goobers. How come I never saw it like that before? Six billion patsies!"

The Twenty-First Century began on this rather odd note.

Selenium Ghosts of the Eighteen Seventies

Introduction by Kelly Robson

I live in the future.

In 1978, when "Selenium Ghosts of the Eighteen Seventies" was first published, I was ten years old. My family lived in the forest-fire-prone foothills of the Canadian Rockies, in the echo path of wolf howls and coyote yips. That close to the mountains, radio signals aren't reliable. Aside from the telephone, our only connection to the outside world was the TV. And oh boy, did we love it.

We had one channel, the Canadian Broadcasting Corporation. The CBC's programming wasn't particularly inspiring—mostly homegrown shows like *The Beachcombers* and *Front Page Challenge,* with a few American shows like *M.A.S.H.* scattered like jewels across prime time. We were always disappointed when the shows went into repeats because we had no alternative. But we were kids. We would watch anything. My brother earned the nickname *pattern-watcher* because when the channel got knocked off the air, he would literally stare at the static pattern.

I would too, from time to time. Occasionally, if I stared long enough, I'd see things in there.

"Selenium Ghosts of the Eighteen Seventies" is an alternate history of television. The narrator is an unnamed historian (probably amateur) who describes the television shows produced by Aurelian Bentley in 1873. These selenium "slow light" dramas are transmitted to television receivers that will repeat anything they receive. Thrillingly, because of the quirks of slow light, the more the receivers repeat the dramas, the better they become. They evolve and grow. The picture becomes clearer. The once-silent productions begin to develop sound. They also develop metacommentary, breaking the fourth wall and letting us into the inner workings of *The Wonderful World of Aurelian Bentley.*

What a thrilling science fictional concept. My brothers and sisters and I would have embraced this technology in 1978. We would have watched those "slow light" dramas until they became so real we could have walked into their world.

This is Lafferty at his most delightful, playing with words and images to build a multilayered story within a story (within a story) that seems real despite its stylized, melodramatic trappings. I try to forgive Lafferty the use of troubling racial epithets (should I?) even though they throw me out of the story (in 1978, no, there was no excuse), because he touches my world to his. Lafferty makes me remember my entertainment-starved youth, where we would have done anything for a TV show that changed and even got better in repeat. And he makes me appreciate anew the wonder of this future I live in, where I carry in my pocket a receiver that will bring me, at a moment's notice, all the television anyone could ever want.

Selenium Ghosts of the Eighteen Seventies

E ven today, the "invention" of television is usually ascribed to Paul Nipkow of Germany, and the year is given as 1884. Nipkow used the principle of the variation in the electrical conductivity of selenium when exposed to light, and he used scanning discs as mechanical effectors. What else was there for him to use before the development of the phototube and the current-amplifying electron tube? The resolution of Nipkow's television was very poor due to the "slow light" characteristics of selenium response and the lack of amplification. There were, however, several men in the United States who transmitted a sort of television before Nipkow did so in Germany.

Resolution of the images of these even earlier experimenters in the field (Aurelian Bentley, Jessy Polk, Samuel J. Perry, Gifford Hudgeons) was even poorer than was the case with Nipkow. Indeed, none of these pre-Nipkow inventors in the television field is worthy of much attention, except Bentley. And the interest in Bentley is in the content of his transmissions and not in his technical ineptitude.

It is not our object to enter into the argument of who really did first "invent" television (it was not Paul Nipkow, and it probably was not Aurelian Bentley or Jessy Polk either); our object is to examine some of the earliest true television dramas in their own queer "slow light" context. And the first of those "slow light" or selenium ("moonshine") dramas were put together by Aurelian Bentley in the year 1873.

The earliest art in a new field is always the freshest and is often the best. Homer composed the first and freshest, and probably the best, epic poetry. Whatever caveman did the first painting, it remains among the freshest as well as the best paintings ever done. Aeschylus composed the first and best tragic dramas, Euclid invented the first and best of the artful mathematics (we speak here of mathematics as an *art* without being concerned with its accuracy or practicality). And it may be that Aurelian Bentley produced the best of all television dramas in spite of their primitive aspect.

Bentley's television enterprise was not very successful despite his fee of one thousand dollars per day for each subscriber. In his heyday (or his hey-month, November of 1873), Bentley had fifty-nine subscribers in New York City, seventeen in Boston, fourteen in Philadelphia, and one in Hoboken. This gave him an income of ninety-one thousand dollars a day (which would be the equivalent of about a million dollars a day in today's terms), but Bentley was extravagant and prodigal, and he always insisted that he had expenses that the world wotted not of. In any case, Bentley was broke and out of business by the beginning of the year 1874. He was also dead by that time.

The only things surviving from *The Wonderful World of Aurelian Bentley* are thirteen of the "slow light" dramas, the master projector, and nineteen of the old television receivers. There are probably others of the receivers around somewhere, and persons coming onto them might not know what they are for. They do not look much like the television sets of later years.

The one we use for playing the old dramas is a good kerosene-powered model which we found and bought for eighteen dollars two years ago. If the old sets are ever properly identified and become collectors' items, the price on them may double or even triple. We told the owner of the antique that it was a chestnut roaster, and with a proper rack installed it could likely be made to serve as that.

We bought the master projector for twenty-six dollars. We told the owner of that monster that it was a chicken incubator. The thirteen dramas in their canisters we had for thirty-nine dollars total. We had to add formaldehyde to activate the dramas, however, and we had to add it to both the projector and the receiver; the formaldehyde itself came to fifty-two dollars. I discovered soon that the canisters with their dramas were not really needed, nor was the master projector. The receiver itself would repeat everything that it had ever received. Still and all, it was money well spent.

The kerosene burner activated a small dynamo that imposed an electrical grid on the selenium matrix and awakened the memories of the dramas.

There was, however, an oddity in all the playbacks. The film-fix of the receiver continued to receive impressions so that every time a "slow light" drama is presented it is different, because of the feedback. The resolution of the pictures *improves* with use and is now much clearer and more enjoyable than originally.

The librettos of the first twelve of the thirteen Bentley dramas are not good, not nearly as good as the librettos of the Jessy Polk and the Samuel J. Perry dramas later in the decade. Aurelian Bentley was not a literary man; he was not even a completely literate man. His genius had many gaping holes in it. But he was a passionately dramatic man, and these dramas which he himself devised and directed have a great sweep and action to them. And even the librettos from which he worked are valuable for one reason. They tell us, though sometimes rather ineptly and vaguely, what the dramas themselves are all about. Without these outlines, we would have no idea in the world of the meaning of the powerful dramas.

There was an unreality, a "ghostliness," about all the dramas, as though they were made by sewer light underground; or as if they were made by poor quality moonlight. Remember that the element *selenium* (the metal that is not a metal), the chemical basis of the dramas, is named from *Selene,* the moon.

Bentley did not use "moving pictures" of quickly succeeding frames to capture and transmit his live presentation dramas. Although Muybridge was in fact working on the zoopraxiscope (the first "moving picture" device) at that very time, his still incomplete work was not known to Aurelian Bentley. Samuel J. Perry and Gifford Hudgeons did use "moving picture" techniques for their primitive television dramas later in the decade; but Bentley, fortunately perhaps, did not. Each of Bentley's thirty-minute live dramas, however it appeared for the first time in the first television receiver, was recorded in one single matrix or frame: and, thereafter, that picture took on a life and growth of its own. It was to some extent independent of sequence (an effect that has been attempted and failed of in several of the other arts); and it had a free way with time and space generally. This is part of the "ghostliness" of the dramas, and it is a large part of their power and charm. Each drama was one evolving moment outside of time and space (though mostly the scenes were in New York City and the Barrens of New Jersey).

Of course there was no sound in these early Bentley dramas, but let us not go too far astray with that particular "of course." "Slow sound" as well as "slow light" is a characteristic of selenium response, and we will soon see that sound did in fact creep into some of the dramas after much replaying. Whether their total effects were accidental or by design, these early television dramas were absolutely unique.

The thirteen "slow light" dramas produced by Aurelian Bentley in the year 1873 (the thirteenth of them, the mysterious *Pettifoggers of Philadelphia*, lacks Bentley's "Seal of Production," and indeed it was done after his death: and yet he appears as a major character in it) were these:

1. *The Perils of Patience, a Damnable Chase.* In this, Clarinda Calliope, who was possibly one of the greatest actresses of American or world drama, played the part of Patience Palmer in the title role. Leslie Whitemansion played the role of Simon Legree. Kirbac Fouet played the part of "the Whip," a sinister character. X. Paul McCoffin played the role of "the Embalmer." Jaime del Diablo played "the Jesuit," one of the most menacing roles in all drama. Torres Malgre played "the Slaver," who carried the forged certificate showing that Patience had a shadow of black blood and so might be returned to slavery on San Croix. Inspiro Spectralski played "the Panther" (Is he a Man? Is he a Ghost?), who is the embodiment of an evil that is perhaps from beyond the world. Hubert Saint Nicholas played the part of "the Guardian," who is really a false guardian.

This *Damnable Chase* is really a galloping allegory. It is the allegory of good against evil, of light against darkness, of inventiveness against crude obtuseness, of life against death, of openness against intrigue, of love against hatred, of courage against hellish fear. For excitement and intensity, this drama has hardly an equal. Time and again, it seemed that the Embalmer, striking out of the dark, would stab Patience with his needle full of the dread embalming fluid and so trap her in the rigidity of living death. Time and again, it seemed that the Whip would cut the flesh of Patience Palmer with his long lash with viper poison on its iron tip that would bring instant death. At every eventuality, it seemed as though Simon Legree or the Slaver would enslave her body, or the Jesuit or the Panther would enslave her soul. And her mysterious Guardian seems always about to save her, but his every attempt to save her has such reverse and disastrous effects as to cast doubt on the honesty and sincerity of the Guardian.

A high point of the drama is the duel of the locomotives that takes place during a tempestuous night in the West Orange Switching Yards. Again and again, Patience Palmer is all but trapped on railroad trestles by thundering locomotives driven by her adversaries (the West Orange Switching Yards seem to consist almost entirely of very high railroad trestles). Patience finally gets control of a locomotive of her own on which to escape, but the locomotives of her enemies thunder at her from every direction so that she is able to switch out of their way only at the last brink of every moment.

The Embalmer attempts to stab her with his needleful of embalming fluid every time their locomotives pass each other with double thunder and only inches to spare. The Whip tries to lash her with his cruel lash with its poisoned tip; and the Slaver threatens her with the outreached forged certificate of color, and only by fantastic cringing can she cringe back far enough to keep from being touched by it as their locomotives roar past each other in opposite directions.

It seems impossible that the racing locomotives can come so close and not hit each other, with their dazzling switching from track to track. And then (Oh, God save us all!) the Panther (Is he a Man? Is he a Devil?) has leaped from his own locomotive to that of Patience Palmer: he is behind her on her own locomotive, and *she does not see him*. He comes closer—but the climax of *The Perils of Patience* is not there in the West Orange Switching Yards. It is at a secret town and castle in the Barrens of New Jersey, a castle of evil repute. In this place the enemies of Patience were assembling a gang of beaters (slack-faced fellows with their tongues cut out), and they were readying bloodhounds to hunt Patience down to her death. She somehow obtains a large wagon piled high with hay and pulled by six large high-spirited horses. With this, she boldly drives, on a stormy night, into the secret town of her enemies and down that jagged road (there was a lightning storm going on that made everything seem jagged) at the end of which was the castle itself. The bloodhounds leap high at her as she passes, but they cannot pull her from the wagon.

But the Panther (Is he a Man? Is he a Beast?) has leaped onto her hay wagon behind her, and *she does not see him*. He comes close behind her—but Patience Palmer is already making her move. Driving unswervingly, carrying out her own intrepid plan, at that very moment she raises a key in her hand very high into the air. This draws the lightning down with a stunning flash, and the hay wagon is set ablaze. Patience leaps clear of the flaming hay wagon at the last possible moment, and the blazing, hurtling inferno crashes into the tall and evil castle to set it and its outbuildings and its whole town ablaze.

This is the flaming climax to one of the greatest chase dramas ever.

This final scene of *The Perils* will be met with often later. Due to the character of the "slow light" or selenium scenes, this vivid scene leaks out of its own framework and is superimposed, sometimes faintly, sometimes powerfully, as a ghost scene on all twelve of the subsequent dramas.

2.   *Thirsty Daggers, a Murder Mystery.* This is the second of the Aurelian Bentley television dramas of 1873. Clarinda Calliope, one of the most talented actresses of her time, played the part of Maud Trenchant, the Girl Detective. The actors Leslie Whitemansion, Kirbac Fouet, X. Paul McCoffin, Jaime del Diablo, Torres Malgre, Inspiro Spectralski, and Hubert Saint Nicholas played powerful and menacing roles, but their identities and purposes cannot be set exactly. One must enter into the bloody and thrilling spirit of the drama without knowing the details.

More even than *The Perils of Patience* does *Thirsty Daggers* seem to be freed from the bonds of time and sequence. It is all one unfolding moment, growing always in intensity and intricacy, but not following a straight line of action. And this, accompanied by a deficiency of the libretto, leads to confusion.

The libretto cannot be read. It is darkened and stained. Chemical analysis has revealed that it is stained with human blood. It is our belief that Bentley sent the librettos to his clients decorated with fresh human blood to set a mood. But time has spread the stains, and almost nothing can be read. This is, however, a highly interesting drama, the earliest murder ever done for television.

It is nearly certain that Maud Trenchant, the Girl Detective, overcomes all the menaces and solves all the crimes, but the finer details of this are lost forever.

3.   *The Great Bicycle Race,* the third of the Bentley television dramas, has that versatile actress Clarinda Calliope playing the lead role of July Meadowbloom in this joyful and allegorical "journey into summertime." It is in *The Great Bicycle Race* that sound makes its first appearance in the Bentley dramas. It is the sounds of all outdoors that are heard in this drama, faintly at first, and more and more as time goes on. These are country and village sounds; they are county fair sounds. Though the sounds seem to be an accidental intrusion (another ghostly side-play of the selenium response magic), yet their quality lends belief to the evidence that the full and original title of this drama was *The Great Bicycle Race, a Pastoral.*

But there are other sounds, sometimes angry, sometimes imploring, sometimes arrogant and menacing—more about them in a bit.

Sheep and cattle sounds are all through the play; goat and horse and swine sounds; the rattle of ducks and geese; all the wonderful noises of the countryside. There are birds and grasshoppers, windmills and wagons, people calling and singing. There are the sounds of carnival barkers and the chants of gamblers and shills. There are the shrieks and giggles of young people.

And then there are those intrusive sounds of another sort, the separate over-lay. These seem to be mostly indoor sounds, but sometimes they are outdoor grandstand sounds also, bristling talk in the reserved shadows of crowd noise and roaring.

"No, no, no. I'll not be had. What sort of a girl do you think I am?"

"All these things I will give you, Clarie. No one else would give you so much. No one else would ever care so much. But now is the time for it. Now is the summer of our lives. Now we cut hay."

"Let's just see the price of a good hay barn first, Aurie. Let's just get some things down on paper right now. We are talking about a summertime check that is as big as all summer. And we are talking about a much larger settlement to back up the other seasons and years."

"Don't you trust me, Clarie?"

"Of course I trust you, Bentley baby. I trust that you will get that trust fund that we are talking about down on paper today. I am a very trusting woman. I believe that we should have a trust fund to cover every condition and circumstance."

Odd talk that, to be mixed in with the sound of *The Great Bicycle Race*.

The race was in conjunction with the Tri-county Fair, which counties were Camden, Gloucester, and Atlantic. The bicycle racers rode their twenty-mile course every afternoon for five afternoons, and careful time was kept. There was betting on each day's race, but there was bigger betting on the final winner with the lowest total time for the five days, and the kitty grew and grew. From the great fairground grandstand, one could see almost all of the twenty-mile course that the riders rode, or could follow it by the plumes of dust. The grandstand was on high ground and the whole countryside was spread out before it. Cattle and mules were paraded and judged in front of that grandstand, before and during and after that daily race; then the race (for the approximate hour that it took to run it) was the big thing. There were seven drivers in the race, and all of them were world famous:

1. Leslie Whitemansion drove on a Von Sauerbronn "Special" of fine German craftsmanship. This machine, popularly known then as the "whizzer," would get you there and it would bring you back. It was very roadworthy and surprisingly fast.

2. Kirbac Fouet was on an Ernest Michaux Magicien, a splendid machine. It had a socket into which a small sail might be fitted to give greater speed on a favorable wind.

3. X. Paul McCoffin was on a British Royal Velocipede. There are two things that may be remarked about the British Royal: it had solid rubber tires (the first rubber-tired bicycle ever), and it had class. It had that cluttered austerity of line that only the best of British products have.

4. Jaime del Diablo was on a Pierre Lallement "Boneshaker" with its iron-tired wooden wheels, the front one much larger than the rear.

5. Torres Malgre was on an American-built Richard Warren Sears Roadrunner, the first all-iron machine. "The only wood is in the heads of its detractors" was an advertising slogan used for the Roadrunner.

6. Inspiro Spectralski (Is he a Man? Is he a Cannon Ball?) was riding a McCracken's Comet. This Comet had won races at several other county fairs around the state.

7. Hubert Saint Nicholas had a machine such as no one in the state had ever seen before. It was a French *bicyclette* named the Supreme. The bicyclette had the pedals fixed to drive the *back* wheel by the ingenious use of a chain and sprocket wheel, and so was not, strictly speaking, a bicycle at all. The true bicycles of the other six racers had the pedals attached directly to the *front* wheels. There was one syndicate of bettors who said the bicyclette had a mechanical advantage, and that Hubert would win on it. But other persons made jokes about this rig whose back wheel would arrive before its front wheel and whose driver would not arrive before the next day.

It was on these great riders that all the six-shot gamblers around were wagering breathtaking sums. It was for them that sports came from as far away as New York City.

Clarinda Calliope played the role of Gloria Goldenfield, the beauty queen of the Tri-county Fair in this drama. But she also played the role of the "Masked Alternate Rider Number Seven." (All the racing riders had their alternates to ride in their places in case of emergency.) And Clarinda also played a third role, that of Rakesly Rivertown, the splurging gambler. Who would ever guess that the raffish Rakesly was being played by a woman? The author and director of *The Great Bicycle Race* did not know anything about Clarinda playing these latter two roles.

The grandstand, the bandstand, the pleasures of a country carnival in the summertime! And the "slow smells" of the selenium-directed matrix just becoming ripe and evocative now! Smell of sweet clover and timothy hay, or hot horses pulling buggies or working in the fields, smells of candy and sausage and summer squash at the eating places at the fair, smells of dusty roads and of green money being counted out and thumped down on betting tables for the bicycle race! And then again there was the override of intrusive voices breaking in on the real summer drama just by accident.

"Clarie, I will do handsomely by you in just a day or so. I have placed very, very heavy bets on the bicycle race, and I will win. I am betting against the wildest gambler in this part of the country, Rakesly Rivertown, and we will have the bet up to a cool million with one more raise. He is betting the field against number seven. And number seven will win."

"I have heard that this Rakesly Rivertown is about the sharpest gambler anywhere, and that he has a fine figure and makes an extraordinary appearance."

"A fine figure! Why, the fraud is shaped like a girl! Yes, he is a sharp gambler, but he doesn't understand mechanics. Number seven, the Supreme, has a rear-wheel drive with gear-ratio advantage. Hubert Saint Nicholas, who is riding number seven, is just toying with the other riders so far to get the bets higher, and he can win whenever he wants to. I will win a million dollars on the race, my love. And I will give it to you, if you act a little bit more like my love."

"Surely your love for me should transcend any results of a bicycle race, Aurie. If you really loved me, and if you contemplated making such a gift to me, you would make it today. That would show that your appreciation and affection are above mere fortune. And, if you can't lose, as you say that you cannot, you will have your money in the same amount won back in two days' time, and you will have made me happy two days longer."

"All right, I guess so then, Clarie. Yes, I'll give it to you today. Right now. I'll write you a check right now."

"Oh, you are a treasure, Aurie. You are a double treasure. You can't guess how double a treasure you are!"

The wonderful Tri-county Fair was near its end, and its Great Bicycle Race with it. It was the last day of the race. Hubert Saint Nicholas on number seven, the Supreme, the French bicyclette with the mechanical advantage, was leading the field by only one minute in total elapsed time going into that last day's racing. There were those who said that Hubert could win any time he wanted to, and that he stayed so close only to keep the bets a-growing.

And the bets did grow. The mysterious gambler with the fine figure and the extraordinary appearance, Rakesly Rivertown, was still betting the field to win against number seven. And a still more mysterious gambler, working through agents, was betting on number seven to *place*, but not to win. These latter bets were quickly covered. Number seven would *win*, unless some terrible calamity overtook that entry; and, in the case of such terrible calamity, number seven would not finish second, would not finish at all most likely.

The seven intrepid racers were off on their final, mad, twenty-mile circuit. Interest was high, especially with moneyed gamblers who followed the riders from the grandstand with their binoculars. At no place was the winding, circuit course more than four miles from the grandstand; and there were only three or four places, not more than three hundred yards in all, where the racers were out of sight of the higher tiers of the grandstand. One of those places was where Little Egg Creek went through Little Egg Meadow. Something mysterious happened near Little Egg Creek Crossing that neither the libretto nor the enacted drama itself makes clear.

Hubert Saint Nicholas, riding the French bicyclette, number seven, the Supreme, with the rear-wheel drive and the mechanical advantage, was unsaddled

from his mount and knocked unconscious. The race master later and offi-
cially entered this incident as "A careless rider knocked off his bicycle by a tree
branch," though Hubert swore that there wasn't a tree branch within a hundred
yards of that place.

"I was slugged by a lurker in the weeds," Hubert said. "It was a criminal and
fraudulent assault and I know who did it." Then he cried, "Oh, the perfidy of
women!" This latter seemed to be an unconnected outcry; perhaps Hubert had
suffered a concussion.

Fortunately (for whom?) the alternate rider for number seven, the Mysterious
(though duly certified) Masked Rider, was in the vicinity of the accident and
took control of the bicyclette, the Supreme, and continued the race. But number
seven, though having a one-minute lead ere the race began, did not win. Number seven did come in second though in total elapsed time.

The Great Bicycle Race is a quaint little drama, with not much plot, but with a
pleasant and bucolic atmosphere that grows more pleasant every time the drama
is played back. It is a thoroughly enjoyable "journey into summertime."

And there were a few more seconds of those intrusive "ghost" voices breaking
into the closing moments of the pastoral drama.

"Clarie, I have been took bad, for a big wad, and I don't know how it happened. There is something funny about it all. There was something funny and
familiar about that Masked Alternate Rider for number seven. (I swear that
I know him from somewhere!) And there has always been something double
funny and familiar about that gambler Rakesly Rivertown. (I swear and be
damned if I don't know *him* from somewhere!)"

"Don't worry about it, Aurie. You are so smart that you will have all that
money made back in no time at all."

"Yes, that's true, I will. But how can I write and produce and direct a drama
and then get taken in it and not know what happened?"

"Don't worry about it, Aurie."

I myself doubt very much whether Aurelian Bentley knew about the "slow
sounds" from nowhere-town that sometimes broke into the playing of his dramas, much less the "slow smells" which now began to give the dramas a character all their own.

4.   *The Voyages of Captain Cook* was the fourth of the Bentley-produced
television dramas of the year 1873. In this, Clarinda Calliope played the role
of Maria Masina, the Queen of Polynesia. If *The Great Bicycle Race* was a journey into summertime, *The Voyages of Captain Cook* was a journey into tropical
paradise.

Hubert Saint Nicholas played Captain Cook. Inspiro Spectralski (Is he a
Man? Is he a Fish?) played the Shark God. Leslie Whitemansion played the Mis-
sionary. X. Paul McCoffin played the Volcano God. Torres Malgre played the

God of the Walking Dead. Jaime del Diablo played Kokomoko, the bronzed surf boy and lover boy who was always holding a huge red hibiscus bloom between his white teeth.

The people of the South Sea Islands of the Captain Cook drama were always eating possum and sweet potatoes and fried chicken (a misconception) and twanging on little banjos (another misconception) and talking southern U.S. Darky Dialect (but these ghost voices were not intended to be heard on the television presentation).

The complete libretto for *The Voyages of Captain Cook* has survived, which makes us grateful for those that have not survived for several of the dramas. The story is replete. It is better to disregard the libretto with its simultaneous curses invoked by the Shark God, the Volcano God, and the God of the Walking Dead, and to give oneself over to the charm of the scenery, which is remarkable, considering that it was all "filmed," or "selenium-matrixed," in the salt swamps of New Jersey.

The anomalous intrusive voices are in this drama again, as they will be in all the subsequent dramas.

"A 'South Sea Bubble,' yes, that's what I want, Aurie, one that can't burst. Use your imagination (you have so very much of it) and your finances (you have so very much of those) and come up with something that will delight me."

"I swear to you, Clarie, as soon as my finances are in a little better order, I will buy any island or group of islands in the Pacific Ocean for you. Do you hear me, Clarie? I will give you any island or group you wish, Hawaii, Samoa, Fiji. Name it and it is yours."

"So many things you promise! But you don't promise them on paper, only on air. Maybe I will find a way to make the air retain the promises you make."

"Not on paper, not on air, Clarie, but in real life. I will make you the real and living Queen of Polynesia."

The essence of the South Sea appeal is just plain charm. It may be that this Bentley drama, *The Voyages of Captain Cook,* was the original charm bush whence many things bloomed. No, in things of this sort, it is not necessary that a scion ever be in contact with its source or even know its source. Without the *Voyages* would there ever have been a Sadie Thompson, would there have been a Nellie Forbush? Would there have been a Nina, daughter of Almayer? Well, they wouldn't have been as they were if Clarinda Calliope hadn't, in a way, played them first. Would there have been a *White Shadows of the South Seas* if there hadn't first been *The Voyages of Captain Cook*? No, of course there wouldn't have been.

5.   *Crimean Days* was the fifth of the Aurelian Bentley television dramas. In this, the multitalented Clarinda Calliope played the role of Florence Nightingale, of Ekmek Kaya, a Turkish lady of doubtful virtue who was the number-four wife and current favorite of the Turkish admiral, of Chiara Maldonado, a

young lady camp follower with the army of Savoy, of Katya Petrova, who was
a Russian princess as well as a triple spy, and of Claudette Boudin, a French
lady journalist. Clarinda also masqueraded as Claudette's twin brother, Claude,
a colonel with the French forces, and as such she led the French to a surprising
victory over the Russians at Eupatoria. The unmasqueraded Claude himself was
played by Apollo Mont-de-Marsan, a young actor making his first appearance
in the Bentley dramas.

The Crimean War was the last war in which the field officers of all sides (Leslie Whitemansion was a British field officer, Kirbac Fouet was a French, Jaime
del Diablo was an officer of the forces of Savoy, Torres Malgre was the Turkish
admiral, Inspiro Spectralski was a general of the Czar, X. Paul McCoffin was a
special observer of the Pope), after their days of tactical maneuver and sometimes bloody conflict, would dress for dinner and have formal dinner together.
And it was at these dinners that Clarinda Calliope, in her various guises, shone.

There was a wonderful and many-leveled table intrigue, and I believe that
more and more of it will come through every time the drama is replayed. And
it was here in this drama that one of the most strange of the Bentley-effect phenomena first appeared. There is unmistakable evidence that some of the subvo-
calizations (thoughts) of the people were now to be heard as "slow sound," which
was really selenium triggered "slow thought." Some of these manifestations were
the role thoughts of the actors so strangely vocalized (Clarinda Calliope, for
instance, could not speak or think in any tongues except English and her own
Pennsylvania Dutch in normal circumstances: but in her triple spy roles we find
her thinking out loud in Turkish and Greek and Russian); and other of the vo-
calizations are the real thoughts of the actors (the amazingly frank intentions of
Leslie Whitemansion and of the new Apollo Mont-de-Marsan as to their lady
loves of the evening after they should have received their two-dollar actors' fee
for the day).

It was a wonderful play and too intricate to be described. This one, above all,
has to be seen. But again there was the anomalous intrusion of voices that were
not a part of the scenes of the play: "Get rid of that Greek Wop kid, Clarie. I
told him he was fired, and he said that he would stick around and work for
nothing. He said he loved the fringe benefits. What are fringe benefits? I told
him I'd run him off, and he said that this was the free state of New Jersey and
that no one would run him off. I won't have him around."

"Oh, Aurie, there isn't any Greek Wop kid. That was me playing that role too.
Am I not talented to play so many roles? And you *will not* fire me from this role.
I will continue to play it, and I will be paid for it. It isn't the principle of the thing
either: it's the two dollars."

"Yes, I understand that much about you. But you say that was you playing the
part of that smart-mouth Apollo Dago Greek? That couldn't be. I've seen you
both at the same time. I've seen you two together too many times. I've seen
you smooching each other."

"Ah, Aurie, that was quite an advanced technique and illusion, not to mention double exposure, that I used there. What other actress could play both roles at once and get away with it?"

"Your techniques and illusions are becoming a little bit too advanced, Clarie. And do not be so sure that you *are* getting away with it."

All through *Crimean Days,* there was some tampering with history going on for dramatic effect. The Light Brigade, for instance, was successful in its famous charge and it won a great victory. But the final outcome of the war was left in doubt. Aurelian Bentley had somehow become a strong partisan of the Russians and he refused to show them being finally defeated by the allies.

6.   *Ruddy Limbs and Flaming Hair* is the sixth of the Bentley television dramas. In this piece, the dramatic Clarinda Calliope plays the part of Muothu, the Maid of Mars, for the Ruddy Limbs and Flaming Hair are on the planet itself. There are some fantastic elements in this piece, as well as amazing scientific accuracy. There is, in fact, a technical precocity that is really stunning. Aurelian Bentley has foreseen circumstances that even the scientific community did not then see, and he has dealt with those circumstances.

He posits, for instance, an atmosphere composed mostly of an eno-magnetized, digammated, attenuated form of oxygen. Being eno-magnetized, that atmosphere would naturally cling to its planet even though the gravity would not be strong enough to retain it otherwise. Being digammated, it would produce no line in the Martian spectrum, would have no corona or optical distortion effect, and could in no way be detected from Earth. And yet a human Earthly would be able to breathe it freely.

This was a good-natured utopian drama of total realization and happiness. The Ruddy Limbs and Flaming Hair apply both allegorically to the planet Mars and literally to the highly dramatic Clarinda Calliope as Muothu. Muothu displayed rather more of the ruddy limbs than were ordinarily shown on Earth, but it was explained that customs on Mars were different.

Ruddy Limbs and Flaming Hair was the last of the dramas in which the apparently tormented and disturbed Aurelian Bentley still showed the strong hand of the master as scenarist, dramaturgist, director, and producer generally. After this we come to the four "Trough of the Wave" dramas, and then the three bewildering and hectic displays on the end of the series.

7.   *The Trenton Train Robbery* is the seventh of the Bentley television dramas, and the first of the four "Trough" plays where Aurelian Bentley and his effects are sunken in the slough of despond and have lost their brightness and liveliness and hope. We will pass through them quickly.

In the *Train Robbery,* the peerless Clarinda Calliope plays Roxana Roundhouse, the daughter of the slain locomotive engineer Timothy (Trainman) Roundhouse. Armed with a repeating rifle, a repeating shotgun, a repeating pistol, and a few pocket-sized bombs, Roxana rides the rods of the crack Trenton Express in the effort to catch or kill the murderers of her father. These murderers have sworn that they will rob that very Trenton Express again.

And Roxana Roundhouse does catch or kill all the murderers of her father. In spite of some good shots of landscapes rushing by, this is not one of Aurelian Bentley's best efforts.

And again the voices of unknown persons creep into the drama: "You've already flayed me, Clarie, and scraped both sides of my pelt for whatever might cling to it. What more do you want from me? Go away with your lover and leave me alone." And then in a fuzzier voice (apparently the "thought voice" made vocal) the same person said or thought: "Oh, if only she *would* go away from me, then I might have a chance! For I will never be able to go away from her."

"Grow more skin, Aurie," the other voice said. "I'm not nearly finished fleecing you and flaying you. Oh, don't look so torn up, Aurie. You know I could never love anyone except you. But a little token of our love is required now and then, and especially now, today. Yes, I know you are going to use your old line, 'I gave you a million dollars last week,' but Aurie, that *was* last week. Yes, I know that you have expenses that the world wots not of. So do I. Believe me, Aurie, I wouldn't ask for these tokens of affection if I didn't want them." And then in a fuzzier voice, a "thought voice," the same person said or thought: "I'll never get another fish like this one and I sure can't afford to lose him. But gentle handling doesn't get it all the time. When the hook in him shows signs of working loose a bit, it has to be set in again with a very hard jerk on the line."

8.   *Six Guns on the Border* is the eighth of the Bentley television dramas. In this drama, Clarinda Calliope (is there no end to her versatility?) plays the part of Conchita Allegre, the half-breed Apache and Mexican girl, on the Arizona border during the Mexican War. Conchita hates the American soldiers who are invading that area. She has them come to her secretly, with promises of love, and then she has them ambushed and killed. She kills many of them herself with her own six gun, and she makes antimacassars out of their skins. The sort of gentlemen that Conchita really likes use a lot of oil on their hair so Conchita needs a lot of antimacassars at her house.

But there are a few of the American officers so awkward and oafish that Conchita simply can't stand to have much to do with them, not even long enough to seduce them and have them killed. These horrible specimens are:

Captain James Polk (played by Leslie Whitemansion).
General Zachary Taylor (played by Kirbac Fouet).
Captain Millard Fillmore (played by X. Paul McCoffin).
Captain Franklin Pierce (played by Jaime del Diablo).
Captain James Buchanan (played by Torres Malgre).
Captain Abraham Lincoln (played by Inspiro Spectralski).
Captain Andrew Johnson (played by Apollo Mont-de-Marsan).

Captain Sam Grant (played by Hubert Saint Nicholas).

There was a lot of historical irony in this play, but maybe it belonged somewhere else.

There was a lot of "Comedy of Manners" stuff in it but it falls a little flat, mostly because the eight oafish officers spared by Conchita were too unmannerly to be in a comedy of manners.

Aurelian Bentley came near the bottom of his form in this piece. But for the energy of Clarinda Calliope (she played five other parts besides that of Conchita) there would have been hardly any drama at all.

And, as always, there were those intrusive voices hovering over the playbacks.

"Clarie, believe me! Believe me! Believe me! I will do all these things for you. I promise it."

"Yes, you promise it to the earless walls and to the earless me. Promise it to the pen and ink and paper here."

"Get rid of that Apollo kid first, Clarie."

"You get rid of him. You have a lot of rough-looking men around."

9. *Clarence Greenback, Confidence Man* was the ninth of the Aurelian Bentley television dramas. Hubert Saint Nicholas played the role of Clarence Greenback, the casino owner. It was the first time that Clarinda Calliope had not played the lead role in a drama. Is it possible that Clarinda had somehow slipped? Or was this another instance of the left lobe of Aurelian Bentley having lost its cunning, and casting badly. The talented prestidigitator of drama did not have his sure touch nowadays. Oh sure, Clarinda played other roles in the drama, but she did not have the lead role.

Clarinda played the role of Gretchen, the sweep-out girl at the casino. She played the role of Maria, the mounting-block girl in the street outside the casino. She played the role of Elsie, the chimney-sweep girl. She played the part of Hennchen, the scullery maid in the third and vilest kitchen of the casino. She played the part of Josephine, the retriever who had to gather up the shattered bodies of the suicides below Suicide Leap Window of the casino and take them to East Potters' Field and dig their graves and bury them. Elsie made a good thing out of her job, from the gold teeth of the late patrons of the casino, but the dramatist and producer did not know about the good thing she had there.

There were hazards in all these different roles.

"No, of course we can't put out the fires for you to clean the chimneys," said Leslie Whitemansion, who was in charge of fireplaces and chimneys at the casino. "Clean them hot." And it was very hot working inside those tall chimneys with the fires roaring below, and Elsie the chimney-sweep girl suffered.

For keeping a copper coin that she found while sweeping out the casino, the sadist Baron von Steichen (played by X. Paul McCoffin) had Gretchen hung up by her thumbs and flogged.

And Maria, the mounting-block girl, who had to stand in the muddy street outside the casino and bend her back for the gentlemen to step on her when they mounted or dismounted their horses, she had it worse on the muddy days. Oh, the great muddy boots of those men! "Maybe they're trying to tell me something," Clarinda Calliope spoke or thought (by slow talk-thought). "I do like subtle people." But a good actress can play any role, and Clarinda has her revenge today. Hardly anyone remembers the plot for *Clarence Greenback, Confidence Man,* but everyone remembers the tribulations of those pretty little servant girls.

And then there were those other intrusive voices of the overlay. It was almost as if they belonged in another sort of drama.

"Clarie, this has to stop. Not counting the special gifts, and they're fantastic, I'm giving you ten times as much as the president of the United States is making."

"I'm ten times as good at acting as he is. And how about *my* special gifts?— and they're fantastic. Why do you have all the private detectives running around the last couple of days? To spy on me?"

"To spy on everything and everyone. To save my life. Frankly, Clarie, I am afraid of being murdered. I have premonitions of being killed, with a knife, always with a knife."

"Like in *Thirsty Daggers, a Murder Mystery*? That one wasn't really very well worked out, and I believe it's one of the things bothering you. Your undermind is looking for a better solution, I believe, for a neater murder. It is seeking to enact a more artistic murder. I believe it will do it. I believe you will come up with quite an artistic murder for yourself. There are good murders and bad murders, you see."

"Clarie, I don't intend to let myself be killed at all, not by either a good or a bad murder."

"Not even for art's sake? It seems it would be worth it, for the perfect murder, Aurie."

"Not when *I'm* the murdered one, Clarie."

Then, a moment later, the female person said or thought something further, in a "slow thought-voice."

"Sometimes persons have perfection thrust upon them in spite of themselves. An artful murder for Aurie would make up for a lot of the mad art that he's been guilty of lately."

10. *The Vampires of Varuma* was the tenth of the Aurelian Bentley television dramas. This is the fourth and last of the "Trough of the Wave" dramas, which show Bentley's dramatic powers in almost complete decline and himself mightily disoriented. Yet, in this bottoming-out, there is a curious resurrection of his powers in a slightly different form. His sense of plotting and story movement did not return yet, but his sense of dramatic horror as motive force was resurrected to its highest pitch.

Clarinda Calliope played Magda the peasant maid, Miss Cheryl Somerset, the governess from England, and the Princess Irene of Transylvania. All three of these had been traveling to Castle Khubav on rational errands by the regular coach of the road; and each of the three had seen all the other passengers dismount hastily, and had then experienced the coach horses being whipped ahead frantically by an invisible coachman, or by no coachman at all. And each of these ladies had arrived, on successive days, in the apparently driverless coach, not at Castle Khubav, but at the dread Castle Beden. And inside the Castle Beden were the seven ("no, not seven, eight" was written into the libretto in a weirdly different hand) insane counts in their castle of evil. These were:

Count Vladmel, played by Leslie Whitemansion.

Count Igork, played by Kirbac Fouet.

Count Lascar, played by X. Paul McCoffin.

Count Chort, played by Jaime del Diablo.

Count Sangressuga, played by Torres Malgre.

Count Letuchaya, played by Inspiro Spectralski (Is he a Man? Is he a Bat?).

Count Ulv, played by Hubert Saint Nicholas.

And then there is another one added in the libretto in that weirdly different hand: Count Prividenne, played by Apollo Mont-de-Marsan.

There is a slipup here somewhere. Apollo is supposed to have been "gotten rid of," to have shuffled off the mortal coil, and the sheriff's report said that he died of indigestion. But if Apollo has not been "gotten rid of" then certainly money was paid in vain.

The seven (or eight) evil counts are sometimes conventional counts in evening clothes and monocles. And sometimes they are huge bat-winged creatures flitting ponderously down the lightning-lit corridors of Castle Beden. The castle, in fact, is the main character in the drama. It does not have formal lighting, as it is lit by lightning all twenty-four hours of every night (there is no daylight at Castle Beden). The floors and walls howl and chains rattle constantly. The counts have sometimes conventional six-inch-long eyeteeth, and then suddenly they will have hollow fangs eighteen inches long and deadly. And there is a constant lot of howling and screaming for what is supposed to be a silent television drama.

A flying count will suddenly fold his bat wings and land on the broad bosom of one of the three maidens and have into her throat with his terrible blood-sucking fangs. And every time it happens, there is a horrible flopping and screeching.

The voice of Clarinda Calliope is heard loud and clear and real in a slow angry sound.

"Dammit, Aurelian, that's real blood they're taking out of my throat."

And came the suave voice of the master dramatist Aurelian Bentley (but the voices shouldn't be breaking in like this): "Right, Clarie. It is on such verisimilitude that I have built my reputation as a master."

Clarinda, in her three roles, seemed to lose quite a bit of blood as the drama went on, and she fell down more and more often. And the drama was a howling and bloody success, no matter that the storyline was shattered in a thousand pieces—for each piece of it was like a writhing blood snake that gluts and gloats.

And then, after the drama itself was ended in a spate of final blood, there came those intrusive voices that seemed to be out of some private drama.

"Aurie, if you are worrying about being killed, how about providing for me before it happens?"

"I leave you half of my kingdom, ah, estate, Clarie, right off the top of it. My word is good for this. And stop falling down."

"I'm weak. It took a lot out of me. Yes, your written word is good on this, Aurie, if it is written and attested to in all the right places. Let's take care of that little detail right now."

"Clarie, my spoken promise is enough, and it is all that I will give. I hereby attest that half of my estate, off the top, belongs to you. Let the eared walls of this room be witnesses to what I say, Clarie. If the walls of this room will swear to it, then surely they will be believed. Now don't bother me for a few days. I will be busy with something else. And stop falling down. It's annoying."

The female person then said or thought something in a fuzzy thought-voice: "Yes, I believe I *can* make the walls of this room attest for me when the time comes. (I might have to put in another amplifying circuit to be sure.) And I believe that the attesting walls will be believed."

The male person then said or thought something in a fuzzy thought-voice: "I have Miss Adeline Addams now. Why should I care about this Calliope clown? It's irritating the way she keeps turning chalk-white and falling down. I never saw anyone make such a fuss over nine quarts of blood. But now I am on a new and more glorious dawn road. Is it not peculiar how a man will fall in love with one woman and out of love with another one at the same time?"

11. *The Ghost at the Opera* is the eleventh of the Aurelian Bentley television dramas in the year 1873. *The Ghost* is based on Verdi's *Il Trovatore*, but Bentley's production is quite original for all that. The role of Leonora is played by Miss Adeline Addams. But the same role is also played by Clarinda Calliope, who was originally selected to play the role by herself. This business of having two different persons playing the same role creates a certain duality, one might almost say a certain duplicity, in the drama.

The "Ghost" is the doubling: it is the inept and stumbling Clarinda trying again and again to sing parts of the Leonora role and failing in it totally and being jerked off stage by the stage manager's crook; and it is the beautiful and brimming genius Adeline Addams coming on and performing the same role brilliantly. This provides the "cruel comedy" that is usually lacking in Verdi; for, without cruelty, only a limited success is ever possible in opera. But Clarinda took some very bad falls from the stageman's crook jerking her off her feet, and besides she was still weak and falling down from all the blood she had lost in her roles in *The Vampires of Varuma*. She was suffering.

"Why do you go through with it, Clarinda?" Hubert Saint Nicholas asked her once in an outside-of-the-play-itself voice. "Why do you allow yourself to be tortured and humiliated like that?"

"Only for the money," Clarinda was heard to say. "Only for the actor's fee of four dollars a day. I am clear broke and I am hungry. But if I can stick it out to the end of the opera, I will have four dollars tonight for my wages."

"Four dollars, Clarinda? The rest of us get only two dollars a day. Are you playing another role that I don't know about?"

"Yes, I am also playing the role of Wilhelmina, the outhouse cleaner."

"But I thought that you had millions from that old tyrant, Clarinda."

"It's gone, Hubie, all gone. I had expenses that the world wotted not of. I gave Apollo most of the money when I was in love with him. And I gave the rest of it to him to do a special favor for me."

"You gave the money to him today? But he was buried yesterday."

"Time seems to go faster as we get older, doesn't it?"

Meanwhile, back on the opera stage, a new Verdi was being hammered out. Leslie Whitemansion was playing Manrico. X. Paul McCoffin was playing Ferrando. Hubert Saint Nicholas was playing Count di Luni. Apollo Mont-de-Marsan was playing the ghost. But was there a ghost in the libretto besides the double ghost of the two females playing the same role? Yes, there was; there was a real ghost in the libretto. It was written in there in a queer "other" hand, really a "ghostly" hand, and it wrote that Apollo was playing the role of the ghost.

So the merry comic opera went along almost to its end. It was just when Manrico was being led to the executioner's block and the evil Count di Luni was gloating in triumph, when everything was finally being shaped up in that drama that had some pleasure for everybody, that a horrible thing happened in one of the loges or boxes that overhung the stage.

Aurelian Bentley was knifed there in his box at the opera. Oh God, this was murder! "Your mind is looking for a better solution, I believe, for a neater murder." Oh, that had been the voice of another sort of ghost. But now, to be slain by the ghost of a man dead only a day or two, and in the presence of several thousands of persons here! (For it was, possibly, none other than Apollo Mont-de-Marsan, who had been "gotten rid of," who was getting rid of Aurelian Bentley.) And again: "There are good murders and bad murders, you see . . . It seems it would be worth it, for art's sake, for the perfect murder." Aurelian Bentley was stabbed to death in his box at the opera there, but even he had to admit, with some appreciation, as he went, that it was done with art.

And immediately, as the opera on stage came to its great conclusion, there welled up cries of "Author, Author, Bentley, Bentley!"

Then the dying (or more likely dead) man rose for the last time, bowed formally, and tumbled out of his box and onto his face on the stage, stark dead, and with the thirsty (now slaked) dagger twinkling between the blades of his shoulders.

What other man had ever made such an exit from or on life's stage! That was Theater! That was Drama!

12.   *An Evening in Newport* was intended to be the twelfth of the Bentley television dramas. But it was never produced; possibly because of the death of its producer. It exists only as a libretto.

There was a high society "drama of manners," as Miss Adeline Addams knew it, as Aurelian Bentley with his quick mind and quick mimicry knew it from his brief brushes with it. But does not a drama or comedy of manners depend largely on the quip and the arch aphorism? How could it be done in silent presentation?

By art, that's how it might be done: by the perfect art of the silent mimes, and Aurelian Bentley was master of that art. By the gestures, by the facial implications, by great silent acting this might be done. Was there any witticism that Adeline Addams could not express with her talented high-society face? Was there any devastating riposte that she could not give with her autocratic hands? It was never tested, but Aurelian believed that she was pretty good.

On the lower level, *An Evening in Newport* was a one-sided duel between Mistress Adeline Addams of Newport, playing the role of Mistress Adela Adams of Newport, and Clarinda Calliope, playing the role of Rosaleen O'Keene, a low, vicious, ignorant, filthy, bad-mannered, fifth parlor maid newly arrived from Ireland. It was a stacked set in favor of Adeline/Adela.

On the higher level, the drama was the passionate portrayal of the total love of a beautiful and wealthy and intelligent and charming and aristocratic young lady (Adeline-Adela) for a man of surpassing genius and ineffable charm, a man of poise and power and heroic gifts, a man the like of whom will hardly appear once in a century. The drama was supposed to take on a note of hushed wonder whenever this man was mentioned, or so the libretto said. The libretto does not identify this exceptional man, but our own opinion is that the librettist, Aurelian Bentley, intended this hardly-once-in-a-century man, the object of the torrid and devoted love of Miss Adeline Addams, to be himself, Aurelian Bentley.

But *An Evening in Newport*, intended to be the surpassing climax of that first and still unsurpassed television series, was never produced.

13.   *Pettifoggers of Philadelphia* is the noncanonical, apocryphal, thirteenth apocalypse of *The Wonderful World of Aurelian Bentley*, that first and greatest television series. There is no libretto to it. There is no formal production, and it does not carry the Bentley "Seal of Production." But it does repose in one of the old television receivers, the one that was Aurelian's own control receiver, the one

that was in Aurelian's own luxurious den where he spent so many hectic hours with Clarinda Calliope and later with Adeline Addams. It reposes there, and it may be seen and heard there.

Though Bentley was already dead when these scenes were ordered and live-presented, yet he walks in them and talks in them. The experience of hearing the thoughts and words of a hovering dead man spoken out loud and of seeing him as if in the flesh is a shattering but dramatic one.

The setting and sole scene of *Pettifoggers of Philadelphia* is that same luxurious den of Aurelian Bentley's, first placed under court seal, but then opened for a meeting which, as one of the parties to it stated, could not validly be held anywhere else. A probate judge was present, and pettifoggers representing several of the parties, and two of the parties themselves. It was a hearing on the disposition of the estate of Aurelian Bentley, of what might be left of that estate, he having died without having made a will. But one of the parties, Clarinda Calliope, insisted that Bentley *had* made a will, that the will *was* in this particular room and no other, that the will in fact *was* this room and the eared and tongued walls of it.

There seemed to be several meetings in this room superimposed on one another, and they cannot be sorted out. To sort them out would have been to destroy their effect, however, for they achieved syntheses of their several aspects and became the true meeting that never really took place but which contained all the other meetings in one theatrical unity.

The pettifogger of a second cousin once removed was there to present the claim of that distant person, as next in kin, to the estate of Aurelian Bentley.

The pettifogger of Adeline Addams of Newport was there to present the claim of Adeline to the estate, claims based on an *irrefutable promise*. This irrefutable promise was the marriage license for Aurelian Bentley and Adeline Addams. It was not signed or witnessed, of course. The marriage, the pettifogger said, had been scheduled to take place on a certain night after the presentation of an opera, that was contained in a television drama, that was contained in a riddle. But Aurelian Bentley had been killed during that opera, which voided the prospect of marriage, but he did not void the promise.

There were pettifoggers there for the different creditors. And all the pettifoggers were from Philadelphia.

And there was Clarinda Calliope representing herself (as Portia, she insisted, and not as a pettifogger), and she claimed rights by a promise too big and too intricate to be put on paper.

There was the probate judge of the private hearing who ambled around the luxurious den flipping a silver dollar in the air and humming the *McGinty's Saloon Waltz*.

"Oh, stop flipping that silly silver dollar and get on with the matter of the probate," Miss Adeline Addams complained to that nitwit judge.

"The silver dollar is the matter of the probate," the judge said. "The dollar is important. It is the soul and body of what this is all about."

The piles of paper began to accumulate on the tables there. There were the documents and attestations of the distant next of kin, of Adeline Addams, and of the creditors in their severality. And not one scrap of paper did Clarinda Calliope put forward.

"Enough, enough," said the judge after the flood of paper had narrowed down to a trickle. "Stop the paper," but he didn't stop flipping that silver dollar or humming that *McGinty's Saloon Waltz*. "All a-sea that's going a-sea, Miss Calliope, it is time you laid a little evidence on the table if you are to be a party to these hearings."

"My evidence is too large and too living to lay on the table," Clarinda said. "But listen, and perhaps look. Due to the magic of the selenium 'slow response' principle, and to the walls of this very room being wired parallel to the receiver in this room, we may be able to bring to you a veritable reconstruction of past words and avowals and persons."

And pretty soon the voice of the once-in-a-century man began, ghostly at first, and then gradually taking on flesh.

"Oh, Aurelian!" Adeline Addams squealed. "Where *are* you?"

"He is here present, in this room where he spent so many wonderful hours with me," Clarinda said. "All right, Aurie baby, talk a little bit clearer and start materializing."

"All these things I will give you, Clarie," came the voice of Aurelian Bentley, and Bentley was there in shadow form of himself. "No one else would give you so much. No one else would ever care so much . . . trust me, Clarie."

Aurelian Bentley was standing there solidly now. It was a three-dimensional projection or re-creation of him, coming into focus from all the eared and eyed and remembering walls of the room that was wired in parallel to the television receiver. Aurelian stood in the midst of them there in his own luxurious den.

"Clarie, I will do handsomely by you . . . a million dollars, my love, and I will give it to you." Oh, these were startling and convincing words coming from the living ghost there! "I swear to you, Clarie . . . I will buy any island or group of islands in the Pacific Ocean for you . . . Hawaii, Samoa, Fiji. Name it and it's yours."

What man ever made such tall promises and with such obvious sincerity?

"Not on paper, not on air, Clarie, but in real life. I will make you the real and living queen."

If they will not listen to one risen from the dead, whom will they listen to?

"Clarie, believe me, believe me, believe me! I will do all things for you. I promise it." How are you going to top something like that?

"I leave you . . . my kingdom, ah, estate, Clarie. My word is good for that."

It was all in the bag, and the drawstring was being tightened on the bag.

"I hereby attest that . . . my estate . . . belongs to you. Let the eared walls of this room be witnesses to what I say, Clarie. If the walls of this room will swear to it, then surely they will be believed."

The image of Aurelian Bentley disappeared, and his sound was extinguished with a sharp snipping sound. Adeline Addams was putting a scissors back into her handbag.

"I've meant to find out what that wire there was for several times," she said. "That sort of shuts it all off when the wire is cut, doesn't it?"

"Here, here, you are guilty of destroying my evidence," Clarinda Calliope said. "You can go to prison for that! You can burn in fire for that!"

A sudden flaming hay wagon with a wild woman driving it rushed into the room and seemed about to destroy everyone in the room. Everyone cringed from it except Clarinda and the probate judge. The flaming hay wagon did crash into all the people of the room, but it did them no damage. It was only a scene from one of the earlier plays. You didn't think that Clarinda had only one circuit in that room, did you? But several of the persons were shaken by the threat.

"Good show," said the probate judge. "I guess it wins, what there is left to win."

"No, no," Adeline cried. "You can't give her the *estate*?"

"What's left of it, sure," said the judge, still flipping the silver dollar.

"It isn't the principle either," said Clarinda, "it's the dollar." She plucked the silver dollar out of the air as the probate judge was still flipping it.

"This *is* the entire residue of the estate, isn't it?" she asked to be sure.

"Right, Calliope, right," the judge said. "That's all that was left of it."

He continued to flip an invisible coin into the air, and he whistled the last, sad bars of the *McGinty's Saloon Waltz*.

"Anybody know where a good actress can get a job?" Clarinda asked. "Going rates, two dollars a day per role." She swept out of the room with head and spirits high. She was a consummate actress.

The other persons fade out into indistinct sounds and indistinct shadows on the old kerosene-powered television receiver.

The prospects of retrieval and revival of the first and greatest of all television series, *The Wonderful World of Aurelian Bentley*, recorded and produced in the year 1873, is in grave danger.

The only true and complete version of the series reposes in one single television receiver; Aurelian Bentley's own control receiver, the one that he kept in his own luxurious den where he spent so many happy hours with his ladies. The original librettos are stored in this set: they are, in fact, a part of this set and they may not, for inexplicable reasons, be removed to any great distance from it.

All the deep and ever-growing side talk, "slow talk," is in this set (All the other sets are mute.) All the final drama *Pettifoggers of Philadelphia* is recorded on this set and is in none of the others. *There is a whole golden era of television recorded in this set*. I bought this old kerosene-burning treasure from its last owner (he did not know what it was: I told him that it was a chestnut roaster) for eighteen dollars. Now, by a vexing coincidence, this last owner has inherited forty acres of land with a fine stand of chestnut trees, and he wants the chestnut roaster back. And he has the law on his side.

I bought it from him, and I paid him for it, of course. But the check I gave him for it was hotter than a selenium rectifier on a shorted circuit. I have to make up the eighteen dollars or lose the receiver and its stored wealth.

I have raised thirteen dollars and fifty cents from three friends and one enemy. I still need four dollars and a half. Oh wait, wait, here is ninety-eight cents in pennies brought in by the "Children for the Wonderful World of Aurelian Bentley Preservation Fund." I still need three dollars and fifty-two cents. Anyone wishing to contribute to this fund had best do so quickly before this golden era of television is lost forever. Due to the fussiness of the government, contributions are not tax-deductible.

It is worth preserving as a remnant of that early era when there were giants on the earth. And, if it is preserved, someday someone will gaze into the old kerosene-powered receiver and cry out in astonishment in the words of the Greatest Bard:

"—what poet-race
Shot such Cyclopean arches at the stars?"

The Primary Education of the Camiroi

Introduction by Samuel R. Delany

R. A. Lafferty was a gadfly.

Paradoxically, he was never a writer I "liked"—and even today I think of him as someone I am always being asked to write about. Because he's so smart, it's always a compliment. (The first time, decades ago, Terry Carr asked me to blurb his novel *Past Master*, I felt that same way.) His works are wryly humorous—though I always realize, moments after the laughter, I am the butt of the joke.

I never met him—he was from Oklahoma and lived his life in Tulsa with his sister, while tales of his alcoholic excess at SF conventions filtered up through the SF community.

"The Primary Education of the Camiroi" is, among other things, a story about linguistic drift as human society spreads more and more widely over more and more diverse landscapes.

Among the surprises the story offers is a fictive revelation that the flowering of ancient Greek Civilization was an "incursion" (an invasion?) of the Camiroi centuries ago.

Camiroi children have to learn to read more and more slowly, rather than faster and faster. (Lafferty's tale was written in the 1950s, when a nation-wide craze for "speed-reading" courses swept the Anglophone world, among the most popular, one from Evelyn Wood. I was a slow reader—I was someone who wondered if I would not profit by taking an Evelyn Wood course . . .) Every once in a while in their topsy-turvy world, a familiar idea swims by ("Can you imagine a person so sick that he would *desire* to hold high office for any great period of time?" One of the reasons I wanted to be a writer in the first place is so that I could observe the effects of politics without being directly responsible for them.) This is in a section of text on education that ends with our learning that the Camiroi children design and construct their own school buildings.

Lafferty had his enthusiasm—the Choctaw Indians of his local area, whom he championed in the mythic novel *Okla Hannali* (1972), published by University of Oklahoma Press—sadly, not a book I have read, though it comes with high praise from writers on the topic such as Dee Brown.

Diogenes the Cynic is the philosopher who suggested, during the time of Plato, that perhaps education would go better if the teachers were beaten when their students did poorly . . .

This is the tradition Lafferty's tales emerge from. And one has a far better understanding of this after one has been a teacher and, perhaps, retired from the position, than before.

The last half dozen pages of the Camiroi's "primary education" are a list of courses, decided up by year, which end with a comment on what this progression might accomplish if it were "constituted" on Earth. The comment contains three recommendations as to how to accomplish these ends. Since they include kidnapping, book burning, and the murdering ("judicious hanging") of "certain malingering students," the tale is both witty and troubling, in the tradition of Swift's "Modest Proposal."

And that is where a good bit of Lafferty's satire originates.

One of my favorite Lafferty anecdotes (I only discovered it on Wikipedia minutes ago) comes from David Langford in the Magazine *SFX* (2002): "[Once a] French publisher nervously asked whether Lafferty minded being compared to G. K. Chesterton [a Catholic author whose 'distributism' got him compared favorably to Marx], and there was a terrifying silence that went on and on. Was the great man hideously offended? Eventually, very slowly, he said: 'You're on the right track, kid,' and wandered away."

Even while I still find the stories unsettling, Lafferty seems on the right track . . .

The Primary Education
of the Camiroi

ABSTRACT FROM JOINT REPORT TO THE GENERAL
DUBUQUE PTA CONCERNING THE PRIMARY EDUCATION OF
THE CAMIROI, Subtitled *Critical Observations of a Parallel Culture
on a Neighboring World, and Evaluations of THE OTHER WAY OF
EDUCATION.*

Extract from the Day Book:

"Where," we asked the Information Factor at Camiroi City Terminal, "is the office of the local PTA?"

"Isn't any," he said cheerfully.

"You mean that in Camiroi City, the metropolis of the planet, there is no PTA?" our chairman Paul Piper asked with disbelief.

"Isn't any office of it. But you're poor strangers, so you deserve an answer even if you can't frame your questions properly. See that elderly man sitting on the bench and enjoying the sun? Go tell him you need a PTA. He'll make you one."

"Perhaps the initials convey a different meaning on Camiroi," said Miss Munch the first surrogate chairman. "By them we mean—"

"Parent Teachers Apparatus, of course. Colloquial English is one of the six Earthian languages required here, you know. Don't be abashed. He's a fine person, and he enjoys doing things for strangers. He'll be glad to make you a PTA."

We were nonplussed, but we walked over to the man indicated.

"We are looking for the local PTA, sir," said Miss Smice, our second surrogate chairman. "We were told that you might help us."

"Oh, certainly," said the elderly Camiroi gentleman. "One of you arrest that man walking there, and we'll get started with it."

"Do what?" asked our Mr. Piper.

"Arrest him. I have noticed that your own words sometimes do not convey a meaning to you. I often wonder how you do communicate among yourselves. Arrest, take into custody, seize by any force physical or moral, and bring him here."

"Yes, *sir*," cried Miss Hanks, our third surrogate chairman. She enjoyed things like this. She arrested the walking Camiroi man with force partly physical and partly moral and brought him to the group.

"It's a PTA they want, Meander," the elder Camiroi said to the one arrested. "Grab three more, and we'll get started. Let the lady help. She's good at it."

Our Miss Hanks and the Camiroi man named Meander arrested three other Camiroi men and brought them to the group.

"Five. It's enough," said the elderly Camiroi. "We are hereby constituted a PTA and ordered into random action. Now, how can we accommodate you, good Earth people?"

"But are you legal? Are you five persons competent to be a PTA?" demanded our Mr. Piper.

"Any Camiroi citizen is competent to do any job on the planet of Camiroi," said one of the Camiroi men (we learned later that his name was Talarium), "otherwise Camiroi would be in a sad shape."

"It may be," said our Miss Smice sourly. "It all seems very informal. What if one of you had to be World President?"

"The odds are that it won't come to one man in ten," said the elderly Camiroi (his name was Philoxenus). "I'm the only one of this group ever to serve as president of this planet, and it was a pleasant week I spent in the Office. Now to the point. How can we accommodate you?"

"We would like to see one of your schools in session," said our Mr. Piper. "We would like to talk to the teachers and the students. We are here to compare the two systems of education."

"There is no comparison," said old Philoxenus, "—meaning no offense. Or no more than a little. On Camiroi, we practice Education. On Earth, they play a game, but they call it by the same name. That makes the confusion. Come. We'll go to a school in session."

"And to a public school," said Miss Smice suspiciously. "Do not fob off any fancy private school on us as typical."

"That would be difficult," said Philoxenus. "There is no public school in Camiroi City and only two remaining on the planet. Only a small fraction of one percent of the students of Camiroi are in public schools. We maintain that there is no more reason for the majority of children to be educated in a public school than to be raised in a public orphanage. We realize, of course, that on Earth you have made a sacred buffalo of the public school."

"Sacred cow," said our Mr. Piper.

"Children and Earthlings should be corrected when they use words wrongly," said Philoxenus. "How else will they learn the correct forms? The animal held sacred in your own near Orient was of the species *bos bubalus* rather than *bos bos*, a buffalo rather than a cow. Shall we go to a school?"

"If it cannot be a public school, at least let it be a typical school," said Miss Smice.

"That again is impossible," said Philoxenus. "Every school on Camiroi is in some respect atypical."

We went to visit an atypical school.

Incident:

Our first contact with the Camiroi students was a violent one. One of them, a lively little boy about eight years old, ran into Miss Munch, knocked her down, and broke her glasses. Then he jabbered something in an unknown tongue.

"Is that Camiroi?" asked Mr. Piper with interest. "From what I have heard, I supposed the language to have a harsher and fuller sound."

"You mean you don't recognize it?" asked Philoxenus with amusement. "What a droll admission from an educator. The boy is very young and very ignorant. Seeing that you were Earthians, he spoke in Hindi, which is the tongue used by more Earthians than any other. No, no, Xypete, they are of the minority who speak English. You can tell it by their colorless texture and the narrow heads on them."

"I say you sure do have slow reaction, lady," the little boy Xypete explained. "Even subhumans should react faster than that. You just stand there and gape and let me bowl you over. You want me analyze you and see why you react so slow?"

"No! No!"

"You seem unhurt in structure from the fall," the little boy continued, "but if I hurt you I got to fix you. Just strip down to your shift, and I'll go over you and make sure you're all right."

"No! No! No!"

"It's all right," said Philoxenus. "All Camiroi children learn primary medicine in the first grade, setting bones and healing contusions and such."

"No! No! I'm all right. But he's broken my glasses."

"Come along Earthside lady, I'll make you some others," said the little boy. "With your slow reaction time you sure can't afford the added handicap of defective vision. Shall I fit you with contacts?"

"No. I want glasses just like those which were broken. Oh heavens, what will I do?"

"You come, I do," said the little boy. It was rather revealing to us that the little boy was able to test Miss Munch's eyes, grind lenses, make frames and have her fixed up within three minutes. "I have made some improvements over those you wore before," the boy said, "to help compensate for your slow reaction time."

"Are all the Camiroi students so talented?" Mr. Piper asked. He was impressed.

"No. Xypete is unusual," Philoxenus said. "Most students would not be able to make a pair of glasses so quickly or competently till they were at least nine."

Random interviews:

"How rapidly do you read?" Miss Hanks asked a young girl.

"One hundred and twenty words a minute," the girl said.

"On Earth some of the girl students your age have learned to read at the rate of five hundred words a minute," Miss Hanks said proudly.

"When I began disciplined reading, I was reading at the rate of four thousands words a minute," the girl said. "They had quite a time correcting me of it. I had to take remedial reading, and my parents were ashamed of me. Now I've learned to read almost slow enough."

"I don't understand," said Miss Hanks.

"Do you know anything about Earth history or geography?" Miss Smice asked a middle-sized boy.

"We sure are sketchy on it, lady. There isn't very much over there, is there?"

"Then you have never heard of Dubuque?"

"Count Dubuque interests me. I can't say as much for the city named after him. I always thought that the Count handled the matters of the conflicting French and Spanish land grants and the basic claims of the Sauk and Fox Indians very well. References to the town now carry a humorous connotation, and 'School-Teacher from Dubuque' has become a folk archetype."

"Thank you," said Miss Smice, "or do I thank you?"

"What are you taught of the relative humanity of the Earthians and the Camiroi and of their origins?" Miss Munch asked a Camiroi girl.

"The other four worlds, Earth (Gaea), Kentauron Mikron, Dahae, and Astrobe were all settled from Camiroi. That is what we are taught. We are also given the humorous aside that if it isn't true we will still hold it true till something better comes along. It was we who rediscovered the Four Worlds in historic time, not they who discovered us. If we did not make the original settlements, at least we have filed the first claim that we made them. We did, in historical time, make an additional colonization of Earth. You call it the Incursion of the Dorian Greeks."

"Where are their playgrounds?" Miss Hanks asked Talarium.

"Oh, the whole world. The children have the run of everything. To set up specific playgrounds would be like setting a table-sized aquarium down in the depths of the ocean. It would really be pointless."

Conference:

The four of us from Earth, specifically from Dubuque, Iowa, were in discussion with the five members of the Camiroi PTA.

"How do you maintain discipline?" Mr. Piper asked.

"Indifferently," said Philoxenus. "Oh, you mean in detail. It varies. Sometimes we let it drift, sometimes we pull them up short. Once they have learned that they must comply to an extent, there is little trouble. Small children are often put down into a pit. They do not eat or come out till they know their assignment."

"But that is inhuman," said Miss Hanks.

"Of course. But small children are not yet entirely human. If a child has not learned to accept discipline by the third or fourth grade, he is hanged."

"Literally?" asked Miss Munch.

"How would you hang a child figuratively? And what effect would that have on the other children?"

"By the neck?" Miss Munch still was not satisfied.

"By the neck until they are dead. The other children always accept the example gracefully and do better. Hanging isn't employed often. Scarcely one child in a hundred is hanged."

"What is this business about slow reading?" Miss Hanks asked. "I don't understand it at all."

"Only the other day there was a child in the third grade who persisted in rapid reading," Philoxenus said. "He was given an object lesson. He was given a book of medium difficulty, and he read it rapidly. Then he had to put the book away and repeat what he had read. Do you know that in the first thirty pages he missed four words? Midway in the book there was a whole statement which he had understood wrongly, and there were hundreds of pages that he got word-perfect only with difficulty. If he was so unsure on material that he had just read, think how imperfectly he would have recalled it forty years later."

"You mean that the Camiroi children learn to recall everything that they read?"

"The Camiroi children and adults will recall for life every detail they have ever seen, read, or heard. We on Camiroi are only a little more intelligent than you on Earth. We cannot afford to waste time in forgetting or reviewing, or in pursuing anything of a shallowness that lends itself to scanning."

"Ah, would you call your schools liberal?" Mr. Piper asked.

"I would. You wouldn't," said Philoxenus. "We do not on Camiroi, as you do on Earth, use words to mean their opposites. There is nothing in our education or on our world that corresponds to the quaint servility which you call liberal on Earth."

"Well, would you call your education progressive?"

"No. In your argot, progressive, of course, means infantile."

"How are the schools financed?" asked Mr. Piper.

"Oh, the voluntary tithe on Camiroi takes care of everything, government, religion, education, public works. We don't believe in taxes, of course, and we never maintain a high overhead in anything."

"Just how voluntary is the tithing?" asked Miss Hanks. "Do you sometimes hang those who do not tithe voluntarily?"

"I believe there have been a few cases of that sort," said Philoxenus.

"And is your government really as slipshod as your education?" Mr. Piper asked. "Are your high officials really chosen by lot and for short periods?"

"Oh yes. Can you imagine a person so sick that he would actually *desire* to hold high office for any great period of time? Are there any further questions?"

"There must be hundreds," said Mr. Piper. "But we find difficulty putting them into words."

"If you cannot find words for them, we cannot find answers. PTA disbanded."

CONCLUSION A: The Camiroi system of education is inferior to our own in organization, in buildings, in facilities, in playgrounds, in teacher conferences, in funding, in parental involvement, in supervision, in in-group out-group accommodation adjustment motifs. Some of the school buildings are grotesque. We asked about one particular building which seemed to us to be flamboyant and in bad taste. "What do you expect from second-grade children?" they said. "It is well built even if of peculiar appearance. Second-grade children are not yet complete artists of design."

"You mean that the children designed it themselves?" we asked.

"Of course," they said. "Designed and built it. It isn't a bad job for children."

Such a thing wouldn't be permitted on Earth.

CONCLUSION B: The Camiroi system of education somehow produces much better results than does the education system of Earth. We have been forced to admit this by the evidence at hand.

CONCLUSION C: There is an anomaly as yet unresolved between CONCLUSION A and CONCLUSION B.

APPENDIX TO JOINT REPORT

We give here, as perhaps of some interest, the curriculum of the Camiroi Primary Education.

FIRST YEAR COURSE:
Playing one wind instrument.
Simple drawing of objects and numbers.
Singing. (This is important. Many Earth people sing who cannot sing. This early instruction of the Camiroi prevents that occurrence.)
Simple arithmetic, hand and machine.
First acrobatics.

First riddles and logic.
Mnemonic religion.
First dancing.
Walking the low wire.
Simple electric circuits.
Raising ants. (Eoempts, not Earth ants.)

SECOND YEAR COURSE:
Playing one keyboard instrument.
Drawing, faces, letters, motions.
Singing comedies.
Complex arithmetic, hand and machine.
Second acrobatics.
First jokes and logic.
Quadratic religion.
Second dancing.
Simple defamation. (Spirited attacks on the character of one fellow student,
    with elementary falsification and simple hatchet-job programming.)
Performing on the medium wire.
Project electric wiring.
Raising bees. (Galelea, not Earth bees.)

THIRD YEAR COURSE:
Playing one stringed instrument.
Reading and voice. (It is here that the student who may have fallen into bad
    habits of rapid reading is compelled to read at voice speed only.)
Soft stone sculpture.
Situation comedy.
Simple algebra, hand and machine.
First gymnastics.
Second jokes and logic.
Transcendent religion.
Complex acrobatic dancing.
Complex defamation.
Performing on the high wire and the sky pole.
Simple radio construction.
Raising, breeding, and dissecting frogs. (Karakoli, not Earth frogs.)

FOURTH YEAR COURSE:
History reading, Camiroi and galactic, basic and geological.
Decadent comedy.
Simple geometry and trigonometry, hand and machine.
Track and field.

Shaggy people jokes and hirsute logic.
Simple obscenity.
Simple mysticism.
Patterns of falsification.
Trapeze work.
Intermediate electronics.
Human dissection.

FIFTH YEAR COURSE:
History reading, Camiroi and galactic, technological.
Introverted drama.
Complex geometries and analytics, hand and machine.
Track and field for fifth form record.
First wit and logic.
First alcoholic appreciation.
Complex mysticism.
Setting intellectual climates, defamation in three dimensions.
Simple oratory.
Complex trapeze work.
Inorganic chemistry.
Advanced electronics.
Advanced human dissection.
Fifth form thesis.

The child is now ten years old and is half through his primary schooling. He is an unfinished animal, but he has learned to learn.

SIXTH YEAR COURSE:
Reemphasis on slow reading.
Simple prodigious memory.
History reading, Camiroi and galactic, economic.
Horsemanship (of the Patrushkoe, not the Earth horse).
Advanced lathe and machine work for art and utility.
Literature, passive.
Calculi, hand and machine pankration.
Advanced wit and logic.
Second alcoholic appreciation.
Differential religion.
First business ventures.
Complex oratory.
Building-scaling. (The buildings are higher and the gravity stronger than on
    Earth; this climbing of buildings like human flies calls out the ingenuity and
    daring of the Camiroi children.)

Nuclear physics and post-organic chemistry.
Simple pseudo-human assembly.

SEVENTH YEAR COURSE:
History reading, Camiroi and galactic, cultural.
Advanced prodigious memory.
Vehicle operation and manufacture of simple vehicle.
Literature, active.
Astrognosy, prediction and programming.
Advanced pankration.
Spherical logic, hand and machine.
Advanced alcoholic appreciation.
Integral religion.
Bankruptcy and recovery in business.
Conmanship and trend creation.
Post-nuclear physics and universals.
Transcendental athletics endeavor.
Complex robotics and programming.

EIGHTH YEAR COURSE:
History reading, Camiroi and galactic, seminal theory.
Consummate prodigious memory.
Manufacture of complex land and water vehicles.
Literature, compendious and terminative. (Creative book-burning following
    the Camiroi thesis that nothing ordinary be allowed to survive.)
Cosmic theory, seminal.
Philosophy construction.
Complex hedonism.
Laser religion.
Conmanship, seminal.
Consolidation of simple genius status.
Post-robotic integration.

NINTH YEAR COURSE:
History reading, Camiroi and galactic, future and contingent.
Category invention.
Manufacture of complex light-barrier vehicles.
Construction of simple asteroids and planets.
Matrix religion and logic.
Simple human immortality disciplines.
Consolidation of complex genius status.
First problems of post-consciousness humanity.
First essays in marriage and reproduction.

TENTH YEAR COURSE:

History construction, active.

Manufacture of ultra-light-barrier vehicles.

Panphilosophical clarifications.

Construction of viable planets.

Consolidation of simple sanctity status.

Charismatic humor and pentacosmic logic.

Hypogyroscopic economy.

Penentaglossia. (The perfection of the fifty languages that every educated Camiroi must know including six Earthian languages. Of course the child will already have colloquial mastery of most of these, but he will not yet have them in their full depth.)

Construction of complex societies.

World government. (A course of the same name is sometimes given in Earthian schools, but the course is not of the same content. In this course the Camiroi student will govern a world, though not one of the first aspect worlds, for a period of three or four months.)

Tenth form thesis.

COMMENT ON CURRICULUM:

The child will now be fifteen years old and will have completed his primary education. In many ways he will be advanced beyond his Earth counterpart. Physically more sophisticated, the Camiroi child could kill with his hands an Earth-type tiger or a cape buffalo. An Earth child would perhaps be reluctant even to attempt such feats. The Camiroi boy (or girl) could replace any professional Earth athlete at any position of any game, and could surpass all existing Earth records. It is simply a question of finer poise, strength and speed, the result of adequate schooling.

As to the arts (on which Earthlings sometimes place emphasis) the Camiroi child could produce easy and unequaled masterpieces in any medium. More important, he will have learned the relative unimportance of such pastimes.

The Camiroi child will have failed in business once, at age ten, and have learned patience and perfection of objective by his failure. He will have acquired the techniques of falsification and conmanship. Thereafter he will not be easily deceived by any of the citizens of any of the worlds. The Camiroi child will have become a complex genius and a simple saint; the latter reduces the index of Camiroi crime to near zero. He will be married and settled in those early years of greatest enjoyment.

The child will have built, from materials found around any Camiroi house, a faster-than-light vehicle. He will have piloted it on a significant journey of his own plotting and programming. He will have built quasi-human robots of great intricacy. He will be of perfect memory and judgment and will be well prepared to accept solid learning.

He will have learned to use his whole mind, for the vast reservoirs which are the unconscious to us are not unconscious to him. Everything in him is ordered for use. And there seems to be no great secret about the accomplishments, only to do everything slowly enough and in the right order: thus they avoid repetition and drill which are the shriveling things which dull the quick apperception.

The Camiroi schedule is challenging to the children, but it is nowhere impossible or discouraging. Everything builds to what follows. For instance, the child is eleven years old before he is given post-nuclear physics and universals. Such subjects might be too difficult for him at an earlier age. He is thirteen years old before he undertakes category invention, that intricate course with the simple name. He is fourteen years old when he enters the dangerous field of panphilosophical clarification. But he will have been constructing comprehensive philosophies for two years, and he will have the background for the final clarification.

We should look more closely at this other way of education. In some respects it is better than our own. Few Earth children would be able to construct an organic and sentient robot within fifteen minutes if given the test suddenly; most of them could not manufacture a living dog in that time. Not one Earth child in five could build a faster-than-light vehicle and travel it beyond our galaxy between now and midnight. Not one Earth child in a hundred could build a planet and have it a going concern within a week. Not one in a thousand would be able to comprehend pentacosmic logic.

RECOMMENDATIONS:

A. Kidnapping five Camiroi at random and constituting them a pilot Earth PTA.
B. A little constructive book-burning, particularly in the education field.
C. Judicious hanging of certain malingering students.

Continued on Next Rock

Introduction by Nancy Kress

Some stories you don't forget.

I first read R. A. Lafferty's "Continued on Next Rock" over forty years ago, in the autumn of 1975. I remember it exactly. I was in graduate school, taking a Master's degree, and I'd signed up for a course in science fiction. The text was *Speculations: An Introduction To Literature Through Fantasy and Science Fiction,* edited by Thomas E. Sanders. It included poetry, three essays, and forty-one stories. I know the exact number because I still have the book. The stories ranged widely, including genre precursors by Nathaniel Hawthorne, Herman Melville, and Rudyard Kipling; 1940s stories by writers such as Walter Van Tilburg Clark, Murray Leinster, and Judith Merril; and a lot of newer stories by then-current stars like Robert Silverberg, Theodore Sturgeon, and Robert Sheckley.

I read the entire volume the first weekend after I purchased it.

Among the stories was "Continued on Next Rock." I read it, puzzled a while, and read it again. This was different. This was *way* different. It was clearly a love story, but not like any I'd ever read. Magdalen and Anteros seemed very strange, if not downright crazy. Actually, they *are* crazy. Sexually obsessed, he chases her through time, leaving amorous poems in strata of ancient rock. She spurns him, in what may or may not be a courtship ritual. Or murder.

The writing was wonderful, the characters inventive, the tone perfectly balanced between wryness and passion, the kind of passion that annihilates. I could not get it out of my head.

A few years later, a different one of my graduate-school professors, who'd become a friend, told me how much he admired R. A. Lafferty. He gave me a bound, uncorrected page-proof copy of *Iron Tears,* the 1992 Lafferty collection from Edgewood Press (I still have this volume, too). I thanked him, but my main reaction was indignation that the fifteen stories in the volume didn't include "Continued on Next Rock."

My admiration for the story, which I just read yet again, has only grown. After all, Anteros's love poems are, if nothing else, unique: "You are the freedom of wild pigs in the sour-grass, and the nobility of badgers. You are the brightness of serpents and the soaring of vultures. You are passion of mesquite bushes on fire with lightning. You are serenity of toads."

As I said—unique courtship poetry. And how come no man has ever told me that I am the nobility of badgers, let alone the serenity of toads? Why not, I ask you?

Maybe if I could have done the things that Magdalen could . . .

Continued on Next Rock

U p in the Big Lime country there is an up-thrust, a chimney rock that is half fallen against a newer hill. It is formed of what is sometimes called Dawson sandstone and is interlaced with tough shale. It was formed during the glacial and recent ages in the bottom lands of Crow Creek and Green River when these streams (at least five times) were mighty rivers.

The chimney rock is only a little older than mankind, only a little younger than grass. Its formation had been up-thrust and then eroded away again, all but such harder parts as itself and other chimneys and blocks.

A party of five persons came to this place where the chimney rock had fallen against a still-newer hill. The people of the party did not care about the deep limestone below: they were not geologists. They *did* care about the newer hill (it was man-made) and they did care a little about the rock chimney; they were archeologists.

Here was time heaped up, bulging out in casing and accumulation, and not in line sequence. And here also was striated and banded time, grown tall, and then shattered and broken.

The five party members came to the site early in the afternoon, bringing the working trailer down a dry creek bed. They unloaded many things and made a camp there. It wasn't really necessary to make a camp on the ground. There was a good motel two miles away on the highway; there was a road along the ridge above. They could have lived in comfort and made the trip to the site in five minutes every morning. Terrence Burdock, however, believed that one could not get the feel of a digging unless he lived on the ground with it day and night.

The five persons were Terrence Burdock, his wife Ethyl, Robert Derby, and Howard Steinleser: four beautiful and balanced people. And Magdalen Mobley who was neither beautiful nor balanced. But she was electric; she was special. They rouched around in the formations a little after they had made camp and while there was still light. All of them had seen the formations before and had guessed that there was promise in them.

"That peculiar fluting in the broken chimney is almost like a core sample," Terrence said, "and it differs from the rest of it. It's like a lightning bolt through the whole length. It's already exposed for us. I believe we will remove the chimney entirely. It covers the perfect access for the slash in the mound, and it is the mound in which we are really interested. But we'll study the chimney first. It is so available for study."

"Oh, I can tell you everything that's in the chimney," Magdalen said crossly. "I can tell you everything that's in the mound too."

"I wonder why we take the trouble to dig if you already know what we will find," Ethyl sounded archly.

"I wonder too," Magdalen grumbled. "But we will need the evidence and the artifacts to show. You can't get appropriations without evidence and artifacts. Robert, go kill that deer in the brush about forty yards northeast of the chimney. We may as well have deer meat if we're living primitive."

"This isn't deer season," Robert Derby objected. "And there isn't any deer there. Or, if there is, it's down in the draw where you couldn't see it. And if there's one there, it's probably a doe."

"No, Robert, it is a two-year-old buck and a very big one. Of course it's in the draw where I can't see it. Forty yards northeast of the chimney would have to be in the draw. If I could see it, the rest of you could see it too. Now go kill it! Are you a man or a *mus microtus*? Howard, cut poles and set up a tripod to string and dress the deer on."

"You had better try the thing, Robert," Ethyl Burdock said, "or we'll have no peace this evening."

Robert Derby took a carbine and went northeastward of the chimney, descending into the draw forty yards away. There was the high ping of the carbine shot. And, after some moments, Robert returned with a curious grin.

"You didn't miss him, Robert, you killed him," Magdalen called loudly. "You got him with a good shot through the throat and up into the brain when he tossed his head high like they do. Why didn't you bring him? Go back and get him!"

"Get him? I couldn't even lift the thing. Terrence and Howard, come with me and we'll lash it to a pole and get it here somehow."

"Oh, Robert, you're out of your beautiful mind," Magdalen chided. "It only weighs a hundred and ninety pounds. Oh, I'll get it."

Magdalen Mobley went and got the big buck. She brought it back, carrying it listless across her shoulders and getting herself bloodied, stopping sometimes to examine rocks and kick them with her foot, coming on easily with her load. It looked as if it might weigh two hundred and fifty pounds; but if Magdalen said it weighed a hundred and ninety, that is what it weighed.

Howard Steinleser had cut poles and made a tripod. He knew better than not to. They strung the buck up, skinned it off, ripped up its belly, drew it, and worked it over in an almost professional manner.

"Cook it, Ethyl," Magdalen said.

Later, as they sat on the ground around the fire and it had turned dark, Ethyl brought the buck's brains to Magdalen, messy and not half-cooked, believing that she was playing an evil trick. And Magdalen ate them avidly. They were her due. She had discovered the buck.

If you wonder how Magdalen knew what invisible things were where, so did the other members of the party always wonder.

"It bedevils me sometimes why I am the only one to notice the analogy between historical geology and depth psychology," Terrence Burdock mused as they grew lightly profound around the campfire. "The isostatic principle applies to the mind and the under-mind as well as it does to the surface and under-surface of the Earth. The mind has its erosions and weatherings going on along with its deposits and accumulations. It also has its up-thrusts and its stresses. It floats on a similar magma. In extreme cases it has its volcanic eruptions and its mountain building."

"And it has its glaciations," Ethyl Burdock said, and perhaps she was looking at her husband in the dark.

"The mind has its hard sandstone, sometimes transmuted to quartz, or half-transmuted into flint, from the drifting and floating sand of daily events. It has its shale from the old mud of daily ineptitudes and inertias. It has limestone out of its more vivid experiences, for lime is the remnant of what was once animate: and this limestone may be true marble if it is the deposit of rich enough emotion, or even travertine if it has bubbled sufficiently through agonized and evocative rivers of the under-mind. The mind has its sulfur and its gemstones—" Terrence bubbled on sufficiently, and Magdalen cut him off.

"Say simply that we have rocks in our heads," she said. "But they're random rocks, I tell you, and the same ones keep coming back. It *isn't* the same with us as it is with the Earth. The world gets new rocks all the time. But it's the same people who keep turning up, and the same minds. Damn, one of the samest of them just turned up again! I wish he'd leave me alone. The answer is still no."

Very often Magdalen said things that made no sense. Ethyl Burdock assured herself that neither her husband, nor Robert, nor Howard, had slipped over to Magdalen in the dark. Ethyl was jealous of the chunky and surly girl.

"I am hoping that this will be as rich as Spiro Mound," Howard Steinleser hoped. "It could be, you know. I'm told that there was never a less prepossessing site than that, or a trickier one. I wish we had someone who had dug at Spiro."

"Oh, he dug at Spiro," Magdalen said with contempt.

"He? Who?" Terrence Burdock asked. "No one of us was at Spiro. Magdalen, you weren't even born yet when that mound was opened. What could you know about it?"

"Yeah, I remember him at Spiro," Magdalen said, "—always turning up his own things and pointing them out."

"*Were* you at Spiro?" Terrence suddenly asked a piece of darkness. For some time, they had all been vaguely aware that there were six, not five, persons around the fire.

"Yeah, I was at Spiro," the man said. "I dig there. I dig at a lot of the digs. I dig real well, and I always know when we come to something that will be important. You give me a job."

"Who are you?" Terrence asked him. The man was pretty visible now. The flame of the fire seemed to leap toward him as if he compelled it.

"Oh, I'm just a rich old poor man who keeps following and hoping and asking. There is *one* who is worth it all forever, so I solicit that one forever. And sometimes I am other things. Two hours ago I was the deer in the draw. It is an odd thing to munch one's own flesh." And the man was munching a joint of the deer, unasked.

"Him and his damn cheap poetry!" Magdalen cried angrily.

"What's your name!" Terrence asked him.

"Manypenny. Anteros Manypenny is my name forever."

"What are you?"

"Oh, just Indian. Shawnee, Choc, Creek, Anadarko, Caddo, and pre-Caddo. Lots of things."

"How could anyone be pre-Caddo?"

"Like me. I am."

"Is Anteros a Creek name?"

"No. Greek. Man, I am a going Jessie, I am one digging man! I show you tomorrow."

Man, he was one digging man! He showed them tomorrow. With a short-handled rose hoe he began the gash in the bottom of the mound, working too swiftly to be believed.

"He will smash anything that is there. He will not know what he comes to," Ethyl Burdock complained.

"Woman, I will *not* smash whatever is there," Anteros said. "You can hide a wren's egg in one cubic meter of sand. I will move all the sand in one minute. I will uncover the egg, wherever it is. And I will not crack the egg. I sense these things. I come now to a small pot of the proto-Plano period. It is broken, of course, but I do not break it. It is in six pieces and they will fit together perfectly. I tell you this beforehand. Now I reveal it."

And Anteros revealed it. There was something wrong about it even before he uncovered it. But it was surely a find, and perhaps it *was* of the proto-Plano period. The six shards came out. They were roughly cleaned and set. It was apparent that they would fit wonderfully.

"Why, it is perfect!" Ethyl exclaimed.

"It is too perfect," Howard Steinleser protested. "It was a turned pot, and who had turned pots in America without the potter's wheel? But the glyphs pressed into it do correspond to proto-Plano glyphs. It is fishy." Steinleser was in a twitchy humor today and his face was livid.

"Yes, it is the ripple and the spinosity, the fish-glyph," Anteros pointed out. "And the sun-sign is riding upon it. It is fish-god."

"It's fishy in another way," Steinleser insisted. "Nobody finds a thing like that in the first sixty seconds of a dig. And there *could not be* such a pot. I wouldn't believe it was proto-Plano unless points were found in the exact site with it."

"Oh, here," Anteros said. "One can smell the very shape of the flint points already. Two large points, one small one. Surely you get the whiff of them already? Four more hoe cuts and I come to them."

Four more hoe cuts, and Anteros *did* come to them. He uncovered two large points and one small one, spearheads and arrowhead. Lanceolate they were, with ribbon flaking. They were late Folsom, or they were proto-Plano; they were what you will.

"This cannot be," Steinleser groaned. "They're the missing chips, the transition pieces. They fill the missing places too well. I won't believe it. I'd hardly believe it if mastodon bones were found on the same level here."

"In a moment," said Anteros, beginning to use the hoe again. "Hey, those old beasts *did smell funny*! An elephant isn't in it with them. And a lot of it still clings to their bones. Will a sixth thoracic bone do? I'm pretty sure that's what it is. I don't know where the rest of the animal is. Probably somebody gnawed the thoracic here. Nine hoe cuts, and then very careful."

Nine hoe cuts; and then Anteros, using a mason's trowel, unearthed the old gnawed bone very carefully. Yes, Howard said almost angrily, it was a sixth thoracic of a mastodon. Robert Derby said it was a fifth or sixth; it is not easy to tell.

"Leave the digging for a while, Anteros," Steinleser said. "I want to record and photograph and take a few measurements here."

Terrence Burdock and Magdalen Mobley were working at the bottom of the chimney rock, at the bottom of the fluting that ran the whole height of it like a core sample. "Get Anteros over here and see what he can uncover in sixty seconds," Terrence offered.

"Oh, him! He'll just uncover some of his own things."

"What do you mean, his own things? Nobody could have made an intrusion here. It's hard sandstone."

"And harder flint here," Magdalen said. "I might have known it. Pass the damned thing up. I know just about what it says, anyhow."

"What it says? What do you mean? But it is marked! And it's large and dressed rough. Who'd carve in flint?"

"Somebody real stubborn, just like flint," Magdalen said. "All right then, let's have it out. Anteros! Get this out in one piece. And do it without shattering it or tumbling the whole thing down on us. He can do it, you know, Terrence. He can do things like that."

"What do you know about his doings, Magdalen? You never saw or heard about the poor man till last night."

"Oh well, I know that it'll turn out to be the same damned stuff."

Anteros did get it out without shattering it or bringing down the chimney column. A cleft with a digging bar, three sticks of the stuff and a cap, and he touched the leads to the battery when he was almost on top of the charge. The blast, it sounded as if the whole sky were falling down in them, and some of those sky-blocks were quite large stones. The ancients wondered why fallen pieces of the sky should always be dark rockstuff and never sky-blue clear stuff. The answer is that it is only pieces of the night sky that ever fall, even though they may sometimes be most of the daytime in falling, such is the distance. And the blast that Anteros set off did bring down rocky chunks of the night sky even though it was broad daylight. They brought down darker rocks than any of which the chimney was composed.

Still, it was a small blast. The chimney tottered but did not collapse. It settled back uneasily on its base. And the flint block was out in the clear.

"A thousand spearheads and arrowheads could be shattered and chipped out of that hunk," Terrence marveled. "That flint block would have been a primitive fortune for a primitive man."

"I had several such fortunes," Anteros said dully, "and this one I preserved and dedicated."

They had all gathered around it.

"Oh the poor man!" Ethyl suddenly exclaimed, but she was not looking at any of the men. She was looking at the stone.

"I wish he'd get off that kick," Magdalen sputtered angrily. "I don't care *how* rich he is. I can pick up better stuff than him in the alleys."

"What are the women chirping about?" Terrence asked. "But those do look like true glyphs. Almost like Aztec, are they not, Steinleser?"

"Nahuat-Tanoan, cousins-german to the Aztec, or should I say cousins-yaqui?"

"Call it anything, but can you read it?"

"Probably. Give me eight or ten hours on it and I should come up with a contingent reading of many of the glyphs. We can hardly expect a rational rendering of the message, however. All Nahuat-Tanoan translations so far have been gibberish."

"And remember, Terrence, that Steinleser is a slow reader," Magdalen said spitefully. "And he isn't very good at interpreting *other* signs either."

Steinleser was sullen and silent. How had his face come to bear those deep livid claw marks today?

They moved a lot of rock and rubble that morning, took quite a few pictures, wrote up bulky notes. There were constant finds as the divided party worked up the shag-slash in the mound and the core-flute of the chimney. There were no more really startling discoveries; no more turned pots of the proto-Plano period; how could there be? There were no more predicted and perfect points of the late Folsom, but there were broken and unpredictable points. No other mastodon thoracic was found, but bones were uncovered of *bison latifrons*, of dire wolf, of coyote, of man. There were some anomalies in the relationship of the things discovered, but it was not as fishy as it had been in the early morning, not as fishy as when Anteros had announced and then dug out the shards of the pot, the three points, the mastodon bone. The things now were as authentic as they were expected, and yet their very profusion had still the smell of a small fish.

And that Anteros was one digging man. He moved the sand, he moved the stone, he missed nothing. And at noon he disappeared.

An hour later he reappeared in a glossy station wagon, coming out of a thicketed ravine where no one would have expected a way. He had been to town. He brought a variety of cold cuts, cheeses, relishes and pastries, a couple of cases of cold beer, and some V.O.

"I thought you were a poor man, Anteros," Terrence chided.

"I told you that I was a rich old poor man. I have nine thousand acres of grassland, I have three thousand head of cattle, I have alfalfa land and clover land and corn land and hay-grazer land—"

"Oh, knock it off!" Magdalen snapped.

"I have other things," Anteros finished sullenly.

They ate, they rested, they worked the afternoon. Magdalen worked as swiftly and solidly as did Anteros. She was young, she was stocky, she was light-burned-dark. She was not at all beautiful (Ethyl was). She could have any man there any time she wanted to (Ethyl couldn't). She was Magdalen, the often unpleasant, the mostly casual, the suddenly intense one. She was the tension of the party, the string of the bow.

"Anteros!" she called sharply just at sundown.

"The turtle?" he asked. "The turtle that is under the ledge out of the current where the backwater curls in reverse? But he is fit and happy and he has never harmed anything except for food or fun. I know you do not want me to get that turtle."

"I do! There's eighteen pounds of him. He's fat. He'll be good. Only eighty yards, where the bank crumbles down to Green River, under the lower ledge that's shale that looks like slate, two feet deep—"

"I know where he is. I will go get the fat turtle," Anteros said. "I myself am the fat turtle. I am the Green River." He went to get it.

"Oh that damned poetry of his!" Magdalen spat when he was gone.

Anteros brought back the fat turtle. He looked as if he'd weigh twenty-five pounds; but if Magdalen said he weighed eighteen pounds, then it was eighteen.

"Start cooking, Ethyl," Magdalen said. Magdalen was a mere undergraduate girl permitted on the digging by sheer good fortune. The others of the party were all archeologists of the moment. Magdalen had no right to give orders to anyone, except her born right.

"I don't know how to cook a turtle," Ethyl complained.

"Anteros will show you how."

"The late evening smell of newly exposed excavation!" Terrence Burdock burbled as they lounged around the campfire a little later, full of turtle and V.O. and feeling rakishly wise. "The exposed age can be guessed by the very timbre of the smell, I believe."

"Timbre of the smell! What is your nose wired up to?" from Magdalen.

And, indeed, there was something time-evocative about the smell of the diggings; cool, at the same time musty and musky, ripe with old stratified water and compressed death. Stratified time.

"It helps if you already know what the exposed age is," said Howard Steinleser. "Here there is an anomaly. The chimney sometimes acts as if it were younger than the mound. The chimney cannot be young enough to include written rock, but it is."

"Archeology is made up entirely of anomalies," said Terrence, "rearranged to make them fit in a fluky pattern. There'd be no system to it otherwise."

"Every science is made up entirely of anomalies rearranged to fit," said Robert Derby. "Have you unriddled the glyph-stone, Howard?"

"Yes, pretty well, better than I expected. Charles August can verify it, of course, when we get it back to the University. It is a non-royal, non-tribal, non-warfare, non-hunt declaration. It does not come under any of the usual radical signs, any of the categories. It can only be categorized as uncategorized or personal. The translation will be rough."

"Rocky is the word," said Magdalen.

"On with it, Howard," Ethyl cried.

"'You are the freedom of wild pigs in the sour-grass, and the nobility of badgers. You are the brightness of serpents and the soaring of vultures. You are passion of mesquite bushes on fire with lightning. You are serenity of toads.'"

"You've got to admit he's got a different line," said Ethyl. "Your own love notes were less acrid, Terrence."

"What kind of thing is it, Steinleser?" Terrence questioned. "It must have a category."

"I believe Ethyl is right. It's a love poem. 'You are the water in rock cisterns and the secret spiders in that water. You are the dead coyote lying half in the stream, and you are the old entrapped dreams of the coyote's brains oozing liquid through the broken eye socket. You are the happy ravening flies about that broken socket.'"

"Oh, hold it, Steinleser," Robert Derby cried. "You can't have gotten all that from scratches on flint. What is 'entrapped dreams' in Nahuat-Tanoan glyphwriting?"

"The solid-person sign next to the hollow-person sign, both enclosed in the night sign—that has always been interpreted as the dream glyph. And here the dream glyph is enclosed in the glyph of the dead-fall trap. Yes, I believe it means entrapped dreams. To continue: 'You are the corn-worm in the dark heart of the corn, the naked small bird in the nest. You are the pustules on the sick rabbit, devouring life and flesh and turning it into your own serum. You are stars compressed into charcoal. But you cannot give, you cannot take. Once again you will be broken at the foot of the cliff, and the word will remain unsaid in your swollen and purple tongue.'"

"A love poem, perhaps, but with a difference," said Robert Derby.

"I never was able to go his stuff, and I tried, I really tried," Magdalen moaned.

"Here is the change of person-subject shown by the canted-eye glyph linked with the self-glyph," Steinleser explained. "It is now a first-person talk. 'I own ten-thousand back-loads of corn. I own gold and beans and nine buffalo horns full of watermelon seeds. I own the loin cloth that the sun wore on his fourth journey across the sky. Only three loin cloths in the world are older and more valued than this. I cry out to you in a big voice like the hammering of herons' (that sound-verb-particle is badly translated, the hammer being not a modern pounding hammer but a rock angling, chipping hammer) 'and the belching of buffaloes. My love is sinewy as entwined snakes, it is steadfast as the sloth, it is like a feathered arrow shot into your abdomen—such is my love. Why is my love unrequited?'"

"I challenge you, Steinleser," Terrence Burdock cut in. "What is the glyph for 'unrequited'?"

"The glyph of the extended hand—with all the fingers bent backward. It goes on, 'I roar to you. Do not throw yourself down. You believe you are on the hanging sky bridge, but you are on the terminal cliff. I grovel before you. I am no more than dog-droppings.'"

"You'll notice he said that and not me," Magdalen burst out. There was always a fundamental incoherence about Magdalen.

"Ah—continue, Steinleser," said Terrence. "The girl is daft, or she dreams out loud."

"That is all of the inscriptions, Terrence, except for a final glyph which I don't understand. Glyph writing takes a lot of room. That's all the stone would hold."

"What is the glyph that you don't understand, Howard?"

"It's the spear-thrower glyph entwined with the time glyph. It sometimes means 'flung forward or beyond.' But what does it mean here?"

"It means 'continued,' dummy. 'Continued,'" Magdalen said. "Do not fear. There'll be more stories."

"I think it's beautiful," said Ethyl Burdock, "—in its own context, of course."

"Then why don't you take him on, Ethyl, in his own context, of course?" Magdalen asked. "Myself, I don't care how many back-loads of corn he owns. I've had it."

"Take whom on, dear?" Ethyl asked. "Howard Steinleser can interpret the stones, but who can interpret our Magdalen?"

"Oh, I can read her like a rock." Terrence Burdock smiled. But he couldn't.

But it had fastened on them. It was all about them and through them: the brightness of serpents and the serenity of toads, the secret spiders in the water, the entrapped dreams oozing through the broken eye socket, the pustules of the sick rabbit, the belching of the buffalo, and the arrow shot into the abdomen. And around it all was the night smell of flint and turned earth and chuckling streams, the mustiness, and the special muskiness which bears the name Nobility of Badgers.

They talked archeology and myth talk. Then it was steep night, and the morning of the third day.

Oh, the sample digging went well. This was already a richer mound than Spiro, though the gash in it was but a small promise of things to come. And the curious twin of the mound, the broken chimney, confirmed and confounded and contradicted. There was time going wrong in the chimney, or at least in the curious fluted core of it; the rest of it was normal enough, and sterile enough.

Anteros worked that day with a soft sullenness, and Magdalen brooded with a sort of lightning about her.

"Beads, glass beads!" Terrence Burdock exploded angrily. "All right! Who is the hoaxer in our midst? I will not tolerate this at all." Terrence had been angry of face all day. He was clawed deeply, as Steinleser had been the day before, and he was sour on the world.

"There have been glass-bead caches before, Terrence, hundreds of them," Robert Derby said softly.

"There have been hoaxers before, hundreds of them," Terrence howled. "These have 'Hong Kong Contemporary' written all over them, damn cheap glass beads sold by the pound. They have no business in a stratum of around the year seven hundred. All right, who is guilty?"

"I don't believe that any one of us is guilty, Terrence," Ethyl put in mildly. "They are found four feet in from the slant surface of the mound. Why, we've cut through three hundred years of vegetable loam to get to them, and certainly the surface was eroded beyond that."

"We are scientists," said Steinleser. "We find these. Others have found such. Let us consider the improbabilities of it."

It was noon, so they ate and rested and considered the improbabilities. Anteros had brought them a great joint of white pork, and they made sandwiches and drank beer and ate pickles.

"You know," said Robert Derby, "that beyond the rank impossibility of glass beads found so many times where they *could not be found,* there is a real mystery about *all* early Indian beads, whether of bone, stone, or antler. There are millions and millions of these fine beads with pierced holes finer than any piercer ever found. There are residues, there are centers of every other Indian industry, and there is evolution of every other tool. Why have there been these millions of pierced beads, and never one piercer? There was no technique to make so fine a piercer. How were they done?"

Magdalen giggled. "Bead-spitter," she said.

"Bead-spitter! You're out of your fuzzy mind," Terrence erupted. "That's the silliest and least sophisticated of all Indian legends."

"But it *is* the legend," said Robert Derby, "the legend of more than thirty separate tribes. The Carib Indians of Cuba said that they got their beads from Bead-spitters. The Indians of Panama told Balboa the same thing. The Indians of the pueblos told the same story to Coronado. Every Indian community had an Indian who was its Bead-spitter. There are Creek and Alabama and Koasati stories of Bead-spitter; see Swanton's collections. And his stories were taken down within living memory.

"More than that, when European trade-beads were first introduced, there is one account of an Indian receiving some and saying, 'I will take some to Bead-spitter. If he sees them, he can spit them too.' And that Bead-spitter did then spit them by the bushel. There was never any other Indian account of the origin of their beads. *All* were spit by a Bead-spitter."

"Really, this is very unreal," Ethyl said. Really it was.

"Hog hokey! A Bead-spitter of around the year seven hundred could not spit future beads, he could not spit cheap Hong Kong glass beads of the present time!" Terrence was very angry.

"Pardon me, yes sir, he could," said Anteros. "A Bead-spitter can spit future beads, if he faces north when he spits. That has always been known."

Terrence was angry, he fumed and poisoned the day for them, and the claw marks on his face stood out livid purple. He was angrier yet when he said that the curious dark capping rock on top of the chimney was dangerous, that it would fall and kill someone; and Anteros said that there was no such capping rock on the chimney, that Terrence's eyes were deceiving him, that Terrence should go sit in the shade and rest.

And Terrence became excessively angry when he discovered that Magdalen was trying to hide something that she had discovered in the fluted core of the chimney. It was a large and heavy shale-stone, too heavy even for Magdalen's puzzling strength. She had dragged it out of the chimney flute, tumbled it down to the bottom, and was trying to cover it with rocks and scarp.

"Robert, mark the extraction point!" Terrence called loudly. "It's quite plain yet. Magdalen, stop that! Whatever it is, it must be examined now."

"Oh, it's just more of the damned same thing! I wish he'd let me alone. With his kind of money he can get plenty of girls. Besides, it's private, Terrence. You don't have any business reading it."

"You are hysterical, Magdalen, and you may have to leave the digging site."

"I wish I could leave. I can't. I wish I could love. I can't. Why isn't it enough that I die?"

"Howard, spend the afternoon on this," Terrence ordered. "It has writing of a sort on it. If it's what I think it is, it scares me. It's too recent to be in any eroded chimney rock formation, Howard, and it comes from far below the top. Read it."

"A few hours on it and I may come up with something. I never saw anything like it either. What did you think it was, Terrence?"

"What do you think I think it is? It's much later than the other, and that one was impossible. I'll not be the one to confess myself crazy first."

Howard Steinleser went to work on the incised stone; and two hours before sundown they brought him another one, a gray soap-stone block from higher up. Whatever this was covered with, it was not at all the same thing that covered the shale-stone.

And elsewhere things went well, too well. The old fishiness was back on it. No series of finds could be so perfect, no petrification could be so well ordered.

"Robert," Magdalen called down to Robert Derby just at sunset, "in the high meadow above the shore, about four hundred yards down, just past the old fence line—"

"—there is a badger hole, Magdalen. Now you have me doing it, seeing invisible things at a distance. And if I take a carbine and stroll down there quietly, the badger will stick his head out just as I get there (I being strongly downwind of him), and I'll blam him between the eyes. He'll be a big one, fifty pounds."

"Thirty. Bring him, Robert. You're showing a little understanding at last."

"But, Magdalen, badger is rampant meat. It's seldom eaten."

"May not the condemned girl have what she wishes for her last meal? Go get it, Robert."

Robert went. The voice of the little carbine was barely heard at that distance. Soon, Robert brought back the dead badger.

"Cook it, Ethyl," Magdalen ordered.

"Yes, I know. And if I don't know how, Anteros will show me." But Anteros was gone. Robert found him on a sundown knoll with his shoulders hunched. The old man was sobbing silently and his face seemed to be made out of dull pumice stone. But he came back to aid Ethyl in preparing the badger.

"If the first of today's stones scared you, the second should have lifted the hair right off your head, Terrence," Howard Steinleser said. "It does, it does. All the stones are too recent to be in a chimney formation, but this last one is an insult. It isn't two hundred years old, but there's a thousand years of strata above it. What time is deposited here?"

They had eaten rampant badger meat and drunk inferior whiskey (which Anteros, who had given it to them, didn't know was inferior), and the muskiness was both inside them and around them. The campfire sometimes spit angrily with small explosions, and its glare reached high when it did so. By one such leaping glare, Terrence Burdock saw that the curious dark capping rock was once more on top of the chimney. He thought he had seen it there in the daytime; but it had not been there after he had sat in the shade and rested, and it had absolutely not been there when he climbed the chimney itself to be sure.

"Let's have the second chapter and then the third, Howard," Ethyl said. "It's neater that way."

"Yes. Well, the second chapter (the first and lowest and apparently the earliest rock we came on today) is written in a language that no one ever saw written before; and yet it's no great trouble to read it. Even Terrence guessed what it was and it scared him. It is Anadarko-Caddo hand-talk graven in stone. It is what is called the Sign Language of the Plains Indians copied down in formalized pictographs. And it *has* to be very recent, within the last three hundred years. Hand-talk was fragmentary at the first coming of the Spanish, and well developed at the first coming of the French. It was an explosive development, as such things go, worked out within a hundred years. This rock has to be younger than its *situs,* but it was absolutely found in place."

"Read it, Howard, read it," Robert Derby called. Robert was feeling fine and the rest of them were gloomy tonight.

"'I own three hundred ponies,'" Steinleser read the rock out of his memory. "'I own two days' ride north and east and south, and one day's ride west. I give you all. I blast out with a big voice like fire in tall trees, like the explosion of crowning pine trees. I cry like closing-in wolves, like the high voice of the lion, like the hoarse scream of torn calves. Do you not destroy yourself again! You are the dew on crazy-weed in the morning. You are the swift crooked wings of the nighthawk, the dainty feet of the skunk, you are the juice of the sour squash. Why can you not take or give? I am the hump-backed bull of the high plains, I am the river itself and the stagnant pools left by the river, I am the raw earth and the rocks. Come to me, but do not come so violently as to destroy yourself.'

"Ah, that was the text of the first rock of the day, the Anadarko-Caddo hand-talk graven in stone. And final pictographs which I don't understand: a shot-arrow sign, and a boulder beyond."

"'Continued on next rock' of course," said Robert Derby. "Well, why *wasn't* hand-talk ever written down? The signs are simple and easily stylized and they were understood by many different tribes. It would have been natural to write it."

"Alphabetical writing was in the region *before* hand-talk was well developed," Terrence Burdock said. "In fact, it was the coming of the Spanish that gave the impetus to hand-talk. It was really developed for communication between Spanish and Indian, not between Indian and Indian. And yet, I believe, hand-talk *was* written down once; it was the beginning of the Chinese pictographs. And there also it had its beginning as communication between differing peoples. Depend on it, if all mankind had always been of a single language, there would never have been any written language developed at all. Writing always began as a bridge, and there had to be some chasm for it to bridge."

"We have one to bridge here," said Steinleser. "That whole chimney is full of rotten smoke. The highest part of it should be older than the lowest part of the mound, since the mound was built on a base eroded away from the chimney formation. But in many ways they seem to be contemporary. We must all be under a spell here. We've worked two days on this, parts of three days, and the total impossibility of the situation hasn't struck us yet.

"The old Nahuatlan glyphs for Time are the Chimney glyphs. Present time is a lower part of a chimney and fire burning at the base. Past time is black smoke from a chimney, and future time is white smoke from a chimney. There was a signature glyph running through our yesterday's stone which I didn't and don't understand. It seemed to indicate something coming down out of the chimney rather than going up it."

"It really doesn't look much like a chimney," Magdalen said.

"And a maiden doesn't look much like dew on crazy-weed in the morning, Magdalen," Robert Derby said, "but we recognize these identities."

They talked a while about the impossibility of the whole business. "There are scales on our eyes," Steinleser said. "The fluted core of the chimney is wrong. I'm not even sure the rest of the chimney is right."

"No, it isn't," said Robert Derby. "We can identify most of the strata of the chimney with known periods of the river and stream. I was above and below today. There is one stretch where the sandstone was not eroded at all, where it stands three hundred yards back from the shifted river and is overlaid with a hundred years of loam and sod. There are other sections where the stone is cut away variously. We can tell when most of the chimney was laid down, we can find its correspondences up to a few hundred years ago. But when were the top ten feet of it laid down? There were no correspondences anywhere to that. The centuries represented by the strata of the top of the chimney, people, those centuries haven't happened yet."

"And when was the dark capping rock on top of it all formed—?" Terrence began. "Ah, I'm out of my mind. It isn't there. I'm demented."

"No more than the rest of us," said Steinleser. "I saw it too, I thought, today. And then I didn't see it again."

"The rock-writing, it's like an old novel that I only half remember," said Ethyl.

"Oh, that's what it is, yes," Magdalen murmured.

"But I don't remember what happened to the girl in it."

"*I* remember what happened to her, Ethyl," Magdalen said.

"Give us the third chapter, Howard," Ethyl asked. "I want to see how it comes out."

"First you should all have whiskey for those colds," Anteros suggested humbly.

"But none of us have colds," Ethyl objected.

"You take your own medicinal advice, Ethyl, and I'll take mine," Terrence said. "I will have whiskey. My cold is not rheum but fear-chill."

They all had whiskey. They talked a while, and some of them dozed.

"It's late, Howard," Ethyl said after a while. "Let's have the next chapter. Is it the last chapter? Then we'll sleep. We have honest digging to do tomorrow."

"Our third stone, our second stone of the day just past, is another and even later form of writing, and it has never been seen in stone before. It is Kiowa picture writing. The Kiowas did their out-turning spiral writing on buffalo skins dressed almost as fine as vellum. In its more sophisticated form (and this is a copy of that) it is quite late. The Kiowa picture writing probably did not arrive at its excellence until influenced by white artists."

"How late, Steinleser?" Robert Derby asked.

"Not more than a hundred and fifty years old. But I have never seen it copied in stone before. It simply isn't stone-styled. There's a lot of things around here lately that I haven't seen before.

"Well then, to the text, or should I say the pictography? 'You fear the earth, you fear rough ground and rocks, you fear moister earth and rotting flesh, you fear the flesh itself, all flesh is rotting flesh. If you love not rotting flesh, you love not at all. You believe the bridge hanging in the sky, the bridge hung by tendrils and woody vines that diminish as they go up and up till they are no thicker than hairs. There is no sky-bridge, you cannot go up on it. Did you believe that the roots of love grow upside down? They come out of deep earth that is old flesh and brains and hearts and entrails, that is old buffalo bowels and snakes' pizzles, that is black blood and rot and moaning underground. This is old and worn-out and bloody Time, and the roots of love grow out of its gore.'"

"You seem to give remarkably detailed translations of the simple spiral pictures, Steinleser, but I begin to get in the mood of it," Terrence said.

"Ah, perhaps I cheat a little," said Steinleser.

"You lie a lot," Magdalen challenged.

"No I do not. There is some basis for every phrase I've used. It goes on: 'I own twenty-two trade rifles. I own ponies. I own Mexico silver, eight-bit pieces. I am rich in all ways. I give all to you. I cry out with big voice like a bear full of mad-weed, like a bullfrog in love, like a stallion rearing against a puma. It is the earth that calls you. I am the earth, woolier than wolves and rougher than rocks. I am the bog earth that sucks you in. You cannot give, you cannot like, you cannot love, you think there is something else, you think there is a sky-bridge you may loiter on without crashing down. I am bristled-boar earth, there is no other. You will come to me in the morning. You will come to me easy and with grace. Or you will come to me reluctant and you be shattered in every bone and member of you. You be broken by our encounter. You be shattered as by a lightning bolt striking up from the earth. I am the red calf which is in the writings. I am the rotting red earth. Live in the morning or die in the morning, but remember that love in death is better than no love at all.'"

"Oh brother! Nobody gets that stuff from such kid pictures, Steinleser," Robert Derby moaned.

"Ah well, that's the end of the spiral picture. And a Kiowa spiral pictograph ends with either an in-sweep or an out-sweep line. This ends with an out-sweep, which means—"

"'Continued on next rock,' that's what it means," Terrence cried roughly.

"You won't find the next rocks," Magdalen said. "They're hidden, and most of the time they're not there yet, but they will go on and on. But for all that, you'll read it in the rocks tomorrow morning. I want it to be over with. Oh, I don't know what I want!"

"I believe I know what you want tonight, Magdalen," Robert Derby said.

But he didn't.

The talk trailed off, the fire burned down, they went to their sleeping sacks.

Then it was long jagged night, and the morning of the fourth day. But wait! In Nahuat-Tanoan legend, the world ends on the fourth morning. All the lives we lived or thought we lived had been but dreams of third night. The loin cloth that the sun wore on the fourth day's journey was not so valuable as one has made out. It was worn for no more than an hour or so.

And, in fact, there was something terminal about fourth morning. Anteros had disappeared. Magdalen had disappeared. The chimney rock looked greatly diminished in its bulk (something had gone out of it) and much crazier in its broken height. The sun had come up a garish gray-orange color through fog. The signature-glyph of the first stone dominated the ambient. It was as if something were coming down from the chimney, a horrifying smoke; but it was only noisome morning fog.

No it wasn't. There was something else coming down from the chimney, or from the hidden sky: pebbles, stones, indescribable bits of foul oozings, the less fastidious pieces of sky; a light, nightmare rain had begun to fall there; the chimney was apparently beginning to crumble.

"It's the damnedest thing I ever heard about," Robert Derby growled. "Do you think that Magdalen really went off with Anteros?" Derby was bitter and fumatory this morning and his face was badly clawed.

"Who is Magdalen? Who is Anteros?" Ethyl Burdock risked.

Terrence Burdock was hooting from high on the mound. "All come up," he called. "Here is a find that will make it all worthwhile. We'll have to photo and sketch and measure and record and witness. It's the finest basalt head I've ever seen, man-sized, and I suspect that there's a man-sized body attached to it. We'll soon clean it and clear it. Gah! What a weird fellow he was!" But Howard Steinleser was studying a brightly colored something that he held in his two hands.

"What is it, Howard? What are you doing?" Derby demanded.

"Ah, I believe this is the next stone in the sequence. The writing is alphabetical but deformed—there is an element missing. I believe it is in modern English, and I will solve the deformity and see it true in a minute. The text of it seems to be—"

Rocks and stones were coming down from the chimney, and fog, amnesic and wit-stealing fog.

"Steinleser, are you all right?" Robert Derby asked with compassion. "That isn't a stone that you hold in your hand."

"It isn't a stone? I thought it was. What is it then?"

"It is the fruit of the Osage orange tree, an American moraceous. It isn't a stone, Howard." And the thing was a tough, woody, wrinkled mock-orange, as big as a small melon.

"You have to admit that the wrinkles look a little bit like writing, Robert."

"Yes, they look a little like writing, Howard. Let us go up where Terrence is bawling for us. You've read too many stones. And it isn't safe here."

"Why go up, Robert? The other thing is coming down."

It was the bristled-boar earth reaching up with a rumble. It was a lightning bolt struck upward out of the earth, and it got its prey. There was explosion and roar. The dark capping rock was jerked from the top of the chimney and slammed with terrible force to the earth, shattering with a great shock. And something else that had been on that capping rock. And the whole chimney collapsed about them.

She was broken by the encounter. She was shattered in every bone and member of her. And she was dead.

"Who—Who is she?" Howard Steinleser stuttered.

"Oh God! Magdalen, of course!" Robert Derby cried.

"I remember her a little bit. Didn't understand her. She put out like an evoking moth but she wouldn't be had. Near clawed the face off me the other night when I misunderstood the signals. She believed there was a sky-bridge. It's in a lot of the mythologies. But there isn't one, you know. Oh well."

"The girl is dead! Damnation! What are you doing grubbing in those stones?"

"Maybe she isn't dead in them yet, Robert. I'm going to read what's here before something happens to them. This capping rock that fell and broke, it's impossible, of course. It's a stratum that hasn't been laid down yet. I always did want to read the future and I may never get another chance."

"You fool! The girl's dead! Does nobody care? Terrence, stop bellowing about your find. Come down. The girl's dead."

"Come up, Robert and Howard," Terrence insisted. "Leave that broken stuff down there. It's worthless. But nobody ever saw anything like this."

"Do come up, men," Ethyl sang. "Oh, it's a wonderful piece! I never saw anything like it in my life."

"Ethyl, is the whole morning mad?" Robert Derby demanded as he came up to her. "She's dead. Don't you really remember her? Don't you remember Magdalen?"

"I'm not sure. Is she the girl down there? Isn't she the same girl who's been hanging around here a couple of days? She shouldn't have been playing on that high rock. I'm sorry she's dead. But just look what we're uncovering here!"

"Terrence. Don't *you* remember Magdalen?"

"The girl down there? She's a little bit like the girl that clawed the hell out of me the other night. Next time someone goes to town they might mention to the sheriff that there's a dead girl here. Robert, did you ever see a face like this one? And it digs away to reveal the shoulders. I believe there's a whole man-sized figure here. Wonderful, wonderful!"

"Terrence, you're off your head. Well, do you remember Anteros?"

"Certainly, the twin of Eros, but nobody ever made much of the symbol of unsuccessful love. Thunder! That's the name for him! It fits him perfectly. We'll call him Anteros."

Well, it *was* Anteros, lifelike in basalt stone. His face was contorted. He was sobbing soundlessly and frozenly and his shoulders were hunched with emotion. The carving was fascinating in its miserable passion, his stony love unrequited. Perhaps he was more impressive now than he would be when he was cleaned. He was earth, he was earth itself. Whatever period the carving belonged to, it was outstanding in its power.

"The live Anteros, Terrence. Don't you remember our digging man, Anteros Manypenny?"

"Sure. He didn't show up for work this morning, did he? Tell him he's fired."

"Magdalen is dead! She was one of us! Dammit, she was the main one of us!" Robert Derby cried. Terrence and Ethyl Burdock were earless to his outburst. They were busy uncovering the rest of the carving.

And down below, Howard Steinleser was studying dark broken rocks before they would disappear, studying a stratum that hadn't been laid down yet, reading a foggy future.

How I Wrote "Continued on Next Rock"
An Afterword by R. A. Lafferty

To ask how any story or tune or statue comes about is to ask "How is it done?"; "What does it take?" Have you heard of the Dutch boy in this country who was going to butcher school, whose schoolmates tried to mix him up? The heart, they told him, that is named the liver; the bladder is called the stomach; the tongue is the coccyx; the loin is known as the chuck; the brisket is the flank; the lungs are named the trotters; and so on. This Dutch kid was very smart, however; he figured out that they were having him, and he figured out the right names for everything, or for almost everything. And he passed his final examination with top grades both in meat-cutting and nomenclature. "How were you able to do it," the instructor asked, "with so many things going against you?" "I've got it up there," the Dutch kid said, and he tapped his head. "Kidneys."

It isn't exactly that one should use kidneys for brains, but the sense of grotesque juxtaposition *does* come in handy. You can't be sure you are looking at something from the right angle till you have looked at it from every angle. How did I write "Continued on Next Rock" then? Upside down and backward, of course. I started with a simple, but I believe novel, idea that had to do with time. Then I involuted the idea of time (making all things contemporary or at least repeating), and I turned the systems of values backward, trying to make the repulsive things appear poetic ("the nobility of badgers, the serenity of toads") and trying to set anti-love up as comparable to love (the flattest thing you can imagine has to have at least two sides; it can have many more). I let the characters that had been generated by this action work out their own way then. After this, I subtracted the original simple but novel idea from the story, and finished things up. (The original idea was a catalyst which could be recovered practically unchanged at the end of the reaction.)

The beginning idea, which I give to anyone who wants it, was simply to have archeologists digging *upward* through certain strata, for rather vague topographic reasons, come to deposits of the fairly recent past, or the very recent past, of the near future (a discarded license plate from fifteen years in the future, for instance), then the more distant future, then to realize that the strata still remaining above them had to contain the remnants of at least a hundred thousand years of unfaked future.

So much for the genesis of one particular short story. Each one is different but each one is anomalous; and there is a reason for that. No normal or reasonable or balanced or well-adjusted person is going to attempt the making of a story or a tune or a statue or a poem; he'll have no need for such abnormal activity. A person has to be somehow deficient or lacking in person or personality or he will not attempt these things. He must be very deficient or lacking if he will succeed at all in them. Every expression in art or pseudo-art is a crutch that a crippled person makes and donates to the healthy world for its use (the healthy world having only the vaguest idea that it even needs crutches).

There are, I know, many apparent glaring exceptions to the rule that only persons who are deficient or lacking in person or personality will contribute any creative content. Believe me, these exceptions are only apparent. There is something badly unbalanced in every one of them.

Carry it one step further, though. One of the legends, unwritten from the beginning and maybe unwritten forever, is about a Quest for the Perfect Thing. But it is really the quest for the normal thing. Can you find, anywhere in the world, behind or before or present, even one person who is really normal and reasonable and balanced and well-adjusted? This is the Perfect Thing, if it or he or she is ever found, and if ever found there will be no further need of any art or attempted art, good or bad.

Enough of such stuff, end of article, if this is an article. I am both facetious and serious in every written word here.

Sky

Introduction by Gwenda Bond

Reading an R. A. Lafferty story is always a bit of a trippy experience—a journey into the odder parts of experience, his perceptively askew perspective a looking glass all its own. But "Sky" is about an actual trip (or a few of them), with all the inspired psychedelia and questionable reality we expect—and desire—from a Lafferty story. The title's Sky isn't the airy horizon above us. No, it's the unusual substance sold by the furry-handed "Sky-Seller" who can't survive in sunlight (or thinks he can't anyway) to ostensible main character Welkin Alauda.

A 1972 Hugo nominee, "Sky" sits at the intersection of the absurd and the transcendental. There are deadpan assurances of fantastical dangers: "You will burn," Welkin told him. "Nobody burns so as when sunning himself on a cloud." There is the observational commentary of some unseen but nonetheless present narrator on both the characters and the grim world that surrounds them; of Welkin we're told "it was said that her bones were hollow and filled with air." The Sky-Diving friends of Welkin discuss time and the universe, existence and falls through it, in perfect rose-colored stoner parlance. We sense the end of a journey coming as we read, and we know it will be quite a crash. Welkin wanders through caverns filled with Amanita mushroom varieties, deadly and hallucinogenic, gathered by not just the Sky-Seller but moles.

The results that follow this final trip linger with the reader. So enjoy this delightful trance of a tale, but, always remember, Sky has its dangers.

Sky

The Sky-Seller was Mr. Furtive himself, fox-muzzled, ferret-eyed, slithering along like a snake, and living under the Rocks. The Rocks had not been a grand place for a long time. It had been built in the grand style on a mephitic plot of earth (to transform it), but the mephitic earth had won out. The apartments of the Rocks had lost their sparkle as they had been divided again and again, and now they were shoddy. The Rocks had weathered. Its once pastel hues were now dull grays and browns.

The five underground levels had been parking places for motor vehicles when those were still common, but now these depths were turned into warrens and hovels. The Sky-Seller lurked and lived in the lowest and smallest and meanest of them all.

He came out only at night. Daylight would have killed him; he knew that. He sold out of the darkest shadows of the night. He had only a few (though oddly select) clients, and nobody knew who his supplier was. He said that he had no supplier, that he gathered and made the stuff himself.

Welkin Alauda, a full-bodied but light-moving girl (it was said that her bones were hollow and filled with air), came to the Sky-Seller just before first light, just when he had become highly nervous but had not yet bolted to his underground.

"A sack of Sky from the nervous mouse. Jump, or the sun will gobble your house!" Welkin sang-song, and she was already higher than most skies.

"Hurry, hurry!" the Sky-Seller begged, thrusting the sack to her while his black eyes trembled and glittered (if real light should ever reflect into them he'd go blind).

Welkin took the sack of Sky, and scrambled money notes into his hands which had furred palms. (Really? Yes, really.)

"World be flat and the Air be round, wherever the Sky grows underground," Welkin intoned, taking the sack of Sky and soaring along with a light scamper of feet (she hadn't much weight, her bones were hollow). And the Sky-Seller darted headfirst down a black well-shaft thing to his depths.

Four of them went Sky-Diving that morning, Welkin herself, Karl Vlieger, Icarus Riley, Joseph Alzarsi; and the pilot was—(no, not who you think, he had already threatened to turn them all in; they'd use that pilot no more)—the pilot was Ronald Kolibri in his little crop-dusting plane.

But a crop-duster will not go up to the frosty heights they liked to take off from. Yes it will—if everybody is on Sky. But it isn't pressurized, and it doesn't carry oxygen. That doesn't matter, not if everybody is on Sky, not if the plane is on Sky too.

Welkin took Sky with Mountain Whizz, a carbonated drink. Karl stuffed it into his lip like snuff. Icarus Riley rolled it and smoked it. Joseph Alzarsi needled it, mixed with drinking alcohol, into his main vein. The pilot, Ronny, tongued and chewed it like sugar dust. The plane named *Shrike* took it through the manifold.

Fifty thousand feet—you can't go that high in a crop-duster. Thirty below zero—ah, that isn't cold! Air too thin to breathe at all—with Sky, who needs such included things as air?

Welkin stepped out, and went up, not down. It was a trick she often pulled. She hadn't much weight; she could always get higher than the rest of them. She went up and up until she disappeared. Then she drifted down again, completely enclosed in a sphere of ice crystal, sparkling inside it and making monkey faces at them.

The wind yelled and barked, and the divers took off. They all went down, soaring and gliding and tumbling; standing still sometimes, it seemed; even rising again a little. They went down to clouds and spread out on them; dark-white clouds with the sun inside them and suffusing them both from above and below. They cracked Welkin's ice-crystal sphere and she stepped out of it. They ate the thin pieces of it, very cold and brittle and with a tang of ozone. Alzarsi took off his shirt and sunned himself on a cloud.

"You will burn," Welkin told him. "Nobody burns so as when sunning himself on a cloud." That was true.

They sank through the black-whiteness of these clouds and came into the limitless blue concourse with clouds above and below them. It was in this same concourse that Hippodameia used to race her horses, there not being room for such coursers to run on Earth. The clouds below folded up and the clouds above folded down, forming a discrete space.

"We have our own rotundity and sphere here," said Icarus Riley (these are their Sky-Diver names, not their legal names), "and it is apart from all worlds and bodies. The worlds and bodies do not exist for as long a time as we say that they do not exist. The axis of our present space is its own concord. Therefore, it being in perfect concord, Time stops."

All their watches had stopped, at least.

"But there *is* a world below," said Karl. "It is an abject world, and we can keep it abject forever if we wish. But it has at least a shadowy existence, and later we will let it fill out again in our compassion for lowly things. It is flat, though, and we must insist that it remain flat."

"This is important," Joseph said with the deep importance of one on Sky. "So long as our own space is bowed and globed, the world must remain flat or depressed. But the world must not be allowed to bow its back again. We are in danger if it ever does. So long as it is truly flat and abject it cannot crash ourselves to it."

"How long could we fall," Welkin asked, "if we had not stopped time, if we let it flow at its own pace, or at ours? How long could we fall?"

"Hephaestus once tumbled through space all day long," Icarus Riley said, "and the days were longer then."

Karl Vlieger had gone wall-eyed from an interior-turned sexual passion that he often experienced in diving. Icarus Riley seemed to be on laughing gas suddenly; this is a sign that Sky is not having a perfect effect. Joseph Alzarsi felt a cold wind down his spine and a series of jerky little premonitions.

"We are not perfect," Joseph said. "Tomorrow or the next day we may be, for we *do* approach perfection. We win a round. And we win another. Let us not throw away our victory today through carelessness. The Earth has bowed his old back a little bit, and we make ready for him! Now, guys, now!"

Four of them (or maybe only three of them) pulled the rings. The chutes unpeeled, flowered, and jerked. They had been together like a sheaf in close conversation. But suddenly, on coming to earth, they were spread out over five hundred yards.

They assembled. They packed their chutes. That would be all the diving for that day.

"Welkin, how did you pack your chute so quickly?" Icarus asked her suspiciously.

"I don't know."

"You are always the slowest one of us, and the sloppiest. Someone always has to reroll your chute for you before it is used again. And you were the last one to land just now. How were you the first one to be packed? How did you roll it so well? It has the earmarks of my own rolling, just as I rolled it for you before we took off this morning."

"I don't know, Icarus. Oh, I think I'll go up again, straight up."

"No, you've sailed and dived enough for one morning. Welkin, did you even open your chute?"

"I don't know."

High on Sky, they went up again the next morning. The little plane named *Shrike* flew up as no plane had ever flown before, up through Storm. The storm-shrouded Earth shrank to the size of a pea-doogie.

"We will play a trick on it," said Welkin. "When you're on Sky you can play a trick on anything and make it abide by it. I will say that the pea-doogie that was the world is nothing. See, it is gone. Then I will select another pea-doogie, that one there, and I will call it the world. And that is the world that we will come down to in a little while. I've switched worlds on the world, and it doesn't know what happened to it."

"It's uneasy, though," Joseph Alzarsi spoke through flared nostrils. "You shook it. No wonder the world has its moments of self-doubt."

They were one million feet high. The altimeter didn't go that high, but Ronald Kolibri, the pilot, wrote out the extended figure in chalk to make it correct. Welkin stepped out. Karl and Icarus and Joseph stepped out. Ronald Kolibri stepped out, but only for a while. Then he remembered that he was the pilot and got back in the plane. They were so high that the air was black and star-filled instead of blue. It was so cold that the empty space was full of cracks and potholes. They dived half a million feet in no time at all. They pulled up laughing.

It was invigorating, it was vivifying. They stamped on the clouds, and the clouds rang like frosty ground. This was the ancestral country of all hoarfrost, of all grained-snow and glare-ice. Here was weather-maker, here was wind-son. They came into caves of ice mixed with moraine; they found antler hatchets and Hemicyon bones; they found coals still glowing. The winds bayed and hunted in packs through the chasms. These were the cold Fortean clouds, and their location is commonly quite high.

They came down below Storm, finding new sun and new air. It was pumpkin-summer, it was deep autumn in the sky.

They dropped again, miles and millennia, to full Sky-summer: the air so blue that it grew a violet patina on it to save the surface. Their own space formed about them again, as it did every day, and time stopped.

But not motion! Motion never stopped with them. Do you realize that nothingness in a void can still be in motion? And how much more they of the great centrality! There was Dynamic; there was sustaining vortex; there was the high serenity of fevered motion.

But is not motion merely a relationship of space to time? No. That is an idea that is common to people who live on worlds, but it is a subjective idea. Here, beyond the possible influence of any worlds, there was living motion without reference.

"Welkin, you look quite different today," Joseph Alzarsi spoke in wonder. "What is it?"

"I don't know. It's wonderful to be different and I'm wonderful."

"It is something missing from you," said Icarus. "I believe it is a defect missing."

"But I hadn't any, Icarus."

They were in central and eternal moment, and it did not end, it could not end, it goes on yet. Whatever else seems to happen, it is merely in parentheses to that moment.

"It is time to consider again," Icarus mused after a while. There is no time or while in the Moment, but there is in the parentheses. "I hope it is the last time we will ever have to consider. We, of course, are in our own space and beyond time or tangent. But the Earth, such as it is, is approaching with great presumption and speed."

"But it's *nothing* to us!" Karl Vlieger suddenly raged out in a chthonic and phallic passion. "We can shatter it! We can shoot it to pieces like a clay pigeon! It cannot rush onto us like a slashing dog. Get down, world! Heel, you cur! Heel, I say!"

"We say to one world 'rise' and it rises, and to another one 'heel' and it heels," Icarus Sky-spoke in his dynamic serenity.

"Not yet," Joseph Alzarsi warned. "Tomorrow we will be total. Today we are not yet. Possibly we *could* shatter the world like a clay pigeon if we wished, but we would not be lords of it if we had to shatter it."

"We could always make another world," said Welkin reasonably.

"Certainly, but this one is our testing. We will go to it when it is crouched down. We cannot allow it to come ravening to us. Hold! Hold there, we order you!"

And the uprushing world halted, cowed.

"We go down," said Joseph. "We will let it come up only when it is properly broken."

("And they inclined the heavens and came down.")

Once more, three of them pulled the rings. And the chutes unpeeled, flowered, and jerked. They had been like a sheaf together in their moment; but now, coming to earth, they were suddenly scattered out over five hundred yards.

"Welkin, you didn't have your chute at all today!" Icarus gaped with some awe when they had assembled again. "That is what was different about you."

"No, I guess I didn't have it. There was no reason to have it if I didn't need it. Really, there was never any reason for me to have used one at all, ever."

"Ah, we *were* total today and didn't know it," Joseph ventured. "Tomorrow none of us will wear chutes. This is easier than I had believed."

Welkin went to the Sky-Seller to buy new Sky that night. Not finding him in the nearer shadows of the Rocks, she went down and down, drawn by the fungoid odor and the echoing dampness of the underground. She went through passages that were man-made, through passages that were natural, through passages that were unnatural. Some of these corridors, it is true, had once been built by men, but now they had reverted and became most unnatural deep-earth caverns. Welkin went down into the total blackness where there were certain small things that still mumbled out a faint white color; but it was the wrong color white, and the things were all of a wrong shape.

There was the dead white shape of Mycelium masses, the grotesqueness of Agaricus, the deformity of Deadly Amanita and of Morel. The gray-milky Lactarius glowed like light-less lanterns in the dark; there was the blue-white of the Deceiving Clitocybe and the yellow-white of the Caesar Agaric. There was the insane ghost-white of the deadliest and queerest of them all, the Fly Amanita, and a mole was gathering this.

"Mole, bring Sky for the Thing Serene, for the Minions tall and the Airy Queen," Welkin jangled. She was still high on Sky, but it had begun to leave her a little and she had the veriest touch of the desolate sickness.

"Sky for the Queen of the buzzing drones, with her hollow heart and her hollow bones," the Sky-Seller intoned hollowly.

"And fresh, Oh I want it fresh, fresh Sky!" Welkin cried.

"With these creatures there is no such thing as fresh," the Sky-Seller told her. "You want it stale, Oh so stale! Ingrown and aged and with its own mold grown moldy."

"Which is it?" Welkin demanded. "What is the name of the one you gather it from?"

"The Fly Amanita."

"But isn't that simply a poisonous mushroom?"

"It has passed beyond that. It has sublimated. Its simple poison has had its second fermenting into narcotic."

"But it sounds so cheap that it be merely narcotic."

"Not merely narcotic. It is something very special in narcotic."

"No, no, not narcotic at all!" Welkin protested. "It is liberating, it is world-shattering. It is Height Absolute. It is motion and detachment itself. It is the ultimate. It is mastery."

"Why, then it is mastery, lady. It is the highest and lowest of all created things."

"No, no," Welkin protested again, "not created. It is not born, it is not made. I couldn't stand that. It is the highest of all uncreated things."

"Take it, take it," the Sky-Seller growled, "and be gone. Something begins to curl up inside me."

"I go!" Welkin said, "And I will be back many times for more."

"No, you will not be. Nobody ever comes back many times for Sky. You will be back never. Or one time. I think that you will be back one time."

They went up again the next morning, the last morning. But why should we say that it was the last morning? Because there would no longer be divisions or days for them. It would be one last eternal day for them now, and nothing could break it.

They went up in the plane that had once been named *Shrike* and was now named *Eternal Eagle*. The plane had repainted itself during the night with new name and new symbols, some of them not immediately understandable. The plane snuffled Sky into its manifolds, and grinned and roared. And the plane went up!

Oh! Jerusalem in the Sky! How it went up!

They were all certainly perfect now and would never need Sky again. *They were Sky.*

"How little the world is!" Welkin rang out. "The towns are like fly-specks and the cities are like flies."

"It is wrong that so ignoble a creature as the Fly should have the exalted name," Icarus complained.

"I'll fix that," Welkin sang. "I give edict: that all the flies on Earth be dead!" And all the flies on Earth died in that instant.

"I wasn't sure you could do that," said Joseph Alzarsi. "The wrong is righted. Now we ourselves assume the noble name of Flies. There are no Flies but us!"

The five of them, including the pilot, Ronald Kolibri, stepped chuteless out of the *Eternal Eagle*. "Will you be all right?" Ronald asked the rollicking plane. "Certainly," the plane said. "I believe I know where there are other *Eternal Eagles*. I will mate."

It was cloudless, or else they had developed the facility of seeing through clouds. Or perhaps it was that, the Earth having become as small as a marble, the clouds around it were insignificant.

Pure light that had an everywhere source! (The sun also had become insignificant and didn't contribute much to the light.) Pure and intense motion that had no location reference. They weren't going anywhere with their intense motion (they already *were* everywhere, or at the supercharged center of everything).

Pure cold fever. Pure serenity. Impure hyper-space passion of Karl Vlieger, and then of all of them; but it was purely rampant at least. Stunning beauty in all things along with a towering cragginess that was just ugly enough to create an ecstasy.

Welkin Alauda was mythic with nenuphars in her hair. And it shall not be told what Joseph Alzarsi wore in his own hair. An always-instant, a million or a billion years!

Not monotony, no! Presentation! Living sets! Scenery! The scenes were formed for the splinter of a moment; or they were formed forever. Whole worlds formed in a pregnant void: not spherical worlds merely, but dodeka-spherical, and those much more intricate than that. Not merely seven colors to play with, but seven to the seventh and to the seventh again.

Stars vivid in the bright light. You who have seen stars only in darkness be silent! Asteroids that they ate like peanuts, for now they were all metamorphic giants. Galaxies like herds of rampaging elephants. Bridges so long that both ends of them receded over the light-speed edges. Waterfalls, of a finer water, that bounced off galaxy clusters as if they were boulders.

Through a certain ineptitude of handling, Welkin extinguished the old sun with one such leaping torrent.

"It does not matter," Icarus told her. "Either a million or a billion years had passed according to the timescale of the bodies, and surely the sun had already come onto dim days. You can always make other suns."

Karl Vlieger was casting lightning bolts millions of parsecs long and making looping contact with clustered galaxies with them.

"Are you sure that we are not using up any time?" Welkin asked them with some apprehension.

"Oh, time still uses itself up, but we are safely out of the reach of it all," Joseph explained. "Time is only one very inefficient method of counting numbers. It is inefficient because it is limited in its numbers, and because the counter by such a system must die when he has come to the end of his series. That alone should weigh against it as a mathematical system; it really shouldn't be taught."

"Then nothing can hurt us ever?" Welkin wanted to be reassured.

"No, nothing can come at us except inside time and we are outside it. Nothing can collide with us except in space and we disdain space. Stop it, Karl! As you do it that's buggery."

"I have a worm in my own tract and it gnaws at me a little," the pilot Ronald Kolibri said. "It's in my internal space and it's crunching along at a pretty good rate."

"No, no, that's impossible. Nothing can reach or hurt us," Joseph insisted.

"I have a worm of my own in a still more interior tract," said Icarus, "the tract that they never quite located in the head or the heart or the bowels. Maybe this tract always was outside space. Oh, my worm doesn't gnaw, but it stirs. Maybe I'm tired of being out of reach of everything."

"Where do these doubts rise from?" Joseph sounded querulous. "You hadn't them an instant ago, you hadn't them as recently as ten million years ago. How can you have them now when there isn't any now?"

"Well, as to that—" Icarus began—(and a million years went by)—"as to that I have a sort of cosmic curiosity about an object in my own past—"—(another million years went by)—"an object called world."

"Well, satisfy your curiosity then," Karl Vlieger snapped. "Don't you even know how to make a world?"

"Certainly I know how, but will it be the same?"

"Yes, if you're good enough. It will be the same if you make it the same."

Icarus Riley made a world. He wasn't very good at it and it wasn't quite the same, but it did resemble the old world a little.

"I want to see if some things are still there," Welkin clamored. "Bring it closer."

"It's unlikely your things are still there," Joseph said, "Remember that billions of years may have passed."

"The things will be there if I put them there," Icarus insisted.

"And you cannot bring it closer since all distance is now infinite," Karl maintained.

"At least I can focus it better," Icarus insisted, and he did. The world appeared quite near.

"It remembers us like a puppy would," Welkin said. "See, it jumps up at us."

"It's more like a lion leaping for a treed hunter just out of reach," Icarus grudged. "But we are *not* treed."

"It can't ever reach us, and it wants to," Welkin piqued. "Let's reach down to it." ("And they inclined the heavens and went down.")

A most peculiar thing happened to Ronald Kolibri as he touched Earth. He seemed to have a seizure. He went slack-faced, almost horror-faced, and he would not answer the others.

"What is it, Ronald?" Welkin begged in kindred anguish. "Oh, what is it? Somebody help him!"

Then Ronald Kolibri did an even more peculiar thing. He began to fold up and break up from the bottom. Bones slowly splintered and pierced out of him and his entrails gushed out. He compressed. He shattered. He splashed. Can a man splash?

The same sort of seizure overtook Karl Vlieger: the identical slack-face horror-face, the same folding up and breaking up from the bottom, the same hideous sequence.

And Joseph Alzarsi went into the same sundering state, baffled and breaking up.

"Icarus, what's happened to them?" Welkin screamed. "What is the slow loud booming?"

"They're dead. How could that be?" Icarus puzzled trembling. "Death is in time, and we are not."

Icarus himself passed through time as he crashed earth, breaking up, spilling out more odiously than any of them.

And Welkin touched earth, crashed, then what? She heard her own slow loud booming as she hit.

(Another million years went by, or some weeks.)

A shaky old woman on crutches was going down the middle-of-the-night passages that are under the Rocks. She was too old a woman to be Welkin Alauda, but not too old for a Welkin who had lived millions of years outside of time.

She had not died. She was lighter than the others, and besides she had done it twice before unscathed. But that was before she had known fear.

Naturally they had told her that she would never walk again; and now most unnaturally she was walking with crutches. Drawn by the fungoid odor and the echoing dampness she went down in the total dark to where small things were growing with the wrong color white and were all of the wrong shape. She wanted one thing only, and she would die without it.

"Sky for salving the broken Crone! Sky for the weal of my hollow bone!" she crackled in an old-woman voice. But it was only her own voice that echoed back to her.

Should a Sky-Seller live forever?

Cliffs That Laughed

Introduction by Gregory Feeley

"Cliffs That Laughed" appeared in the March 1969 issue of *Magazine of Horror*, surely one of Lafferty's less likely markets (it was edited by Robert A. W. Lowndes, who had published some of Lafferty's earliest stories and who doubtless knew enough to ask for more). It was reprinted in Lafferty's second collection, 1972's *Strange Doings,* but has scarcely been seen since. It certainly cannot be called a horror story, although what Freud called "the horror of incest" definitely plays a role. But what kind of story is it?

It's a tale told in a bar, at least in part—but interleaved with another tale, told decades earlier to the same narrator, by a Malay storyteller he met while stationed in Indonesia, who gained new inspiration when he gained access to American comic books. The storyteller's tale, which begins with "flute notes ascending" and ends with "flute notes descending," offers a pleasing sense of unity, but the other story, about three soldiers who disappeared on an Indonesian island in 1945, "keeps interposing itself" upon it. In the end, however, the two tales complete each other, forming a deeply bizarre saga that the narrator (his protestations notwithstanding) weaves into a third tale, the one we read.

The tale's elements will be familiar for Lafferty fans: a bloodthirsty but colorful pirate; a willful young woman intent on withholding sexual favors; a fell scheme foiled by a clever trick. Neither will these readers be surprised by the rather idealized portrait of pirates, nor with what Andrew Ferguson calls Lafferty's "lurid depictions of death and dismemberment." What does startle us is that the trick turns on the incest taboo, something Lafferty never otherwise wrote about. The brutal but poetic Willy Jones finally wins over Margaret, daughter of a man he murdered, and succeeds in consummating his love, but when he disregards her warning not to resume pirating, she exacts a grotesque vengeance upon his return to their sinister island, which forever frustrates his desire to "board" his wife lest he unwittingly commit the abomination of incest. Since her trick requires both Margaret and her nubile—indeed indistinguishable—daughter (born and bred during Willy's twenty-year absence) to be at once dead and alive, the grotesque family romance seethes with the Freudian *unheimlich* or uncanny, and leads in time to father, mother, and daughter banding perversely together to attract other men to the island and then slaughter them as they "frolicked" with the two beautiful women.

This tangle of rage and baffled lust—the impulse to incest deflected into murderous resolve—gets its sequel in the tale told in the bar, by an American soldier who alone escaped from Willy Jones Island in 1945 and now, after twenty years' journeying home, wishes for nothing but to go back again. A Malay folk tale updated by *Wonder Woman* (complete with numerous elements common to incest myths, such as identical mother and daughter and a questing figure who was declared dead yet is still alive) turns into the evocation of a composite Belle Dame Sans Merci, who leaves the men she encounters wracked by sexual enthrallment and desolation. It is a strange short story even for Lafferty, and this is without mentioning the "golems" (who are clearly something else) or the uncanny intermediate condition that haunts the text, such as the "middle state" between life and death (which mother and daughter now inhabit) or the "middle land" that the soldier traverses beneath the earth.

And what does the title signify? There are no cliffs in the story. The soldier now returning to his death remembers the two women as being "like volcanoes" and declares that "we climbed them like mountains. Man, the uplift on them! The shoulders were cliffs that laughed. The swaying—"

It's an odd image (it does not sound like shoulders that he is praising) and recalls a short story Lafferty published a year later, "The Cliff Climbers," in which the eponymous cliff—which the narrator tells us at the outset is actually "a spire"—clearly (like the "up-thrust" or "rock chimney" in "Continued on Next Rock," also published in 1970) stands as a synecdoche, too blatant for readers to overlook, for a centuries-long male desire, one that (as in "Continued on Next Rock") proves destructive to both pursuer and pursued.

Lafferty's use of "cliff" as an image of displaced sexuality remains finally mysterious, as do his reasons for offering a different version of the three soldiers' disappearance in his 1971 novel *The Devil is Dead*. "There is only one story in the world," the storyteller reminds us, and the version proffered in "Cliffs That Laughed" gives us myth, humor, and virtuosity. For utter clarity, you need look to another writer.

Cliffs That Laughed

Between ten and ten-thirty of the morning of October 1, 1945, on an island that is sometimes called Pulau Petir and sometimes Willy Jones Island (neither of them its map name), three American soldiers disappeared and have not been seen since.

"I'm going back there, I tell you! It was worth it. The limbs that laughed! Let them kill me! I'll get there! Oh, here, here, I've got to get hold of myself.

"The three soldiers were Sergeant Charles Santee of Orange, Texas; Corporal Robert Casper of Gobey, Tennessee; and PFC Timothy Lorrigan of Boston which is in one of the eastern states. I was one of those three soldiers.

"I'm going back there if it takes me another twenty years!"

No, no, no! That's the wrong story. It happened on Willy Jones Island also, but it's a different account entirely. That's the one the fellow told me in a bar years later, just the other night, after the usual "Didn't I used to know you in the Islands?"

"One often makes these little mistakes and false starts," Galli said. "It is a trick that is used in the trade. One exasperates people and pretends to be embarrassed. And then one hooks them."

Galli was an hereditary storyteller of the Indies. "There is only one story in the world," he said, "and it pulls two ways. There is the reason part that says, 'Hell, it can't be' and there is the wonder part that says, 'Hell, maybe it is.'" He was the storyteller, and he offered to teach me the art.

For we ourselves had a hook into Galli. We had something he wanted.

"We used the same stories for a thousand years," he said. "Now, however, we have a new source, the American Comic Books. My grandfather began to use these in another place and time, and I use them now. I steal them from your orderly tents, and I have a box full of them. I have *Space Comics* and *Commander Midnight*; I have *Galactic Gob* and *Mighty Mouse* and the *Green Hornet* and the *Masked Jetter*. My grandfather also had copies of some of these, but drawn by older hands. But I do not have *Wonder Woman*, not a single copy. I would trade three-for-one for copies of her. I would pay a premium. I can link her in with an island legend to create a whole new cycle of stories, and I need new stuff all the time. Have you a *Wonder Woman*?"

When Galli said this, I knew that I had him. I didn't have a *Wonder Woman*, but I knew where I could steal one. I believe, though I am no longer sure, that it was *Wonder Woman Meets the Space Magicians*.

I stole it for him. And in gratitude Galli not only taught me the storyteller's art, but he also told me the following story:

"Imagine about flute notes ascending," said Galli. "I haven't my flute with me, but a story should begin so to set the mood. Imagine about ships coming out of the Arabian Ocean, and finally to Jilolo Island, and still more finally to the very island on which we now stand. Imagine about waves and trees that were the great-great-grandfathers of the waves and trees we now have."

It was about the year 1620, Galli is telling it, in the late afternoon of the high piracy. These Moluccas had already been the rich Spice Islands for three hundred years. Moreover, they were on the road of the Manila galleons coming from Mexico and the Isthmus. Arabian, Hindu, and Chinese piracy had decayed shamefully. The English were crude at the business. In trade the Dutch had become dominant in the Islands and the Portuguese had faded. There was no limit to the opportunities for a courageous and dedicated raider in the Indies.

They came. And not the least of these new raiding men was Willy Jones.

It was said that Willy Jones was a Welshman. You can believe it or not as you like. The same thing has been said about the Devil. Willy was twenty-five years old when he finally possessed his own ship with a mixed crew. The ship was built like a humpbacked bird, with a lateen sail and suddenly appearing rows of winglike oars. On its prow was a swooping bird that had been carved in Muskat. It was named the *Flying Serpent*, or the *Feathered Snake*, depending on what language you use.

"Pause a moment," said Galli. "Set the mood. Imagine about dead men variously. We come to the bloody stuff at once."

One early morning, the *Feathered Snake* overtook a tall Dutchman. The ships were grappled together, and the men from the *Snake* boarded the Dutch ship. The men on the Dutchman were armed, but they had never seen such suddenness and savagery as shown by the dark men from the *Snake*. There was slippery blood on the decks, and the croaking of men being killed. "I forgot to tell you that this was in the passage between the Molucca Sea and the Banda," Galli said.

The *Snake* took a rich small cargo from the Dutch ship, a few able-bodied Malay seamen, some gold specie, some papers of record, and a dark Dutch girl named Margaret. These latter things Willy Jones preempted for himself. Then the *Snake* devoured that tall Dutchman and left only a few of its burning bones floating in the ocean.

"I forgot to tell you that the tall Dutch ship was named the *Luchtkastell*," Galli said.

Willy Jones watched the *Luchtkastell* disappearing under the water. He examined the papers of record, and the dark Dutch girl Margaret. He made a sudden decision: he would cash his winnings and lay up for a season.

He had learned about an island in the papers of record. It was a rich island, belonging to the richest of the Dutch spice men who had gone to the bottom with the *Luchtkastell*. The fighting crew would help Willy Jones secure the island for himself; and in exchange, he would give them his ship and the whole raiding territory and the routes he had worked out.

Willy Jones captured the island and ruled it. From the ship he kept only the gold, the dark Dutch girl Margaret, and three golems which had once been ransom from a Jew in Oman.

"I forgot to tell you that Margaret was the daughter of the Dutch spice man who had owned the island and the tall ship and who was killed by Willy," Galli said, "and the island really belonged to Margaret now as the daughter of her father."

For one year Willy Jones ruled the small settlement, drove the three golems and the men who already lived there, had the spices gathered and baled and stored (they were worth their weight in silver), and built the Big House. And for one year he courted the dark Dutch girl Margaret, having been unable to board her as he had all other girls.

She refused him because he had killed her father, because he had destroyed the *Luchtkastell* which was Family and Nation to her, and because he had stolen her island.

This Margaret, though she was pretty and trim as a *kuching*, had during the affair of the *Feathered Snake* and the *Luchtkastell* twirled three seamen in the air like pinwheels at one time and thrown them all into the ocean. She had eyes that twinkled like the compounded eyes of the devil-fly; they could glint laughter and fury at the same time.

"Those girls were like volcanoes," the man said. "Slim, strong mountains, and we climbed them like mountains. Man, the uplift on them! The shoulders were cliffs that laughed. The swaying—"

No, no! Belay that last paragraph! That's from the ramble of the fellow in the bar, and it keeps intruding.

"I forgot to tell you that she reminds me of *Wonder Woman*," Galli said.

Willy Jones believed that Margaret was worth winning unbroken, as he was not at all sure that he could break her. He courted her as well as he could, and he used to advantage the background of the golden-green spicery on which they lived.

"Imagine about the Permata bird that nests on the moon," Galli said, "and which is the most passionate as well as the noblest-singing of the birds. Imagine about flute notes soaring."

Willy Jones made this tune to Margaret:

> *The Nutmeg Moon is the third moon of the year.*
> *The Tides come in like loose Silk all its Nights.*
> *The Ground is animated by the bare Feet of Margaret*
> *Who is like the* Pelepah *of the* Ko-eng *Flower.*

Willy made this tune in the Malaya language in which all the words end in *ang*.

"Imagine about water leaping down rocky hills," Galli said. "Imagine about red birds romping in green groves."

Willy Jones made another tune to Margaret:

> *A Woman with Shoulders so strong that a Man might ride upon them*
> *The while she is still the little Girl watching for the black Ship*
> *Of the Hero who is the same age as the Sky,*
> *But she does not realize that I am already here.*

Willy made this tune in the Dutch language in which all the words end in *lijk*.

"Imagine about another flute joining the first one, and their notes scamper like birds," Galli said.

Willy Jones made a last tune to Margaret:

> *Damnation! That is enough of Moonlight and Tomorrows!*
> *Now there are mats to plait, and* kain *to sew.*
> *Even the smallest crab knows to build herself a house in the sand.*
> *Margaret should be raking the oven coals and baking a* roti.
>
> *I wonder why she is so slow in seeing this.*

Willy made this tune in the Welsh language in which all the words end in *gwbl*.

When the one year was finished, they were mated. There was still the chilliness there as though she would never forgive him for killing her father and stealing her island; but they began to be in accord.

"Here pause five minutes to indicate an idyllic interlude," Galli said. "We sing the song *Bagang Kali Berjumpa* if you know the tune. We flute, if I have my flute."

The idyllic interlude passed.

Then Willy's old ship, the *Feathered Snake*, came back to the Island. She was in a pitiful state of misuse. She reeked of old and new blood, and there were none left on her but nine sick men. These nine men begged Willy Jones to become their captain again to set everything right.

Willy washed the nine living skeletons and fed them up for three days. They were fat and able by then. And the three golems had refitted the ship.

"All she needs is a strong hand at the helm again," said Willy Jones. "I will sail her again for a week and a day. I will impress a new crew, and once more make her the terror of the Spice Islands. Then I will return to my island, knowing that I have done a good deed in restoring the *Snake* to the bloody work for which she was born."

"If you go, Willy Jones, you will be gone for many years," said the dark Dutch Margaret.

"Only one at the most," said Willy.

"And I will be in my grave when you return."

"There is no grave could hold you, Margaret."

"Aye, it may not hold me. I'll out of it and confront you when you come back. But it gives one a weirdness to be in the grave for only a few years. I will not own you for my husband when you do come back. You will not even know whether I am the same woman that you left, and you will never know. I am a volcano, but I banked my hatred and accepted you. But if you leave me now, I will erupt against you forever."

But Willy Jones went away in the *Flying Serpent* and left her there. He took two of the golems with him, and he left one of them to serve Margaret.

What with one thing and another, he was gone for twenty years.

"We were off that morning to satisfy our curiosity about the Big House," the fellow said, "since we would soon be leaving the island forever. You know about the Big House. You were on Willy Jones Island too. The Jilolos call it the House of Skulls, and the Malaya and Indonesia people will not speak about it at all.

"We approached the Big House that was not more than a mile beyond our perimeter. It was a large decayed building, but we had the sudden feeling that it was still inhabited. And it wasn't supposed to be. Then we saw the two of them, the mother and the daughter. We shook like we were unhinged, and we ran to them.

"They were so alike that we couldn't tell them apart. Their eyes twinkled like the compounded eyes of a creature that eats her mate. Noonday lightning! How it struck! Arms that swept you off your feet and set your bones to singing! We knew that they were not twins, or even sisters. We knew that they were mother and daughter.

"I have never encountered anything like them in my life. Whatever happened to the other two soldiers, I know it was worth it to them. Whatever happened to them? I don't care if they kill me! They were perfect, those two women, even though we weren't with them for five minutes."

"Then it was the Badger."

No, no, no! That's the wrong story again. That's not the story Galli told me. That's part of the story the fellow told me in the bar. His confused account keeps interposing itself, possibly because I knew him slightly when we were both soldiers on

Willy Jones Island. But he had turned queer, that fellow. "It is the earthquake belt around the world that is the same as the legend belt," he said, "and the Middle-world underlies it all. That's why I was able to walk it." It was as though he had been keel-hauled around the world. I hadn't known him well. I didn't know which of the three soldiers he was. I had heard that they were all dead.

"Imagine about conspiracy stuff now," said Galli. "Imagine about a whispering in a pinang grove before the sun is up."

"How can I spook that man?" Margaret asked her golem shortly after she had been abandoned by Willy Jones. "But I am afraid that a mechanical man would not be able to tell me how."

"I will tell you a secret," said the golem. "We are not mechanical men. Certain wise and secret men believe that they made us, but they are wrong. They have made houses for us to live in, no more. There are many of us unhoused spirits, and we take shelter in such bodies as we find. That being so, I know something of the houseless spirits in the depth of every man. I will select one of them, and we will spook Willy Jones with that one. Willy is a Welshman who has become by adoption a Dutchman and a Malayan and a Jilolo man. There is one old spook running through them all. I will call it up when it is time."

"I forgot to tell you that the name of Margaret's golem was Meshuarat," Galli said.

After twenty years of high piracy, Willy Jones returned to his island. And there was the dark Dutch Margaret standing as young and as smoldering as when he had left. He leaped to embrace her, and found himself stretched flat on the sand by a thunderous blow. He was not surprised, and was not (as he had at first believed) decapitated. Almost he was not displeased. Margaret had often been violent in her love-making.

"But I will have you," Willy swore as he tasted his own blood delightfully in his mouth and pulled himself up onto hands and knees. "I have ridden the Margaret-tiger before."

"You will never ride my loins, you lecherous old goat," she rang at him like a bell. "I am not your wife. I am the daughter that you left here in the womb. My mother is in the grave on the hill."

Willy Jones sorrowed terribly, and he went to the grave.

But Margaret came up behind him and drove in the cruel lance. "I told you that when you came back you would not know whether I was the same woman you had left," she chortled, "and you will never know!"

"Margaret, you are my wife!" Willy Jones gasped.

"Am I of an age to be your wife?" she jibed. "Regard me! Of what age do I seem to be?"

"Of the same age as when I left," said Willy. "But perhaps you have eaten of the besok nut and so do not change your appearance."

"I forgot to tell you about the besok nut," said Galli. "If one eats the nut of the besok tree, the tomorrow tree, the time tree, that one will not age. But this is always accompanied by a chilling unhappiness."

"Perhaps I did eat it," said Margaret. "But that is my grave there, and I have lain in it many years, as has she. You are prohibited from touching either of us."

"Are you the mother or the daughter, Witch?"

"You will never know. You will see us both, for we take turns, and you will not be able to tell us apart. See, the grave is always disturbed, and the entrance is easy."

"I'll have the truth from the golem who served you while I was gone," Willy swore.

"A golem is an artificial man," said Galli. "They were made by the Jews and Arabs in earlier ages, but now they say that they have forgotten how to make them. I wonder that you do not make them yourselves, for you have advanced techniques. You tell them and you picture them in your own heroic literature," (he patted the comic books under his arm), "but you do not have them in actuality."

The golem told Willy Jones that the affair was thus:

A daughter had indeed been born to Margaret. She had slain the child, and had then put it into the middle state. Thereafter, the child stayed sometimes in the grave, and sometimes she walked about the island. And she grew as any other child would. And Margaret herself had eaten the besok nut so that she would not age.

When mother and daughter had come to the same age and appearance (and it had only been the very day before that, the day before Willy Jones had returned), then the daughter had also eaten the besok nut. Now the mother and daughter would be of the same appearance forever, and not even a golem could tell them apart.

Willy Jones came furiously onto the woman again.

"I was sure before, and now I am even more sure that you are Margaret," he said, "and now I will have you in my fury."

"We both be Margaret," she said. "But I am not the same one you apprehended earlier. We changed places while you talked to the golem. And we are both in the middle state, and we have both been dead in the grave, and you dare not touch either of us ever. A Welshman turned Dutchman turned Malayan turned Jilolo has this spook in him four times over. The Devil himself will not touch his own daughters."

The last part was a lie, but Willy Jones did not know it.

"We be in confrontation forever then," said Willy Jones. "I will make my Big House a house of hate and a house of skulls. You cannot escape from its environs, neither can any visitor. I'll kill them all and pile their skulls up high for a monument to you."

Then Willy Jones ate a piece of bitter bark from the pokok ru.

"I forgot to tell you that when a person eats bark from the pokok ru in anger, his anger will sustain itself forever," Galli said.

"If it's visitors you want for the killing, I and my mother-daughter will provide them in numbers," said Margaret. "Men will be attracted here forever with no heed for danger. I will eat a telor tuntong of the special sort, and all men will be attracted here even to their death."

"I forgot to tell you that if a female eats the telor tuntong of the special sort, all males will be attracted irresistibly," Galli said. "Ah, you smile as though you doubted that the besok nut or the bark of the pokok ru or the telor tuntong of the special sort could have such effects. But yourselves come now to wonder drugs like little boys. In these islands they are all around you and you too blind to see. It is no ignorant man who tells you this. I have read the booklets from your orderly tents: *Physics without Mathematics, Cosmology without Chaos, Psychology without Brains*. It is myself, the master of all sciences and disciplines, who tells you that these things do work. Besides hard science, there is soft science, the science of shadow areas and story areas, and you do wrong to deny it the name.

"I believe that you yourself can see what had to follow, from the dispositions of the Margarets and Willy Jones," Galli said. "For hundreds of years, men from everywhere came to the Margarets who could not be resisted. And Willy Jones killed them all and piled up their skulls. It became, in a very savage form, what you call the Badger Game."

Galli was a good-natured and unhandsome brown man. He worked around the army base as translator, knowing (besides his native Jilolo), the Malayan, Dutch, Japanese, and English languages, and (as every storyteller must) the Arabian. His English was whatever he wanted it to be, and he burlesqued the speech of the American soldiers to the Australians, and the Australians to the Americans.

"Man, it was a Badger!" the man said. "It was a grizzle-haired, glare-eyed, flat-headed, underslung, pigeon-toed, hook-clawed, clam-jawed Badger from Badger Game Corner! They moved in on us, but I'd take my chances and go back and do it again. We hadn't frolicked with the girls for five minutes when the things moved in on us. I say things; I don't know whether they were men or not. If they were, they were the coldest three men I ever saw. But they were directed by a man who made up for it. He was livid, hopping with hatred. They moved in on us and began to kill us."

No, No, that isn't part of Galli's story. That's some more of the ramble that the fellow told me in the bar the other evening.

It has been three hundred years, and the confrontation continues. There are skulls of Malayan men and Jilolo men piled up there; and of Dutchmen and Englishmen and of Portuguese men; of Chinamen and Filipinos and Goanese; of Japanese, and of the men from the United States and Australia.

"Only this morning there were added the skulls of two United States men, and there should have been three of them," Galli said. "They came, as have all others, because the Margarets ate the telor tuntong of the special sort. It is a fact that with a species (whether insect or shelled thing or other) where the male gives his life in the mating, the female has always eaten of this telor tuntong. You'd never talk the males into such a thing with words alone."

"How is it that there were only two United States skulls this morning, and there should have been three?" I asked him.

"One of them escaped," Galli explained, "and that was unusual. He fell through a hole to the middle land, that third one of them. But the way back from the middle land to one's own country is long, and it must be walked. It takes at least twenty years, wherever one's own country is; and the joker thing about it is that the man is always wanting to go the other way.

"That is the end of the story, but let it not end abruptly," Galli said. "Sing the song *Chari Yang Besar* if you remember the tune. Imagine about flute notes lingering in the air."

"I was lost for more than twenty years, and that's a fact," the man said. He gripped the bar with the most knotted hands I ever saw, and laughed with a merriment so deep that it seemed to be his bones laughing. "Did you know that there's another world just under this world, or just around the corner from it? I walked all day every day. I was in a torture, for I suspected that I was going the wrong way, and I could go no other. And I sometimes suspected that the middle land through which I traveled was in my head, a derangement from the terrible blow that one of the things gave me as he came in to kill me. And yet there are correlates that convince me it was a real place.

"I wasn't trying to get home. I was trying to get back to those girls even if it killed me. There weren't any colors in that world, all gray tones, but otherwise it wasn't much different from this one. There were even bars there a little like the Red Rooster."

(I forgot to tell you that it was in the Red Rooster bar that the soldier from the islands told me the parts of his story.)

"I've got to get back there. I think I know the way now, and how to get on the road. I have to travel it through the middle land, you know. They'll kill me, of course, and I won't even get to jazz those girls for five minutes; but I've got to get back there. Going to take me another twenty years, though. That sure is a weary walk."

I never knew him well, and I don't remember which of the names was his. But a man from Orange, Texas, or from Gobey, Tennessee, or from Boston, in one of the eastern states, is on a twenty-year walk through the middle land to find the dark Dutch Margarets, and death.

I looked up a couple of things yesterday. There was Revel's recent work on Moluccan narcotics. He tells of the besok nut which *does* seem to inhibit aging but which induces internal distraction and hypersexuality. There is the pokok ru whose bitter bark impels even the most gentle to violent anger. There is one sort of telor tuntong which sets up an inexplicable aura about a woman eater and draws all males overpoweringly to her. There is much research still to be done on these narcotics, Revel writes.

I dipped into Mandrago's *Earthquake and Legend and the Middle World*. He states that the earthquake belt around the world is also the legend belt, and that one of the underlying legends is of the underlying land, the middle world below this world where one can wander lost forever.

And I went down to the Red Rooster again the next evening, which was last evening, to ask about the man and to see if he could give me a more cogent account. For I had re-remembered Galli's old story in the meanwhile.

"No, he was just passing through town," the barman said. "Had a long trip ahead of him. He was sort of a nutty fellow. I've often said the same thing about you."

That is the end of the other story, but let it not end suddenly. Pause for a moment to savor it. Sing the song *Itu Masa Dahulu* if you remember the tune.

Imagine about flute notes falling. I don't have a flute, but a story should end so.

Seven-Day Terror

Introduction by Connie Willis

"Seven-Day Terror" was not my first introduction to R. A. Lafferty—that was "Slow Tuesday Night"—but it instantly became my favorite Lafferty story and remains so to this day, in spite of intense competition from "The Hole on the Corner," the aforementioned "Slow Tuesday Night," and "Thus We Frustrate Charlemagne."

"Seven-Day Terror" is part of the proud tradition of science fiction stories like C. L. Moore and Henry Kuttner's "Mimsy Were the Borogoves" and Ray Bradbury's "Zero Hour" which are about children and how they see the world entirely differently from adults, a way of seeing that grants them incomprehensible and sometimes dangerous powers. But Lafferty's children stand alone in their audacity, precociousness, and ruthless common sense.

And wisdom: Clarissa's absolutely right about the dangers of letting scientific discoveries like the disappearer fall into irresponsible hands, i.e., those of adults.

And even though this story is as lighthearted as Lafferty comes, his wry awareness of how the world works is still present. Officer Comstock, for instance, has a knack for "getting near the heart of dark matters. This is why he was walking a beat out in the boondocks instead of sitting in a chair downtown."

But mostly Lafferty's just having fun here, and so are we. The Willoughby kids, from Clarence down to three-year-old Cyril, are charmingly incorrigible, the dialogue's hilarious, and we get to meet the "esteemed" scientist Willy McGilly and his pals (who pop up in several Lafferty stories). Plus, there are oatmeal boxes, gold watches, floods, fireplugs, cats, local officials, beer cans, and an ending you should have seen coming but didn't. In other words, Lafferty at his best. So sit back and prepare to have a really good time.

Seven-Day Terror

I s there anything you want to make disappear?" Clarence Willoughby asked his mother.

"A sink full of dishes is all I can think of. How will you do it?"

"I just built a disappearer. All you do is cut the other end out of a beer can. Then you take two pieces of red cardboard with peepholes in the middle and fit them in the ends. You look through the peepholes and blink. Whatever you look at will disappear."

"Oh."

"But I don't know if I can make them come back. We'd better try it on something else. Dishes cost money."

As always, Myra Willoughby had to admire the wisdom of her nine-year-old son. She would not have had such foresight herself. He always did. "You can try it on Blanche Manners's cat outside there. Nobody will care if it disappears except Blanche Manners."

"All right."

He put the disappearer to his eye and blinked. The cat disappeared from the sidewalk outside.

His mother was interested. "I wonder how it works. Do you know how it works?"

"Yes. You take a beer can with both ends cut out and put in two pieces of cardboard. Then you blink."

"Never mind. Take it outside and play with it. You hadn't better make anything disappear in here till I think about this."

But when he had gone his mother was oddly disturbed.

"I wonder if I have a precocious child. Why, there's lots of grown people who wouldn't know how to make a disappearer that would work. I wonder if Blanche Manners will miss her cat very much?"

Clarence went down to the Plugged Nickel, a pot house on the corner.

"Do you have anything you want to make disappear, Nokomis?"

"Only my paunch."

"If I make it disappear it'll leave a hole in you and you'll bleed to death."

"That's right, I would. Why don't you try it on the fireplug outside?"

This in a way was one of the happiest afternoons ever in the neighborhood. The children came from blocks around to play in the flooded streets and gutters, and if some of them drowned (and we don't say that they *did* drown) in the flood (and brother! it was a flood), why, you have to expect things like that. The fire engines (whoever heard of calling fire engines to put out a flood?) were apparatus-deep in water. The policemen and ambulance men wandered around wet and bewildered.

"Resuscitator, resuscitator, anybody wanna resuscitator," chanted Clarissa Willoughby.

"Oh, shut up," said the ambulance attendants.

Nokomis, the bar man in the Plugged Nickel, called Clarence inside.

"I don't believe, just for the moment, I'd tell anyone what happened to that fireplug."

"I won't tell if you won't tell," said Clarence.

Officer Comstock was suspicious. "There's only seven possible explanations: one of the seven Willoughby kids did it. I dunno how. It'd take a bulldozer to do it, and then there'd be something left of the plug. But however they did it, one of them did it."

Officer Comstock had a talent for getting near the truth of dark matters. This is why he was walking a beat out here in the boondocks instead of sitting in a chair downtown.

"Clarissa!" said Officer Comstock in a voice like thunder.

"Resuscitator, resuscitator, anybody wanna resuscitator?" chanted Clarissa.

"Do you know what happened to that fireplug?" asked Officer C.

"I have an uncanny suspicion. As yet it is no more than that. When I am better informed I will advise you."

Clarissa was eight years old and much given to uncanny suspicions.

"Clementine, Harold, Corinne, Jimmy, Cyril," he asked the five younger Willoughby children. "Do you know what happened to that fireplug?"

"There was a man around yesterday. I bet he took it," said Clementine.

"I don't even remember a fireplug there. I think you're making a fuss about nothing," said Harold.

"City hall's going to hear about this," said Corinne.

"Pretty dommed sure," said Jimmy, "but I won't tell."

"Cyril!" cried Officer Comstock in a terrible voice. Not a terrifying voice, a terrible voice. He felt terrible now.

"Great green bananas," said Cyril, "I'm only three years old. I don't see how it's even my responsibility."

"Clarence," said Officer Comstock.

Clarence gulped.

"Do you know where the fireplug went?"

Clarence brightened. "No, sir. I don't know where it went."

A bunch of smart alecs from the water department came out and shut off the water for a few blocks around and put some kind of cap on in place of the fireplug. "This sure is going to be a funny-sounding report," said one of them.

Officer Comstock walked away discouraged. "Don't bother me, Miss Manners," he said. "I don't know where to look for your cat. I don't even know where to look for a fireplug."

"I have an idea," said Clarissa, "that when you find the cat you will find the fireplug in the same place. As yet it's only an idea."

Ozzie Murphy wore a little hat on top of his head. Clarence pointed his weapon and winked. The hat was no longer there, but a little trickle of blood was running down the pate.

"I don't believe I'd play with that any more," said Nokomis.

"Who's playing?" said Clarence. "This is for real."

This was the beginning of the seven-day terror in the heretofore obscure neighborhood. Trees disappeared from the parks; lamp posts were as though they had never been; Wally Waldorf drove home, got out, slammed the door of his car, and there was no car. As George Mullendorf came up the walk to his house his dog Pete ran to meet him and took a flying leap to his arms. The dog left the sidewalk but something happened; the dog was gone and only a bark lingered for a moment in the puzzled air.

But the worst were the fireplugs. The second plug was installed the morning after the disappearance of the first. In eight minutes it was gone and the flood waters returned. Another one was in by twelve o'clock. Within three minutes it had vanished. The next morning fireplug number four was installed.

The water commissioner was there, the city engineer was there, the chief of police was there with a riot squad, the president of the Parent-Teachers Association was there, the president of the university was there, the mayor was there, three gentlemen of the FBI, a newsreel photographer, eminent scientists, and a crowd of honest citizens.

"Let's see it disappear now," said the city engineer.

"Let's see it disappear now," said the police chief.

"Let's see it disa—It did, didn't it?" said one of the eminent scientists.

And it was gone and everybody was very wet.

"At least I have the picture sequence of the year," said the photographer. But his camera and apparatus disappeared from the midst of them.

"Shut off the water and cap it," said the commissioner. "And don't put in another plug yet. That was the last plug in the warehouse."

"This is too big for me," said the mayor. "I wonder that Tass doesn't have it yet."

"Tass has it," said a little round man. "I am Tass."

"If all of you gentlemen will come into the Plugged Nickel," said Nokomis, "and try one of our new Fire Hydrant Highballs you will all be happier. These are made of good corn whiskey, brown sugar, and hydrant water from this very gutter. You can be the first to drink them."

Business was phenomenal at the Plugged Nickel, for it was in front of its very doors that the fireplugs disappeared in floods of gushing water.

"I know a way we can get rich," said Clarissa several days later to her father,

Tom Willoughby. "Everybody says they're going to sell their houses for nothing and move out of the neighborhood. Go get a lot of money and buy them all. Then you can sell them again and get rich."

"I wouldn't buy them for a dollar each. Three of them have disappeared already, and all the families but us have their furniture moved out in their front yards. There might be nothing but vacant lots in the morning."

"Good, then buy the vacant lots. And you can be ready when the houses come back."

"Come back? Are the houses going to come back? Do you know anything about this, young lady?"

"I have a suspicion verging on a certainty. As of now I can say no more."

Three eminent scientists were gathered in an untidy suite that looked as though it belonged to a drunken sultan.

"This transcends the metaphysical. It impinges on the quantum continuum. In some way it obsoletes Boff," said Dr. Velikof Vonk.

"The contingence of the intransigence is the most mystifying aspect," said Arpad Arkabaranan.

"Yes," said Willy McGilly. "Who would have thought that you could do it with a beer can and two pieces of cardboard? When I was a boy I used an oatmeal box and red crayola."

"I do not always follow you," said Dr. Vonk. "I wish you would speak plainer."

So far no human had been injured or disappeared—except for a little blood on the pate of Ozzie Murphy, on the lobes of Conchita when her gaudy earrings disappeared from her very ears, a clipped finger or so when a house vanished as the front doorknob was touched, a lost toe when a neighborhood boy kicked a can and the can was not; probably not more than a pint of blood and three or four ounces of flesh all together.

Now, however, Mr. Buckle the grocery man disappeared before witnesses. This was serious.

Some mean-looking investigators from downtown came out to the Willoughbys. The meanest-looking one was the mayor. In happier days he had not been a mean man, but the terror had now reigned for seven days.

"There have been ugly rumors," said one of the mean investigators, "that link certain events to this household. Do any of you know anything about them?"

"I started most of them," said Clarissa. "But I didn't consider them ugly. Cryptic, rather. But if you want to get to the bottom of this just ask me a question."

"Did you make those things disappear?" asked the investigator.

"That isn't the question," said Clarissa.

"Do you know where they have gone?" asked the investigator.

"That isn't the question either," said Clarissa.

"Can you make them come back?"

"Why, of course I can. Anybody can. Can't you?"

"I cannot. If you can, please do so at once."

"I need some stuff. Get me a gold watch and a hammer. Then go down to the drug store and get me this list of chemicals. And I need a yard of black velvet and a pound of rock candy."

"Shall we?" asked one of the investigators.

"Yes," said the mayor. "It's our only hope. Get her anything she wants."

And it was all assembled.

"Why does she get all the attention?" asked Clarence. "I was the one who made all the things disappear. How does she know how to get them back?"

"I knew it!" cried Clarissa with hate. "I knew he was the one that did it. He read in my diary how to make a disappearer. If I was his mother I'd whip him for reading his little sister's diary. That's what happens when things like that fall into irresponsible hands."

She poised the hammer over the mayor's gold watch, now on the floor.

"I have to wait a few seconds. This can't be hurried. It'll only be a little while."

The second hand swept around to the point that was preordained for it before the world began. Clarissa suddenly brought down the hammer with all her force on the beautiful gold watch.

"That's all," she said. "Your troubles are over. See, there is Blanche Manners's cat on the sidewalk just where she was seven days ago."

And the cat was back.

"Now let's go down to the Plugged Nickel and watch the fireplugs come back."

They had only a few minutes to wait. It came from nowhere and clanged into the street like a sign and a witness.

"Now I predict," said Clarissa, "that every single object will return exactly seven days from the time of its disappearance."

The seven-day terror had ended. The objects began to reappear.

"How," asked the mayor, "did you know they would come back in seven days?"

"Because it was a seven-day disappearer that Clarence made. I also know how to make a nine-day, a thirteen-day, a twenty-seven-day, and an eleven-year disappearer. I was going to make a thirteen-year one, but for that you have to color the ends with the blood from a little boy's heart, and Cyril cried every time I tried to make a good cut."

"You really know how to make all of these?"

"Yes. But I shudder if the knowledge should ever come into unauthorized hands."

"I shudder, too, Clarissa. But tell me, why did you want the chemicals?"

"For my chemistry set."

"And the black velvet?"

"For doll dresses."

"And the pound of rock candy?"

"How did you ever get to be mayor of this town if you have to ask questions like that? What do you think I wanted the rock candy for?"

"One last question," said the mayor. "Why did you smash my gold watch with the hammer?"

"Oh," said Clarissa, "that was for dramatic effect."

Boomer Flats

Introduction by Cat Rambo

In "Boomer Flats," which originally appeared in *If Magazine* in 1971, Lafferty expands on the internal mythology of his work and returns to familiar themes. Evolution, and how humans fit into it through spontaneous evolutionary leaps, features in other stories such as "Ginny Wrapped in the Sun" and "In Deepest Glass." Lafferty asserted that storytelling was a manifestation of ancestry and that storytellers belonged "to the old 'red-bone people.'" The journey to Boomer Flats brings the reader to a strange town where those people walk daily.

To those who know who Ivan Sanderson is, the clue is there from the very first line: eminent scientists Arpad Arkabaranan, Willy McGilly, and Dr. Velikof Vonk, declaring themselves his spiritual offspring, are in search of Fortean phenomena, specifically the ABSM (Abominable Snowman). It's a literal wild-goose chase, as McGilly notes, referring to the hundreds of mud geese in flight across the sky.

This sort of linguistic play, the metaphorical made real, ripples through the story, and even sometimes slides it over into poetry's realm, such as the repeated reassurance Crayola Catfish gives the eminent scientists about their drinks, "They're fixing them for you now. I'll bring them after a while."

Boomer Flats is a shadow town, an echo of the town of Boomer. "Something a little queer and primordial about the whole place!" Lafferty warns the reader, who already knows we're wandering in strange territory.

The three eminent scientists know it too. Dr. Velikof Vonk's eyes grin "out of deep folk memory," as he begins to drink what Crayola has brought him: a clay cup that "smelled strongly of river, perhaps of interstadial river." The drinks, the Green Snake Snorters, move the trio into a strange mythopoetic world in washes, like a television show's set where each cut-away and back reveals odder and odder details changed and added. The prose becomes stranger and stranger at the same time, moving into deeper and deeper waters of wordplay. That shabby man playing dominoes is a bear. Pieces are falling off a man called the Comet. And then, the giants enter, standing around the edges of the room in their black hats. This is where the legends dwell, almost as though Boomer Flats is the secret heart of Lafferty's cosmos.

The three eminent scientists are specifically identified as three Magi, but what they find is not an answer in the form of the Christ Child, but more and more questions about the world itself. Instead the ending turns back to story's heart in a way that pulls the reader further in and farther out, so to speak. This is Lafferty at his luminiferous best, slipstream before the term was ever invented.

Boomer Flats

I n the tracks of our spiritual father Ivan Sanderson we may now have trailed a clutch of ABSMs to their lair," the eminent scientist Arpad Arkabaranan was saying in his rattling voice. "And that lair may not be a mountain thicket or rain forest or swamp, but these scrimpy red clay flats. I would almost give my life for the success of this quest, but it seems that it should have a more magnificent setting."

"It looks like a wild-goose chase," the eminent scientist Willy McGilly commented. But no, Willy was not downgrading their quest. He was referring to the wild geese that rose about them from the edges of the flats with clatter and whistle and honk. This was a flight-way, a chase of theirs. There were hundreds of them if one had the fine eyes to pick them out from the background. "Mud geese," Willy said. "We don't see as many of them as when I was a boy."

"I do not, and I am afraid that I will not, believe in the ABSMs," said the eminent scientist Dr. Velikof Vonk, stroking his—(no he didn't, he didn't have one)—stroking his jaw, "and yet this is the thing that I also have most desired, to find this missing link finally, and to refute all believers in the other thing."

"We can't see the chain for the links," said Willy McGilly. "I never believed that any of them was missing. There's always been too many of them for the length of the chain: that's the trouble."

"I've traveled a million miles in search of them," said Arpad. "I've pretty well probed all the meager ribs of the world in that travel. My fear has always been that I'd miss them by a trick, even that in some unaccountable way I wouldn't know them when I found them. It would be ironic if we did find them in such a place as this: not a wild place, only a shabby and overlooked place."

"My own fear has been that when I finally gazed on one I would wake with a start and find that I had been looking in a mirror," said Velikof. "There must be some symbolism here that I don't understand. What is your own anticipation of them, Willy?"

"Oh, coming back to people I've always liked. There used to be a bunch of them on the edge of my hometown," Willy McGilly said. "Come to think of it, there used to be a bunch of them on the edge of every hometown. Now they're more likely to be found right in the middle of every town. They're the scrubs, you know, for the bottoming of the breed."

"What are you talking about, Willy?" Arpad asked sharply.

What they were all talking about was ABSMs.

Every town in the south part of that county has a shadow or secondary. There is Meehan, and Meehan Corners; Perkins, and Perkins Corner; Boomer, and Boomer Flats. The three eminent scientists were driving the three miles from Boomer to Boomer Flats looking for the bones, and hopefully even the living flesh, of a legend. It was that of the missing link, of the Abominable Snowman, the ABSM. It wasn't snowy country there, but the so-called Snowmen have been reported in every sort of climate and countryside. The local legend, recently uncovered by Arpad, was that there was a non-African non-Indian "people of color" living in the neighborhood of Boomer Flats, "between the sand-bush thickets and the river." It was said that they lived on the very red mud banks of the river, and that they lived a little in the river itself.

Then Dr. Velikof Vonk had come onto a tape in a bunch of anthropological tapes, and the tape contained sequences like this:

"What do they do when the river floods?"

"Ah, they close their noses and mouths and ears with mud, and they lie down with big rocks on their breasts and stay there till the flood has passed."

"Can they be taught?"

"Some of the children go to school, and they learn. But when they are older then they stay at home, and they forget."

"What sort of language do they talk?"

"Ah, they don't seem to talk very much. They keep to themselves. Sometimes when they talk it is just plain Cimarron Valley English."

"What do they eat?"

"They boil river water in mud clay pots. They put in wild onions and greenery. The pottage thickens then, I don't know how. It gets lumps of meat or clay in it, and they eat that too. They eat frogs and fish and owls and thicket filaments. But mostly they don't eat very much of anything."

"It is said that they aren't all of the same appearance. It is even said that they are born, ah, shapeless, and that—ah—could you tell me anything about that?"

"Yeah. They're born without much shape. Most of them never do get much shape. When they have any, well actually their mothers lick them into shape, give them their appearance."

"It's an old folk tale that bears do that."

"Maybe they learned it from the bears then, young fellow. There's quite a bit of bear mixture in them, but the bears themselves have nearly gone from the flats and thickets now. More than likely the bears learned it from them. Sometimes the mothers lick the cubs into the shape of regular people for a joke."

"That is the legend?"

"You keep saying legend. I don't know anything about legend. I just tell you what you ask me. I'll tell you a funny one, though. One of the mothers who was getting ready to bear happened to get ahold of an old movie magazine that some fishers from Boomer had left on the river edge. There was a picture in it of the prettiest girl that anyone ever saw, and it was a picture of all of that girl. This mother was tickled by that picture. She bore a daughter then, and she licked her into the shape and appearance of the girl in the movie magazine. And the girl grew up looking like that and she still looks like that, pretty as a picture. I don't believe the girl appreciates the joke. She is the prettiest of all the people, though. Her name is Crayola Catfish."

"Are you having me, old fellow? Have those creatures any humor?"

"Some of them tell old jokes. John Salt tells old jokes. The Licorice Man tells really old jokes. And man, does the Comet ever tell old jokes!"

"Are the creatures long-lived?"

"Long-lived as we want to be. The elixir comes from these flats, you know. Some of us use it, some of us don't."

"Are *you* one of the creatures?"

"Sure, I'm one of them. I like to get out from it sometimes though. I follow the harvests."

This tape (recorded by an anthropology student at State University who, by the way, has since busted out of anthropology and is now taking hotel and restaurant management) had greatly excited the eminent scientist Dr. Velikof Vonk when he had played it, along with several hundred other tapes that had come in that week from the anthropology circuit. He scratched his—(no he didn't, he didn't have one)—he scratched his jowl and he phoned up the eminent scientists Arpad Arkabaranan and Willy McGilly.

"I'll go, I'll go, of course I'll go," Arpad had cried. "I've traveled a million miles in search of it, and should I refuse to go sixty? This won't be it, this can't be it, but I'll never give up. Yes, we'll go tomorrow."

"Sure, I'll go," Willy McGilly said. "I've been there before, I kind of like those folks on the flats. I don't know about the biggest catfish in the world, but the biggest catfish stories in the world have been pulled out of the Cimarron River right about at Boomer Flats. Sure, we'll go tomorrow."

"This may be it," Velikof had said. "How can we miss it? I can almost reach out and scratch it on the nose from here."

"You'll find yourself scratching your own nose, that's how you'll miss it. But it's there and it's real."

"I believe, Willy, that there is a sort of amnesia that has prevented us finding them or remembering them accurately."

"Not that, Velikof. It's just that they're always too close to see."

So the next day the three eminent scientists drove over from T-Town to come to Boomer Flats. Willy McGilly knew where the place was, but his pointing out of the way seemed improbable: Velikof was more inclined to trust the information of people in Boomer. And there was a difficulty there.

People kept saying, "This is Boomer. There isn't exactly any place called Boomer Flats." Boomer Flats wasn't on any map. It was too small even to have a post office. And the Boomer people were exasperating in not knowing about it or knowing the way to it.

"Three miles from here, and you don't know where it is?" Velikof asked one of them angrily.

"I don't even know *that* it is," the Boomer man had said in his own near anger. "I don't believe that there *is* such a place."

Finally, however, other men told the eminent scientists that there sort of was such a place, sort of a place. Sort of a road going to it too. They pointed out the same improbable way that Willy McGilly had pointed out.

The three eminents took the road. The flats hadn't flooded lately. The road was sand, but it could be negotiated. They came to the town, to the sort of town, in the ragged river flats. There was such a place. They went to the Cimarron Hotel which was like any hotel anywhere, only older. They went into the dining room, for it was noon.

It had tables, but it was more than a dining room. It was a common room. It even had intimations of old elegance in blued pier mirrors. There was a dingy bar there. There was a pool table there, and a hairy man was playing rotation with the Comet on it. The Comet was a long gray-bearded man (in fact, comet means a star with a beard) and small pieces were always falling off him. Clay-colored men with their hats on were playing dominos at several of the tables, and there were half a dozen dogs in the room. Something a little queer and primordial about those dogs! Something a little queer and primordial about the whole place!

But, as if set to serve as distraction, there was a remarkably pretty girl there, and she might have been a waitress. She seemed to be waiting, either listlessly or profoundly, for something.

Dr Velikof Vonk twinkled his deep eyes in their orbital caves: perhaps he cogitated his massive brain behind his massive orbital ridges: and he arrived, by sheer mentality, at the next step.

"Have you a menu, young lady?" he asked.

"No," she answered simply, but it wasn't simple at all. Her voice didn't go with her prettiness. It was much more intricate than her appearance, even in that one syllable. It was powerful, not really harsh, deep and resonant as caverns, full and timeless. The girl was big-boned beneath her prettiness, with heavy brindled hair and complex eyes.

"We would like something to eat," Arpad Arkabaranan ventured. "What do you have?"

"They're fixing it for you now," the girl said. "I'll bring it after a while."

There was a rich river smell about the whole place, and the room was badly lit.

"Her voice is an odd one," Arpad whispered in curious admiration. "Like rocks rolled around by water, but it also has a touch of springtime in it, spring-time of a very peculiar duality."

"Not just a springtime; it's an interstadial time," Willy McGilly stated accu-rately. "I've noticed that about them in other places. It's old green season in their voices, green season between the ice."

The room was lit only by hanging lamps. They had a flicker to them. They were not electric.

"There's a lot of the gas-light era in this place," Arpad gave the opinion, "but the lights aren't gas lights either."

"No, they're hanging oil lamps," Velikof said. "An amusing fancy just went through my head that they might be old whale-oil lamps."

"Girl, what do you burn in the hanging lamps?" Willy McGilly asked her.

"Catfish oil," she said in the resonant voice that had a touch of the green in-terstadial time in it. And catfish oil burns with a clay-colored flame.

"Can you bring us drinks while we wait?" Velikof of the massive head asked.

"They're fixing them for you now," the girl said. "I'll bring them after a while."

Meanwhile on the old pool table the Comet was beating the hairy man at rotation. Nobody could beat the Comet at rotation.

"We came here looking for strange creatures," Arpad said in the direction of the girl. "Do you know anything about strange creatures or people, or where they can be found?"

"You are the only strange people who have come here lately," she told them. Then she brought their drinks to them, three great sloshing clay cups or bulbous stems that smelled strongly of river, perhaps of interstadial river. She set them in front of the eminents with something like a twinkle in her eyes; something like, but much more. It was laughing lightning flashing from under the ridges of that pretty head. She was awaiting their reaction.

Velikof cocked a big deep eye at his drink. This itself was a feat. Other men hadn't such eyes, or such brows above them, as had Velikof Vonk. They took a bit of cocking, and it wasn't done lightly. And Velikof grinned out of deep folk memory as he began to drink. Velikof was always strong on the folk memory bit.

Arpad Arkabaranan screamed, rose backward, toppled his chair, and stood aghast while pointing a shaking finger at his splashing clay cup. Arpad was dis-turbed.

Willy McGilly drank deeply from his own stirring vessel.

"Why, it's Green Snake Snorter!" he cried in amazement and delight. "Oh drink of drinks, thou're a pleasure beyond expectation! They used to serve it to us back home, but I never even hoped to find it here. What great thing have we done to deserve this?"

He drank again of the wonderful splashing liquor while the spray of it filled the air. And Velikof also drank with noisy pleasure. The girl righted Arpad's chair, put Arpad into it again with strong hands, and addressed him powerfully to his cresting breaker. But Arpad was scared of his lively drink. "It's alive, it's alive," was all that he could jabber. Arpad Arkabaranan specialized in primitives, and primitives by definition are prime stuff. But there wasn't, now in his moment of weakness, enough prime stuff in Arpad himself to face so pleasant and primitive a drink as this.

The liquid was sparkling with bright action, was adequately alcoholic, something like choc beer, and there was a green snake in each cup. (Velikof in his notebook states that they were green worms of the species *vermis ebrius viridis*, but that is only a quibble. They were snakelike worms and of the size of small snakes, and we will call them snakes.)

"Do get with it, Arpad," Willy McGilly cried. "The trick is to drink it up before the snake drinks it. I tell you though that the snakes can discern when a man is afraid of them. They'll fang the face off a man who's afraid of them."

"Ah, I don't believe that I want the drink," Arpad declared with sickish grace. "I'm not much of a drinking man."

So Arpad's green snake drank up his Green Snake Snorter, noisily and greedily. Then it expired—it breathed out its life and evaporated. That green snake was gone.

"Where did he go?" Arpad asked nervously. He was still uneasy about the business.

"Back to the catfish," the girl said. "All the snakes are spirits of catfish just out for a little ramble."

"Interesting," Velikof said, and he noted in his pocket notebook that the *vermis ebrius viridis* is not a discrete species of worm or snake, but is rather spirit of catfish. It is out of such careful notation that science is built up.

"Is there anything noteworthy about Boomer Flats?" Velikof asked the girl then. "Has it any unique claim to fame?"

"Yes," the girl said. "This is the place that the comets come back to."

"Ah, but the moths have eaten the comets," Willy McGilly quoted from the old epic.

The girl brought them three big clay bowls heaped with fish eggs, and these they were to eat with three clay spoons. Willy McGilly and Dr. Velikof Vonk addressed themselves to the rich meal with pleasure, but Arpad Arkabaranan refused.

"Why, it's all mixed with mud and sand and trash," he objected.

"Certainly, certainly, wonderful, wonderful," Willy McGilly slushed out the happy words with a mouth full of delicious goop. "I always thought that something went out of the world when they cleaned up the old shantytown dish of shad roe. In some places they cleaned it up; not everywhere. I maintain that roe at its best must always have at least a slight tang of river sewage."

But Arpad broke his clay spoon in disgust. And he would not eat. Arpad had traveled a million miles in search of it but he didn't know it when he found it; he hadn't any of it inside him so he missed it.

One of the domino players at a near table (the three eminents had noticed this some time before but had not fully realized it) was a bear. The bear was dressed as a shabby man, he wore a big black hat on his head; he played dominos well; he was winning.

"How is it that the bear plays so well?" Velikof asked.

"He doesn't play at all well," Willy McGilly protested. "I could beat him. I could beat any of them."

"He isn't really a bear," the girl said. "He is my cousin. Our mothers, who were sisters, were clownish. His mother licked him into the shape of a bear for fun. But that is nothing to what my mother did to me. She licked me into pretty face and pretty figure for a joke, and now I am stuck with it. I think it is too much of a joke. I'm not really like this, but I guess I may as well laugh at me just as everybody else does."

"What is your name?" Arpad asked her without real interest.

"Crayola Catfish."

But Arpad Arkabaranan didn't hear or recognize the name, though it had been on a tape that Dr. Velikof Vonk had played for them, the same tape that had really brought them to Boomer Flats. Arpad had now closed his eyes and ears and heart to all of it.

The hairy man and the Comet were still shooting pool, but pieces were still falling off the Comet.

"He's diminishing, he's breaking up," Velikof observed. "He won't last another hundred years at that rate."

Then the eminents left board and room and the Cimarron Hotel to go looking for ABSMs who were rumored to live in that area.

ABSM is the code name for the Abominable Snowman, for the Hairy Woodman, for the Wild Man of Borneo, for the Sasquatch, for the Booger-Man, for the Ape-Man, for the Bear-Man, for the Missing Link, for the nine-foot-tall Giant things, for the living Neanderthals. It is believed by some that all of these beings are the same. It is believed by most that these things are no thing at all, no where, not in any form.

And it seemed as if the most were right, for the three eminents could not find hide nor hair (rough hide and copious hair were supposed to be marks by which the ABSMs might be known) of the queer folks anywhere along the red bank of the Cimarron River. Such creatures as they did encounter were very like the shabby and untalkative creatures they had already encountered in Boomer Flats. They weren't an ugly people: they were pleasantly mud-homely. They were civil and most often they were silent. They dressed something as people had dressed seventy-five years before that time—as the poor working people had dressed then. Maybe they were poor, maybe not. They didn't seem to work very much. Sometimes a man or a woman seemed to be doing a little bit of work, very casually.

It may be that the red-mud river was full of fish. Something was splashing and jumping there. Big turtles waddled up out of the water, caked with mud even around their eyes. The shores and flats were treacherous, and sometimes an eminent would sink into the sand-mud up to the hips. But the broad-footed people of the area didn't seem to sink in.

There was plenty of greenery (or brownery, for it had been the dusty weeks) along the shores. There were muskrats, there were even beavers, there were skunks and possums and badgers. There were wolf dens and coyote dens digged into the banks, and they had their particular smells about them. There were dog dens. There were coon trees. There were even bear dens or caves. But no, that was not a bear smell either. What smell was it?

"What lives in these clay caves?" Velikof asked a woman who was digging river clams there.

"The Giants live in them," she said. Well, they were tall enough to be Giants' caves. A nine-footer need hardly stoop to enter one.

"We have missed it," Arpad said. "There is nothing at all to be found here. I will travel farther, and I may find it in other places."

"Oh, I believe we are right in the middle of it," Velikof gave the opinion.

"It is all around us, Arpad, everything you wanted," Willy McGilly insisted.

But Arpad Arkabaranan would have none of the muddy water, none of the red sand or the red sand caves, nothing of anything here. The interest had all gone out of him. The three of them went back to the Cimarron Hotel without, apparently, finding primitive creature or missing link at all.

They entered the common room of the hotel again. Dominos were set before them. They played draw listlessly.

"You are sure that there are no odd creatures around this place?" Arpad again asked the girl Crayola Catfish.

"John Salt is an odd creature and he comes from this place," Crayola told them. "The Licorice Man is an odd creature, I suppose. So is Ape Woodman: he used to be a big-time football player. All three of them had regular-people blood in them; I suppose that's what made them odd. They were almost as odd as you three creatures. And the Comet playing pool there is an odd one. I don't know what kind of blood he has in him to make him odd."

"How long has he been around here?" Velikof asked.

"He returns every eighty-seven years. He stays here about three years, and he's already been here two of them. Then he goes off on another circuit. He goes out past the planets and among the stars."

"Oh? And how does he travel out there?" Velikof asked with cocked tongue and eye.

"With horse and buggy, of course."

"Oh there, Comet," Willy McGilly called. "Is it true that you travel out among the stars with horse and buggy?"

"Aye, that I do," the long gray-bearded man named Comet called back, "with a horse named Pee-gosh and a buggy named Harma. It's a flop-eared horse and a broken buggy, but they take me there."

"Touch clay," said Crayola Catfish, "for the lightning."

They touched clay. Everything was of baked clay anyhow, even the dominos. And there had been lightning, fantastic lightning dashing itself through every crack and cranny of the flimsy hotel. It was a lightning brighter than all the catfish-oil lamps in the world put together. And it continued. There was clattering sequence thunder, and there was a roaring booming sound that came from a few miles west of the thunder.

The Giants came in and stood around the edges of the room. They were all very much alike, like brothers. They were tall and somber, shabby, black-bearded to the eyes, and with black hats on their heads. Unkempt. All were about nine feet tall.

"Shall I sound like a simpleton if I ask if they are really giants?" Velikof questioned.

"As your eyes tell you, they are the Giants," Crayola said. "They stay here in the out-of-the-way places even more than the rest of us. Sometimes regular people see them and do not understand that they are regular people too. For that there is scandal. It was the scent of such a scandal, I believe, that brought the three of you here. But they are not apes or bears or monsters. They are people too."

"They are of your own same kindred?" Velikof asked.

"Oh yes. They are the uncles, the old bachelors. That's why they grow tall and silent. That's why they stand around the edges of the room. And that is why they dig themselves caves into the banks and bluffs instead of living in huts. The roofs of huts are too low for them."

"It would be possible to build taller huts," Willy McGilly suggested.

"It would be possible for you, yes," Crayola said. "It would not be possible for them. They are set in their ways. They develop a stoop and a gait because they feel themselves so tall. They let their hair grow and overflow, all over their faces and around their eyes, and all over their bodies also. They are the steers of the species. Having no children or furniture, what can they do but grow tall and ungainly like that? This happens also to the steers of cattle and bears and apes, that they grow tall and gangling. They become bashful, you see, so sometimes it is mistakenly believed that they are fierce."

The roaring and booming from west of the thunder was becoming louder and nearer. The river was coming dangerously alive. All of the people in the room knew that it was now dark outside, and it was not yet time to be night.

The Comet gave his pool cue to one of the bashful giants and came and sat with the eminents.

"You are Magi?" he asked.

"I am a magus, yes," Willy McGilly said. "We are called eminent scientists nowadays. Velikof here also remains a magus, but Arpad has lost it all this day."

"You are not the same three I first believed," the old Comet said. "Those three passed me several of my cycles back. They had had word of an Event, and they had come from a great distance as soon as they heard it. But it took them near two thousand years to make the trip and they were worried that myth had them as already arriving long ago. They were worried that false Magi had anticipated them and set up a preventing myth. And I believe that is what did happen."

"And your own myths, old fellow, have they preceded you, or have you really been here before?" Willy McGilly asked. "I see that you have a twisty tongue that turns out some really winding myths."

"Thank you, for that is ever my intent. Myths are not merely things that were made in times past: myths are among the things that maintain the present in being. I wish most strongly that the present should be maintained: I often live in it."

"Tell us, old man, why Boomer Flats is a place that the comets come back to?" Willy said.

"Oh, it's just one of the post stations where we change horses when we make our orbits. A lot of the comets come to the Flats: Booger, Donati, Encke, 1914c, and Halley."

"But why to Boomer Flats on the little Cimarron River?" Willy inquired.

"Things are often more than they seem. The Cimarron isn't really so little a river as you would imagine. Actually it is the river named Ocean that runs around all the worlds."

"Old Comet, old man with the pieces falling off of you," Dr. Velikof Vonk asked out of that big head of his, "can you tell us just who are the under-people that we have tracked all around the world and have probably found here no more than seventy miles from our own illustrious T-Town?"

"A phyz like you have on you, and you have to ask!" the old Comet twinkled at Velikof (a man who twinkled like that had indeed been among the stars; he had their dust on him). "You're one of them, you know."

"I've suspected that for a long time," Velikof admitted. "But who are they? And who am I?"

"Wise Willy here said it correctly to you last night; that they were the scrubs who bottom the breed. But do not demean the scrubs: they are the foundation. They are human as all of us are human. They are a race that underlies the other several races of man. When the bones and blood of the more manifest races grow too thin, then they sustain you with the mixture of their strong kingship: the mixing always goes on, but in special eras it is more widespread. They are the link that is never really missing, the link between the clay and the blood."

"Why are they, and me if I were not well-kempt and eminent, sometimes taken to be animals?" Velikof asked. "Why do they always live in such outlandish places?"

"They don't always. Sometimes they live in very inlandish places. Even wise Willy understands that. But it is their function to stand apart and grow in strength. Look at the strong bone structure of that girl there! It is their function to invent forms—look at the form her mother invented for her. They have a depth of mind, and they have it particularly in those ghostly areas where the other races lack it. And they share and mingle it in those sudden motley ages of great achievement and vigor. Consider the great ages of Athens, of Florence, of Los Angeles. And afterward, this people will withdraw again to gather new strength and bottom."

"And why are they centered here in a tumble-down hotel that is like a series of old daguerreotypes?" Willy McGilly asked. "Will you tell us that there is something cosmic about this little old hotel, as there is about this little old river?"

"Aye, of course there is, Willy. This is the hotel named Xenodocheion. This is the special center of these Xenoi, these strangers, and of all strangers everywhere. It isn't small; it is merely that you can see but a portion of it at one time. And then they center here to keep out of the way. Sometimes they live in areas and neighborhoods that regularized humanity has abandoned (whether in inner-city or boondock). Sometimes they live in eras and decades that regularized humanity has abandoned: for their profundity of mind in the more ghostly areas, they have come to have a cavalier way with time. What is wrong with that? If regular people are finished with those days and times, why may not others use them?"

The roaring and booming to the west of the thunder had become very loud and very near now, and in the immediate outdoors there was heavy rain.

"It is the time," the girl Crayola Catfish cried out in her powerful and intricate voice. "The flash flood is upon us and it will smash everything. We will all go and lie down in the river."

They all began to follow her out, the Boomer Flats people, and the Giants among them; the eminents, everybody.

"Will you also lie down in the river, Comet?" Willy McGilly asked. "Somehow I don't believe it of you."

"No, I will not. That isn't my way. I will take my horse and buggy and ascend above it."

"Ah, but Comet, will it look like a horse and buggy to us?"

"No, it will look quite other, if you do chance to see it."

"And what are you really, Comet?" Velikof asked him as they left him. "What species do you belong to?"

"To the human species, of course, Velikof. I belong to still another race of it; another race that mixes sometimes, and then withdraws again to gather more strength and depth. Some individuals of us withdraw for quite long times. There are a number of races of us in the wide cousinship, you see, and it is a necessity that we be strangers to each other for a good part of the time."

"Are you a saucerian?"

"Oh saucerian be damned, Velikof! Harma means chariot or it means buggy; it does not mean saucer. We are the comets. And our own mingling with the commonalty of people has also had quite a bit to do with those sudden incandescent eras. Say, I'd like to talk with you fellows again some time. I'll be by this way again in about eighty-seven years."

"Maybe so," said Dr. Velikof Vonk.

"Maybe so," said Willy McGilly.

The eminents followed the Boomer Flats people to the river. And the Comet, we suppose, took his horse and buggy and ascended out of it. Odd old fellow he was; pieces falling off him; he'd hardly last another hundred years.

The red and black river was in surging flood with a blood-colored crest bearing down. And the flats—they were just too flat. The flood would be a mile wide here in one minute and everywhere in that width it would be deep enough and swift enough to drown a man. It was near dark: it was near the limit of roaring sound. But there was a pile of large rocks there in the deepening shallows: plenty of rocks: at least one big heavy rock for every person.

The Boomer Flats people understood what the rocks were for, and the Giants among them understood. Two of the eminents understood; and one of them, Arpad, apparently did not. Arpad was carrying on in great fear about the dangers of death by drowning.

Quickly then, to cram mud into the eyes and ears and noses and mouths. There is plenty of mud and all of it is good. Spirits of Catfish protect us now!—it will be only for a few hours, for two or three days at the most.

Arpad alone panicked. He broke and ran when Crayola Catfish tried to put mud in his mouth and nose to save him. He ran and stumbled in the rising waters to his death.

But all the others understood. They lay down in the red roaring river, and one of the Giants set a heavy rock on the breast of every person of them to hold them down. The last of the Giants then rolled the biggest of the rocks onto his own breast.

So all were safe on the bottom of the surging torrent, safe in the old mud-clay cradle. Nobody can stand against a surging flood like that: the only way is to lie down on the bottom and wait it out. And it was a refreshing, a deepening, a renewing experience. There are persons, both inside and outside the orders, who make religious retreats of three days every year for their renewal. This was very like such a retreat.

When the flood had subsided (this was three days later), they all rose again, rolling the big rocks off their breasts; they cleared their eyes and ears and mouths of the preserving mud, and they resumed their ways and days.

For Velikof Vonk and for Willy McGilly it had been an enriching experience. They had found the link that was not really lost, leaving the other ninety-nine meanwhile. They had grown in cousinship and wisdom. They said they would return to the flats every year at mud-duck season and turtle-egg season. They went back to T-Town enlarged and happy.

There is, however, a gap in the Magi set, due to the foolish dying of Arpad Arkabaranan. It is not of scripture that a set of Magi should consist of only three. There have been sets of seven and nine and eleven. It is almost of scripture, though, that a set should not consist of less than three. In the Masulla Apocalypse it seems to be said that a set must contain at the least a Comet, a Commoner, and a Catfish. The meaning of this is pretty muddy, and it may be a mistranslation.

There is Dr. Velikof Vonk with his huge head, with his heavy orbital ridges, with the protruding near-muzzle on him that makes the chin unnecessary and impossible, with the great back-brain and the great good humor. He is (and you had already guessed it of him) an ABSM, a neo-Neanderthal, an unmissing link, one of that branch of the human race that lives closest to the clay and the catfish.

There is Willy McGilly who belongs (and he himself has come to the realization of this quite lately) to that race of mankind called the Comets. He is quite bright, and he has his periods. He himself is a short-orbit comet, but for all that he has been among the stars. Pieces fall off of him; he leaves a wake; but he'll last a while yet.

One more is needed so that this set of Magi may be formed again. The other two aspects being already covered, the third member could well be a regularized person. It could be an older person of ability, an eminent. It could be a younger person of ability, a pre-eminent.

This person may be you. Put your hand to it if you have the surety about you, if you are not afraid of green snakes in the cup (they'll fang the face off you if you're afraid of them), or of clay-mud, or of comet dust, or of the rollicking world between.

Old Foot Forgot

Introduction by John Scalzi

So, here's a quick story of mine, relevant to this particular story.

My wife became pregnant when I was twenty-nine years old, and when she told me the news

a) I was ecstatic;

b) I suddenly begun waking up at three in the morning every night with the thought "dude, you're totally gonna die one day" ricocheting through my brain.

You don't need to be a genius of psychology to figure this one out. With the advent of our child, I was no longer the final generation on the family chain; a new link would be forged and I would be inevitably pulled into eternity's maw. I would survive by passing along my genes, not by living forever, which, up to age twenty-nine apparently, was my unspoken assumption.

I got over it. My kid's pretty great and I don't mind shuffling off the mortal coil, because I helped make her, and also I wrote a few books people might still read after I'm gone. I'm doing OK.

But that jolt of awareness I got at twenty-nine pops up again every now and then, in a slightly different way. I don't mind so much that I will die. But I'm sad that I will no longer *exist*. I enjoy existing. Existing is pretty neat. And while I'm pretty sure that when I no longer exist I won't mind (I didn't mind not existing before I was born, after all), right now I'm put out about it. I mean, I put a lot of effort into developing a sense of self, here, people. I don't get to take it with me? That's some bullshit right *there*, I tell you.

It's selfish of me but I don't mind that little bit of selfishness. It won't help me in the end, but until then it gets me along.

As I said, this story is relevant to "Old Foot Forgot," which is a story that makes me both happy and sad. Happy because clearly Lafferty got where I was coming from. Sad because, well. Oblivion *awaits*, doesn't it?

Fine. Bring it on (eventually). Until then: hey, I'm *here*, man. And I like it.

Old Foot Forgot

"Dookh-Doctor, it is a sphairikos patient," Lay Sister Moira P. T. de C. cried happily. "It is a genuine spherical alien patient. You've never had one before, not in good faith. I believe it is what you need to distract you from the—ah—happy news about yourself. It is good for a Dookh-Doctor to have a different patient sometimes."

"Thank you, lay sister. Let it, him, her, fourth case, fifth case, or whatever come in. No, I've never had a sphairikos in good faith. I doubt if this one is, but I will enjoy the encounter."

The sphairikos rolled or pushed itself in. It was a big one, either a blubbery kid or a full-grown one. It rolled itself along by extruding and withdrawing pseudopods. And it came to rest grinning, a large translucent rubbery ball of fleeting colors.

"Hello, Dookh-Doctor," it said pleasantly. "First I wish to extend my own sympathy and that of my friends who do not know how to speak to you for the happy news about yourself. And secondly I have an illness of which you may cure me."

"But the sphairikoi are never ill," Dookh-Doctor Drague said dutifully.

How did he know that the round creature was grinning at him? By the colors, of course; by the fleeting colors of it. They were grinning colors.

"My illness is not of the body but of the head," said the sphairikos.

"But the sphairikoi have no heads, my friend."

"Then it is of another place and another name, Dookh-Doctor. There is a thing in me suffering. I come to you as a Dookh-Doctor. I have an illness in my Dookh."

"That is unlikely in a sphairikos. You are all perfectly balanced, each a cosmos unto yourself. And you have a central solution that solves everything. What is your name?"

"Krug Sixteen, which is to say that I am the sixteenth son of Krug; the sixteen fifth case son, of course. Dookh-Doc, the pain is not in me entirely; it is in an old forgotten part of me."

"But you sphairikoi have no parts, Krug Sixteen. You are total and indiscriminate entities. How would you have parts?"

"It is one of my pseudopods, extended and then withdrawn in much less than a second long ago when I was a little boy. It protests, it cries, it wants to come back. It has always bothered me, but now it bothers me intolerably. It screams and moans constantly now."

"Do not the same ones ever come back?"

"No. Never. Never exactly the same ones. Will exactly the same water ever run past one point in a brook? No. We push them out and we draw them back. And we push them out again, millions of times. But the same one can never come back. There is no identity. But this one cries to come back, and now it becomes more urgent. Dookh-Doc, how can it be? There is not one same molecule in it as when I was a boy. There is nothing of that pseudopod that is left; but parts of it have come out as parts of other pseudopods, and now there can be no parts left. There is nothing remaining of that foot; it has all been absorbed a million times. But it cries out! And I have compassion on it."

"Krug Sixteen, it may possibly be a physical or mechanical difficulty, a pseudopod imperfectly withdrawn, a sort of rupture whose effects you interpret wrongly. In that case it would be better if you went to your own doctors, or doctor: I understand that there is one."

"That old fogey cannot help me, Dookh-Doc. And our pseudopods are always perfectly withdrawn. We are covered with the twinkling salve; it is one-third of our bulk. And if we need more of it we can make more of it ourselves; or we can beg some of it from a class four who makes it prodigiously. It is the solvent for everything. It eases every possible wound; it makes us round as balls; you should use it yourself, Dookh-Doc. But there is one small foot in me, dissolved long ago, that protests and protests. Oh, the shrieking! The horrible dreams!"

"But the sphairikoi do not sleep and do not dream."

"Right enough, Dookh-Doc. But there's an old dead foot of mine that sure does dream loud and wooly."

The sphairikos was not grinning now. He rolled about softly in apprehension. How did the Dookh-Doctor know that it was apprehension? By the fleeting colors. They were apprehension colors now.

"Krug Sixteen, I will have to study your case," said the Dookh-Doctor. "I will see if there are any references to it in the literature, though I don't believe that there are. I will seek for analogy. I will probe every possibility. Can you come back at the same hour tomorrow?"

"I will come back, Dookh-Doc," Krug Sixteen sighed. "I hate to feel that small vanished thing crying and trembling."

It rolled or pushed itself out of the clinic by extruding and then withdrawing pseudopods. The little pushers came out of the goopy surface of the sphairikos and then were withdrawn into it completely. A raindrop falling in a pond makes a much more lasting mark than does the disappearing pseudopod of a sphairikos.

But long ago, in his boyhood, one of the pseudopods of Krug Sixteen had not disappeared completely in every respect.

"There are several jokers waiting," Lay Sister Moira P. T. de C. announced a little later, "and perhaps some valid patients among them. It's hard to tell."

"Not another sphairikos?" the Dookh-Doctor asked in sudden anxiety.

"Of course not. The one this morning is the only sphairikos who has ever come. How could there be anything wrong with him? There is never anything wrong with a sphairikos. No, these are all of the other species. Just a regular morning bunch."

So, except for the visitation of the sphairikos, it was a regular morning at the clinic. There were about a dozen waiting, of the several species; and at least half of them would be jokers. It was always so.

There was a lean and giddy subula. One cannot tell the age or sex of them. But there was a tittering. In all human or inhuman expression, whether of sound, color, radioray, or osmerhetor, the titter suggests itself. It is just around the corner, it is just outside, it is subliminal, but it is there somewhere.

"It is that my teeth hurt so terrible," the subula shrilled so high that the Dookh-Doctor had to go on instruments to hear it. "They are tromping pain. They are agony. I think I will cut my head off. Have you a head-off cutter, Dookh-Doctor?"

"Let me see your teeth," Dookh-Doctor Drague asked with the beginnings of irritation.

"There is one tooth jump up and down with spike boot," the subula shrilled. "There is one jag like poisoned needle. There is one cuts like coarse rough saw. There is one burns like little hot fires."

"Let me see your teeth," the Dookh-Doctor growled evenly.

"There is one drills holes and sets little blasting powder in them," the subula shrilled still more highly. "Then he sets them off. Ow! Good night!"

"Let me see your teeth!!"

"Peeef!" the subula shrilled. The teeth cascaded out, half a bushel of them, ten thousand of them, all over the floor of the clinic.

"Peeef," the subula screeched again, and ran out of the clinic.

Tittering? (But he should have remembered that the subula have no teeth.) Tittering? It was the laughing of demented horses. It was the jackhammer braying of the dolcus, it was the hysterical giggling of the ophis (they were a half a bushel of shells of the little stink conches and they were already beginning to rot), it was the clown laughter of the arktos (the clinic would never be habitable again; never mind, he would burn it down and build another one tonight).

The jokers, the jokers, they did have their fun with him, and perhaps it did them some good.

"I have this trouble with me," said a young dolcus, "but it make me so nervous to tell it. Oh, it do make me nervous to tell it to the Dookh-Doc."

"Do not be nervous," said the Dookh-Doctor, fearing the worst. "Tell me your trouble in whatever way you can. I am here to serve every creature that is in any trouble or pain whatsoever. Tell it."

"Oh but it make me so nervous. I perish. I shrivel. I will have accident I am so nervous."

"Tell me your trouble, my friend. I am here to help."

"Whoops, whoops, I already have accident! I tell you I am nervous."

The dolcus urinated largely on the clinic floor. Then it ran out laughing.

The laughing, the shrilling, the braying, the shrill giggling that seemed to scrape the flesh from his bones. (He should have remembered that the dolcus do not urinate; everything comes from them hard and solid.) The hooting, the laughing! It was a bag of green water from the kolmula swamp. Even the aliens gagged at it, and their laughter was of a pungent green sort.

Oh well, there were several of the patients with real, though small, ailments, and there were more jokers. There was the arktos who—(Wait, wait, that particular jokerie cannot be told with human persons present; even the subula and the ophis blushed lavender at the rawness of it. A thing like that can only be told to arktos themselves.) And there was another dolcus who—

Jokers, jokers, it was a typical morning at the clinic.

One does whatever one can for the oneness that is greater than self. In the case of Dookh-Doctor Drague it meant considerable sacrifice. One who works with the strange species here must give up all hope of material reward or material sophistication in his surroundings. But the Dookh-Doctor was a dedicated man.

Oh, the Dookh-Doctor lived pleasantly and with a sort of artful simplicity and dynamic involvement in the small articles of life. He had an excited devotion and balanced intensity for corporate life.

He lived in small houses of giolach-weed, woven with careful double-rappel. He lived in each one for seven days only, and then burned it and scattered the ashes, taking always one bitter glob of them on his tongue for reminder of the fleetingness of temporal things and the wonderfulness of the returning. To live in one house for more than seven days is to become dull and habitual; but the giolach-weed will not burn well till it has been cut and plaited for seven days, so the houses set their own terms. One half day to build, seven days to inhabit, one half day to burn ritually and scatter, one renewal night under the speir-sky.

The Dookh-Doctor ate raibe, or he ate innuin or ull or piorra when they were in season. And for the nine days of each year when none of these were in season, he ate nothing at all.

His clothing he made himself of colg. His paper was of the pailme plant. His printer used buaf ink and shaved slinn stone. Everything that he needed he made for himself from things found wild in the hedgerows. He took nothing from the cultivated land or from the alien peoples. He was a poor and dedicated servant.

Now he stacked some of the needful things from the clinic, and Lay Sister Moira P. T. de C. took others of them to her own giolach house to keep till the next day. Then the Dookh-Doctor ritually set his clinic on fire, and a few moments later his house. This was all symbol of the great nostos, the returning. He recited the great rhapsodies, and other persons of the human kind came by and recited with him.

"That no least fiber of giolach die," he recited, "that all enter immediately the more glorious and undivided life. That the ashes are the doorway, and every ash is holy. That all become a part of the oneness that is greater than self.

"That no splinter of the giuis floorboards die, that no glob of the chinking clay die, that no mite or louse in the plaiting die. That all become a part of the oneness that is greater than self."

He burned, he scattered, he recited, he took one glob of bitter ash on his tongue. He experienced vicariously the great synthesis. He ate holy innuin and holy ull. And when it was finished, both of the house and the clinic, when it had come on night and he was homeless, he slept that renewal night under the speir-sky.

And in the morning he began to build again, the clinic first, and then the house. "It is the last of either that I shall ever build," he said. The happy news about himself was that he was a dying man and that he would be allowed to take the short way out. So he built most carefully with the Last Building Rites. He chinked both the buildings with special uir clay that would give a special bitterness to the ashes at the time of final burning.

Krug Sixteen rolled along while the Dookh-Doctor still built his final clinic, and the sphairikos helped him in the building while they consulted on the case of the screaming foot. Krug Sixteen could weave and plait and rappel amazingly with his pseudopods; he could bring out a dozen of them, a hundred, thick or thin, whatever was needed, and all of a wonderful dexterity. That globe could weave.

"Does the forgotten foot still suffer, Krug Sixteen?" Dookh-Doctor Drague asked it.

"It suffers, it's hysterical, it's in absolute terror. I don't know where it is; it does not know; and how I know about it at all is a mystery. Have you found any way to help me, to help it?"

"No. I am sorry, but I have not."

"There is nothing in the literature on this subject?"

"No. Nothing that I can identify as such."

"And you have not found analogy to it?"

"Yes, Krug Sixteen, ah— In a way I *have* discovered analogy. But it does not help you. Or me."

"That is too bad, Dookh-Doc. Well, I will live with it; and the little foot will finally die with it. Do I guess that your case is somewhat the same as mine?"

"No. My case is more similar to that of your lost foot than to you."

"Well, I will do what I can for myself, and for it. It's back to the old remedy then. But I am already covered deep with the twinkling salve."

"So am I, Krug Sixteen, in a like way."

"I was ashamed of my affliction before and did not mention it. Now, however, since I have spoken of it to you, I have spoken of it to others also. There is some slight help, I find. I should have shot off my big bazoo before."

"The sphairikoi have no bazoos."

"Folk-joke, Dookh-Doc. There is a special form of the twinkling salve. My own is insufficient, so I will try the other."

"A special form of it, Krug Sixteen? I am interested in this. My own salve seems to have lost its effect."

"There is a girlfriend, Dookh-Doc, or a boyfriend person. How shall I say it? It is a case four person to my case five. This person, though promiscuous, is expert. And this person exudes the special stuff in abundance."

"Not quite my pot of ointment I'm afraid, Krug Sixteen; but it may be the answer for you. It is special? And it dissolves everything, including objections?"

"It is the most special of all the twinkling salves, Dookh-Doc, and it solves and dissolves everything. I believe it will reach my forgotten foot, wherever it is, and send it into kind and everlasting slumber. It will know that it is itself that slumbers, and that will be bearable."

"If I were not—ah—going out of business, Krug Sixteen, I'd get a bit of it and try to analyze it. What is the name of this special case four person?"

"Torchy Twelve is its name."

"Yes. I have heard of her."

Everybody now knew that it was the last week in the life of the Dookh-Doctor, and everyone tried to make his happiness still more happy. The morning jokers outdid themselves, especially the arktos. After all, he was dying of an arktos disease, one never fatal to the arktos themselves. They did have some merry and outrageous times around the clinic, and the Dookh-Doctor got the sneaky feeling that he would rather live than die. He hadn't, it was plain to see, the right attitude. So Lay Priest Migma P. T. de C. tried to inculcate the right attitude in him.

"It is the great synthesis you go to, Dookh-Doctor," he said. "It is the happy oneness that is greater than self."

"Oh I know that, but you put it on a little too thick. I've been taught it from my babyhood. I'm resigned to it."

"Resigned to it? You should be ecstatic over it! The self must perish, of course, but it will live on as an integral atom of the evolving oneness, just as a drop lives on in the ocean."

"Aye, Migma, but the drop may hang onto the memory of the time when it was cloud, of the time when it was falling drop, indeed, of the time when it was brook. It may say, 'There's too damned much salt in this ocean. I'm lost here.'"

"Oh, but the drop will want to be lost, Dookh-Doctor. The only purpose of existence is to cease to exist. And there cannot be too much of salt in the evolving oneness. There cannot be too much of anything. All must be one in it. Salt and sulfur must be one, undifferentiated. Offal and soul must become one. Blessed be oblivion in the oneness that collapses on itself."

"Stuff it, lay priest. I'm weary of it."

"Stuff it, you say? I don't understand your phrase, but I'm sure it's apt. Yes, yes, Dookh-Doctor, stuff it all in: animals, people, rocks, grass, worlds, and wasps. Stuff it all in. That all may be obliterated into the great—may I not coin a word even as the master coined them?—into the great stuffiness!"

"I'm afraid your word is all too apt."

"It is the great quintessence, it is the happy death of all individuality and memory, it is the synthesis of all living and dead things into the great amorphism. It is the—"

"It is the old old salve, and it's lost its twinkle," the Dookh-Doctor said sadly. "How goes the old quotation? When the salve becomes sticky, how then will you come unstuck?"

No, the Dookh-Doctor did not have the right attitude, so it was necessary that many persons should harass him into it. Time was short. His death was due. And there was the general fear that the Dookh-Doctor might not be properly lost.

He surely came to his time of happiness in grumpy fashion.

The week was gone by. The last evening for him was come. The Dookh-Doctor ritually set his clinic on fire, and a few minutes later his house.

He burned, he scattered, he recited the special last-time recital. He ate holy innuin and holy ull. He took one glob of most bitter ash on his tongue: and he lay down to sleep his last night under the speir-sky.

He wasn't afraid to die.

"I will cross that bridge gladly, but I want there to be another side to that bridge," he talked to himself. "And if there is no other side of it, I want it to be *me* who knows that there is not. They say, 'Pray that you be happily lost forever. Pray for blessed obliteration.' I will *not* pray that I be happily lost forever. I would rather burn in a hell forever than suffer happy obliteration! I'll burn if it be *me* that burns. I want me to be me. I will refuse forever to surrender myself."

It was a restless night for him. Well, perhaps he could die easier if he were wearied and sleepless at dawn.

"Other men don't make such a fuss about it," he told himself (the self he refused to give up). "Other men are truly happy in obliteration. Why am I suddenly different? Other men desire to be lost, lost, lost. How have I lost the faith of my childhood and manhood? What is unique about me?"

There was no answer to that.

"Whatever is unique about me, I refuse to give it up. I will howl and moan against that extinction for billions of centuries. Ah, I will go sly! I will devise a sign so I will know me if I meet me again."

About an hour before dawn the Lay Priest Migma P. T. de C. came to Dookh-Doctor Drague. The dolcus and the arktos had reported that the man was resting badly and was not properly disposed.

"I have an analogy that may ease your mind, Dookh-Doctor," the Lay Priest whispered softly, "ease it into great easiness, salve it into great salving—"

"Begone, fellow, your salve has lost its twinkle."

"Consider that we have never lived, that we have only seemed to live. Consider that we do not die, but are only absorbed into great selfless self. Consider the odd sphairikoi of this world—"

"What about the sphairikoi? I consider them often."

"I believe that they are set here for our instruction. A sphairikos is a total globe, the type of the great oneness. Then consider that it sometimes ruffles its surface, extrudes a little false-foot from its soft surface. Would it not be odd if that false-foot, for its brief second, considered itself a person? Would you not laugh at that?"

"No, no. I do not laugh." And the Dookh-Doctor was on his feet.

"And in much less than a second, that pseudopod is withdrawn back into the sphere of the sphairikoi. So it is with our lives. Nothing dies. It is only a ripple on the surface of the oneness. Can you entertain so droll an idea as that the pseudopod should remember, or wish to remember?"

"Yes. I'll remember it a billion years for the billion who forget."

The Dookh-Doctor was running uphill in the dark. He crashed into trees and boles as though he wished to remember the crashing forever. "I'll burn before I forget, but I must have something that says it's me who burns!"

Up, up by the spherical hills of the sphairikoi, bawling and stumbling in the dark. Up to a hut that had a certain fame he could never place, to the hut that had its own identity, that sparkled with identity.

"Open, open, help me!" the Dookh-Doctor cried out at the last hut on the hill.

"Go away, man!" the last voice protested. "All my clients are gone, and the night is almost over with. What has this person to do with a human man anyhow?"

It was a round twinkling voice out of the roweled dark. But there was enduring identity there. The twinkling, enduring-identity colors, coming from the chinks of the hut, had not reached the level of vision. There was even the flicker of the I-will-know-me-if-I-meet-me-again color.

"Torchy Twelve, help me. I am told that you have the special salve that solves the last problem, and makes it know that it is always itself that is solved."

"Why, it is the Dookh-Doc! Why have you come to Torchy?"

"I want something to send me into kind and everlasting slumber," he moaned. "But I want it to be *me* who slumbers. Cannot you help me in any way?"

"Come you in, the Dookh-Doc. This person, though promiscuous, is expert. I help you—"

The World as Will and Wallpaper

Introduction by Samuel R. Delany

Along with "The Primary Education of the Camiroi," this was one of the first tales by Raphael Aloysius Lafferty (1914–2002) I read.

Where it appeared, however, I have no notion. Possibly that's because today I know so much more about the intellectual context that informs his story than I did when I first read it, and it is easy to let the context overwhelm the tale. One suspects that is part of the story's project. But in whose anthology—Judith Merril's? Terry Carr's?—I first read this piece, I have no notion at all.

I once taught a Clarion workshop at Tulane (where the students included George R. R. Martin), and I wondered if somehow Lafferty himself might be in evidence. He wasn't. And the class was in some confusion because the young man who had set up the whole thing had also pulled out at the last minute. It's interesting that even at that time Lafferty as a myth was so in evidence.

But what of the tale to hand?

William Morris (1834–1896) was intelligent, rich, and multitalented. He was a committed socialist, and the author of a number of fantasies, including *News from Nowhere* and *The World Beyond the Wood*. He supported a number of other artists, including Edward Burne-Jones, and he designed ornate wallpapers still used today; as well, he printed sumptuous illustrated editions of books such as the Kelmscott *Works of Geoffrey Chaucer*. He is one of the most written-about men of his times, and he is the avatar of the hero of Lafferty's futuristic tale of a trip through the City of the World.

As much or more than any famous Victorian figure, it's easy to see how the nature of Morris's fame is entirely an accident of a social position.

Lafferty's title riffs on the German philosopher Arthur Schopenhauer's (1788–1860) two-volume philosophical treatise *The World as Will and Representation*. Schopenhauer is known for the extreme pessimism of his philosophy and the beauty of his writing.

Like a Wallace Shawn play, Lafferty's tale takes place in a stressed future and moves from there to its distressing end.

The story begins from a seeming common-sense challenge to the classical description of a city, straight out of Jane Jacobs ("a concentration of persons that is not economically self-contained . . .") and sets it at the limit of its growth: "The World City is economically self-contained."

By the story's end, Lafferty's own pessimism is running neck and neck with

Schopenhauer's. Lafferty's Catholicism was a topic often referred to by fans and critics: the other writer who sits in my mind as a (severely lapsed) Catholic is Thomas Disch. And I wonder to what extent that can be read as part of the cultural context that informs both writers.

Lafferty's is a story of bookies and talkies and readies, where the World City is a tidy place because it tips and tilts with the tides it floats on, and Willy, whose "name game" is based on William Morris, goes to explore with Kandy Kalosh and later Fairhair Farquhar, the World City which is, of course, much too large for them to see more than a fraction of—though what of it that's revealed, with each narrative move, is more and more distressing.

In all, "The World as Will and Wallpaper" offers a grim view of what a world as it approaches its end times requires to be self-sustaining.

The World as Will and Wallpaper

A template, a stencil, a plan.
Corniest, orniest damsel and man,
Orderly, emptily passion and pity,
All-the-World, All-the-World, All-the-World City.

—13th Street Ballad

There is an old dictionary-encyclopedia that defines a City as "... a concentration of persons that is not economically self-contained." The dictionary-encyclopedia being an old one, however (and there is no other kind), is mistaken. The World City *is* economically self-contained.

It was William Morris who read this definition in the old book. William was a bookie, or readie, and he had read parts of several books. But now he had a thought: if all the books are old, then things may no longer be as the books indicate. I will go out and see what things are like today in the City. I will traverse as much of the City as my life allows me. I may even come to the *Wood Beyond the World* that my name-game ancestor described.

William went to the Permit Office of the City. Since there was only one City, there might be only one Permit Office, though it was not large.

"I want a permit to traverse as much of the City as my life allows me," William told the permit man. "I even want a permit to go to the *Wood Beyond the World*. Is that possible?"

The permit man did a little skittish dance around William, "like a one-eyed gander around a rattlesnake." The metaphor was an old and honored one, one of the fifty-four common metaphors. They both understood it: it didn't have to be voiced. William was the first customer the permit man had had in many days, though, so the visit startled him.

"Since everything is permitted, you will need no permit," the permit man said. "Go, man, go."

"Why are you here then?" William asked him. "If there are no permits, why is there a Permit Office?"

"This is my niche and my notch," the permit man said. "Do away with me and my office and you begin to do away with the City itself. It is the custom to take a companion when you traverse the City."

Outside, William found a companion named Kandy Kalosh and they began to traverse the City that was the World. They began (it was no more than coincidence) at a marker set in stone that bore the words "Beginning of Stencil 35,352." The City tipped and tilted a bit, and they were on their way. Now this is what the City was like:

It was named Will of the World City, for it had been constructed by a great and worldwide surge of creative will. Afterward, something had happened to that surge, but it did not matter; the City was already created then.

The City was varied, it was joyful, it was free, and it covered the entire world. The mountains and heights had all been removed, and the City, with its various strips of earth and sweet water and salt water, floated on the ocean on its interlocking floaters. As to money values, everything was free; and everything was free as to personal movement and personal choice. It was not really crowded except in the places where the people wanted it crowded, for people do love to congregate. It was sufficient as to foodstuff and shelter and entertainment. These things have always been free, really; it was their packaging and traffic that cost, and now the packaging and traffic were virtually eliminated.

"Work is joy" flashed the subliminal signs. Of course it is. It is a joy to stop and turn into an area and work for an hour, even an hour and a half, at some occupation never or seldom attempted before. William and Kandy entered an area where persons made cloth out of clamshells, softening them in one solution, then drawing them out to filaments on a machine, then forming (not weaving) them into cloth on still another machine. The cloth was not needed for clothing or for curtains, though sometimes it was used for one or the other. It was for ornamentation. Temperature did not require cloth (the temperature was everywhere equitable) and modesty did not require it, but there was something that still required a little cloth as ornament.

William and Kandy worked for nearly an hour with other happy people on the project. It is true that their own production was all stamped "Rejected" when they were finished, but that did not mean that it went all the way back to the clamshells, only back to the filament stage.

"Honest labor is never lost," William said as solemnly as a one-horned owl with the pip.

"I knew you were a readie, but I didn't know you were a talkie," Kandy said. People didn't talk much then. Happy people have no need to talk. And of course honest labor is never lost, and small bits of it are pleasurable.

This portion of the City (perhaps all portions of the City) floated on an old ocean itself. It had, therefore, a slight heave to it all the time. "The City is a tidy place" was an old and honored saying. It referred to the fact that the City moved a little with the tides. It was a sort of joke.

The two young persons came ten blocks; they came a dozen. For much of this traverse the City had been familiar to William but not to Kandy. They had been going west, and William had always been a westing lad. Kandy, however, had always wandered east from her homes, and she was the farthest west that she had ever been when she met William.

They came to the 14th Street Water Ballet and watched the swimmers. These swimmers were very good, and great numbers of curiously shaped fish frolicked with them in the green salt-fresh pools. Anyone who wished to could, of course, swim in the Water Ballet, but most of the swimmers seemed to be regulars. They were part of the landscape, of the waterscape.

William and Kandy stopped to eat at an algae-and-plankton quick-lunch place on 15th Street. Indeed, Kandy worked there for half an hour, pressing the plankton and adding squirts of special protein as the people ordered it. Kandy had worked in quick-lunch places before.

The two of them stopped at the Will of the World Exhibit Hall on 16th Street. They wrote their names with a stylus in wax when they went in, or rather William wrote the names of both of them for Kandy could not write. And because he bore the mystic name of William, he received a card out of the slot with a genuine Will of the World verse on it:

This City of the World is wills
Of Willful folk, and nothing daunts it.
With daring hearts we hewed the hills
To make the World as Willy wants it.

Really, had it taken such great will and heart to build the City of the World? It must have or there would not have been a Will of the World Exhibit Hall to commend it. There were some folks, however, who said that the building of the World City had been an automatic response.

Kandy, being illiterate (as the slot knew), received a picture card.

They stopped at the Cliff-Dweller Complex on 17th Street. This part of the City was new to William as well as to Kandy.

The cliffs and caves were fabricated and not natural cliff dwellings, but they looked very much as old cliff dwellings must have looked. There were little ladders going up from one level to the next. There were people sitting on the little terraces with the small-windowed apartments behind them. Due to the circular arrangement of the cliff dwellings, very many of the people were always visible to one another. The central courtyard was like an amphitheater. Young people played stickball and Indian ball in this area. They made music on drums and whistles. There were artificial rattlesnakes in coils, artificial rib-skinny dogs, artificial coyotes, artificial women in the act of grinding corn with hand querns. And also, in little shelters or pavilions, there were real people grinding simulacrum corn on apparatus.

Kandy Kalosh went into one of the pavilions and ground corn for fifteen minutes. She had a healthy love for work. William Morris made corndogs out of simulacrum corn and seaweeds. It was pleasant there. Sometimes the people sang simulacrum Indian songs. There were patterned blankets, brightly colored, and woven out of bindweed. There were buffoons in masks and buffoon suits who enacted in-jokes and in-situations that were understood by the cliff-dwelling people only, but they could be enjoyed by everyone.

"All different, all different, every block different," William murmured in rapture. It had come on evening, but evening is a vague thing. It was never very bright in the daytime or very dark at night. The World City hadn't a clear sky but it had always a sort of diffused light. William and Kandy traveled still farther west.

"It is wonderful to be a world traveler and to go on forever," William exulted. "The City is so huge that we cannot see it all in our whole lives and every bit of it is different."

"A talkie you are," Kandy said. "However did I get a talkie? If I were a talkie too I could tell you something about that every-part-of-it-is-different bit."

"This is the greatest thing about the whole World City," William sang, "to travel the City itself for all our lives, and the climax of it will be to see the *Wood Beyond the World*. But what happens then, Kandy? The City goes on forever, covering the whole sphere. It cannot be bounded. What is beyond the *Wood Beyond the World*?"

"If I were a talkie I could tell you," Kandy said.

But the urge to talk was on William Morris. He saw an older and somehow more erect man who wore an armband with the lettering "Monitor" on it. Of course only a readie, or bookie, like William would have been able to read the word.

"My name-game ancestor had to do with the naming as well as the designing of the *Wood Beyond the World*," William told the erect and smiling man, "for I also am a William Morris. I am avid to see this ultimate wood. It is as though I have lived for the moment."

"If you will it strongly enough, then you may see it, Willy," the man said.

"But I am puzzled," William worried out the words, and his brow was furrowed. "What is beyond the *Wood Beyond the World*?"

"A riddle, but an easy one." The man smiled. "How is it that you are a readie and do not know such simple things?"

"Cannot you give me a clue to the easy riddle?" William begged.

"Yes," the man said. "Your name-game ancestor had to do with the designing of one other particular thing besides the *Wood Beyond the World*."

"Come along, readie, come along," Kandy said.

They went to the West Side Show Square on 18th Street. Neither of them had ever been to such a place, but they had heard rumors of it for there is nothing at all like the West Side Show Square on 18th Street.

There were the great amplifiers with plug-ins everywhere. Not only were the instruments plugged in, but most of the people were themselves plugged in. And ah! The wonderful setting was like the backside of old tenements all together in a rough circuit. There were period fire escapes that may even have been accurate. They looked as though persons might actually climb up and down on them. Indeed, light persons had actually done this in the past, but it was forbidden now as some of the folks had fallen to death or maiming. But the atmosphere was valid.

Listen, there was period washing on period clotheslines! It was flapped by little wind machines just as though there were a real wind blowing. No wonder they called this the show square. It was a glum-slum, a jetto-ghetto, authentic past time.

The performing people (and all the people on that part of 18th Street seemed to be performing people) were dressed in tight jeans and scalloped or ragged shirts, and even in broken shoes full of holes. It must have been very hot for them, but art is worth it. It was a memento of the time when the weather was not everywhere equitable.

There were in-dramas and in-jokes and in-situations acted out. The essence of the little dramas was very intense hatred for a group or class not clearly defined. There were many of those old-period enemy groups in the various drama locations of the City.

The lights were without pattern but they were bright. The music was without tune or melody or song or chord but it was very loud and very passionate. The shouting that took the place of singing was absolutely livid. Some of the performers fell to the ground and writhed there and foamed at their mouths.

It was a thing to be seen and heard—once. William and Kandy finally took their leave with bleeding ears and matter-encrusted eyes. They went along to 19th Street where there was a Mingle-Mangle.

It was now as dark as it ever got in the City but the Mangle was well lighted. Certain persons at the Mangle laughingly took hold of William and Kandy and married them to each other. They had bride and groom crowns made of paper and they put them on their heads.

Then they wined and dined them, an old phrase. Really, they were given fine cognac made of fish serum and braised meat made of algae but also mixed with the real chopped flesh of ancients.

Then William and Kandy padded down in the great Pad Palace that was next to the Mangle. Every night there were great numbers of people along that part of 19th Street, at the Mingle-Mangle and at the Pad Palace, and most of these folks were friendly, with their glazed eyes and their dampish grins.

2.

Pleasant most special to folks of the club!
Pleasant for manifold minions and hinds of it!
Stuff them with plankton and choppings and chub!
Simple the City and simple the minds of it.

—*20th Street Ballad*

The world's resources are consumed disproportionately by the intelligent classes. Therefore we will keep our own numbers drastically reduced. The wan-wits have not strong reproductive or consuming urge so long as they are kept in reasonable comfort and sustenance. They are happy, they are entertained; and when they are convinced that there is no more for them to see, they become the ancients and go willingly to the choppers. But the 2 percent or so of us superior ones are necessary to run the world.

Why then do we keep the others, the simple-minded billions? We keep them for the same reason that our ancestors kept blooms or lands or animals or great houses or trees or artifacts. We keep them because we want to, and because there is no effort involved.

But a great effort was made once. There was an incredible surge of will. Mountains were moved and leveled. The sky itself was pulled down, as it were. The Will of the World was made manifest. It was a new act of creation. And what is the step following creation when it is discovered that the Commonality is not worthy of the City created? When it is discovered also that they are the logical cattle to fill such great pens? The next step is hierarchies. The Angels themselves have hierarchies, *and we are not less.* It is those who are intelligent but not quite intelligent enough to join the Club who are imperiled and destroyed as a necessity to the operation of the City. At the Summit is always the Club. It is the Club in the sense of a bludgeon and also of an organization.

Will of the World Annals—Classified Abstract

In the morning, Kandy Kalosh wanted to return to her home even though it was nearly twenty blocks to the eastward. William watched her go without sorrow. He would get a westering girl to go with him on the lifelong exploration of the endlessly varied City. He might get a girl who was a talkie or even a readie, or bookie.

And he did. She was named Fairhair Farquhar, though she was actually dark of hair and of surface patina. But they started out in the early morning to attain (whether in a day or a lifetime) the *Wood Beyond the World.*

"But it is not far at all," Fairhair said (she was a talkie). "We can reach it this very evening. We can sleep in the *Wood* in the very night shadow of the famous Muggers. Oh, is the morning not wonderful! A blue patch was seen only last week, a real hole in the sky. Maybe we can see another."

They did not see another. It is very seldom that a blue (or even a starry) hole can be seen in the greenhouse glass–gray color that is the sky. The Will of the World had provided sustenance for everyone, but it was a muggy and sticky World City that provided almost equally warm from pole to pole, cloyingly fertile in both the land strips and the water strips, and now just a little bit queasy.

"Run, William, run in the morning!" Fairhair cried, and she ran while he shuffled after her. Fairhair did not suffer morning sickness but most of the world did: it had not yet been bred out of the races. After all, it was a very tidy world.

There was a great membrane or firmament built somewhere below, and old ocean was prisoned between this firmament and the fundamental rock of Gehenna-earth. But the ocean-monster tossed and pitched and was not entirely tamed: he was still old Leviathan.

Along and behind all the streets of the World City were the narrow (their width not five times the length of a man) strips, strips of very nervous and incredibly fertile land, of salt water jumping with fish and eels and dark with tortoise and so thick with blue-green plankton that one could almost walk on it, of fresh water teeming with other fish and loggy with snapping turtles and snakes, of other fresh water almost solid with nourishing algae, of mixed water filled with purged shrimp and all old estuary life; land strips again, and strips of rich chemical water where people voided themselves and their used things and from which so many valuable essences could be extracted; other strips, and then the houses and buildings of another block, for the blocks were not long. Kaleidoscope of nervous water and land, everywhere basic and everywhere different, boated with boats on the strange overpass canals, crossed by an infinity of bridges.

"And no two alike!" William sang, his morning sickness having left him. "Every one different, everything different in a world that cannot be traversed in a lifetime. We'll not run out of wonders!"

"William, William, there is something I have been meaning to tell you," Fairhair tried to interpose.

"Tell me, Fairhair, what is beyond the *Wood Beyond the World*, since the world is a globe without bounds?"

"The World Beyond the Wood is beyond the *Wood Beyond the World*," Fairhair said simply. "If you want the *Wood*, you will come to it, but do not be cast down if it falls short for you."

"How could it fall short for me? I am a William Morris. My name-game ancestor had to do with the naming as well as the designing of the *Wood*."

"Your name-game ancestor had to do with the designing of another thing also," Fairhair said. Why, that was almost the same thing as the monitor man had said the day before. What did they mean by it?

William and Fairhair came to the great Chopper House at 20th Street. The two of them went in and worked for an hour in the Chopper House.

"You do not understand this, do you, little William?" Fairhair asked.

"Oh, I understand enough for me. I understand that it is everywhere different."

"Yes, I suppose you understand enough for you," Fairhair said with a touch of near sadness. (What they chopped up in the Chopper House was the ancients.) They went on and on along the strips and streets of the ever-changing city. They came to 21st Street and 22nd and 23rd. Even a writie could not write down all the marvels that were to be found at every street. It is sheer wonder to be a world traveler.

There was a carnival at 23rd Street. There were barkies, sharkies, sparkies, darkies, parkies, and markies; the visitors were the markies, but it was not really bad for them. There was the very loud music even though it was supposed to be period tingle-tangle or rinky-dink. There was a steam calliope with real live steam. There were the hamburger stands with the wonderful smell of a touch of garlic in the open air, no matter that it was ancient chopper meat and crinoid-root bun from which the burgers were made. There were games of chance, smooch houses and cooch houses, whirly rides and turning wheels, wino and steino bars and bordellos, and Monster and Misbegotten displays in clamshell-cloth tents.

Really, is anyone too old to enjoy a carnival? Then let that one declare himself an ancient and turn himself in to a Chopper House.

But on and on; one does not tarry when there is the whole World City to see and it not be covered in one lifetime. On 24th (or was it 25th?) Street were the Flesh Pots; and a little beyond them was the Cat Center. One ate and drank beyond reason in the Flesh Pots region and also became enmeshed in the Flesh Mesh booths. And one catted beyond reason in the honeycomb-like cubicles of the Cat Center. Fairhair went and worked for an hour at the Cat Center; she seemed to be known and popular there.

But on and on! Everywhere it is different and everywhere it is better.

Along about 27th and 28th Streets were the Top of the Town and Night-Life Knoll, those great cabaret concentrations. It was gin-dizzy here; it was yesterday and tomorrow entangled with its great expectations and its overpowering nostalgia; it was loud as the West Side Show Square; it was as direct as the Mingle-Mangle or the Pad Palace. It was as fleshy as the Flesh Pots and more catty than the Cat-Center. Oh, it was the jumpingest bunch of places that William had yet seen in the City.

Something a little sad there, though; something of passion and pity that was too empty and too pat. It was as though this were the climax of it all, and one didn't *want* it to be the climax yet. It was as if the Top of the Town and Night-Life Knoll (and not the *Wood Beyond the World*) were the central things of the World City.

Perhaps William slept there awhile in the sadness that follows the surfeit of flesh and appetite. There were other doings and sayings about him, but mostly his eyes were closed and his head was heavy.

But then Fairhair had him up again and rushing toward the *Wood* in the still early night.

"It is only a block, William, it is only a block," she sang, "and it is the place you have wanted more than any other." (The *Wood* began at 29th Street and went on, it was said, for the space of *two* full blocks.) But William ran badly and he even walked badly. He was woozy and confused, not happy, not sad, just full of the great bulk of life in the City. He'd hardly have made it to his high goal that night except for the help of Fairhair. But she dragged and lifted and carried him along in her fine arms and on her dusky back and shoulders. He toppled off sometimes and cracked his crown, but there was never real damage done. One sometimes enters the *Wood Beyond* in a sort of rhythmic dream, grotesque and comic and jolting with the sway of a strong friend and of the tidy world itself. And William came in with his arms around the neck and shoulders of the girl named Fairhair, with his face buried in her hair itself, with his feet touching no ground.

But he knew it as soon as they were in the *Wood*. He was afoot again and strong again in the middle of the fabled place itself. He was sober? No, there can be no sobriety in the *Wood*; it has its own intoxication.

But it had real grass and weeds, real trees (though most of them were bushes), real beasts as well as artificial, real spruce cones on the turf, real birds (no matter that they were clattering crows) coming in to roost.

There was the carven oak figure of old Robin Hood and the tall spar-wood form of the giant lumberjack Paul Bunyan. There was the Red Indian named White Deer who was carved from cedarwood. There was maple syrup dripping from the trees (is that the way they used to get it?), and there was the aroma of slippery elm with the night dampness on it.

There were the famous Muggers from the mugger decades. They were of papier-mâché, it is true, and yet they were the most fearsome. There were other dangerous beasts in the *Wood,* but none like the Muggers. And William and Fairhair lay down and wept in the very night shadow of the famous Muggers for the remainder of the enchanted night.

3.

"Wander-bird, wander-bird, where do you fly?"
"All over the City, all under the sky."

"Wandr'ing through wonders of strippies and streets,
Changing and challenging, bitters and sweets."

"Wander-bird, squander-bird, should not have budged:
City is sicko and sky is a smudge."

—1st Street Ballad

"Run, William, run in the morning!" Fairhair cried, and she ran while William (confused from the night) shuffled after her.

"We must leave the *Wood*?" he asked.

"Of course *you* must leave the *Wood*. You want to see the whole world, so you cannot stay in one place. You go on, I go back. No, no, don't you look back or you'll be turned into a salt-wood tree."

"Stay with me, Fairhair."

"No, no, you want variety. I have been with you long enough. I have been guide and companion and pony to you. Now we part."

Fairhair went back. William was afraid to look after her. He was in the world beyond the *Wood Beyond the World*. He noticed though that the street was 1st Street and not 31st Street as he had expected.

It was still wonderful to be a world traveler, of course, but not quite as wonderful as it had been one other time. The number of the street shouldn't have mattered to him. William had not been on any 1st Street before. Or 2nd.

But he had been on a 3rd Street before on his farthest trip east.

Should he reach it again on his farthest trip west? The world, he knew (being a readie who had read parts of several books), was larger than that. He could not have gone around it in thirty blocks. Still, he came to 3rd Street in great trepidation.

Ah, it was not the same 3rd Street he had once visited before; almost the same but not exactly. An ounce of reassurance was intruded into the tons of alarm in his heavy head. But he was alive, he was well, he was still traveling west in the boundless City that is everywhere different.

"The City is varied and joyful and free," William Morris said boldly, "and it is everywhere different." Then he saw Kandy Kalosh and he literally staggered with the shock. Only it did not quite seem to be she.

"Is your name Kandy Kalosh?" he asked as quakingly as a one-legged kangaroo with the willies.

"The last thing I needed was a talkie," she said. "Of course it isn't. My name, which I have from my name-game ancestor, is Candy Calabash, not at all the same."

Of course it wasn't the same. Then why had he been so alarmed and disappointed?

"Will you travel westward with me, Candy?" he asked.

"I suppose so, a little way, if we don't have to talk," she said.

So William Morris and Candy Calabash began to traverse the City that was the world. They began (it was no more than coincidence) at a marker set in stone that bore the words "Beginning of Stencil 35,353," and thereat William went into a sort of panic. But why should he? It was not the same stencil number at all. The World City might still be everywhere different.

But William began to run erratically. Candy stayed with him. She was not a readie or a talkie, but she was faithful to a companion for many blocks. The two young persons came ten blocks; they came a dozen.

They arrived at the 14th Street Water Ballet and watched the swimmers. It was almost, but not quite, the same as another 14th Street Water Ballet that William had seen once. They came to the algae-and-plankton quick-lunch place on 15th Street and to the Will of the World Exhibit Hall on 16th Street. Ah, a hopeful eye could still pick out little differences in the huge sameness. The World City had to be everywhere different.

They stopped at the Cliff-Dweller Complex on 17th Street. There was an artificial antelope there now. William didn't remember it from the other time. There was hope, there was hope.

And soon William saw an older and somehow more erect man who wore an armband with the word "Monitor" on it. He was not the same man, but he had to be a close brother of another man that William had seen two days before.

"Does it all repeat itself again and again and again?" William asked this man in great anguish. "Are the sections of it the same over and over again?"

"Not quite," the man said. "The grease marks on it are sometimes a little different."

"My name is William Morris," William began once more bravely.

"Oh, sure. A William Morris is the easiest type of all to spot," the man said.

"You said—no, another man said that my name-game ancestor had to do with designing of another thing besides the *Wood Beyond the World*," William stammered. "What was it?"

"Wallpaper," the man said. And William fell down in a frothy faint.

Oh, Candy didn't leave him there. She was faithful. She took him up on her shoulders and plodded along with him, on past the West Side Show Square on 18th Street, past the Mingle-Mangle and the Pad Palace, where she (no, another girl very like her) had turned back before, on and on.

"It's the same thing over and over and over again," William whimpered as she toted him along.

"Be quiet, talkie," she said, but she said it with some affection.

They came to the great Chopper House on 20th Street. Candy carried William in and dumped him on a block there.

"He's become ancient," Candy told an attendant. "Boy, how he's become ancient!" It was more than she usually talked.

Then, as she was a fair-minded girl and as she had not worked any stint that day, she turned to and worked an hour in the Chopper House. (What they chopped up in the Chopper House was the ancients.) Why, there was William's head coming down the line! Candy smiled at it. She chopped it up with loving care, much more care than she usually took.

She'd have said something memorable and kind if she'd been a talkie.

Funnyfingers

Introduction by Andrew Ferguson

Ask a few readers of Lafferty what they treasure him for, and you'll get a lot of the same answers. He will make you laugh, uproariously. He will show you new possibilities inherent in language—not just in English, but many others as well. He will provide you a vantage point on this world (and other worlds, to boot) that flips you inside out, inverting everything you thought you knew about the workings of fiction.

What they won't mention as often—partly because he doesn't do it that much, and partly because it hurts so much when he does—is that he will break your heart wide open.

"Funnyfingers" is, at its most basic level, a tale of doomed love. It isn't spoiling anything to say that in an introduction, either, because as he often does, Lafferty tells us what's going to happen right from the start. Here it's in an epigram alluding to Orpheus, something you don't do unless a Eurydice is about to be lost. With admirable narrative economy, the main character immediately thereafter poses the central question that will lead to her romantic impasse—who, or what, am I?—and then the reader is given several valid answers: she is a somewhat exasperating and precocious little girl, and she is also a young Dactyl, a creature of myth, one of a number who gave humankind ironworking, arithmetic, and the alphabet and who (in their adult years) remain responsible for manufacturing letters and numbers and pieces for the entire world.

The story plays out from there, though the narrative beats and resolution are hardly formulaic. However, Lafferty is as usual concerned with much more than just the central relationship of his unhappy couple: he's exploring humanity's relationship with its stories, as well as his own particular relation as a channel for those myths. While Lafferty's personal relationship experience was limited to what he could glean from others, he nonetheless understood that much of what we love about another is the stories we construct around them, myths that are deeply personal even as they partake of the universal. But when what you love is a story—or you yourself *are* a story—the deck is stacked against you from the start.

As the young lovers in "Funnyfingers" realize to their dismay, our stories will outlive us, and in particular they will outlive their own tellers. The result is a curious (if typically Laffertian) inversion of the Orpheus legend: it's not the stories who must be left behind to the darkness, but us. When Oread Funnyfingers traipses through the mine, assembling iron dogs or iron boys or iron philoso-phies, it's us she's putting together. And when she disassembles them at the end of play, it's us she puts back in the spare-part bins. And, in the end, though we too feel heartbreak at the conclusion of our all-too-brief parts, it is Oread and it is Pluto, the stories themselves, who will weep iron tears.

Funnyfingers

"—and Pluto, Lord of Hell, wept when Orpheus played to him that lovely phrase from Gluck—but these were iron tears."

—H. Belloc, *On Tears of the Great*

Who am I?" Oread Funnyfingers asked her mother one day, "and, for that matter, what am I?"

"Why, you are our daughter," the mother Frances Funnyfingers told her, "or have you been talking to someone?"

"Only to myself and to my uncles in the mountain."

"Oh. Now first, dear, I want you to know that we love you very much. There was nothing casual about it. We chose you, and you are to us—"

"Oh, take it easy, Mother. I know that I'm adopted. And I'm sure that you both love me very much; you tell me so often enough. But what am I really?"

"You are a little girl, Oread, a somewhat exasperating and precocious little girl."

"But I don't feel precocious. I feel like a rock-head. How can I be a little bit like Papa and not anything like anyone else at all? What was the connection between myself and Papa?"

"There wasn't any at first, Oread, not like that. We were looking for a child since we could not have one of our own. I fell in love with you at first sight because you reminded me of Henry. And Henry fell in love with you at first sight because you reminded him of Henry. Henry was always the favorite person of both myself and Henry. That's a joke, dear. But not entirely; my husband is so delightfully boyish and self-centered. Now run out and play."

"No, I think I'll run in and play."

"Oh, but it's so dark and dirty and smoky in there."

"And it's so light and unsmoky everywhere else, Mama," Oread said, and she ran inside the mountain to play.

Well, the house and the shop of Henry Funnyfingers backed onto the mountain. It was really only a low but steep foot-hill to the Osage Hills. This was on the northwest fringe of the city. The shop was the typewriter repair shop of Henry the father of Oread. You wouldn't know that from the sign out front, though. The sign said "Daktylographs Repaired Here, Henry Funnyfingers."

The shop part of the building was half into and under the hill. Behind the shop was a dimly lit parts room that was entirely under the hill. And behind this were other parts rooms, one after the other, rock-walled and dark, rockier and darker as one went on, all deep under the hills. And these continued, on and on, as tunnel and cavern without apparent end.

In these places of total darkness, if only one knew where to reach in which pot, there was to be found every part for every sort of machine in the world; or so Henry Funnyfingers said.

Oread ran through room after room, through passage after passage in the blackness. She drew parts from the pots and the furnaces as she ran. She put the parts together, and it barked remindfully. "What have I forgotten?" Oread asked. "Ah, Rusty, I've given you only one ear. I'm sorry." She took the other ear from the Other Ear Pot as she ran past, and she put it on him. Then she had an iron dog complete. It would run and play and bark after her in the tunnels under the mountain.

"Oh Kelmis, Oh Acmon, Oh Damnae all three!
Come out of the mountain and play with me."

Oread sang that. Sometimes the three Mountain Uncles were busy (they had to make numbers and letters and pieces for the whole world) and couldn't come to play. But almost always one of them came, and Kelmis came today. Kelmis was the smoky smelly one, but Oread didn't mind that. He was full of stories, he was full of fun, he was full of the hot darkness-fire from which anything can be made. It was great fun there through all the afternoon and evening, as they are called out in the light. But then Kelmis had to go back to work.

Oread and the iron dog Rusty ran back up the passages toward the house. She took the dog apart as they went back and put each piece into its proper pot. Last of all she put its bark in the bark pot, and she came up through the shop and into the inside of the house for supper.

"Oh, Oread, however do you get so smoky and smelly?" mother Frances Funnyfingers asked her. "Why don't you play out in the sunshine like other girls do? Why don't you play with other girls and boys?"

"I made an iron boy to play with once, Mama," Oread said. "You wouldn't believe how he carried on or the things he wanted to do. I had the devil's own time taking him apart again. That's the last boy I ever make, I tell you. They're tricky."

"Yes, as I remember it, they are," Frances conceded. "Whatever do you make your stories out of, Oread?"

"Oh, I make them out of iron," Oread told her seriously. "Iron is what everything is made out of first. The pieces are all there in the pots and the furnaces. You just put them together."

"Pieces of stories, Oread?"

"Oh yes."

"Iron stories, girl?"

"Oh, yes, yes, iron stories."

"You are funny-fingers and funny-face and funny-brains," the mother told her. "I think I'll have you eat your supper off an iron plate with iron spoon and knife."

"Oh, may I? I'll go make them," Oread cried.

"Make me a set while you're at it," father Henry Funnyfingers said.

"No, Oread. Sit down and eat your supper from what we have, both of you." Frances Funnyfingers loved her husband and her daughter, but sometimes they puzzled her.

We cannot honestly say that Oread grew up; we can hardly say that she grew older. She finally started school when she was nine years old, and she looked as though she were four or five. Going to school was only for seemliness anyhow. Oread already knew everything. She got on well. She was a peculiar little girl, but she didn't know it. She gave disconcerting answers in class, but nobody could say that they were wrong answers. What difference does it make which end you start and answer at? She was a strange, smiling little girl, and she was liked by most of her schoolmates. Those who didn't like her, feared her; and why should anyone fear so small a creature as Oread Funnyfingers? They feared her because she said, "Be good to me or I'll make an iron wolf to eat you up." She would have done it, and they knew she would have done it.

And she always got her homework and got it right. She had, what seemed to her mother, an unscholarly way of doing it, though. She would take her books or her printed assignments. She would walk singing through the shop, through the parts room, through the other parts rooms behind that, and down into the passages in the toes of the hills.

"Oh Kelmis, Oh Acmon, Oh Damnae all three,
Make ready all pots where the answers may be."

Oread would sing so. Then she would pick the iron answers out of the answer pots. She'd put them together by subjects. She would stamp them onto her papers, and they would mark all the answers correct in her handwriting. So she would have the Catechism, the Composition, the questions on the Reading, the Arithmetic all perfect. Then she'd drop all the iron answers back into the answer pots where they would melt themselves down to iron slag again.

"Don't you think that's cheating?" her mother would ask her. "What if all the other children got their homework that way?"

"They couldn't unless they were funnyfingers," Oread said. "The hot iron answers would burn their hands clear off unless they were funnyfingers. No, it isn't cheating. It's just knowing your subject."

"I guess so then," mother Frances said. There were so many things she didn't understand about her husband Henry ("He's boyish, like a boy, like an iron boy," she'd say), and about her daughter ("She's like an owl, like a little owl, a little iron owl"). Neither Henry nor Oread liked the daylight very much, but they always faced it as bravely as they could.

One day Oread found her mother in tears, yet there was happy salt in them.

"Look," the mother Frances said. She had a valentine, an iron valentine that Henry had given her. There was an iron heart on it and an iron verse:

"When you are dead five hundred years
Who once were full of life,
I'll think of you with salty tears,
And take another wife."

"Oh, it's nice, Mama," Oread said.

"But of iron?" Frances asked.

"Oh yes, the very first rimes were made out of iron, you know."

"And what of the five hundred years?"

"I think it's considerate that he would wait five hundred years after you die to take another wife."

"Yes, I suppose so, Oread." But Frances wasn't completely at ease with her family.

Henry always made a good living from his typewriter repair shop, or rather he made a good living from his parts stocks in the rooms behind. Other dealers and repairmen, not just of typewriters but of everything, came to him for parts. His prices were reasonable, and there was never a part that he didn't have. A dealer would rattle off the catalog number of something for a tractor or a hay-baler or a dishwasher. "Just a minute," Henry Funnyfingers would say, and he would plunge into his mysterious back rooms. He had a comical little song he would croon to himself as he went:

"Oh Kelmis, Oh Acmon, Oh Damnae all three,
Now this is the number, Oh make it for me!"

And in a second, with the last word of the song just out of his mouth, he'd be back with the required part still hot in his hand. He never missed. Parts of combines, parts of electric motors, parts for Fords, he could come up with all of them instantly with only a catalog number or the broken piece itself or even a vague description to go on. And he did repair typewriters quicker and better than anyone in town. He wasn't rich, he was fearful of becoming rich; but he did well, and nobody in the Funnyfinger family wanted for anything.

When they were in the sixth grade, Oread had a boyfriend. He was a Syrian boy named Selim Elia. He was dark and he was handsome. He looked the veriest little bit as though he were made of iron; that was the main reason that Oread liked him. And he seemed to suspect entirely too much about the funnyfingers; she thought that was a reason that she'd better like him.

"When you grow up (Oh, Oread, will you ever grow up?) I'm going to marry you," Selim said boldly.

"Of course I'll grow up. Doesn't everyone?" Oread said. "But you won't be able to marry me."

"Why not, little horned owl?"

"I don't know. I just feel that we won't be grown up at the same time."

"Hurry up then, little iron-eyes, little basilisk-eyes," Selim said. "I will marry you."

They got along well. Selim was very protective of little Oread. They liked each other. What is wrong with people liking each other?

When in the eighth grade, Oread made a discovery about Sister Mary Dactyl, the art teacher for all the grades. Sister Mary D seemed to be very young. "But she can't be that young," Oread told Selim. "Some of the mythological things she draws, they've been gone a long time. She has to be old to have seen them."

"Oh, she draws them from old stories and old descriptions," Selim said, "or she just draws them out of her imagination."

"A couple of them she didn't draw out of her imagination," Oread insisted. "She had to have seen them." That, however, wasn't the discovery.

Sister was drawing something very rapidly one day, and she forgot that some-one with very rapid eyes might be watching her hands. Oread saw, and she waited around after class.

"You are a funnyfingers," she said to Sister. "All your fingers are triple-jointed like mine. They can move fast as light like mine. I bet you can pick up iron parts out of the hot pots without getting burned."

"Sure I can," said Sister M.D.

"But are you a funnyfingers all the way?" Oread asked. "Papa says that, in the old language, our name Funnyfingers meant both funny-fingers and funny-toes. Are you?"

"Sure I am," said the very young-looking Sister Mary Dactyl. She took off her shoes and stockings. Sisters didn't do that very often in the classroom then. Now, of course they go everywhere barefooted and in nothing but a transparent short shift, but that wasn't so when Oread Funnyfingers was still in the eighth grade.

Yes, Sister was a funny-toes also. She had the triple-jointed fast-as-vision toes. She could do more things with her toes than other people could do with their fingers.

"Did you have a little hill or mountain when you were young, I mean when you were a girl?" Oread asked her.

"Oh, yes, yes, I have it still, an interior mountain."

"How old are you, sister who always looks so young and pretty?"

"Very old, Oread, very old."

"*How* old?"

"Ask me again in eight years, Oread, if you still want to know."

"In eight years? Oh, all right, I will."

High school went by, four years just like a day. Selim had made a big twisted hammered iron thing that said "Selim Loves Oread." He suspected something very strongly about the iron. But he wasn't a funny-fingers, so it took him three weeks instead of three seconds to make the thing. Many other things happened in those four years, but they were all happy things so there is no use mentioning them.

When they were in and almost through college (Oread still looked like a nine- or ten-year-old, and this was maddening) they were into some very intricate courses. Selim was a veritable genius, and Oread always knew in which pots the answers might be found, so the two of them qualified for the profound fields. It is good to have a piece of the deep raw knowledge as it births, it is good to see the future lifted out of the future pots.

"We have come to the point where we must invent a whole new system of concepts and symbols," said the instructor of one powerful course one day. "Little girl, what are you doing in this room," he added to Oread. "This is a college building and a college course."

"I know it. We've been through this every day for a year," she said.

"We are as much at a crossroads as was mankind when the concept of a crossroads was first invented," the instructor continued. "If that concept (excluding choice pictured graphically with simple diverging lines) had not been invented, mankind would have remained at that situation, unchoosing and merely accepting. There are dozens of cases where mankind has remained in a particular situation for thousands of years for failure to invent a particular concept. I suspect that is the situation here; we have not moved in a certain area because we have not entertained the possibility of movement in that area. A whole new concept is needed, but I cannot even conceive what that concept should be."

"Oh, I'll make it for you tonight," Oread said.

"Has that little girl wandered into the class again today?" the instructor asked with new irritation. "Oh yes, I remember now, you always come up with some sort of proof that you're an enrolled member of the class and that you're twenty-one years old. You're not, though. You're just a little girl with little-girl brains."

"Oh, I know it," Oread said sadly, "but I'll still make the thing for you tonight."

"Make what thing, little girl?"

"The new concept, and the symbol set that goes with it."

"And just what does one make a concept out of?" that man asked her with near exasperation.

"I'll make it mostly out of iron, I think," Oread said. "I'll use whatever is in the pots, but I guess it will be mostly iron."

"Oh God help us!" the man cried out.

"Such a nice expression," Oread told him, "and somebody had told me that you were an unbeliever."

"Actually," said the instructor, controlling himself and talking to the rest of the class and not to Oread Funnyfingers. "Actually, these things often appear simple in retrospect. So may this be if ever we are able to make it retro. The ABCs, the alphabet isn't very hard, is it? Yes, Mr. Levkovitch, I know all about those hard letters after C. A little humor, it is said, is a tedious thing. But the alphabet was a hard thing when mankind stood at the foothills—"

"*En daktulos,* at the toes of, that's what the original form of the expression was," Oread told him.

"Be quiet, little girl," the instructor muttered darkly. "—when mankind stood at the foothills of the alphabetical concept and looked up at the mountain, it was hard then."

"Yes, the first alphabets were all made out of hammered iron," Oread told the world, "and they were quite hard."

"The same was the case with simple arithmetic," said the instructor, disregarding Oread with a deep sigh. "It is easy as we look back on it in its ordered simplicity. But when it was only a crying need and not yet a real concept, then it was hard, very hard."

"Sure, it was made out of iron too," Oread whispered to Selim. "Why does he get so mad when I tell him about things being made out of iron?"

"It's just a weakness of the man, Oread," Selim whispered. "We'll have to accept it."

"And so we are probably at an end," the instructor was ending his class for the day. "If we cannot come up with a new dimension, with a new symbolism, with a new thought and a new concept (having no idea at all what they should be) then we might as well end this class forever. We might as well, as a matter of likely fact, end the world forever. And on that somber note I leave you till tomorrow, if there should be a tomorrow."

"Don't worry, Mr. Zhelezovitch," Oread said. "I'll make it for you tonight."

2.

The name Daktuloi (Fingers) is variously explained from their number being five or ten, or because they dwelt at the foot (*en daktulois*) of Mount Ida. The original number seems to have been three: i.e., Kelmis the smelter, Damnameneus the hammer, and Acmon the anvil. This number was afterward increased to five, then to ten . . . and finally to one hundred.

— *Harper's Dictionary of Classical Literature and Antiquities*

In the forests of Phrygian Ida there lived cunning magicians called the Dactyls. Originally there were three of them. Celmis, Damnameneus, and the powerful Acmon who in the caves of the mountains was the first to practice the art of Hephaestus and who knew how to work blue iron, casting it into the burning furnace. Later their number increased. From Phrygia they went to Crete where they taught

the inhabitants the use of iron and how to work metals. To them
is also attributed the discovery of arithmetic and the letters of the
alphabet.

—*Larousse Encyclopedia of Mythology*

It is also said of the Dactyls (the Finger-Folk inside the hills) that
they live very long lives and retain their youthful appearance for
very many years.

—Groff Crocker, *Mear-Daoine*

Just after closing time that evening, Oread Funnyfingers went by City Museum
to see Selim. Selim Elia worked as night watchman there to help pay his way
through the University. There really wasn't much to do on the job. He sat at a big
administrator's desk and studied all night. Studying all night every night is how
he got to be a genius. Oread had brought some sandwiches with her.

"Peanut-butter and jelly sandwiches made out of iron," Selim joked.

"No, they're not of iron," Oread said solemnly. "One would need iron teeth to
eat an iron sandwich."

"Surely a funnyfingers could manage iron teeth."

"Oh, our third set comes in iron, but for me that should be many years yet."

"Oread, I want to marry you."

"Everyone calls you a cradle-robber."

"I know they do. And yet we're almost exactly the same age."

"There's so many people here," Oread said. "Terra Cotta People, Marble
People, Sandstone People, Basalt People, Raffia People, Wooden People, Wax
People. I will have to find out from my uncles which ones are real. Some of them
aren't, you know; some of them never lived at all."

"We have one of your friends or uncles here, Oread, in wax. Over here."

"I know where. You have all three of my uncles here in wax," Oread said. "You
might not recognize them from the forms of their names on the plaques, though.

"*Oh Kelmis, Oh Acmon, Oh Damnae all three,*
Come out of your cases and play with me.

"I don't think they'll come out though, Selim, since they're made out of wax
instead of iron. Effigies should always be made out of iron."

"What do their names mean, Oread?"

"*Oh Smelter, Oh Anvil, Oh Hammer all three,*
Come out of your cases and play with me.

"No, they won't come out. I'd have to be a bee-brain to evoke anything out
of wax."

"Oread, I love you very much."

"No, they won't come out at all. I'll have them come over here themselves
some night and make iron effigies of themselves. Then you can get rid of those
silly wax ones."

"Little iron-ears, I said that I loved you very much."

"Oh, I heard you. You won't be alarmed when they come out some night to make the effigies? They're kind of funny-looking."

"So are you, Oread. No, I won't be alarmed. Why should a Syrian be alarmed over fabulous people? We're fabulous people ourselves. And if they're your uncles they cannot be dangerous."

"Sure they can. I am. You said yourself that I'd set the flaming ducks after you again. I go home now, Selim, to get my homework made, and also to make that concept-symbol system for Mr. Zhelezovitch the instructor. It's important, isn't it?"

"I'll go with you, Oread. Yes, it's important to Zhelly and to the class and the course. It's true that he might as well end the class forever if he doesn't find it. But it isn't true that we might as well end the world if we don't find it. It's not quite that important."

"Who will watch the museum if you leave? I want very much to make this correctly and understandably for Mr. Zhelezovitch. I am a Funnyfinger, and making things for people is the whole business and being of the funnyfingers."

"Oh, tell Kelmis to watch the place for me. Will it take long for them and you to make the concept?"

"*Oh watch it for Selim, and watch it real nice,*

Oh Kelmis, from rotters and robbers and mice.

"Sure, he'll watch it for you. Even a Waxman-Kelmis will be faithful in that. Oh no, they never take very long to make anything for anybody any more." (Time had slipped by, though not much of it; Selim had a sporty car that he drove like a flaming rocket; and it wasn't very far to the northwest side of town. They were out at the Funnyfingers' place now, and into the back, back rooms that turned into tunnels.) "They never take very long to make things anymore," Oread was continuing, "not since that time, you know, when God got a little bit testy with them on Sinai when there was a little delay. They first made the tablets out of iron entirely, and they wouldn't do. They had to make them out of slate-stone with the iron letters inset in it, and the iron had to be that alloy known as command iron. Since then they are all pretty prompt with everyone, and they follow instructions exactly. You never know who it really is who places an order.

"Kelmis has the original all-iron set. I'll get him to show them to you some time."

"Where do you get your stories, Oread?"

"I tell my mother that I make them out of iron."

"And where do you really get them?"

"I make them out of iron."

Selim talked easily with the three uncles while they wrought and hammered the white-hot parts that Oread was to assemble into a symbol concept.

"How is it that you work inside a little hill in Oklahoma?" he asked them.

"Shouldn't you be in the forests or hills of Phrygian Ida? How did you come to leave the Old Country?"

"This is the Old Country, and we haven't left it," powerful Acmon said. "Everything underground anywhere is part of the Old Country. All hills and mountains of the world connect down in their roots, in their toes, and they make a single place. We *are* in Mount Ida, we are in Crete, we are in Oklahoma. It is all one."

They made the pieces. And Oread, dipping the parts out of the white-hot iron as if it were water, put them together to make the thing. It was a new concept-symbol system, and it looked as if it would work.

And it looked much more as if it would work the next afternoon. Mr. Zhelezovitch the instructor was almost out of his mind with it. The graduate students and the regular students (for this was one of those advanced, mixed classes) crowded about it and went wild. The implications of the new thing would tumble in their minds for weeks; the class would be a marathon affair going on and on as the wonderful new things were put to work to uncover still more wonderful things. The stars were out when Oread and Selim left the class, and no one else would leave it at all that night. But these two had something between them, and it might take another new concept to solve it.

"Oread, give me your answer," Selim was saying again. "I want to marry you."

"Make a wish on a star then. On that one where I'm pointing."

"Triple jointed funnyfingers, who can tell where you're pointing?"

"On that male star there between the several eunuch stars."

"Yes, I see the one you mean, Oread. I make a wish. Now, when will you answer me?"

"Within a half hour. I go to question two people first."

Oread left there at a run. She went home. She talked to her mother.

"Mama, why is my father so boyish? Is he really just a boy?"

"Yes he is, Oread. Just a boy."

"After some years would he be a man, really, and not just a pleasant young kid?"

"I think so, Oread, yes."

"Then after some years you two could have children of your own? Being a funnyfingers isn't an obstacle?"

"I'll never know that, Oread. When he is grown up I will be long dead."

Oread ran out of there and ran to the convent that was behind the school she used to attend. She entered and went upstairs and down a hallway. She knew where she was going. One funnyfingers can always find another one. Besides, the eight years was up. She opened the door and found Sister Mary Dactyl playing solitaire with iron cards.

"*How* old?" Oread asked.

"Three hundred and fifty-eight years," said Sister M.D. without looking up. "Were I not vowed, I would be coming to the family age now."

Oread ran all the way back to where Selim was still waiting in the street under the stars. She was crying, she was bawling.

"The answer is no," she blubbered. Selim, under the stars, was as white-faced as it is possible for a Syrian to be. But he must not give up.

"Oread, I love you more than you can know," he said. "Maybe we can make a different answer out of iron," he proposed in desperate jest.

"This *is* the iron answer," she bawled, "and the answer is no." She ran away too fast to follow.

Deep under the hills Oread was crying. She was weeping big hot tears. They weren't, however, iron tears that she wept. That part is untrue.

The tears were actually of that aromatic flux of salt and rosin that wrought-iron workers employ in their process.

Thieving Bear Planet

Introduction by Jeff VanderMeer

"Anomalies are messy," R. A. Lafferty writes at the beginning of "Thieving Bear Planet," and the reader might be forgiven for thinking Lafferty was referring to his own career and body of work. But, in fact, he's referring to the alien thieving bears of the title, which follow their own peculiar set of rules. Too often science fiction gives us humans in uncanny bear suits, so to speak, when it comes to aliens. But Lafferty in this story and several others manages to create deeply strange and original alien encounters that both unsettle the reader and send up traditional science fiction approaches.

As ever with Lafferty, too, he manages feats of compression that are beyond most writers. Take the deliberately blithe reference to a *Directory and Delineation of Planets,* which, in offering an entry on the Thieving Bear Planet, tries from the start to impose a cage of logic on the unknowable, with its catalog of the usual planetary attributes, even if it destabilizes its authority in the same instant by including irrational statements from a former explorer of the planet. Or take Lafferty's riotous description of the current expedition's gastronome's delight of a meal—which proves to be a great set-up to the stealing of the thieving bears, who are not just robbing the explorers' very stomachs of plain old pork-and-beans, but a sumptuous feast, that the reader may feel the loss quite viscerally. These are lovely stories within the main story, little whirlpools of magnificent narrative energy.

"Visceral" is a key word when thinking of Lafferty's triumphs, alongside "weird." In, again, a condensed tale-like form Lafferty accomplishes what some space operas take trilogies to get to. A space opera, in its finest form, is just a mimic: a commercial delivery system for some of the strangest moments and situations in science fiction. (See: early Alastair Reynolds, for example.) With Lafferty, the traditional tropes of SF—alien contact, alien invasion, the noble exploration of space—are jewels he likes to put beneath tattered overturned cups, daring the reader to bet on where in the world the true treasure lies. But beware—when you pin down the location of that treasure, it'll likely change shape, grow legs, and hop off the table.

This applies even to the thieving bears of the title, who take on a marvelous initial form, able to fly not so much because of having lightweight bones but because they're almost like drifting toupees in structure. The mimicry they are capable of seems cute at first and then horribly brutal as the explorers become caught up in events they cannot control. Yet even then, Lafferty isn't content, restless. It would have been easy enough for him to take the initial set-up to a very satisfying conclusion, but instead he roughs up and destabilizes his own story with the second act, which makes the reader question . . . well, everything. Is all that occurs just a joke by the thieving bears? Is there some other animating impulse at work? How is it that this Jenga-like structure Lafferty creates doesn't fall and crash to the ground?

Along with many other complexities, then, "Thieving Bear Planet" chronicles the impossibility of comprehension of the alien, the war between the logical and illogical in ourselves that spills out into the cosmos beyond—all in the context of the certain knowledge that human beings will never know *everything* about this world, let alone the next, or the universes we inhabit. And that there is something wonderful about that fact.

Not many writers could grapple with such ideas and create a story that's both so creepy and so funny and *in the moment,* but as in Lafferty's best work in general, the author manages to channel a narrative momentum and a kind of joy in the very act of outrageous and madcap invention that provides unity, depth, and, yes, even a kind of beautiful closure.

Thieving Bear Planet

"Deliver me from carks and cares,
Deliver me from Thieving Bears."
                    —John Chancel, *Logs and Epilogs of Sector 24*

A simple explanation was needed for the conditions on Thieving Bear Planet. It was needed because, as the great Reginald Hot had phrased it, "Anomalies are messy."

Every decade or so, somebody with a passion for regularity takes over the administration of the *Directory and Delineation of Planets,* that massive cataloging operation, and makes a new survey of the anomalies. And there was not any way that such a survey could miss Thieving Bear Planet.

"It offers no threat to human life or activity, no danger to bodily health, and only slight danger to mental health," the great John Chancel had written about it a century before this. "It has almost uniformly ideal climate, though it is not a place to generate sudden wealth. It is serene in environment and in ecological balance, and it is absolutely caressing in its natural beauty. But it does have a strange effect on some of its visitors. It forces them to write things that are untrue, as it is forcing me to do at this moment." That was an odd thing to write in a ship's log.

And, as one later old hand put it, "There is nothing to conquer here. It is a poorly endowed and counterproductive world. And everything goes wrong here. I will say this for it: things go wrong here in the most pleasant way possible. But they do go wrong."

Now another expedition consisting of six explorers—George Mahoon (he was wrestler-big, and with a groping, grappling, leverage-seeking wrestler-mind); Elton Fad (he was long on information and short on personal incandescence); Benedict Crix-Crannon (buff and charming, and he knew all the jobs of the expedition); Luke Fronsa (he was a "comer," as they said in the department, but wasn't he a little bit overage in grade as a "comer" now?); Selma Last-Rose (what can you say after you say that somebody has everything?); Gladys Marclair (pleasant, capable, but she wasn't a genius, and genius was really required for an explorer); and Dixie Late-Lark (sheer Spirit, she!)—had set down on Thieving Bear Planet. These were not the most experienced explorers in the Service, but they were among the newest and freshest. And they had already demonstrated that they were top people at clearing up anomalies.

"It's a pleasant place, but not good for much," George Mahoon said before they had been there ten minutes. "Why didn't the earlier explorers simply say that it was 'Only marginally or submarginally productive, indicated by fast scans to be poor in both radioactive and base metals and also in rare earths and fossil fuels, not recommended for development in the present century when so many better places are available,' or some such thing as that? Why did they put so much stuttering gibberish in their reports? I'm going to like it here, though. It's nice for a brief vacation."

"Oh, I'm going to like it too," Selma Last-Rose spoke in her curious rat-a-tat-tat voice. "There must be a puzzle here, and I like puzzles. And there's a minor mystery in this 'Plain of the Old Spaceships.' I may as well solve that."

They had landed in a clear place on the Plain of the Old Spaceships. Here there were remarkable full-scale drawings or schematics of old spaceships, twelve of them in two-thirds of a circle, from the earliest to the latest, going clockwise on the ground. What medium these schematics were done in was not certain, but the lush grass refrained from growing on the lines of them and so marked them off. The "drawings" showed the circle-spheres of the spaceships and their fore and aft bulges. They gave accurate indication of the interior bulkheads. This was really a life-sized museum of ships that lacked only substance and the dimension of height.

"I recall two passages in the log of the ship *Sorcerer* about this plain or meadow," Elton Fad said. "The first of them stated, 'Some of our party believe that the plain of the ships was actually done by the Thieving Bears in a historical marker sort of response, but I myself do not credit the little beasties with that much intelligence.' And there was a later entry in another hand, 'The Thieving Bears really *did* make those schematics-in-the-grass memorials of all the space-ships that had been here, but they didn't do it in any way that we had imagined.' But that latter log entry, like latter entries of several of the explorers, had been written in something other than ink.

"Well, *I'll* imagine a few ways that the little buggers could have done it, and I'll test it somehow. I'll ask them how they did it. If the tittering little obscenities have any intelligence at all, I'll find a way to ask them."

The "tittering little obscenities," the Thieving Bears, were not much like bears. They were more like large flying squirrels, and they did glide on the winds, apparently for sport. They were more like pack rats (the *Neotoma cinerea* of Earth) both in appearance and in their thieving ways, but larger. It was old John Chancel who had named the species "*Ursus furtificus,* the Thieving Bears." Oh, the explorers had their introduction to the thieving of the little animals within five minutes of planet-landing. The creatures came into the ship itself and got into places that should have been impossible to them. They stole Selma's candy and

Dixie's snuff. They stole (by drinking it on the spot) George Mahoon's "He-Man Scent—Cinnamon," thirteen bottles of it, but they did not drink any of the other scents. They went wild over mustard, emptying whole containers of it and then wheezing in delicious agony from the effect. Elton Fad tried to drive them away with heavy sticks. They fastened onto the sticks while he swung them and ate them right up to his hands. They were funny, but they could become infuriating. They stole six of Dixie Late-Lark's French horror story novels.

That wouldn't be fatal to her. She had lots of them.

"They're going to sample them," Dixie said. (She herself looked a little bit like one of those Thieving Bears.) "They'll be the test. If they do read them and appreciate them, it'll prove that they're intelligent creatures and have better reading tastes than my crewmates. That will be a start in analyzing them, something to put into the electronic notebooks."

Could the Thieving Bears talk? That was not determined for sure within the first ten or even twenty minutes.

"Say 'Good morning,' fuzzy head," Selma rattled at one of the creatures.

"Say good morning, fuzzy head," it bear-barked back at her. Well, it had the right number of syllables, and the right rhythm and stress. And the bear-barks did resemble Selma's rattling words. And whenever the bears answered one of the persons, it answered in that person's own timbre. The bears began to imitate the people quickly, and there was never any doubt as to which person was being imitated.

The tittering that went with the imitations, though! Ooooh, that could become tiresome after a little while. "Tittering little obscenities," yes.

Could the Thieving Bears read? 'Twould be known in a bit, maybe. The bears had gotten into those big lockers that were full of comic books and had stolen big bunches of them. These comic books from the Trader Planets were now collector's items on Old Earth, and they generated quite a profit. The wonderful things should be collector's items everywhere.

Some of the big Thieving Bears were "reading" those comic books to some of the little Thieving Bears, reading them in the Thieving Bears' own barking talk. And some of the little bears would bark their excitement and incredulity at parts of the narration and would come and look at the pictures and the worded balloons themselves. And then there would be that damned tittering!

It was clear that the big bears believed that they were reading, and that the little bears believed they were understanding. But the wording in the comic book balloons was in the Gno-Pidgin dialect of the Trader Planets, and people from the Traders had never been to Thieving Bear Planet. It was almost too much to believe that "Sangster's Syndrome Intuitive Translation" was being practiced by animals below the level of conceptual thinking. Then some of the little bears were clearly acting out episodes from the comic books (very subtle episodes, according to Benedict Crix-Crannon, who had total knowledge of the content of all the comic books from the lockers). Well, there was no easy explanation for that.

The explorers treated themselves to a bonus meal within an hour of their arrival, after things were pretty well settled down. On a new world, they did this only when they had complete confidence that everything was under control. It was a traditional Earth-hearty meal, though it was from a packet of such bonus meals that had been packaged on Trader Planet Number Four. There were ten-centimeter-thick Cape buffalo steaks, mountains of Midland mushrooms, Camiroi currants and Astrobe apples, Elton eels, Wrack World rye bread, "Galaxy" brand goat butter, Rain Mountain coffee, Rumboat cordials, and Ganymede cigars ("They have an aroma that outlasts the Everlasting Hills," a testimonial said of those perfectos).

"Logs of earlier explorers say that there is no real enjoyment in eating on Thieving Bear Planet because of the harassment of the bears," Benny Crix-Crannon gloated. "Well, I'm enjoying this meal (another bumper of Rumboat cordial, Luke, please), and I'd like to see anybody take that enjoyment away from me." And yet the enjoyment and savor of that grand meal began to disappear almost at that moment. How? Oh, it was just that all the items of their enjoyment were being mysteriously stolen away from them.

"All the rest of Dixie's snuff has been stolen by the bears now," Gladys said. "That's too bad. She loves it so much. If all her idiosyncrasies are stolen away, it's as if she is stolen away too."

"And another thirty or so of Dixie's French horror story novels have been stolen by the bears," Elton Fad grumbled. "She's bound to be frustrated by that. We should insist on fair play from the bears."

"Her gold snuffboxes have been stolen, too," Selma Last-Rose lamented. "How mean of the bears! The snuffboxes were valuable, even for the gold."

"And her hookah pipe is gone," Luke Fronsa complained. "What will the bears steal next?"

"I don't know," George Mahoon wondered, "but Dixie Late-Lark has herself been stolen now, or at least she's gone. She could not have gone out unrecorded, for the ship is on full security. And yet the ship itself registers that she is no longer on board. She was sitting between you and Selma, was she not, Gladys?"

"She was, yes, just a moment ago, on the chair between the two of us. But there isn't any chair between us now, and there couldn't have been; there isn't any room for one. She must have been sitting on something else. Oh, that damned tittering! I wonder how they stole her and what they did with her."

"Be rational, Gladys," Luke said. "There's no way the little bears could have stolen Dixie Late-Lark."

"Then where did she go? And how?"

"I don't know," Mahoon admitted, "and I don't believe that any of us know. All at once, it doesn't seem very important. Ah, I'm queasy. Yes, and I'm *hungry*. After a perfect bonus meal, I shouldn't be either. Fortunately, I had plugged myself into the ship's monitor, because of early reports of anomalies on Thieving Bear Planet, reports of the well-feeling and the wits of the explorers being stolen away. All right, monitor, what has gone wrong with me?"

The ship's monitor spilled it all out. It was in coded chatter. "But we all understand the coded chatter just like our mother's milk," as Dixie had once said. All of them were completely tuned to the code of their own ship. And each of them put it into words automatically.

"Essential food value suddenly stolen from your ingested food," the monitor chattered. "Pepsin stolen from your stomach, thalmatite stolen from your thalamus, thyroxine stolen from your pharynx, Cape buffalo essence stolen from your esophagus and stomach, mushrooms and currants and apples stolen from your lower stomach and small intestine, rum alcohol stolen from your stomach and ileum and bloodstream, and normal blood alcohol and blood sugar stolen as part of the same theft. Slurry of rye bread and butter and coffee stolen from your paunch and antrum stomach. Essence of Elton eels stolen from some saltwater swamp of you. And at the same time, insulin and glucagon are stolen from your pancreas, hepatocytes and bile salts from your bile duct and duodenum; and words, ideas, and inklings have been swiped from several parts of your brain. No wonder you're queasy and hungry at the same time."

"Thank you, ship's monitor," George Mahoon said. "Well, it seems that I've been infected by some microbe or germ or virus. I'll take a few of the anti-anti pills to quell the infection."

"Forget the anti-anti pills, George!" Elton Fad cried angrily. "I think we should take a couple of steel bars and teach the Thieving Bears a lesson. There are microbes and germs and viruses infecting me too, but they are about half my own size and are known as the Thieving Bears. Damn those tittering little idiots! They're beginning to intrude too intimately with their thefts and their eatings; but I don't know how they're doing these things so interiorly. Sometimes I wish I'd gone into the family business and never become an explorer at all." Elton Fad's family was in eels: they were big and rich people in eels.

A little doll made out of wax and rags, with thorns and pins and needles sticking clear through it, and with its throat cut horribly, came sailing through the air and landed on the table where all the explorers had just finished their fine meal that had lost its power just after passing its climax. The tortured little doll had Dixie Late-Lark's face on it. Its mouth was wide open and it was screaming silently and horribly.

"At least we know that the bears can read and absorb world-French," Gladys Marclair laughed. And they all laughed. "They couldn't have learned about the *poupées-fetiches,* the fetish dolls, anywhere except from Dixie's French horror stories. Why, it's *Stridente Mimi,* Screaming Mimi herself. That's really Dixie's theme story. Oh, I wish that Dixie would come back so she could see this comical takeoff of herself. Shut your mouth, doll-Dixie!"

Gladys pushed her forefinger against the mouth of the little fetish doll to close it, but the doll bit her finger suddenly, viciously, terribly, and set the blood gushing from it. When Gladys got her finger loose again, the doll opened its mouth wide once more and continued to scream silently and horribly from a now blood-dribbling mouth. It has long been noted that fetish dolls seem to have a life of their own.

That little comic interlude cheered them all a bit, and they left the table in a happier state. And they went out from the ship.

Oh, the Thieving Bears wanted to play games, did they! Well, the explorers would beat them at their games, and they would solve all the mysteries about them at the same time. But the explorers had now come to regard the bears as more complex and as more nearly intelligent than they had previously seemed. They were still tittering little stinkers, though. The Thieving Bears were bigger than police dogs and a little bit smaller than Great Danes. They were toothless and clawless and apparently harmless. How can you worry about such tittering and giggling things?

"Quick! Come quick!" Selma Last-Rose was calling, in a queer voice on the edge of panic. "Come quick! I've found Dixie."

The Thieving Bears, however large they seemed, gave the impression of being nearly weightless. They had to be nearly weightless to glide on the wind the way they did. They seemed to be mostly—well, it wasn't hair and it wasn't feathers— they seemed to be mostly made out of a fluffy and deep-piled covering with not much body inside it.

"Come, come, somebody come!" Selma was still calling in her rattling voice. "Dixie is dead."

The bears had to be ninety percent fluffy covering and no more than ten percent body. Otherwise, big as they seemed, they couldn't have gotten through some of the holes that they did go through.

"Horribly, horribly dead," Selma was chanting in a little-girl singsong voice. "Horribly, horribly dead. Oh please, somebody come and help me look at her. I can hardly manage to look at her all by myself."

Dead Dixie Late-Lark was an exact life-sized replica of her own many times-transfixed fetish doll. Her throat was just as flamboyantly and terribly cut as the doll's had been. The same thorns and pins and needles ran through her, but now they were meter-long thorns and two-meter-long needles. And her mouth was very wide open, as had been that of the doll; and Dixie was likewise screaming horribly and silently.

And a tittering, a giggling in the Thieving Bears' fashion, was coming from her silently screaming mouth and also from her laid-open throat. How ghastly!

The horror was broken a bit, or diverted into a wondering exasperation, by Benny Crix-Crannon's voice booming, "Here's another one of them. This one's better done. It's good!"

Yes, it was another horribly dead Dixie Late-Lark, with her throat cut even more savagely, with her poor body transfixed with even longer thorns and needles, with the tittering and giggling from her wide-open and silently screaming mouth even more disconcerting.

In all, they found seven life-sized versions of Dixie Late-Lark horribly and ritually murdered. Then all seven of them jumped up, turned into rather young Thieving Bears, and ran away tittering. And the very stones of that planet seemed to join in that tittering and giggling.

But where was Dixie Late-Lark herself? Was that not a pertinent question? More pertinent questions may have been: why did all the explorers stop wondering what had happened to their colleague Dixie Late-Lark? And why did they now feel that her disappearance was unimportant?

"I have lost my judgment," George Mahoon lamented. "I've still got most of the pieces of things in my mind, but I can no longer put them together. Putting things together is what judgment is. One of you others will have to take over the captaincy of this expedition."

"Oh, bother the captaincy!" Gladys Marclair rejected it. "Expeditions would be better without captains anyhow. And you can't lose something that you never had, George. Let's play 'Ask the Question' with this situation. And let's wonder why no bunch, coming here, has played it before. This is an Earth-sized planet and remarkably monotonous. On its look-alike continents, there are hundreds and thousands of little low plains or meadows comparable to this Plain of the Old Spaceships. Why have all the expeditions to this world, from that of John Chancel to our own, landed here within one thousand meters of each other? Instructions for exploration landing sites have always been 'Random selection, tempered with intelligence.' And another instruction has been 'Examine new ground wherever possible.' For whose convenience have we all landed in this one place? Oh, your diminished judgment, George! Probably somebody has been eating the hippo out of your hippocampus (I've always believed that the 'little hype' is the center of the judgment as well as of the memory), so now you're not as well hyped as you were. What if hardly any of the area of this planet has been checked out?"

"Oh, we made sixteen scanning circuits of Thieving Bear Planet before we landed," George Mahoon said. "Sixteen circuits will give a very good recorded sample. And some of the previous expeditions made the full sixty-four scanning circuits, and the full scan doesn't miss much."

"Do we believe that the Thieving Bears are to be found in all parts of this planet, George?" Selma Last-Rose asked.

"I don't know. Do we believe it, Benny?"

"Oh no. The Thieving Bears are strictly small-species and small-area creatures. Their crankinesses as well as their brilliancies indicate that they have far too small a gene-pool. They have to stay close together in a small area to 'keep warm' in the special (of a species) identity-survival sense."

"As to myself, I've lost more than my judgment," Luke Fronsa mourned. "I've lost all my ideas, and all that I have left now are notions. Somebody is eating all my ideas right out of my head and leaving only the hulls of them. Did you know that notions are only the shells or hulls of ideas after the meat is eaten out of them?"

The bears were toothless, and they were playful. Sometimes they came gliding in on the air, and they might be practically invisible when the light was in their favor. They came gliding in or ambling in, and they tagged the people gently as a breath. But whenever they touched the people, however briefly or lightly, they left what seemed to be very small entering marks. And they also left a redness, like the stings of nettles. One of the explorers (no matter which one; they had begun to run together, even in their own regard) said that the Thieving Bears were really a species of giant insects, insects with strange appetites and always hungry.

Seven days and nights went by very rapidly. It was a giddy world in this respect, fast-spinning: for seven days and nights on Thieving Bear Planet were the equivalent of only about eighteen hours on Old Earth or sixteen hours on Astrobe. And the fast-spin did make a difference on Thieving Bear. It was because of the fast-spin that there were no large treelike plants, not even any very large bushes. There were small bushes, and there was the non-gramineous grass.

2.

> People without an accompaniment of ghosts are a deprived people. They will descend to almost any depth of "oriental" cultishness or modish superstition or silliness or astrological depravity to hide the fact that they have lost their ghosts.
>   Ghosts without an accompaniment or "neighborness" of people are similarly deprived, and they will cast themselves into the most bizarre roles or forms to try to create a company for themselves.
>   Both of these conditions are unhealthy.
> —Terrance Taibhse, *Introduction to Ghost Stories of Sector 24*

The storminess of Thieving Bear Planet wouldn't have permitted any botanical constructs taller than small bushes. And the fast-spin of Thieving Bear compelled certain surface conditions for that world. On most worlds, the hills go up. On Thieving Bear Planet, the hills went down.

The upper levels of all the continents of Thieving Bear were flat and lush, and sometimes they were swept by violent winds. And down from them, the hills ran to the sheltered plains or meadows or circle-valleys (such as was the Plain of the Old Spaceships), and on these lower levels the winds were less violent.

Two of the seven short nights just past had been "electric nights," and the ghosts walked on electric nights. The electric nights were highlighted (literally) by massive thunderstorms and plasmal displays. (The odds are that these storms are more violent than the storms where you come from.) The lightning piled up on the high places, roaring like lazaruslions. Then it rolled down the hills like waterfalls and formed hot and spitting pools on the lower plains and meadows.

The ghosts were always there, but some of them were ordinarily like empty balloons. On the electric nights, they filled up with lightning and manifested themselves. But others of the ghosts were always low-key, living out their endless nights and days till they would finally fade away after a long era. One of the ghosts was that of John Chancel, one of the earlier visitors to Thieving Bear Planet, usually called the "discoverer" of Thieving Bear, but now he said that this wasn't true. During the second of the electric nights, Chancel's ghost sat in the cockpit room of the ship with the explorers and lovingly handled the eight hundred knobs, wheels, levers, push buttons, keyboards, and voice boxes that commanded the ship. The ships hadn't been so sophisticated in his day.

"I catch onto all the new and enjoyable advances in ship control quicker than 'he' would," Chancel's ghost spoke softly. "Oh, he has the physical brains with him, most of them; but I have the intuition. And he, we, were never very good on brains anyhow. We had the mystique and the personality, we had the intuition, we guessed a lot, and we faked a lot. But we were never a well-linked personality."

"Just how does one become a ghost?" Gladys Marclair asked. "Besides dying, I mean, is there any way to bring it about?"

"It happens, in many cases, long before death. I was his ghost here for twenty years (Earth years) before Chancel died elsewhere. He left his (my) ghost here on his second landing. He came back here for me several times after that, but I wouldn't rejoin him or go away with him. He had become quite cranky in his ways, and I in mine. There would have been everlasting conflict if we had joined. But it was also psychic disaster (more for him than for me) for us to be separated.

"It's not at all rare for a living person to be separated from his ghost. I see that two of you six have become separated from your own ghosts, and none of you can guess which two of you it is. On Thieving Bear, the conditions seem to be favorable for these split-ups. It leaves a great hunger (yes, a physical hunger) in the ghosts who are left behind. But each planet has its own ghostliness that is different from that of other places. Even Old Earth has remnants and tatters of ghostliness, and it isn't a hungry world. As a prophet said, 'Happy the world that has iron meadows and rich essences on which the spirits may feed, and then go to sleep.' But we spirits are most often sleepless here."

"What happened to Dixie Late-Lark?" Gladys Marclair asked this pleasant ghost.

"Oh, she's a ghost of a different sort. There never was any Dixie Late-Lark as a person. There were only the six of you who arrived here. Dixie was your *esprit de group*, your group effigy, and also a manifestation of your 'goofiness syndrome.' But we made her visible to you for the first time. And you recognized her and accepted her in your unthinking way. This 'unthinking way' has become part of the environment of Thieving Bear Planet. She was the toothsome imaginative essence of all of you, the capriciousness or coltishness of you, and that made her very appetizing. We love essence. It's so concentrated."

"Why did you make her visible?" Selma asked.

"Because we like to see what we're eating."

"Who or what are the Thieving Bears?" Luke Fronsa asked Chancel's ghost.

"Oh, they're a sort of tumbleweed, a sort of nettle. Ghosts use them to get around in some of the time; so I myself am often a Thieving Bear. It is only on the electric nights that we can inflate ourselves with enough plasm to look like ourselves. We walk here a lot because we are always hungry and restless. Ghosts in places that are richer in organics and metals and minerals stay well fed by a sort of osmosis, so they walk and stir very little. They sleep their decades and centuries away. Notice it sometimes that active ghosts are only to be found in deprived regions. One of my counterparts has hardly stirred in a hundred years. I can feel my counterparts, but there's not much of them to feel."

"Where do the *little* Thieving Bears come from?"

"From a very early landing, perhaps the earliest, for they were here when I arrived. It was an ill-advised settlement expedition of men, women, and children. Then all died of starvation, not knowing how to turn the lush grass into food. They were the first of the hungry ghosts. It was their crying hunger that has drawn all the ships to land in this one place. 'Come let us eat you' is their cry, and it is still a most passionate cry."

"You spoke of your 'counterparts' a moment ago," George Mahoon said. "Did John Chancel generate more ghosts than one? Is he himself restless and hungry?"

"Oh, I myself (the central John Chancel) have gone to my glory. But all of us great ones leave multiple ghosts behind us. He (I) left at least two others besides myself. We have a sort of awareness of each other, a loose feeling. He had real greatness (unlikely as it seems), and I didn't. And yet this is the paradox: he saw himself entirely from the outside, and he loved what he saw; I saw us from the inside, and I wasn't impressed. And we were not the first man on as many planets as is claimed for us. We were not the first man here. There were already Thieving Bears here when we came, ghosts of earlier explorers. But John Chancel had the greatness; and the earlier explorers had it not. So Chancel was credited with many first landings.

"Good luck to you, ladies and gentlemen, when you lift off in your capsule this electric morning. There are several entries that you must make in your log immediately after lift-off, or you will forget them and never make them at all. And you will have to make these entries in something other than ink."

"Why should we lift off in our capsule?" Elton Fad asked. "We use the capsule only when the ship is inoperative."

"It's inoperative now and forever," the ghost of John Chancel said. "Well, it's a good ship and it eased the hunger of a lot of us. You'd better lift off in the capsule as soon as possible now. We try to play fair, but we'll be feeding on it very soon if it's still here."

That John Chancel was a nice fellow, even in his fading ghost form.

But a much more violent ghost (right at that electric dawn after the second electric night) was the ghost of Manbreaker Crag. After the second of the electric nights had ended, Manbreaker decided to remain apparent out of sheer stubbornness. They had all been feeling the powerful presence of this Manbreaker Crag for some time.

"I'm the only one here of any moment or weight," Manbreaker's ghost spoke in a rough sort of roar. "I'm not a person to crawl into pieces of nettle or tumble-weed or any weeds except my own mortal weeds. I'm not one to take on the form of a cutie giggling bear or other toy. I am not a ghost, nor any part of a ghost story. Ghost stories are for children and cutie bears. I am a simple dead man who is restless and hungry on this mineral-poor world. On electric nights, I go get my own body where I keep it. I enter it and I inflate it with the crackling lightning and the electricity that has gathered here. I'm a hungry dead man with a dead man's temper. Don't mess with me!"

"Don't mess with us, fellow," George Mahoon spoke sharply. "Our ship seems to be in a very weakened condition and we have to be getting out of here quickly. Stay out of the way, grave-rot oaf, and be quiet. Elton, go sharpen this, and then bring it back to me along with a heavy sledgehammer. I think I know how to deal with hungry dead men."

George Mahoon handed a thick and heavy hardwood dowel pin to Elton Fad. It was about the length and heft of a baseball bat.

"The other ones, the real ghosts, which is to say the *real unreal ones,* have their little self-saving fables that they recite when they feed on people and the pos-sessions of people," the hungry, long-dead man, Manbreaker Crag, roared. The only speaking voice he possessed was this sort of dogged roar. "They say, 'We do not steal important things out of your minds. We steal only funny-shaped, trifling things. Serious people like you are better off without them. Our gain is your gain.' That is what they are telling you, but they lie. What we eat out of your minds are the most serious things that your minds are capable of holding. What we steal and eat out of your bodies are the tastiest things in your bodies. We come to table on you, and we feast on you. What we eat out of your ships and your stores are the most nourishing and sophisticated things you have brought, wotto metal, data gelatin, electronic reta, codified memories and processes. We eat these things because we are hungry. And I eat them more ravenously than do any of the others. I eat the essence of minds and leave gibbering idiocy in its place. I eat the bodies of whole people where they stand."

"Is everything possible transferred from the ship to the capsule?" big George Mahoon asked his party.

"It is," several of them answered.

"I will eat the essence of your capsule-boat just as all of us on Thieving Bear have eaten the essence of your ship," dead Manbreaker Crag roared.

"Is it sharpened?" Mahoon asked as he took the thick hardwood dowel from the returning Elton Fad.

"It is sharpened," Elton said, "but something has gone wrong with it. It loses weight as I stand here. They feed across short distances."

"Scrawny ship captain, I think I'll eat you as you stand there," dead Manbreaker roared at Captain Mahoon. "You'd make a big bite, but I'll eat you."

Big George Mahoon felled bigger dead-man Manbreaker Crag with a powerful blow to his dead face. Then he put the point of the sharpened dowel pin ("Yes, Elton, I believe that he ate the heart out of it, but how could it have been prevented?" Mahoon asked) to the region of the heart of Manbreaker and struck the pin a heavy blow with the big sledgehammer. But the wooden pin or stake came apart into weak splinters and pieces of worm-eaten (or zombie-eaten) wood.

"Ah well, we'll have to leave him as he is," Mahoon said. "I don't know any other way to kill a man who's already dead."

The six explorers got into the capsule-boat then and lifted off. They looked down on the ship they had left behind them then, and it crumbled down and became a part of its own outline and schematic. It became one more of the token spaceships that formed that part-circle that gave the name Plain of the Old Spaceships to that curious site. Those drawn outlines of the old spaceships, they were the old spaceships. There must have been a lot of good eating in each of them, though.

"To the log!" George Mahoon howled. "I feel it all slipping out of my memory so fast! Each one of us take a long log page and write as rapidly as possible. Get it down, before we lose it as earlier explorers lost it."

"No use lamenting that there is no 'ink' in any stylus or pen or log pencil laid out or still boxed," Selma Last-Rose rattled. "No use lamenting that even the electronic ink is eaten out of every recorder and that the remembering jelly is eaten out of every memory pot. The hungers of the Thieving Bears are unaccountable. All the earlier logs had a few words written in something other than ink. If we all write as fast as we can, we may get more than a few words down. We may even get the explanation down onto the log sheets before it fades completely from our minds."

They all opened their veins and wrote on the long log sheets in their own blood. It was sticky going. So many free-flowing things had been eaten out of their blood that it was now viscous and thick. But they made it do. They got the explanation all down, even though (when it was shown to them later) they hardly remembered writing it.

A simple explanation had been needed for the conditions on Thieving Bear Planet. It was needed because, as the great Reginald Hot had once phrased it, "Anomalies are messy."

And that simple explanation is herewith given, more or less as it was written in thick blood in the log book.

Days of Grass, Days of Straw

Introduction by Gary K. Wolfe

"Days of Grass, Days of Straw" first appeared in *New Dimensions 3*, the third in a series of rather adventurous anthologies edited by Robert Silverberg throughout the 1970s. Coming close on the heels of science fiction's controversial New Wave, Silverberg's series was clearly out to recognize new voices and new literary approaches to science fiction and fantasy, and Lafferty had stories in each of the first four volumes. The volume with "Days of Grass, Days of Straw" also included two stories which would become widely reprinted, Hugo Award–winning classics, Ursula K. Le Guin's "The Ones Who Walk Away from Omelas" and James Tiptree, Jr.'s "The Girl Who Was Plugged In" (Tiptree was of course later revealed to be a pseudonym of Alice Sheldon). Each of those would be reprinted dozens of times in the coming decades, but Lafferty's story—despite now being regarded as one of his best and most strikingly visionary by aficionados—was reprinted only in a few of his own collections. It did, however, get translated into Dutch and inspired the 2004 song *Dagen van gras, dagen van stro* (a literal translation of the title) by the performer Spinvis (Erik de Jong). Spinvis's lyrics have only an elliptical connection with Lafferty's story, but the point is that Lafferty's best stories, even when not widely familiar, manage to find their way into unexpected corners of the culture and leave traces there.

The story itself is one that some readers find challenging—within the first two lines, a city street morphs into a road, then a trail, then a mere path, and our protagonist Christopher finds himself in a pre-urban, pre-industrial landscape with features resembling Native American legends and Oklahoma tall tales. Even his own name doesn't ring true, and half-recognized people and places never quite coalesce into a more traditionally realized fantasy landscape. Yet he feels revived and invigorated, as though the world had been "pumped full of new juice." "Things were mighty odd here," he notices in an observation that may well sound familiar to anyone reading a Lafferty story for the first time. "There was just a little bit of something wrong about things."

We eventually learn that Christopher hasn't crossed into a fantasy world at all, but rather to a different kind of time—a "day of grass," one of the "overflowing and special days apart from the regular days," which are called days of straw. Although these special days are "Days out of Count" in terms of history and the calendar, they are earned at great cost by prophets and "prayer-men," who wrestle with God to gain them. Called by different names in different cultures, these "rich days, full of joy and death, bubbling with ecstasy and blood" may include entire seasons, and although "nobody has direct memory of being in them or living in them," we give them pallid names like Indian Summer. Lafferty's stunning vision of a more vital and perhaps more dangerous world just beyond the one we know, but somehow folded into it, is one of his most haunting recurrent themes.

Days of Grass, Days of Straw

1.

Fog in the corner and fog in his head:
Gray day broken and bleeding red.

—Henry Drumhead, *Ballads*

Christopher Foxx was walking down a city street. No, it was a city road. It was really a city trail or path. He was walking in a fog, but the fog wasn't in the air or the ambient: it was in his head. Things were mighty odd here. There was just a little bit of something wrong about things.

Oceans of grass for one instance. Should a large and busy city (and this was clearly that) have blue-green grass belly-high in its main street? Things hardly remembered: echoes and shadows, or were they the strong sounds and things themselves? Christopher felt as though his eyeballs had been cleaned with a magic cleaner, as though he were blessed with new sensing in ears and nose, as though he went with a restored body and was breathing a new sort of air. It was very pleasant, but it was puzzling. How had the world been pumped full of new juice?

Christopher couldn't recall what day it was; he certainly didn't know what hour it was. It was a gray day, but there was no dullness in that gray. It was shimmering pearl-gray, of a color bounced back by shimmering water and shimmering air. It was a crimson-edged day, like a gray squirrel shot and bleeding redly from the inside and around the edges. Yes, there was the pleasant touch of death on things, gushing death and gushing life.

Christopher's own name didn't sound right to him. He didn't know what town he was in. Indeed he'd never before seen a town with all the storefronts flapping in the wind like that. Ah, they'd curl and bend, but they wouldn't break. A town made of painted buckskin, and yet it was more real than towns made of stone and concrete.

He saw persons he almost knew. He started to speak and only sputtered. Well, he'd get a newspaper then; they sometimes gave information. He reached in his pocket for a coin, and discovered that he didn't have regular pockets. He found a little leather pouch stuck in his belt. What's this? What else was stuck in his belt? It was a breechclout with the ends fore and aft passing under his belt.

Instead of pants he had a pair of leggings and a breechclout, three-piece pants. Oh, oh, what else?

Oh, he wore a shirt that seemed to be leather of some sort. He wore soft shoes that were softer than slippers. He was hatless, and his hair came forward over his shoulders in two tight long braids. He had dressed casually before, but he didn't remember ever dressing like this. How were the rest of the people dressed? No two alike, really, no two alike.

But he did bring a coin out of that leather pouch that was stuck in his belt. A strange coin. It wasn't metal: it was made of stone, and made roughly. On the face of it was the head and forequarters of a buffalo. On the reverse side was the rump of a buffalo. The words on the obverse of it read WORTH ONE BUFFALO, and on the reverse they read MAYBE A LITTLE BIT LESS.

"And where do I put a coin in this contraption?" Christopher asked himself angrily and loudly. A hand extended itself, and Christopher put the coin in the hand. The hand belonged to an old wrinkled brown man, swathed in robes and folds of blackened leather, and sitting in the dust.

The old man gave Christopher a newspaper, or gave him something anyhow. It was on leather that was almost board-stiff. It was illustrated, it was printed in a variety of hands; and here and there it had a little hair growing out of it as though its leather were imperfectly scraped.

"Wait, your change," the old brown man said. He gave Christopher seven small coins. These were neither metal nor stone: they were clay baked in the sun. The obverse of each was the head and fore of a badger, puffed and bristled and hissing in high defense. And the reverse was the reared rump of the same badger in embattled clawed stance.

"Price go down a little but not a whole badger," the old man said. "Take three puffs. It's close as I can get to even change." Wondering at himself, Christopher took three strong rich smoky puffs from the old pipe of the old man. He felt that he had received full value then. It was about all that he felt satisfied with. But is it wrong to feel unsatisfied, which is unsated? Christopher thought about it.

He went over and sat on a bale of rags outside the shop with the sign HOT ROAST DOG FOR SALE OR GIVE. The bale of rags seemed somehow lively; it was as if there was no division between the animate and the inanimate this day. He tried to make something out of the strange newspaper or the strange day, or the newly strange man who was apparently himself.

Oh, the newspaper was interesting. It could be read one way or another: by picture, by stylized pictograph, by various writings and printings. Here were anecdotes; wooly, horny, bottomlessly funny anecdotes: and they were about people that Christopher knew, or almost knew. And all the people passing by (Christopher realized it with a chuckling gasp) were also people that he knew or almost knew. Well, what made them so different then? They looked like familiar people, they smelled like familiar people (which the familiar people erstwhile had not done), they had the familiar name that came almost to the edge of the tongue.

"But what town is this? What day is this? What is the context?" Christopher wailed out loud. "Why is everything so strange?"

"Kit-Fox, you call me?" Strange Buffalo boomed at him. Strange Buffalo was a big and boisterous man and he had always been a good friend of Christopher. He had? Then why did he look so different? And why was his real name, or his other name, now unremembered?

"Will the buffalo go to war, do you think, Kit-Fox?" Strange Buffalo asked him. "Do you believe that the two great herds of them will go to war? They come near to each other now and they swear that neither will give way."

"No, there will be only the pushing and goring of a few thousand bulls, not much else," Christopher said. "The buffalo simply haven't the basis for a real war." He was surprised at his own knowledge of the subject.

"But the buffalo have human advisers now," Strange Buffalo said. "It began with the betting, of course, but now we can see that there is real cause of conflict on both sides. I dabble in this myself and have some good ideas. We are tying spear-shafts to the horns of some of the big bulls and teaching them to use them. And we're setting up big bows and teaching them to bend them with their great strength, but they haven't any accuracy at all."

"No, I don't believe they were meant to have a real war. It's a wonderful dust they raise, though, when they all come together. It makes you glad to be alive. And the thunder of their millions of hoofs!" (There was the distant sound of morning thunder.) "Or is that a thundering in the mountains?" Kit-Fox—ah, Christopher was asking.

"Well, there *is* quite a clatter in the mountains this morning, Kit," Strange Buffalo was saying in happy admiration. "The deep days, the grass days like this one aren't come by easily. It's a wonder the mountains aren't knocked to pieces when the big prophets pray so noisily and wrestle so strong. But, as the good skin says, we must work out our salvation in fear and thundering."

"Is it not 'In fear and trembling'?" Christopher asked as he lounged on the lively bale of rags.

"No, Kit-Fox, no!" Strange Buffalo pealed at him. "That's the kind of thing they say during the straw days; not here, not now. In the Cahooche shadow-writing it says 'In fear and chuckling,' but the Cahooche words for thunder and chuckling are almost the same. On some of the Kiowa antelope-skin drawings, 'In scare-shaking and in laughter-shaking.' I like that. I wish I could pray and wrestle as wooly and horny as the big ones do. Then I'd get to be a prophet on the mountain also, and I'd bring in more days of grass. Yes, and days of mesquite also."

"The mountain is a funny one this morning, Strange Buffalo. It doesn't reach clear down to the ground," Christopher said. "There's a great space between, and there are eagles flying underneath it."

"Ah, it'll fall back after a while, Kit-Fox, when they have won or lost the wrestling for the day; after they have generated sufficient juice for this day, for I see that they have already won it and it will be a day of grass. Let's go have a rack of roast dog and a gourd of choc beer," Strange Buffalo proposed.

"In a minute, Strange Buffalo. I am in the middle of a puzzle and I have this fog in my head. What day is this?"

"It's one of the days of grass, Kit-Fox. I just told you that."

"But which one, Strange Buffalo? And what, really, are 'days of grass'?"

"I believe that it is the second Monday of Indian Summer, Kit-Fox," Strange Buffalo was saying as he gave the matter his thought and attention. "Or it may be the first Monday of Blue-Goose Autumn. We're not sure, though, that it is a Monday. It sounds and tastes more like a Thursday or an aleikaday."

"It sure does," Christopher—ah, Kit-Fox agreed.

A laughing, dying man was carried past by four hale men. This fortunate one had been smashed by bear or rolled on by horse or gored by buffalo, and the big red blood in him was all running out. "It works," the happy dying man cried out. "It works. I got a little too close to him and he ripped me to pieces, but it works. We are really teaching those big bulls to use the spears lashed to their horns. Others will carry on the work and the fun. I bet that I've had it."

"A little blood to bless me!" Strange Buffalo cried out, and the dying man splashed him with the rich and rigorous blood.

"For me also," Kit-Fox begged, and the dying man smeared him with blood on the brow and breast and shoulders and loins. Two other friends, Conquering Sharp-Leaf and Adoration on the Mountain, came and were blessed with the blood. Then the man died and was dead.

"There is nothing like the fine rich blood to make a grass day sing in your head and in your body," Strange Buffalo exulted. "On the straw days they try to hide the blood or they bleed in a dark corner."

(What was all this about the grass days and the straw days? There was now a sordid dull-dream quality, a day-of-straw quality that kept trying to push itself in. "For a little while," it begged, "to reestablish rigor and rule and reason for just a little while." "Go away," said the day-of-grass quality. "The wrestle was won this morning, and this is a day out of the count.")

Kit-Fox and Strange Buffalo went in, past the booths and work areas of the coin-makers, past the stands of the eaglewing-bone-whistle makers, and into the shop which had roast dog for sale or give. Strange Buffalo had a shoulder of dog and Kit-Fox had a rack of ribs. There was fried bread also, and hominy and pumpkin. There was choc beer dipped with gourd dippers out of a huge crock. Thousands of people were there. It was crowded and it was supposed to be. The man named Mountain twinkled in the air. Why had they not noticed that about him before?

Folks rolled up the walls and tied them. Now the strong smoke and savor could visit all the places, and the folks in every shop could see into every other shop. It was full morning and beginning to get warm.

"But I still want to know the date," Kit-Fox insisted, not quite converted to the day of grass, not quite clear of the head-fog that accompanies the sullen burning of the straw days. "What newspaper is this that doesn't have a date? I want a date!"

"Look at it. It tells," said Strange Buffalo.

"You want a date, honey?" the top of the newspaper writhed in sudden flickering of day-fire print. "Phone 582-8316 and I give you a real date." Then the day-fire print was gone.

"I hope I can remember that number," Kit-Fox said anxiously. "Strange Buffalo, where is there a telephone exchange?"

"They are the same and single and right outside past the booths," Strange Buffalo said. "You were sitting upon it when I came upon you. And you, you old straw-head, you thought it was a bale of rags."

Kit-Fox went outside, past the booths of the stone-buffalocoin makers and the clay-badger-coin makers, past the tents of the porcupine-quill dealers, to what he had thought was a bale of rags, a lively bale of rags as he now remembered it. Well, it was an ample lady in her glad rags and she was the telephone exchange lying there in the grass.

"I want to call number 582-8316," Kit-Fox said uneasily.

"Here are a handful of dice," the glad-rags lady told him. "Arrange them here in the short grass and make any number you want."

"But proper dice have numbers only to six," Kit-Fox protested, "and some of the numbers are higher."

"Those are improper dice, they are crooked dice," the lady said. "They have numbers more than six and numbers less than one. Number out your telephone number in the short grass with them."

"Are you sure this is the way to dial a number?" Kit-Fox asked.

"Sure I'm not sure," the lady said. "If you know a better way, do it that way. Worth a try, kid, worth a try."

Kit-Fox numbered out his numbers in the short grass.

"Now what do I do?" he asked.

"Oh, talk into the telephone here."

"That buckskin bag is a telephone?"

"Try it, try it. Drop a badger coin in and try it."

Kit-Fox dropped the coin into the telephone. "Hello, hello," he said.

"Hello, hello," the lady answered. "That's my number you called. You want a date, I wait for you awhile. Believe me, I get pretty tired of waiting pretty soon."

"I don't think this is a telephone exchange at all," Kit-Fox grumbled.

"How else I can get guys so easy to drop badger-coins in a buckskin bag," the lady said. "Come along, lover man, we will have a grand time this day."

The lady was full-bodied and jolly. Kit-Fox remembered her from somewhere.

"Who are you?" he asked her.

"I'm your wife in the straw days," she said, "but this is a grass day. They're harder to find, but they're more fun when you find one. They have something to do with grandfather's brother and that wrestling of his."

"Days of grass, days of straw," Kit-Fox said as he embraced the lady passionately. "How about a hay day?"

"You mean a heyday? Those are special. We hope to make them more often, if only the wrestle is better. They're fuller of juice than the grass days even. We try to make one now."

They made a heyday together (together with a whole nation of people); and it went on and on. Day-Torch (that was the lady in the glad rags, the lady who was Kit-Fox's wife during the straw days) bought an eagle-wing-bone whistle from a dealer, and she whistled happy haunting tunes on it. The people followed Kit-Fox and Day-Torch out of town, out to the oceans of buffalo grass and blue-stem grass. They torched everything that was dry and set the blue-black smoke to rolling. But the fundamental earth was too green to burn.

All mounted horses and took lances. They went out after buffalo. Word was brought to them that some of the newly armed buffalo bulls wanted to schedule battle with them. And the battle was a good one, with gushing blood and broken-open bodies, and many on each side were killed.

Strange Buffalo was killed. That big boisterous man died with a happy whoop.

"Strange Buffalo, indeed," one of the buffalo bulls said. "He looks like a man to me."

When the ground there had become too soggy and mired in blood, they adjourned the battle till the next day of grass, or the one after that. Bloody battles are fine, but who wants to spend a whole day on one? There are other things. Kit-Fox and Day-Torch and a number of other folks went to higher ground.

There was a roaring river on the higher ground, the biggest river ever and the loudest.

"Oh be quiet," Day-Torch said. "You've got the tune wrong." The great river ceased to roar. Day-Torch whistled the right tune on the eagle-wing-bone whistle. Then the river resumed its roaring, but in this right tune now. This mightiest of all rivers was named Cottonwood Creek.

Henry Drumhead added his beat to the tune. Then the folks had a rain dance till the sharp rain came down and drenched them through. They had a sun dance then, till the sun dried up the mud and began to burn the hides of the people. They had a cloud dance then. They had an antelope dance till enough antelope came to provide a slaughter and a feast. They had a pit dance, a fire dance, a snake dance, and an ashes dance: the ashes from pecan wood and hickory wood are a better condiment than salt to go with roast antelope. They had a feast dance. Then (after a while) a shakedown dance. They had a thunder dance and a mountain dance.

Say, it is spooky to come to the foot of the mountain itself and see the great gap between it and the ground! Rocks and boulders fell off of the bottom of the mountain and killed many of the people below. And, from the mountain itself, a broken, bloody, and headless torso fell down to the earth.

Helen Hightower—ah, that is to say the glad-rag lady Day-Torch—set up a rakish screaming, "The head, the head, somebody forgot the head!"

There was a thunderous grumbling, a mountain-shaking irritation, but the bloody head did come down and smash itself like a bursting pumpkin on the earth.

"A lot of times they forget to throw the head down if you don't remind them," Day-Torch said.

The meaning of the fallen torso and head was that there was now one less prophet or wrestler on the mountain; that there was now an opportunity for one more man to ascend to glory and death.

Several of the men attempted it by various devices, by piling cairns of stones to climb upon, by leaping into the air to try to grab one of the dangling roots of the mountain, by hurling lances with trailing lianas to fasten quivering in the bottom of the mountain. They played it out in the garish day there where all the colors were so bright that they ached. Many of the men fell to their deaths, but one ascended. There is always one who is able to ascend to the great wrestle when there is an empty place to receive him.

And the one who ascended was—no, no, you'll not have his name from us yet.

Something was mighty odd here. There was just a little bit of something right about things.

2.

Draftsman, draftsman, what do you draw?
Dog days, draggy days, days of straw.

—*Ballads*, Henry Drumhead

3.

Indian Summer. A period of warm or mild weather late in autumn or in early winter.

—*Webster's Collegiate*

So *Webster's Collegiate* defines it, but Webster's hasn't the humility ever to admit that it doesn't know the meaning of a word or phrase. And it doesn't know the meaning of this one.

There are intervals, days, hours, minutes that are not remembered directly by anyone. They do not count in the totality of passing time. It is only by the most sophisticated methods that even the existence of these intervals may be shown.

There are whole seasons, in addition to the four regular seasons that are supposed to constitute the year. Nobody knows where they fit in, there being no room for them anywhere in the year; nobody has direct memory of being in them or living in them. Yet, somehow, they have names that have escaped these obliterations. The name of one of the misfit seasons is Indian Summer.

("Why can't the Indians have their summer in the summertime like the rest of us?" comes a high voice with a trace of annoyance. Not a high-pitched voice: a high voice.)

But all that is neither here nor there. It is yonder, and we will come to it.

Christopher Foxx was walking down a city street. Things were mighty even here, mighty neat. There was just a little bit of something wrong about their rightness.

The world was rubbed, scrubbed, and tubbed; it was shaved, paved, and saved; it was neat, sweet, and effete. Ah, the latter was possibly what was wrong with it, if anything could be wrong with perfection. The colors were all flat (flat colors had been deemed best for nerves and such), and the sounds were all muted. Christopher, for a moment, wished for a color that shrieked and for a sound that blazed. He put the thought resolutely out of his head. After all, he had for wife Helen Hightower, and he suffered much criticism because of her gaudiness and exuberance.

Christopher took a paper from the slot on the corner, noted that it was a day in May (he had a queer feeling that he had been uneasy about the date, and yet all that registered with him was that it fell within a familiar month). He entered the North Paragon Breakfast Club. It was there that the Symposium would begin (it would last the whole day and into the night, and be held at various sites) on the multiplex subject "Spatial and Temporal Underlays to the Integrated World, with Insights as to Their Possible Reality and Their Relationship to the World Unconscious and to the Therapeutic Amnesia; with Consideration of the Necessity of Belief in Stratified Worlds, and Explorations of the Orological Motif in Connection with the Apparent Occurrence of Simultaneous Days." It would have been an exciting subject if Excitement had not become another of the muted things.

Buford Strange was already at the North Paragon, and with him were Adrian Montaigne and Vincent Rue.

"I have already ordered for ourselves and for yourself, Christopher," Buford said. "It is sheldrake, and I hope that you like it. They will not prepare it for fewer than four persons. 'We can't go around killing quarter ducks,' they say."

"That is all right," Christopher said meekly. He glanced at the other three nervously. There was surely something familiar about them all.

Great blue mountain thunder! Why shouldn't there be! He had worked with these men daily for several years. But, no, no, his edgy mind told him that they were familiar in some other and more subtle way. He glanced at the paper which he had taken from the corner slot outside. Something like quick flame ran across the top of it and was gone too quickly to verify. But was it possible that the flame had said "You want a date, honey? You phone—" Of course it was not possible. Clearly, at the top of the paper it was printed A DAY IN MAY. Clearly? Was that clear enough for a date?

"What date is this?" Christopher asked the three of them.

"May the eighth, of course," Adrian answered him. "You've got today's *Journal* in your hand and still you ask?"

Well now it was printed clearly there, May 8, and there was no nonsense about "a day in May"; still less was there anything like "You want a date, honey?"

Some wild-looking children burst into the North Paragon Breakfast Club.

"Straw-Men! Straw-Men!" they cried at the four gentlemen there. "Straw-Men! Straw-Men!" The children buffeted the four men a bit, did other extravagant things that are since forgotten, and then they went out of the Breakfast Club again: or at least they disappeared; they were no longer there.

"Why should they have done that?" Adrian asked, puzzled. "Why should they have called us that, and done the other things?"

"Why should *who* have called us *what*?" Vincent asked, even more puzzled.

"I don't know," Adrian said dryly. "It seemed that someone was here and said or did something."

"You're witless, Adrian," Vincent chided. "Nobody was here."

"Straw-Man," Christopher Foxx said softly. "I remember the word now and I couldn't remember it before. I woke up this morning trying to remember it. It seemed to be the key to a dream that was slipping away in spite of my trying to hang on to it. I have the key word now, but it fits nothing. The dream is gone forever."

"We will come back to this subject later in our discussions," Buford Strange said. "I believe that your word 'Straw-Man,' Christopher, is a part of the underlay, or perhaps of the overlay, that pertains to our world and our study. There is a good chance that certain children, or perhaps dwarfs or gnomes, entered here several moments ago. Did any of you notice them?"

"No," said Vincent Rue.

"No one entered," said Adrian Montaigne.

"No. I didn't see anyone," said Christopher Foxx.

"Yet I believe that a group *did* come in," Buford Strange continued suavely. "It was a group unusual enough to be noticed. Then why didn't we notice it? Or why did we forget, within a short moment, that we had seen it at all? I believe it was because the group was in a different sort of day. I am nearly sure that it is a group that lives in either St. Martin's Summer or in the Kingfisher Days. Ah, here is the sheldrake ready with all the trimmings! Drool and be happy. We shall never know such moment again."

It was a momentous fowl, no question of that. It was good, it was rich, it was overflowing with juice. It was peer of the fowl that are found in the land named St. Succulentus's Springtime. (What? What? There is a land named that?)

The four noble men (they were ennobled by the circumstance) fell to eating with what, in days of another sort, might almost be called gusto. It was a royal bird and was basted with that concoction of burst fruits and crushed nuts and peppers and ciders and holy oils and reindeer butter that is called—(wait a bit)—

"Do you know that the sheldrake is really a mysterious creature?" Buford Strange asked as he ate noisily (nobody eats such royal fare in quiet). Buford acted as if he knew a secret.

"It is not a mysterious creature at all," Adrian countered (he knew it was, though). "It is only the common European duck."

"It is not *only* the common European duck," Buford said strongly. "In other days it may be quite uncommon."

"What are you saying, Buford?" Vincent Rue asked him. "In what other days?"

"Oh, I believe, possibly, in what the Dutch call *Kraanzomer,* Crane-Summer. Are we agreed that the other days, the days out of count, are topic rather than temporal?"

"We are not even agreed that there *are* days out of count," Christopher objected.

"Drakes' teeth, by the way, while rare, are not unknown," Adrian Montaigne popped the statement out of his mouth as if in someone else's voice. He seemed startled at his own words.

"Drake is really the same word as *Drakos,* a dragon," Christopher Foxx mumbled. "Ah, I was going to say something else but it is gone now."

"Waiter, what is the name of the excellent stuff with which the drake is basted and to which it is wedded?" Vincent Rue asked in happy wonder.

"Dragons' sauce," said the waiter.

"Well, just what is the mystery, the uncommonness of the sheldrake, Buford?" Christopher asked him.

"I don't seem to remember," that man said. "Ah, let us start our discussion with my, our, failure to remember such things. Vincent, did you not have a short paper prepared on 'Amnesia, the Holes in the Pockets of the Seamless Garment'?"

"I forget. Did I have such a paper prepared? I will look in my own pockets."

Meanwhile, back on the mountain, back on the thundering mountain there were certain daring and comic persons rushing in and out and counting coup on the Wrath of God. It is a dangerous game. These were the big prophets who prayed so violently and sweated so bloodily and wrestled so strongly. It was they who fought for the salving or the salvation of the days, in fear and in chuckling, in scare-shaking and in laughter-shaking. The thundering mountain was a funny one this morning. It didn't reach clear to the ground. There was a great space between, and there were eagles flying under it. And the day, the day, was it really the first Monday of Blue-Goose Autumn? Was it really a Monday at all? Or was it a Thursday or an aleikaday?

It was like another morning of not long before. The eagles remember it; the clouds remember it; the mountain wrestlers remember it dimly, though some of the memory has been taken away from them.

Remember how it is written on the holy skins: "If you have faith you shall say to the mountain 'Remove from here and cast thyself into the sea' and it will do it." Well, on that morning they had tried it. Several of the big prophets and wrestlers tried it, for they *did* have faith. They groaned with travail and joy, they strove mightily, and they did move the mountain and make it cast itself into the sea.

But the thunders made the waters back off. The waters refused to accept or to submerge the mountain. The prayer-men and wrestlers had sufficient faith, but the ocean did not. Whoever had the last laugh on that holy morning?

The strivers were timeless, of the prime age, but they were often called the "grandfathers' brothers" by the people. They were up there now, the great prophets and prayer-men and wrestlers. One of these intrepid men was an Indian and he was attempting to put the Indian Sign on God himself. God, however, was like a mist and would not be signed.

"We will wrestle," the Indian said to God in the mist, "we will wrestle to see which of us shall be Lord for this day. I tell you it is not thick enough if only the regular days flow. I hesitate to instruct you in your own business, and yet someone must instruct you. There must be overflowing and special days apart from the regular days. You have such days, I am sure of that, but you keep them prisoned in a bag. It is necessary now that I wrest one of them from you."

They wrestled, inasmuch as a man slick with his own sweat and blood may wrestle with a mist: and it seemed that the Indian won the lordship of a day from God. "It will be a day of grass," the Indian said. "It will be none of your dry and juiceless days." The Indian lay exhausted with his fingers entwined in the won day: and the strength came back to him. "You make a great thing about marking every sparrow's fall," the Indian said then. "See that you forget not to mark this day."

The thing that happened then was this: God marked the day for which they had wrestled, but he marked it on a different holy skin in a different place, not on the regular skin that lists the regular days. This act caused the wrested day to be one of the Days out of Count.

Prophets, wrestlers, praying-men of other sorts were on the mountain also. There were black men who sometimes strove for kaffir-corn days or ivory-tree days. There were brown island men who wrestled for sailfish days or wild-pig days. There were pinkish north-wood men who walked on pine needles and balsam; there were gnarled men out of the swampy lands; there were town men from the great towns. All of these strove with the Lord in fear and in chuckling.

Some of these were beheaded and quartered, and the pieces of them were flung down violently to earth: it is believed that there were certain qualities lacking in these, or that their strength had finally come to an end. But the others, the most of them, won great days from the Lord, Heydays, Halcyon or Kingfisher Days, Maedchensommer Days, St. Garvais Days, Indian Summer Days. These were all rich days, full of joy and death, bubbling with ecstasy and blood. And yet all were marked on different of the holy skins and so they became the Days out of Count.

"Days out of the Count," Buford Strange was saying. "It's an entrancing idea, and we have almost proved it. Seasons out of the count! It's striking that the word for putting a condiment on should be the same word as a division of the year. Well, the seasons out of the count are all well seasoned and spiced. There are whole multiplex layered eras out of the count. The ice ages are such. I do not say 'were such'; I say 'are such.'"

"But the ice ages are real, real, real," Helen Hightower insisted. (Quite a few long hours had passed in the discussions, and now Helen Hightower, the wife of Christopher Foxx, was off her work at the telephone exchange and had put on her glad rags and joined the scholars.)

"Certainly they are real, Helen," Buford Strange said. "If only I were so real! I believe that you remember them, or know them, more than most of us do. You have a dangerously incomplete amnesia on so many things that I wonder the thunder doesn't come and take you. But in the days and years and centuries and eras of the straight count there are no ice ages."

"Well then, how, for instance, would local dwellers account for terminal moraines and glacial till generally?" asked Conquering Sharp-Leaf—ah, Vincent Rue.

(They were at the University, in that cozy room in the psychology department where Buford Strange usually held forth, the room that was just below the special effects room of Professor Timacheff.)

"How did they account for such before the time of modern geology?" Buford asked. "They didn't. There would be a new boulder one morning that had not been there the day before. The sheep-herder of the place would say that the moon had drawn it out of the ground, or that it had fallen from the sky."

"You're crazy, Buford," Adrian Montaigne said with a certain affection. "Why the ice ages then? Why should they have happened, even in times out of count? Why should they have left their footprints in the times within the count?" Adrian had very huge and powerful hands. Why had they not noticed this before?

"I believe there was a dynasty of great and muscular prophets and ghost-wrestlers who wanted to call out the terrible days of Fimbul Winter," Buford said in a hushed voice. "I don't know why they wanted such things, or why they sweated blood and wrestled prodigies to obtain them. They were men, but they are remembered as the frost giants."

"Oh my grand, grand uncles!" Day-Torch—Helen Hightower, rather, cried out. "Days of snow! Days of ice! Millions of them!"

"You are saying that certain archetypes—" Kit-Fox began.

"Shook the pillars of Heaven till the snow and ice fell down for a million days, for a million days out of the count," Buford Strange finished.

"Strange Buffalo, ah, Buford, you are crazy," Christopher Foxx chided much as Adrian had. Christopher was talking, but the queerly smiling Adrian had now become the presence in the room. Adrian had the curious under-rutile of the skin of one who has sweated blood in prayer and buffoonery and passion. Why had they not noticed that of him before?

"I could almost believe that *you* were one of the great challengers yourself, Strange," Christopher said to Buford, but he was looking at Adrian.

"You strike me as with a lance, Kit," Buford said sadly. "You uncover my mortification. For I failed. I don't know when it was. It was on a day out of the count. I failed a year ago or ten thousand years ago. I could not make it among the great ones. I was not cast out to my death: I was never in. There was room for me, and an opportunity for the ascent, but I failed in nerve. And one who has aspired to be a champion or prophet cannot fall back to be an ordinary man. So I am less than that: I am short of manhood. But, sadly, I do remember and live in other sorts of days."

"I believe that the aberrant days are simultaneous with the prosaic days," Adrian Montaigne mused. Adrian was quite a large man. Why had they not noticed that before?

"No, no, they are not simultaneous," Buford was correcting him. "There are the days out of the count and there are the days in the count. Those out of count are outside of time so they cannot be simultaneous with anything. You have to see it that way."

"You see it your way and I'll see it mine." Adrian was stubborn. "Consider some of the aberrant times or countries: St. Garvais' Springtime, St. Martin's Summer (the saints in these names were mountain prophets and wrestlers, but some of them were not at all saintly in their violence), Midas March (the very rich need their special season also: it is said that, in their special month, they are superiorly endowed in all ways), Dog Days, Halcyon Days, Dragon Days, Harvest May (what in the world is harvested in May?), All-Hallow Summer, Days of Ivory, Days of Horn, Indian Summer, Wicklow Week, Apricot Autumn, Goose Summer, Giant-Stone Days, Day of the Crooked Mile, the season called Alcedonia by the Latins. I tell you that all these days are happening at the same time!" This man named Adoration on the Mountain, or rather Adrian Montaigne, had a reckless sort of transcendence about him now.

"No, they do not all happen at the same time," Strange Buffalo was saying, "for the aberrant days of them are not in time. They are places and not times."

"Are there no nighttime hours in the times out of time?" Vincent Rue asked.

"No. Not in the same sense. They are in another province entirely," Buford said.

There was thunder in the special effects room of Professor Timacheff on the floor just above them, cheerful, almost vulgar thunder. Timacheff taught some sensational (sense response and also melodramatic) courses up there. But how did he get such special effects anyhow?

"They do happen at the same time," Adrian Mountain insisted, and he was laughing like boulders coming together. Quite a few things seemed to be happening to Adrian all at the same time. "They are all happening right now. I am sitting with you here this minute, but I am also on the mountain this minute. The thunder in the room above, it is real thunder, you know. And there is a deeper, more distant, more raffish thunder behind it which primitives call God's-Laughter Thunder."

"This gets out of hand now," Vincent Rue protested. "It is supposed to be a serious symposium on spatial and temporal underlays. Several of you have turned it into a silly place and a silly time. You are taking too anthropomorphic a view of all these things, including God. One does not really wrestle with God in a bush or a mist, or ride in wildly on a pony and count coup on God. Even as an atheist I find these ideas distasteful."

"But we are *anthropoi,* men," Adrian proclaimed. "What other view than an anthropomorphic view could we take? That we should play the God-game, that we should wrestle with a God-form and try to wrest lordship of days from him, that we should essay to count coup on God, I as a theist do not find at all distasteful.

"Why! One of them is failing now! It happens so seldom. I wonder if I have a chance."

"Adrian, what are you talking about?" Vincent demanded.

"How could *you* do it, Adrian, when I could not?" Buford Strange asked.

"Remember me when you come to your place, Adrian," Day-Torch cried. "Send me a day. Oh, send me a day-fire day."

"And me also, Adrian," Kit-Fox begged. "I would love to do it myself, but it isn't given to everyone."

There was a strong shouting in the room above. There was the concussion of bodies, and the roaring of mountain winds.

"What in all the crooked days is Professor Timacheff doing up there this evening?" Vincent Sharp-Leaf asked angrily. "And what things are you doing here, Adrian? You look like a man set afire."

"Make room for me! Oh, make room for me!" Adrian of the Mountain cried out in a voice that had its own crackling thunder. He was in the very transport of passion and he glistened red with his own bloody sweat. "One is failing, one is falling, why doesn't he fall then?"

"Help with it, Kit-Fox! And I help also," Day-Torch yowled.

"I help!" Kit-Fox yelped. The room shuddered, the building shuddered, the whole afternoon shuddered. There was a rending of boulders, either on the prophet's mountain or in the special effects room of Professor Timacheff above them. There was a great breaking and entering, a place turning into a time.

There came a roaring like horses in the sky. Then was the multiplex crash

(God save his soul, his body is done for) of bloody torso and severed limbs falling into the room from a great height, splintering the table at which the five of them sat, breaking the room, splattering them all with blood. But the ceiling above was unbreached and unharmed and there was no point of entry.

"I am not man enough even to watch it," Buford Strange gurgled, and he slumped sideways unconscious.

"Timacheff, you fool!" Vincent Rue bawled to the space above them. "Watch your damned special effects! You're wrecking the place!"

Unquestionably, that Timacheff was good. He used his special effects in classes on phenomenology that he taught up there.

"The head, the head! Don't let them forget the head!" Day-Torch cried in a flaming voice.

"I just remembered that Timacheff is out of town and is holding no classes today," Kit-Fox muttered in vulpine wonder.

"Make room for me! Oh, make room for me!" Adrian Mountain boomed. Then he was gone from the midst of them. He would be a factor, though, "in days to come."

"The head, the head!" Day-Torch flamed and scorched.

Christopher and Vincent tried to straighten up the unconscious Buford Strange. They shook him, but he came apart and one arm came off him. He was revealed as a straw-man filled with bloody straw, and no more.

"Why, he's naught but a poorly made scarecrow," Christopher Foxx said in wonder. "He was right that one who falls back from it cannot become an ordinary man again. He will be less than man."

"That's funny. He always looked like a man to me," Vincent Rue said.

"The head, the head! You forget the head. Let the head fall down!" Day-Torch cried.

And the head fell down.

It smashed itself like a bursting pumpkin on the broken floor.

4.

Under the town is a woolier town,
And the blood splashed up and the head fell down.

—*Ballads*, Henry Drumhead